I0660525

Children of Dreams

Heir to the Firstborn, Volume 6

Elizabeth Schechter

Published by Elizabeth Schechter, 2022.

Children of Dreams

Copyright © 2022 Elizabeth Schechter

Published by Raven's Wing Books

Editor: Michael Schechter

Cover design by GetCovers

Raven's Wing Books

ravens-wing-books.com

ISBN: 978-1-952598-47-0

Table of Contents

This one is for Nicole, for Corey, and for Chrissy.

Worlds begin.

Worlds end.

Worlds begin again

So it is with worlds.

This world is ending. Thanks for being there for the space between

Chapter One

The sky was dark overhead, but there were birds singing, which told Aria that the sun was at least starting to think about rising for the day. She stood outside the dispensary and watched as the last of the supplies were loaded into carts, feeling a tightness easing in her chest.

Finally, they were leaving.

It had only been four days since Owyn had first started feeling the urgent need to leave Terraces, but that urgency had quickly spread to the other Smoke Dancers. There was no vision that went with the feeling, no reason any of them could give for the urgency had quickly become unbearable. It had been four interminable days where they had worked frantically to redraw maps and resupply their provisions. Four endless days to finish necessary arrangements for clothing, boots, and horses. Four excruciating days during which each of the Smoke Dancers had grown more and more anxious, more and more irritable. More and more frustrated, as each delay only added to the growing need.

They needed to *leave*.

And now they were going, as soon as the sun rose. The coaches were ready. The carts were loaded. The horses would be saddled as soon as everyone was awake.

She heard a footstep behind her. Then a cough.

"Can I come closer?" Aven asked softly. "Or will you yell at me again?"

Aria turned. "Aven, I'm sorry." She held her hand out. He took it and let her tug him close.

"I know," he said, and leaned down to rest his forehead against hers. "I know this has been hard on you."

"That doesn't mean that I should have shouted at you," Aria murmured, breathing him in. She'd slept alone the previous night, for just that reason. "That's not fair to you. And I missed you."

"I missed you, too. But, did it help?" Aven asked. He kissed her lips, a fleeting brush of skin on skin. "You slept last night. I came in to check on you, and you were asleep. Deep enough you didn't even move when I kissed you good night. It was the first time you've slept through the night in four days. So maybe it was worth it."

Aria sighed and stepped into his embrace, resting her head on his shoulder. "You're right. I didn't notice. And I'm still sorry. Sorry I shouted, and sorry we have to leave. I'd have liked more time here. More time to be safe before we go on."

"I know, but we clearly don't have that time," Aven murmured into her hair. "We'll do the best we can."

Aria nodded. "Are the others awake?"

"Owyn is making breakfast, and I've been told that you're coming to eat." Aven let her go and grinned. "He didn't sound like he was giving you a choice."

"This is Owyn, and involves feeding people. Did you think there would be a choice?" Aria took Aven's offered hand, and leaned into his arm as they started walking. He moved easily, without a limp, until they reached the stairs. Then he slowed, and she saw in his face a hint of...strain? Pain?

"What's wrong?" she asked as they reached the top. Aven looked back at the stairs and grimaced.

"Stairs," he answered. "Walking is fine. That doesn't hurt. Dancing actually feels good. The little bit of riding I did while I was getting to know Pewter seems fine. But my change is...odd. There's a deep ache, and a pull in the muscles while I'm in between land and sea. And stairs...they're not comfortable. I thought it might be irritation in the tendons."

"And Jehan said what?" Aria asked as they started walking. "Have you done anything? Has he?"

"Fa and Grandmother examined me yesterday." Aven took her hand again and ran his thumb over her fingers. "It appears that the reconstruction of the bones has given me an early case of joint ail in the hip. The cushioning between the bones is too thin, and Grandmother says it can't be built back up. So far, I'm only feeling it in my change and on stairs, but eventually, I'll feel it more."

"You didn't tell me!"

"I was going to over supper last night. And then you yelled at me, and I decided I'd wait until you weren't going to snap at me."

"Oh," Aria murmured, feeling her face warm. "Aven—"

"We'll be on the road today," he said softly. "It'll be fine once we're moving again. Owyn said so."

Aria leaned into his arm again. "I'm still sorry."

"I know, love." Aven kissed the top of her head. "I know."

The door to their house was open, and Aria could hear Treesi's voice from inside. "We should wait for them to get back!"

"There's plenty of food," Owyn answered.

"Good," Aven called. "Because we are hungry." He paused to let Aria enter first, and she walked into their front room, and into Treesi's arms. She kissed her Earth Companion, then went on to the table where Alanar and Othi were already sitting.

"Where is Del?" Aria asked as she sat down. Aven took the chair next to her.

"He volunteered to go through the rooms and make sure we didn't forget anything," Owyn said as he came to the table, carrying a large pot. "Here you go. That nut porridge you like."

"It smells wonderful," Aria said. Owyn came to her chair and leaned down to kiss her, and she ran her fingers through his curls. "How are you feeling, my Fire?"

"A little less...jangled," he said. "We're leaving. The pressure is easing." He held a chair out next to Othi for Treesi, then went to the head of the corridor. "Del! Come and eat!"

Aria heard clattering on the stairs, and Del came out to join them at the table. As Owyn started serving porridge, Del made his way around the table, kissing them all good morning, then sat down on Alanar's right.

"Is everything packed?" Alanar asked.

Del nodded. "*I think so,*" he signed. "*I think Trista got everything. At least, I didn't see anything. But everyone should make one last pass of their own rooms. We can't turn around if we forget something important.*"

Aven translated as he mixed sea oak into his porridge. "I think everything of mine was packed last night. All that's left in my room are my swords."

"Are you riding today, or will you be in the coach?" Owyn asked as he took the chair on Alanar's left.

"I thought I might ride," Aven answered. "I'm still getting to know Pewter. So maybe I'll ride until we get to Cliffside. That's only...what?" He looked at Treesi. "An hour or two?"

"With a mule cart? About two hours." Treesi answered. "Maybe three, if Bunny was being lazy. With all of the settlers coming with us today? Call it three or four."

Aven nodded. "I can ride for that long, I think."

"And if you can't, we stop, and you get in the coach," Owyn said. He ate a spoonful of porridge, then cocked his head to the side. "Three hours. It took...the Usurper four days to walk that, to bring Mem here."

"It was an extraordinary act of love," Aria murmured. "One for which I'm grateful."

"We all are," Alanar agreed. "Now, are the others ready to go? Has anyone seen them this morning?"

Aven turned to Aria. "You were out and about. Did you see my parents? Or Steward?"

Aria nodded. "I saw Steward. And...it's strange, but he seemed to be in a foul mood this morning. Worse than the Smoke Dancers have been the past few days."

"What?" Owyn gasped. "Really? That's possible?"

"I'd never have expected it of him. I said good morning, and he growled at me," Aria admitted, looking down at her bowl. Then she jumped as a growl rumbled around the table in four-part guttural harmony.

"He did what?" Aven snarled. He rested both hands flat on the table and stood up. "Where is he?"

"Aven!" Aria stared at him. "Sit down. You are not going...just sit down!" She reached out and covered his hand with her own. "Sit. And calm down. All of you." She waited until Aven had taken his seat once more before continuing. "He apologized almost immediately. But something is very wrong. I cannot imagine what, and he would not tell me anything." She looked over at Del, who was clearly furious. "Del? Do you know?"

Del shook his head. *"I'll find out,"* he signed. *"Once we're finished, I'll go find him. I'm packed already. I'll bring my bag down before I go, and I'll meet you at the coach."*

Aria nodded. "Thank you." She smiled as she looked around the table. "My loves. That was impressive. If someone so much as frowns at me while we Progress, will you growl at them like that?"

"They might faint," Othi said. "That's the most fierce I've ever heard you, Treesi." He grinned at her. "You should forget trying to come up with threats. Just growl at me when you're angry."

Treesi looked at him curiously. "Would it work?"

Othi's grin grew feral. "Well, it would definitely get my attention..." he drawled. Treesi giggled, and the mood around the table lightened.

"What's the plan for today?" Alanar asked. "Are we camping at Cliffside tonight?"

"We thought about it," Owyn answered. "But I don't think Mem or Steward would sleep if we did. We'll be camping rough tonight, maybe seeing if there's anyone out there." He looked thoughtful. "It took us twelve days to get from Forge to Terraces. How long do you think it will take us to get...well, not back, but to the Eastern Trade Road? That's where we're splitting up."

"Probably twelve days," Aven answered. "Maybe longer. It depends on what we find along the way."

Aria nodded as conversation lulled and was replaced by the sounds of breakfast — spoons and knives clattering on pottery, cups clinking and the soft splash of tea being poured.

"I am heartily tired of leaving places," she murmured. "Once we get back to the Palace, let's never leave again."

"I like that idea," Alanar agreed. "Except we can't. Well, some of us can't. I have to come to Terraces to help Jehan. The

Companions each have to take their season. We'll have to travel sometimes."

"*Can we wait a year?*" Del signed. "*I'm tired of picking up and moving, too. And honestly, taking my season? Where would I go? I've never been to the Solstice village, and I can't go to the high mountains. For an Airborn, I'm awfully land-bound.*"

"Del makes a good point," Aven agreed. "Where do you take your season when...well, if there's no place for you to go? Owyn can't go to Forge, and Del has no connection to the Air tribes."

"We'll have to ask," Aria answered. "For now, we should finish eating."

"Don't worry about helping me clean up, Del," Owyn added. "You go find some answers. Let us know if we all get to growl at Steward."

DEL WANDERED DOWN THE stairs to the main level, and headed toward the tunnel that led to the stable. If Steward was anywhere, he'd be overseeing the horses, a theory proved by the time Del was halfway down the tunnel — he could hear his father's voice, echoing off the rocks.

"When I said I wanted to oversee all of the preparations, I meant all of them!"

Del stopped, suddenly uncertain. He hadn't heard that tone in his father's voice since the last time they'd had to deal with Risha. Something really was wrong.

And he'd told his Heir that he'd find out what it was. He swallowed, and continued down the tunnel, which opened out into the large stable caverns. One of the grooms was holding Freckles by the bridle.

"I can strip his tack," the man said. "And you can examine it. I promise, there weren't anything wrong with it. Teasil told me what you said happened on the road. I'm not letting that happen again. Not to a horse in my care."

Steward scowled and turned, and saw Del. He straightened, taking a deep breath. Then he turned to the groom.

"If you'd be so kind?" he asked, in a much milder tone. "I apologize for snapping. My temper today—"

"You've got all of this to deal with," the groom interrupted, gesturing with his free hand. "I'm not surprised you're snappish this early in the morning. Here, you hold his head, and I'll get this rig off of him so you can check it. Do we need to check any others? Mountain, or Pewter? Or that pretty mare?"

"Del, do you want to check Lady while we do this?" Steward asked.

Del nodded and walked around the edge of the stable toward the box stall where he could see his mare. He whistled, then laughed as she came to him and rubbed her nose against his sleeve. He took some dried apple slices from his pocket and fed them to her, then checked her tack, which seemed to be just fine. Lady nudged his arm, looking for more apples, and he fed the last of them to her before leaving the stall and going to where his father was helping the groom resaddle Freckles.

"Thank you," Steward said. "Given all the trouble we had—"

"I understand completely. Now, all the horses will be ready right here for you, and Captain Leesam will be back in a minute to make sure that no one messes with them. The carts and the coaches are down the tunnel near the mouth, and all the baggage is ready and guarded." The groom ran his hand down Freckles' neck. "I'll be missing this sweet boy. And tell the Waterborn to take good care of Pewter, will you?"

"I will do that. Thank you." Steward looked away, and Del saw Leesam and Karse coming down the tunnel toward them.

"Right, Steward," Leesam said. "I've got men stationed at the coaches, and I'll wait here until the Heir and her Companions come to take their mounts. I think we're safe enough."

"And you're as broody as an old hen today," Karse added. "Steward, what's gnawing at you?"

Steward scowled. "It's...it's nothing." He sighed. "I need to make sure the others are ready." He started walking down the tunnel that led back into Terraces. Del waved at Karse and followed, trotting to catch up with him.

"Fa," Del murmured as he fell in next to Steward. Steward jerked and turned to look at him. Then he smiled.

"I'm still not used to that," he said.

"*You growled at Aria,*" Del signed.

"She told you?"

"*And then had to hurry and tell us you apologized before Aven came after you,*" Del answered. "*And he wouldn't have been alone. You almost had all four of us after you. What is it?*"

Steward sighed. "Never you mind it. It's an old man's fancies, and worth just as much."

Del growled softly. "Fa!"

Steward's lips twitched. "I should annoy you more, just to hear you," he said. Then he sighed again. "She said no."

Del stopped walking. "*No?*"

Steward turned to look at him, and started signing. "*Rhexa told me no. Told me that she enjoys being with me, but she doesn't want me to court her. She doesn't want to marry again.*" He signed. "She's worried it will be another disaster," he finished aloud.

Del blinked, then hugged his father tightly. Steward hugged him back, then let him go.

"I have work to do, to get us on the road," he said, his voice thick. He started signing again, "*And...well, you can tell them. Let them know. But...tell them not to pester Rhexa about it. It's between her and me, and I won't have anyone bothering her over her decision. I can just hear Owyn telling her that she's chosen badly."*

Del nodded, and they started walking again, the sound of their footsteps echoing off the tunnel walls. A third set of footsteps rang behind them, and Del glanced back to see that Karse was following them.

"Need to come get my wolf," he said as he caught up with them. "And...look, Steward, what's going on? You're not like this usually. You're going to get your head handed to you before too long—"

"According to Del, I just avoided it," Steward said with a rueful laugh. "And...it's personal, Karse."

Karse nodded, then pitched his voice low. "She turned you down, hm?"

Steward stopped and stared. "You knew?"

Karse's laughter echoed down the tunnel. "You thought you were being discreet, didn't you? Steward, the only people who didn't know you and Rhexa were sparking were the people not in this town. Maybe." He clapped Steward on the back. "You weren't exactly subtle, either of you. So, want to talk?"

Steward glanced at Del, then nodded. "Let me make sure the last plans are ready, then...yes." He frowned. "Who else knew?"

"We'll go grab Mem," Karse answered. "Keep the group small." He nodded to Del. "Go on and make sure your Heir is awake, yeah?"

"She was probably awake before you were today," Del signed, then waved as headed out of the tunnels. He heard his father translating, and Karse's laughter.

Hopefully, talking to Karse would help.

Owyn was waiting at the door when Del reached the house. "Well?" he asked, stepping back and letting Del enter.

"*I'll tell everyone at once,*" Del answered, not bothering to sign. "*Do you need help with anything?*"

"Nah, everything is cleaned up, and I've packed up the leftover food to take down to Katrin so she can reallocate it. I've swept my room and yours, and brought the bags down." He nodded toward one of the low couches, where Del could see a pile of familiar bags. Owyn turned and went to the head of the corridor, raising his voice to shout, "Del is back!"

The first person to appear was Alanar, coming out of the kitchen. Del watched as he walked down the corridor and into the front room – he was trailing one hand along the wall as he walked. Del glanced at Owyn, who nodded.

"Vir," Del said slowly.

"How did you know it was me?" Virrik asked in his rolling accent. He grinned. "I like how you say my name."

"*You've got your hand on the wall,*" Del signed, waiting for Owyn to translate. "*Alanar doesn't do that. He doesn't need to.*"

"I know, and I can't figure out how he does it," Virrik admitted. "Now, should I step back? And...ah...I'm out of wall. Help?"

"When the others get here," Owyn answered. He went to Virrik's side. "Table or couch?"

"The table, please," Virrik answered. He held his hand out, and Owyn took it and led him over to the table, holding a chair out for him at the foot of the table. Del came over to sit down on his right, while Owyn took the chair on his left. Del reached out and took Virrik's hand; Virrik smiled and raised Del's fingers to his lips, kissing them.

"I wish I'd known you when my body was my own," he said. "I'd love to know what you look like." He turned toward Owyn. "What you both look like. What any of you look like." He paused and cocked his head to the side. "Someone on the stairs. I'll step back now."

Del squeezed Virrik's fingers, and felt him shudder. Then he smiled.

"Virrik promises not to listen," Alanar said. His voice had returned to his usual accent. "Not that there's anyone he can tell."

"I do not mind if Virrik listens," Aria said as she came into the room. "He offers good advice." She sat down at the head of the table. Aven went to lay his swords down on the couch with the bags, then sat down on her left.

"Othi and Treesi will be a moment," he said. "Are we ready to leave once we're done here?"

"I think we are," Owyn answered. "I'll bring the leftover food to Katrin on our way to the stables."

Treesi came into the sitting room, coming straight to the table. Othi followed her, stopping to put another bag on the couch. He sat down between her and Owyn, and rested his hands on the table. Aria nodded, and turned to look at Del.

"What did you learn?"

Del took a deep breath. "*Rhexa said no,*" he signed.

Chapter Two

"Oh, no," Owyn breathed. "Why? Why would she do that?"

Del shook his head. *"I'm not entirely clear on it. And he doesn't want us to pester her about it. It's her choice, and he's abiding by it. Even though he doesn't like it."*

"So that's why he's upset," Aven murmured. "I wouldn't have expected that. Not with how we all know they feel about each other." He turned in his chair as someone knocked on the door. "Come in!"

The door opened, and Rhexa came inside. She stopped short when she saw them all sitting at the table.

"Well, I wasn't expecting you all to be awake and ready," she said brightly. "I was thinking I'd be your wake-up call. And…" she paused, looking at each of them. Then she sighed. "You know already. Did he come last night to tell you?"

"It happened last night?" Owyn asked. "No, he didn't. We didn't know until Del went and talked to him, on account of he's out of sorts enough to growl at Aria. And it was either ask him what's wrong, or let Aven thump him."

Rhexa laughed. "Oh, that's silly. Aven wouldn't do that…" Her voice trailed off as Aven nodded. "You would? But…" She shook her head. "No. You're not allowed to thump him. And it's none of your business. We're both adults."

"It is none of our business, but he is one of mine. As are you," Aria said. "And we worry. He does care for you—"

"And I'm not even four months a widow," Rhexa interrupted. "After a disastrous marriage that ended with her betraying all of us. I can't commit to something yet, Aria. I'm not sure where my head is. Not yet. So I told him no, and I told him that I'd see him again when you came back to Terraces after the Progress, and that we'd see where my head was then." She sniffed. "Honestly, it's no different from what he was proposing. He'd have to come back to me after the Progress anyway. I don't understand why he doesn't see it that way."

"There is a difference," Othi said. "If you'd said yes, he'd know for certain that he had someone to come back to." He looked at Treesi and took her hand. "I understand that. It's what brought me home."

Rhexa shook her head. "I...I can't give him that. Not yet. He doesn't like my answer, but that's the only one I can give him. And I don't want to end this visit with an argument. Not with all of you."

Owyn stood up and walked around the table. "Auntie, we're not looking for an argument. We were worried about him, and now we're worried about the both of you. We just want you happy. And...well, we thought you were happy with him."

"I was happy with Baryl, too," Rhexa said, toying with the button at the throat of her shirt. "Owyn, every time I thought I was happy with someone, it came around and bit me. I trusted Baryl, and she betrayed me. Twice. I...I need to be sure this time. I need to go slowly. And I need to not make promises that will bite me again." She frowned slightly. "And you all need to mind your own business!" she added. "I love you all, but this is mine to do."

Owyn nodded. "All right. Are...are you going to be all right, when we go?"

Rhexa made a face at him. "Do I have a choice?" she asked. "I'll be all right, because I have to be all right. For everyone out in this city who is counting on me to make things all right for them." She paused. "But I'll miss you," she added with a soft smile. "And I'll miss him. Maybe I'll be able to give him a better answer when you come back." Her smile widened. "And I can't wait to meet the baby."

AVEN AND OTHI CARRIED most of the baggage, while Owyn carried the basket of food they hadn't eaten. Rhexa walked alongside him as they went down the stairs.

"I appreciate that you worry about me," she said. "But you don't have to. I'll be fine. And by the time you come back, I think I'll have a better idea of what I want." She stopped at the bottom of the stairs. "I'll walk with you to the dispensary. You're not supposed to be going alone, anyway."

Owyn snorted. "I'm fine, Auntie. Terraces—"

"If you're about to say Terraces is safe, then I'll remind you about Lear," Rhexa interrupted. "I'll walk with you, and then we can meet the others in the stables."

"*I'll come,*" Del whispered in Owyn's mind. "*Unless you want a private talk with your aunt?*"

Owyn glanced over his shoulder. "Del says he'll come with us. Allie, do you want to stay with us or go to the stables?"

"I'll come with you," Alanar answered.

"We'll see you in the stables," Aria said. "Don't take too long."

"I won't," Owyn said. He started toward the dispensary, with Rhexa on his left, and Del and Alanar on his right. They didn't say anything until after he'd delivered the basket to Katrin, and accepted a hug in return.

"Aria and Del both said this morning that they're tired of leaving places," he said as they started walking toward the healing center. "Tired of picking up just when we'd gotten comfortable. I know we have to, but I agree with them. I'm tired of traveling."

"Oh, I can't even imagine," Rhexa said. "I had a hard enough time when we came to Terraces, and that was only the once. Constantly picking up and leaving everything behind? This is...what? The fourth time for you? In a year? I don't know how you can do it."

Owyn started counting on his fingers. "Forge to here. Here to the Palace. The Palace back here...well, going the long way." He heard Alanar wince, and nodded. "Sorry, Allie. Then from here back to the Palace. And now the Progress. Five times." He shrugged. "But it's not like we have a choice."

"And we also don't have to like it," Alanar added. "The Mother can tell us we have to move. She can't make us like it. We can't be the only Companions to complain about the travel. Do you think it gets repetitive?" He chuckled. "I wonder if She gets bored with hearing us complain?"

Del snorted. "*I wonder. Has a Companion ever said no?*"

"No to...what? To being a Companion?" Owyn stared at Del, who nodded. "Can you even do that?" He frowned. "Would you want to?"

Del took his hand, and his mental voice was soft. "*I wouldn't give any of you up. But I'm curious. Being a Companion is life-changing. Shouldn't we have a say in having our lives changed?*"

Owyn nodded slowly. "That's an interesting question. We can ask Granna."

"What was the question?" Alanar asked.

"Why people chosen to be Companions don't have a say in it," Owyn answered, and Alanar laughed.

"Oh," he said, nodding. "I understand. 'Why me? Why not someone else?'"

Del shook his head. "No," he said aloud.

Alanar's brows rose. "Then I'm misunderstanding."

"I think I understand," Rhexa said. "Being the Heir, or being a Companion isn't something you decide to be. It's who you are, because you're chosen for it. But Del is asking why you can be chosen without having a choice in the matter." She paused. "I'm not sure how you could be given that choice, really. I don't suppose the Mother can interview all the potential candidates, the way I can for assistants. Or maybe She does, and you just don't know." Rhexa laughed. "Honestly, it's all far too esoteric for me. I don't deal well with...well, things I can't put a finger on. Give me plans and schematics and ways to take care of people any day."

"That's what we're doing, really," Owyn said, glancing at Del. "We're making plans and trying to take care of people." He pulled his hand out of Del's, then put his arm around Del's shoulders. "Taking care of each other, too."

"*I am still curious,*" Del murmured in Owyn's head. "*I wonder what that would mean for the lore? If taking the wrong road in the Progress is bad, what would having someone turn down their gem foretell?*"

"If taking the wrong road means disaster, then I imagine having someone say no to their gem would mean even worse disaster," Owyn answered. "Which...yeah, that's ridiculous. What's going to make a disaster worse?"

"*Wine-soaked cherries,*" Del answered immediately.

THE STABLES WERE FULL of people and an unusual amount of noise, and Owyn winced as they got there.

"*This isn't good for the horses,*" Del said in Owyn's mind. "*All of these people should be outside.*" He stopped walking. "*I don't see Aria. This...is this all guards? Shouldn't guards know better?*"

"What is going on here?" Rhexa demanded, raising her voice slightly. At the sound, everyone else fell silent. "Where's Teasil?" Rhexa continued. "Why is everyone standing here making all this noise? You should all be outside, not scaring the horses!"

"What are you all still doing in here?" Teasil snapped as he and Karse came out of the stable. Teasil was leading a pair of ponies. "I told you to wait out in the yard...Governor!"

"I was wondering why you were letting all of these guards scare your horses, Teasil," Rhexa said. "They're not listening?"

"And they all of them should know better. Every single one of them," Karse growled. "Right. Outside, all of you. March!"

A few minutes later, the stable was empty. Teasil took a deep breath and let it out.

"Told them to wait for us outside," he grumbled. "Why didn't they listen? Let's get these lads saddled."

"Ponies for Copper and Danir?" Rhexa asked.

"Thought it would be a good idea," Karse answered. "Part of their training. They should know how to ride, and how to care for their horses. Talked to Teasil, and he said he had this pair that the boys could have." He turned and smiled at Teasil. "I appreciate this, Teasil."

"It's a good idea for them to know," Teasil agreed. "Although that Danir, he won't be on a pony for long, or I don't know boys. He's got some growth coming on." He grinned. "Copper, he'll be solid when he's grown, but Danir? He's going to be tall."

"We'll worry about that when his trousers start getting shorter," Karse said. "Wouldn't be the first time one of my men had to learn how to move all over again because he grew a span or two." He shook his head. "Going to have to talk to Steward about adding horsemanship to the new Palace Guard training, because that lot weren't any of them mine from Forge, they weren't Waterborn, and they weren't old Palace guards. The old guards know horses, mine know better than to raise a fuss like that in a stable, and Water follow orders the first time." He shook his head. "Del, I left Steward with Memfis and Meris, and they'll be along shortly. I know you were going to ask me that."

Del nudged Owyn's arm. "*Tell him thank you?*"

"Del says thank you," Owyn translated. "Are they the last ones?"

Karse nodded. "Everyone else is waiting out by the coaches," he said. "They'll be the last ones. Del, you know horses. Will you saddle these lads for me? I need to have a word with Rhexa."

Rhexa arched a brow. "If this is what I think it is, you do not need to have a word with me."

Karse grinned. "Thought you might say that. No, this isn't about Steward. You're a grown adult, and so is he. That's all your business. No, I needed to talk to you about Lee."

Rhexa blushed. "Captain, I'm so sorry. I—"

Karse laughed and held his hand up. "No need to apologize. I imagine you've got a lot of that this morning?" He glanced at Owyn. "Nah, I sat down with Steward and Memfis, and we talked. He told us what you told him, about why you said no. And honestly, I can't disagree with your reasoning. So no lectures from me. No, this is about Leesam. He's a good guard. One of the better ones I've trained. But he's green, and he admits it. He's never been in charge of something on this scale before. He needs support."

Rhexa nodded. "What can I do? We've never had official guards in Terraces before. We've never needed them before."

"That's it. You don't know how to command the guard, and he isn't used to taking orders from someone who doesn't know what orders to give." He took a sealed letter out of his pocket. "I talked this over with him, and he knows I'm suggesting this to you. Lee needs a Commandant, and you need someone who knows how to organize a guard." He handed the letter to Rhexa. "You send that to the Palace next time Destria comes."

Rhexa looked down at the letter. "And what will happen then?"

"Then you'll get a commandant. His name is Grison—"

"The new armorer?" Owyn blurted. "Grison One-Arm? Him?"

Karse grinned. "Yeah, him. You're not old enough to remember when Grison One-Arm had two arms, and was Commandant of the Forge Council Guard. And you're really not old enough to remember when Captain Grison took one know-it-all trainee and kicked him into shape."

"And was that know-it-all trainee named Karse?" Rhexa asked.

"Might have been," Karse admitted, and winked at Rhexa, making her laugh. "I was greener than green when I joined the Guard, and Captain Grison could have thrown me back. But he said he saw something in me and he kept at it until other folks saw it, too. Best commander I ever had. When he showed up at the Palace with a load of refugees? You could have dropped me."

"Is that why you were so insistent that we find him a place?" Steward walked up to them, followed by Memfis and Lady Meris. "You never did say. Why are we talking about Grison?" He nodded to Rhexa. "Good morning. They...no one's been pestering you, have they?"

"Not much, and they all mean well," Rhexa answered. "So I'll let it go. I'll walk out with you, and see you off."

Karse started walking. "I'm talking about Grison because Lee is still too new to command to be good at it. We saw where that went — he should have gotten wind about Lear long before it came down to assassination attempts, and he should have checked with Persis before Owyn did. He needs support to come into his own, and Grison...well, he's wasted as an armorer, but he won't take a subordinate role, especially not under someone he trained. He's too proud for that. But if you offer him the position of Guard Commandant, with Lee as Captain? He'll take that. And he'll push Lee to his full potential."

"And you're sure Lee's fine with this?" Owyn asked. "Because Aunt Rhexa don't need bad blood among the guard."

"Lee jumped at the chance to learn from Grison," Karse assured them. "He's excited for it."

They walked out of the stables and into the sunlight, and Owyn saw Del, who was introducing the boys to their ponies. Aria, Treesi, Othi and Aven were near one of the coaches with Afansa, who had Howl sleeping in her arms. Jehan and Aleia were with Pirit, Skela and Zarai. There were strangers off to one side, surrounding carts loaded with bundles and boxes, and there were guards milling around, walking their horses. Wren saw them and came toward them.

"Good morning, Captain," he called. "The advance riders went out about an hour ago, and the settlers are ready to move. We're just waiting on you."

"Where are we stopping tonight?" Owyn asked.

"Remember where we camped, when we stopped to go to market?" Memfis asked. "South of Cliffside? Near there."

Owyn coughed. "Ah...we left an awful lot of bodies around there. Most of a squad? Palace uniforms, but they weren't the Usurper's men. They were Risha's. But...yeah...that might be...I don't know...kind of a gruesome camp?"

Steward frowned and looked at Memfis. "Did you tell me that? Did we warn the riders?"

"No, and no," Memfis answered. "In that order."

Karse snorted. "Right. Wren, send a courier. Warn them what they're riding into?"

"I'll go myself, if that's all right, Captain?"

Karse nodded. "Very good. Off with you."

Wren saluted and led his horse away; once he was far enough from the others, he mounted and rode off.

"Let's get loaded," Steward said. "Who is riding, and who is in the coach?"

"Aven said he wanted to ride, to get the feel for it again," Alanar said. "Wyn, do you mind if I stay in the coach today? I'm tired."

"My tossing and turning kept you awake, huh?" Owyn grimaced. "Sorry, Allie."

"You didn't yell at me, the way Aria did to Aven," Alanar said, keeping his voice low. "I'll take the tossing and turning to an empty bed." He leaned down and kissed Owyn, then turned toward Rhexa. "You have to promise not to work too hard, Auntie."

"And you have to promise to be careful out there," Rhexa answered. "I'll see you when you come back." She hugged him, then turned to Owyn. "And you," she said. "You promise me that you'll be careful!"

"I promise, Auntie!" Owyn said, hugging her tightly. "I promise! You...you take care of yourself. And Trinket. You take care of her, too."

"And she'll take care of me." Rhexa laughed. "Let me say the rest of my goodbyes."

Owyn stood back and watched as Rhexa moved through the crowd, laughing and giving hugs and kisses, making her way slowly through the crowd until she was back with Owyn.

"You'd best go on," she said. He could hear the tears hiding in her voice. He smiled and hugged her again.

"I love you, Auntie," he whispered. "Go have a good cry, and we'll see you when the Progress is done."

She hiccupped, and hugged him tightly. "Don't you make me cry in front of everyone!" she whispered back. "I'll be fine. You should go."

Owyn kissed her cheek and let her go, and wasn't surprised to see Steward standing next to them.

"Governor," he said softly. "When the Progress is over—"

"I'll hopefully have an answer for you," she said. Then she smiled. "But you have to come back to get it. I'm not putting it into a letter."

Steward blinked. Then he smiled. "Then I'll see you after we've returned," he said. He held out his hand, and she looked at it as if she'd never seen one before.

"Really?" she asked, her voice dry. "A handshake?" She took his hand, stepped in close, and kissed him soundly on the lips. She stepped back, and he just looked at her.

"Really?" he asked, mimicking her tone. He reached out, grabbed her hand, and pulled her to him, wrapping one arm around her and kissing her with enough passion that Alanar whistled softly.

"You can tell?" Owyn whispered.

"I can feel them both from here," Alanar whispered back. "Someone needs to separate them, or we're not leaving until tomorrow."

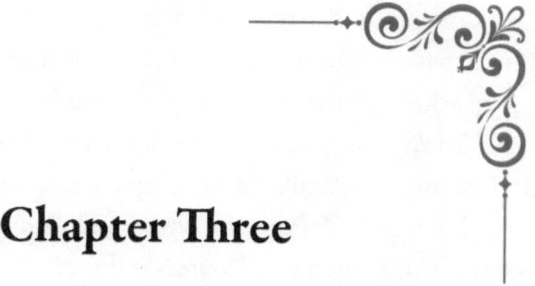

Chapter Three

I t had been long enough since Aven had last ridden a horse without pain that he was certain he'd forgotten how. But the gray mare that Teasil had picked out for him was gentle, and her gait was smooth. Riding her was actually enjoyable, and he was starting to think he could stay in the saddle until they reached Cliffside.

And he was surprised at how good it felt to be back in the saddle.

"How does it feel, Ven?"

Aven turned to see that his father had ridden up next to him. "It feels good."

Jehan nodded. "You're more relaxed. More than I've seen in a long time."

"Not being in pain will do that."

Jehan laughed. "True. Don't push, though. We have the rest of the Progress ahead of us. When we stop next, it's time to get back in the coach."

"I thought I'd wait until we got to Cliffside," Aven said.

"I just said don't push." Jehan sounded a little more stern. "You're not ready for three hours of riding." He grinned. "I'm not sure that I'm ready for three hours of riding. So when we stop, you and I will both get in the coach and I'll start teaching you about tattoo removal."

Aven looked at his father. "You could tell me now."

Jehan shook his head. "No. Consider it an incentive. Or bribery. You decide." He nodded. "Othi will have to stop, too. I've been watching him. He's too stiff. He'll be feeling that tomorrow."

"He might be feeling that by the time we reach Cliffside," Aven said. "After my first day in the saddle, I couldn't walk." He smiled at the memory of lurching around the campfire. "We did warn him not to try to sleep in the saddle."

"That sounds like a story," Jehan said. "Did you learn to sleep in the saddle?"

"I failed miserably at learning to sleep in the saddle," Aven said. "However, I am an expert at falling off my horse."

Jehan burst out laughing, loud enough that Aven had to calm his horse.

"Sorry," Jehan apologized.

"She'll get used to us." Aven looked around. "Fa, maybe you can tell me. I was in healing trance the last time I came this way, but it's greener than I remember. Is it?"

"I haven't been this way in more years than you've been alive," Jehan said. "So I don't know." He looked around. "It is very green. Steward would probably know. We can ask him." Jehan urged his horse forward, and Aven followed him. He lingered by the coach so he could look in the window. Inside were Aria, Alanar and Treesi, and it looked as though all three of them were asleep.

They found Steward near the front of the Progress, riding with Karse and Del. Steward looked over at them.

"You're looking good, Aven," he said. "It's good to see you without painlines."

"Painlines?" Aven glanced at his father. "What are painlines?"

"Wrinkles that show up when you're in pain," Jehan answered. "He's right. Yours are gone."

"I didn't realize that I had them," Aven admitted. "Steward, is it usually this green?"

Steward looked at him. "You came up this way from Forge, didn't you?"

"When we were on this road, I was in healing trance after having my head broken." Aven touched his chest, and the lump under his shirt at his collarbone. "And this broken. So I didn't actually see anything between Cliffside and Terraces."

Steward nodded. "It is greener here, I think. But it's been a time since I last rode this way myself."

"*It's all greener,*" Del signed, letting his reins fall. "*I noticed it after we left the Palace. I don't think I've ever seen this much green.*"

Karse nodded. "Good. We need a good harvest." He grinned as Del laughed. "I'm getting there. I'm learning."

"Where are the boys?" Jehan asked. "And Howl?"

"Howl is here." Karse reached down and touched a large saddlebag. "He's getting used to riding, and Sentry is getting used to having him there. The boys are with Owyn and Othi, learning how to ride. Aleia is with them, I think. And Memfis. He's getting the feel for it again."

"Who's teaching them to ride?" Aven asked. "Owyn?"

"Owyn said he wasn't that good. No, they've got Keelan with them. I'd have asked Wren to watch them, but he rode on." He gestured toward the road. "What are we looking at? How many men did Owyn kill?"

"You'll have to ask Owyn," Aven answered. "And I'm not entirely sure he knows." He shifted in the saddle, looking around. "We're just going to leave the settlers at Cliffside? No guards or anything?"

"Leesam sent guards to make sure they're settled in," Karse answered. "Headed by another one of mine. Westir. You remember him?"

"Not really?" Aven answered. "Was he there when we went after Owyn?"

"Yes. There's going to be a guard outpost there that reports back to Terraces every ten days." He looked around. "I'm going to ride back down the line, see if there's any need to stop."

"And if we do stop..." Jehan let his voice trail off, and Aven sighed.

"Yes, Fa."

ARIA STEPPED OUT OF the coach and stretched, spreading her wings wide, then tipped her face back and closed her eyes.

"How much further to Cliffside?" she heard Alanar ask.

"An hour or so?" Owyn answered. "Want to ride with me?"

"I would like to ride," Aria said. "I should get used to riding again." She turned to see Owyn staring at her. "What?"

"Are you sure you should?" he asked. "I mean—" He gestured vaguely at his own abdomen.

"I'm going to have to, once we go to Forge," Aria pointed out. "And I haven't ridden since Treesi and I rode to Forge before the Smoking Mountain erupted. I need to know if I still can, or if we need to change plans."

Owyn looked thoughtful. "All right. I'll go see about your horse." He turned, and nearly bumped into Aven. "You going to ride with us, Fishie?"

"Who's us?" Aven asked.

"Me, Allie and Aria."

Aven turned to look at Aria. "You're going to ride?"

"Just for a little," Aria said. "I'll need to be able to ride when we go to Forge. I haven't in months. I need to remember how."

Aven scowled. "I told my father I'd ride in the coach with him until we reach Cliffside. I promised I wouldn't push too hard my first day back in the saddle."

"Then you will not, my Water," Aria said. She put her arms around his neck, smiling as he rested his hands on her sides. "We can ride together tomorrow. And once we leave Cliffside, I will join you in the coach."

Aven nodded, tipping his head forward to rest his forehead against hers. She closed her eyes and smiled, breathing in the breath of his lungs, breathing out her love for him.

Then he jumped, looking down between them. He looked startled.

"What is it?" she asked.

Aven burst out laughing. "She kicked me!"

"She?" Aria stepped back, looking down at herself, realizing what Aven said, what he meant. She rested one hand on her belly and felt the baby press back. Their baby. Their *daughter*. The idea made her feel as though she was flying. She looked up at Aven. "She? Really?"

For a moment, it seemed as if Aven wasn't understanding what she was saying. Then Owyn laughed. "It's a girl?"

Aven looked at him and his jaw dropped. "I...oh," he stammered. "I fucked it up! I promised you I wasn't going to tell." He looked away. "Aria—"

"You don't have to apologize, Aven," Aria said. She reached out, and when he'd taken her hands, she pulled him close and wound her arms around his neck again. "I am not angry. Truly." She smiled up at him. "Now we get to decide her name, don't we?"

"You made me promise not to tell," Aven repeated. "I spoiled it."

"How many times have I asked, since I made the mistake of making you promise?" Aria trailed her fingertips down the back of his neck. "I never should have asked that of you."

"And we don't have to tell anyone else," Owyn said. "I mean, Allie and Treesi, you both know, right?"

"Of course we know," Alanar said. "Jehan knows. But we've not told anyone. No one knows other than the healers, and now you and Aria." He looked thoughtful. "Are you going to tell anyone, Aria? Your grandmother, or Del, or anyone?"

"I..." Aria paused and looked up at Aven. "Just Del, I think. It's not fair that he be the only Companion to not know."

"You don't want to tell Mother Meris?" Aven asked. "I think we should."

Aria closed her eyes, thinking. Then she nodded. "You're right. But that's all. No one else." She laughed and kissed Aven. "Thank you."

"For making a mistake?" he asked.

"For forgetting and letting me know," she corrected. "I won't ask you to keep secrets from me again. Now, let's go tell Grandmother." She looked over at Owyn and Alanar. "Will you come with us?"

"No, this is yours and Aven's," Owyn said. He reached out and took Alanar's hand. "You go on."

OWYN SMILED AS ALANAR wrapped his arms around him, leaning back into his husband's chest as he watched Aven and Aria walk away hand-in-hand. The radiant look on Aria's face reminded him that he might have forgotten something.

"Allie, I think I forgot to tell you," he said, keeping his voice low. "When you were working on Aven...well...I was working on Aria."

"Working on...oh?" Alanar chuckled. "I was wondering when that was going to happen. And you didn't tell me why?"

"Let's see...we both have been sort of busy, and it slipped my mind with the whole we need to leave right fucking now vision that wasn't a vision." Owyn tipped his head back. "I should have told you bedtime stories while we still had the privacy to do it."

"You can tell me later," Alanar said, kissing the top of Owyn's head. "Can you hear her now?"

"No. Something changed when I tested, we think. I can feel her. Like right now? She's so happy it's making me giddy just being near her. But I can't hear her the way I can you or Aven or Del." Owyn took a deep breath. "Allie, she asked me for a baby. She wants her next one to be mine."

Alanar tensed a little. "Really? I...do you think I can be there when that happens? Will you mind?"

"You'll have to ask Aria," Owyn said. "I won't, but she might. You don't mind, do you?"

"Mind? That she loves you enough to want your child?" Alanar put his hands on Owyn's shoulders and turned him so they were facing each other. "Of course I don't mind. If I was equipped to do it, I would do it. Because that...that's forever."

Owyn blinked. "You want children? This is the first you've ever said!"

Alanar shrugged. "I never thought about it before. But...if there was a way for us to have a baby? I'd do it." He paused. "We could. We could find someone to carry the baby for us. Someone we both like. It's done in Terraces."

Owyn forgot how to breathe for a moment. "I...we could? I mean...I know we could, but we *could*?"

Alanar laughed. "Broke your brain, didn't I?" he asked. "Owyn, we can discuss this more after the Progress. But yes, we could. And yes, I would. If you wanted to."

Owyn swallowed. "We're going to have to have a long talk. Because...yeah, we need to talk this through."

Alanar smiled. "I'm not going anywhere. Let's go find my boots. Then we can go get the horses."

Owyn turned and looked at the coach. "I'm not sure where the boots are. Let's find Trista."

Jehan joined them while Owyn helped the serving girl assigned to the Companions go through bags and boxes.

"What are you looking for?" he asked.

Owyn sat back on his heels. "Allie's boots. He was going to ride a bit with me, until we got to Cliffside. But we can't find his boots." He looked over at the girl. "Trista, we didn't forget them, did we?"

She shook her head. "I...I could have sworn I packed them myself. In this case here." She pointed. "But they're not there, and nothing is folded the way I fold things. The shirts are folded flat. I don't do that. I roll them. And none of these things look familiar." She shook her head. "Fireborn, I don't know."

Jehan came over to look at the case. "Trista, go and tell Karse what you just told us," he said softly. "He should be near the front of the line. Have him come back with you."

She nodded. "Yes, Senior Healer." She ran off, and Jehan crouched next to the case. He looked into it, then got up and walked away, coming back with a stick. He poked it into the case, frowning.

"What are you doing?" Owyn asked.

"You stay over there," Jehan said softly. He scowled. "I think there's something in here that shouldn't be. It feels like there is. But I want Karse to check."

Owyn frowned and looked at Alanar. "Trista and I both went through that case. If there's something in there, it would have got me already." He took a deep breath. "They're trying for me again, aren't they? Why take Allie's boots?"

"Because that means I can't go with you to Forge," Alanar answered. "There's nowhere between here and...well, there's nowhere for me to have boots made to replace them."

Owyn blinked. "Then...oh, fuck. Someone knows we're splitting up to follow Axia's Way." He turned to see Karse coming toward them with Trista.

"Missing boots?"

"And a tampered with case," Jehan said. "Come look." He handed the stick to Karse. "I think Owyn and Trista were very lucky just now."

Karse poked the stick into the case, then looked at the case from the side. "Trista, go fetch a blanket, will you? And an extra bag, or a box. Something."

When Trista came back with a blanket, Karse pulled the contents of the case out, tossing them to the side. Then he moved the case onto the blanket. Owyn looked at the pile of scattered clothes.

"There are clothes missing," he said. "My wedding shirt should be there. I don't see it. Is there anything in our clothes?"

"No, but this case is shorter inside than it is outside," Karse answered. He gestured for Owyn to come closer, and pointed with the stick. "See that?"

Owyn looked closely. "Is...is that a hinge?"

"Looks like it," Karse said. "Let's see what happens when I open it. Stand back." He looked around and waited until everyone had moved away, then tipped the case onto its side. The false bottom swung open, and a large, black snake tumbled out.

"Widowmaker!" Karse yelped. He kicked the case the rest of the way over, trapping the snake inside the upside-down box. He walked slowly around the case, then looked at Owyn and shook his head. "That...yeah, someone doesn't care about collateral damage."

"That's one of the snakes that took Mem's arm," Owyn said softly. "How...how could they get it in there without...I don't know...dying?"

Karse sighed. "There are ways to handle snakes. If you know what you're doing, it wouldn't be hard. Trista, I need you to think. Did this case come with us from the Palace, or did you get it in Terraces?"

Trista came a little closer. "I...it looks like one of the ones from the Palace, but none of those had a fake bottom. Is there a mark on the bottom? A maker mark?"

Karse shook his head. "Nothing there."

"Then that case didn't come from the Palace," Trista said. She folded her arms over her chest. "All the luggage was prepared special, and they all had the maker's mark. That's a copy."

Karse nodded. "Right. Trista, why don't you repack those things into something new?" He pointed at the pile of clothes. "If there's anything in there worth saving, and it's not all rags. And I'll get rid of this." He gathered the blanket tightly around the box and tied the corners into knots. "I'll have to report to Steward, and to Aria—"

"I'll tell Aria," Owyn blurted. "Just...she's really happy right now, and...well, I don't want to spoil that." He looked up at Alanar. "I'm sorry, Allie."

Alanar wrapped his arms around Owyn. "It's not your fault, love."

"Fireborn?" Trista called. She was kneeling next to the pile of clothes. "These aren't your things. All of these...I don't know who these things belong to." She picked up one item. "I'd never let you wear these. They're rags!"

Jehan came and stood over her. "So...someone swapped out the real box with an identical one? Which means that Owyn and Alanar's clothes are somewhere back in Terraces." He looked over at Owyn and Alanar. "I don't think it would violate the lore to send someone back to find it. As long as you don't go back?"

"Check with Steward," Alanar said. "When we tell him—"

"Tell me what?" Steward asked as he came toward them. "We should be moving out shortly." He looked at the pile of ragged clothing. "What is this?"

Karse pointed at the chest. "They tried again. That's a good copy of one of our cases, and there was a Widowmaker inside. Would sending someone back for the real chest violate the lore?"

"No," Steward answered. "And they'll be able to catch up with us when we make camp tonight. But let me make sure I understand this. Someone smuggled a duplicate case into the luggage?"

"Sometime between when I packed the real case, and when it was loaded onto the cart," Trista said. "Steward, I swear I packed the real case!"

"And who took it from you?" Steward asked.

Trista frowned. "There were a lot of people helping. I didn't know all of them. Governor Rhexa said she'd picked all of them, though." She looked around. "We should check the other cases. Just to be safe."

Steward nodded. "Karse, if you would?" He looked at Trista, then turned to face Owyn and Alanar. "Do you want someone new assigned to you?"

"What?" Owyn gasped. He glanced at Trista, seeing the shocked look on her face. "No! That wasn't her fault! And she was going through the box, too. It could have killed her as easy as me! She's doing a good job of taking care of us."

"And now she'll do a better job of it," Steward added. "Trista, from here on out, anything having to do with the Fireborn or his husband doesn't leave your sight. Understood?"

"Yes, Steward," Trista said.

"Alanar, you can ride in the coach with me and Aven," Jehan said. "I'm going to teach him how to remove tattoos."

"Oh?" Alanar grinned. "That sounds like an interesting lecture."

"Who said anything about lecture?" Jehan asked. "Othi and Treesi will be riding with us. We're starting today."

Chapter Four

Lady Meris was sitting just outside her coach, accompanied by Memfis, Afansa, Copper and Danir. The boys were regaling her with stories of their first day of riding, and she smiled through her laughter as Aven and Aria approached.

"My darlings, you both look so very happy," she said. "What is it?"

Aven looked at Aria and grinned. The sting of having forgotten to be careful was eased by how radiantly happy it had made Aria. "Could we have a word with you, Mother Meris?" he asked. "In private?"

Afansa laughed. "I'll take the boys. We'll go find Karse and see if he needs any help with Howl. Memfis, come with us?"

Memfis slowly got to his feet. "I'm not used to riding anymore," he grumbled. "I'll be joining you in the coach, Meris."

"Good. We can discuss what we need to teach Owyn about projecting," Meris said. "Your reading is more recent than mine." She waited until the others had walked away, then looked up at Aven and Aria. "A private discussion? Sit. Tell me what's so important, my darlings?"

Aven helped Aria sit in Afansa's chair, then sat on the ground at her feet. "I...ah...forgot I was supposed to be keeping the baby's gender a secret," Aven admitted. "So it isn't a secret to Aria anymore. We're keeping it to just the Companions and the healers, though. And we wanted you to know, too."

Meris arched a brow. "You actually told Aria?"

"I forgot!" Aven laughed.

"The baby is a girl," Aria added in a quiet voice. "We're not telling anyone else. Just you."

"A girl?" Meris laughed. "Well, I'm not sure why I'm surprised. I knew it would be one or the other! Do you know her name yet?" She looked thoughtful. "Another Liara for the Air tribe?"

"No," Aven answered. Aria looked at him, clearly surprised. "We haven't talked about it yet, but Water—"

"Oh, of course!" Meris interrupted. "I remember now. Hara explained it to me, when she was carrying her first. I'd forgotten that."

"Forgotten what?" Aria asked. "Why should we not name her Liara?"

"Because Water doesn't reuse names," Aven answered. "To reuse a name is to give the child that person's fate, for good or ill. At least, that's what I was taught. So we change the names. Something close, to honor whoever we're naming the child for, but nothing identical."

"Such as Aven for Abin," Meris said, and Aven nodded.

"Exactly. So if we wanted to name her for your mother, or Mother Liara of old, we would change it, just a little." He took Aria's hand. "We should have had this talk already."

"That would have been difficult," Aria said. "With you not telling me. Or would we have picked a name for a boy and a name for a girl?"

"We can always use the unused name later," Aven answered. Aria blushed.

"I told Owyn I wanted the next one to be his," she said softly. "If you don't mind?"

Aven blinked. "I...why should I mind? Aria, this is our family. Our children are our children, no matter who sires them or bears them." He looked at Meris. "Isn't that how it should be?"

"That is how it should be, but in truth, it rarely is that way," Meris said. "I can't say there was ever a Firstborn who didn't favor their children by one Companion over the others. To our regret, I'm afraid. However, I can't say I've ever seen a tighter bond than the one you all share." She held her hand out. "Help me up, Aven?"

Aven got to his feet, pausing for a moment once he was upright to marvel at being able to move. Meris smiled fondly at him as he helped her up. Once she was standing, she hugged him tightly; he smiled and returned the embrace, wrapping his arms around her.

"Thank you," she murmured, sounding almost as if she was holding back a sob. "For...for everything."

"Mother Meris?" he whispered. "What's wrong?"

She shook her head, and let him go. "Nothing," she answered. "Nothing is wrong. Everything...everything is as it should be."

Aven made himself step back, wanting more than anything to hug her again, so he could examine her. There had been something...something that tickled at the edges of his healing senses. But Meris was perfectly healthy for a woman of her age — she'd been fully examined by Pirit and pronounced hale enough to make the journey. So there was no reason for him to examine her again without her permission. He turned to help Aria to her feet, and watched as Aria went to embrace her great-grandmother.

He was imagining things. Meris was fine.

But he'd still mention it to his father.

"Aven!"

Aven laughed, turning at the sound of his father's voice. "I should have been thinking of the Mother walking up with the answers to all of our problems," he said as Jehan joined him. "I was just about to come find you."

Jehan smiled, but it didn't reach his eyes. "Have you seen your mother?"

"I have," Meris called. "Aleia was with Treesi and Othi. I think they were discussing the differences in tribal wedding customs."

"Oh, good. I needed to find them, too." Jehan looked around. "We'll be leaving shortly, I think. Aven, walk with me for a moment."

Aven glanced at Aria, who didn't seem to have noticed Jehan's distraction. She smiled and turned back to talk to Meris, so Aven followed his father and whispered, "What's wrong?"

"Another attempt on Owyn," Jehan whispered back. "He's fine. Everyone is fine. But this one...this was careless. And stupid. Careless and stupid."

"What happened?"

"Whoever it was replaced Owyn and Alanar's case with a good forgery. When they went in looking for Alanar's boots, your servant noticed it was wrong. And when they emptied it, they found a fake bottom and a Widowmaker snake."

"And everyone is fine?" Aven repeated. He looked around. "Fa—"

"I was with him when they found the false bottom, and I didn't let them do anything until Karse was with us. Owyn and Alanar and Trista were all clear." Jehan took a deep breath. "Karse is dealing with the snake. Which is back in the box. We have no real idea as to how it happened. Trista doesn't have any idea as to how the change happened, and she's beside herself, both at the attempt and the fact that Alanar and Owyn's things appeared to have been left behind." He smiled slightly. "We're sending riders back to see if they can find the real case."

"Which hopefully wasn't destroyed," Aven said.

"Truth. We'll be a long way from a tailor." Jehan nodded. "We're starting to get everyone ready. We'll be leaving as soon as we can."

Aven looked back at Aria. "Why are you telling me and not us? Why not tell Aria?"

"Because Owyn said she's in a very good mood, and he didn't want to spoil it. He says he'll tell her." Jehan looked over at Aria and Meris, then back at Aven. "So you finally told her?"

Aven chuckled. "I sort of forgot to keep it to myself," he admitted. "We're not telling anyone other than Companions and Mother Meris."

Jehan laughed. "Do you mind if I tell your mother?" he asked. "I haven't told her. She's a little vexed at me over it."

"I'll ask Aria," Aven answered. "I don't mind, but she might."

"It can wait," Jehan said. "Now, go get ready. We'll have all the healers in one coach for the lecture and practicum on tattoo removal."

"We're starting to work on Othi today?"

Jehan nodded. "That's why I was looking for him and Treesi."

KARSE STEPPED BACK and watched the fire licking at the sides of the case, watched the paint blacken and peel. He needed to go find Howl — the wolf had run off into the trees, heading back toward the coaches. But he wanted to be sure the fire stayed small. He heard a footstep behind him, and spoke without turning.

"I'll stay and make sure it burns out. So you can ride out without me."

"Which leads to the question of why you're burning a piece of luggage in the first place?"

Karse looked over his shoulder. "Mem! I thought you were Steward." He turned to face Memfis and Afansa. "Where are the boys?"

"Howl met us halfway," Afansa answered. "Why are you burning a case?" She frowned slightly. "That...isn't that Owyn's?"

"It is and it isn't," Karse answered. "Clever fake. I'm sending people back to Terraces to find the real one. Steward says that won't violate the lore. But this...someone really doesn't care who they kill as long as they get your son, Memfis."

"What? Is Owyn all right?"

"He's fine," Karse said. "He and Alanar and Trista are all fine, but someone...Memfis, there was a false bottom in that case. And...the fuck who wants your boy dead put a Widowmaker in there."

"What?" Memfis croaked. "I...Karse, why didn't anyone come and tell me?" He looked over his shoulder. "Do Aven and Aria know?"

"No." Karse shook his head. "Owyn said that Aria was in a really good mood, and he didn't want to spoil it. So he was going to tell her himself. I know. Jehan knows. Owyn and Alanar and Trista know, and Steward knows."

Afansa walked closer to fire, then crouched to sit on her heels. "Karse, this...I don't understand. This seems...entirely brainless." She looked up. "We're traveling with four of the best healers in the world. Three of them are with Owyn practically all the time. What did this idiot think this was going to do?" She stood up. "This...this doesn't make sense. The caltrop was at least somewhat clever. Luring Owyn off and shooting him? Not quite as clever. More brute than brains. This...this was entirely too complicated to work!"

Karse blinked. Then he grinned. "If you're interested, I could make a guard out of you in no time sharpened."

"You mean I'm right?" Afansa asked.

"I mean you've just pointed out that we're not dealing with a single person. We've got at least three." Karse shook his head. "One of them thinks. One of them overthinks, and one of them is a mad dog."

"Which one worries you the most?" Memfis asked.

"Not sure yet." Karse took a deep breath. "I can't tell if I'm more worried about the mad dog or the thinker. The mad dog will take bigger risks, and make bigger mistakes. But the mad dog might poison the lot of us, on the odd chance that they get Owyn. The thinker...they're going to watch us...and they're going to wait until we give them an opening."

"Karse, are you sure it's three?" Afansa asked. "If it's three, then if we stop one, the others will get desperate."

Karse looked at the case that was now burning merrily. "I don't know, Fan...Afansa. There's no way I can know. Not until one of them fucks up. For all we know, it is one, taking any opportunity they can get."

"There's a scary thought," Memfis grumbled. "Is Owyn going back into a coach when we start again? Either of you know? If he's supposed to ride, maybe I can convince him to not, and to come keep me and Meris company."

"I doubt you'd be able to," Karse told him. He walked over to the fire and picked up a stick, poking the burning case. "He and Aria are riding this afternoon. Alanar was supposed to ride with them. That's what started this. They went into the case for his boots. I'll ask Del to ride with them." He broke the stick and threw it into the flames. "Which means I need to talk to Del. And I can't leave the fire. Will one of you go find him and send him to me?"

"I'll go find him," Afansa said. She moved to stand at Karse's side, looking at the fire. "Do you think it's dead? The snake?"

"By now? Probably." Karse folded his arms over his chest and let out a long breath. "I'll let it burn a bit longer. Until the case collapses. Then I'll put this out. When I catch up with you, maybe I'll ride with Owyn and Aria, too."

"Because that won't make her at all suspicious," Afansa said with a laugh. She turned to go back to the coaches, then paused. She turned back, stretched up, and kissed Karse on the cheek. "Thank you, Captain," she murmured. Then she walked away. Karse stared at her as she disappeared from view.

"You look like you just got hit with a board," Memfis said softly.

"I...yeah," Karse stammered. "Yeah...I...that's about right, yeah."

OWYN SANG SOFTLY TO Freckles as he finished getting the horse ready. He double checked the saddle girth, then straightened and ran his hand over the gelding's neck. "Ready for a good ride, Freckles?" he asked.

"Does he ever answer you?" Alanar asked. He and Trista were standing nearby, close enough to talk, but not so close that Alanar's bare feet would be in any danger.

"I...I'm not sure I'd know?" Owyn answered. "I don't think he does, but it could be that I just don't speak horse." He laughed as Freckles snorted. "I don't!"

Trista giggled. "Freckles seems to think that's a failing on your part."

"He'd be right," Owyn said. He took Freckles' reins and led him over to a familiar mare. "Ready to go, Star? Aria's going to be happy to see you."

"Why?" Alanar asked.

"Because when we left Forge, Granna gave us all horses. Freckles was mine. Star was Aria's. And she's been in the stables at Terraces ever since we got there." He took Star's reins in his other hand, looked at Alanar and Trista, then smiled when he saw someone behind them. "Del!"

Del waved. Then he whistled as he came up next to Alanar. Alanar grinned and put his arm around Del's shoulders. "Want to come in the healer coach with me?" he asked. "We'll be learning about how to remove tattoos. It'll be interesting."

Del shook his head and started signing. "*I heard Aria and Owyn were going to ride,*" he said. "*I'm going to ride with them.*"

Owyn translated, then paused. "Who told you?" he asked, keeping his voice low.

Del grinned. "*Karse. Just now. He said you weren't in any danger. But he wants me to ride with you.*"

Owyn nodded. "You rode all morning," he said. "Are you up for another long ride?" He laughed at the sour look on Del's face. "Right. I keep forgetting. You're used to this. Where's Lady?"

"*I'm going to get her. I'll meet you.*" Del hugged Alanar, then pulled away from him and walked down the line of horses.

"You didn't translate," Alanar said. They started walking, and Trista put herself between Alanar and the horses. "Who told him?"

"Karse," Owyn answered.

"When are you going to tell Aria?" Trista asked.

"I'll tell her before we ride out," Owyn answered. "Because if I tell her when we're riding, she'll get upset and that will upset Star. And if I wait and tell her later, she'll get upset because I waited. So I'll tell her when I see her." He looked around. "She and Aven were supposed to be with Granna. Trista, will you take Allie to the healer coach from there?"

They hadn't gone far when they heard Aria laughing. He led the horses around the coach, and saw Aria sitting with Meris. Both of them were giggling over something, and Owyn smiled. It was good to hear her laugh.

Too bad it was time to spoil her mood.

"I brought your horse, Aria," he called. Aria looked up and smiled at him, and her radiant happiness was like standing in sunshine. He felt it right to his core, and for a moment, he was tempted to not tell her. To let her keep being happy.

But she'd never forgive him for hiding it. And he wouldn't forgive himself. He tied the reins off to the back of the coach, kissed Alanar, and watched him and Trista walk away. Then he went over to sit down at Aria's feet.

"So..." he said in a low voice. "I have to spoil your mood. I'm sorry."

Aria coughed, sitting up a little straighter. "What happened?"

"Someone switched out our case. Mine and Allie's. We found it when we went looking for his boots." Owyn kept his voice low. "No one was hurt. We're all fine. But...there was a snake in the fake case." He took a deep breath. "A Widowmaker snake." Aria's mood shifted from happy to rage between one breath and the next, and he hurried to repeat himself, taking her hands in his. "Aria, we're fine."

A warm hand settled on his shoulder. "No one was hurt?" Meris repeated.

"No one," Owyn said. "And Karse said he'd deal with the snake. So the only thing someone really managed to do is be a nuisance, because now Allie and I don't have any clothes except for what we're wearing."

Aria arched a brow, and her rage started to ease. "Is that really so much of a nuisance?" she asked. Owyn grinned up at her.

"Well...there are varying degrees of nuisance," he answered slowly. "Depending on the audience." He squeezed her fingers, then let her hands go. "Karse said he'd sent someone back to Terraces, to see if the case is still there."

"So you should have something in a day or two."

Owyn nodded. "Karse said maybe even before we ride out tomorrow." Aria felt calmer now, and he thought that the distraction of Owyn and Alanar both lacking clothing seemed to be helping. "I hope they do find it," he said. "My wedding shirt was in there. The one you made for me."

Aria frowned. "Oh. And...I think we used the entire bolt of fabric. I wouldn't be able to make another for you."

"You made that one for me," Owyn said. "And if you wanted, you could make a different one. You know...with all your spare time." He looked at the coach, and realized that Aria did have time. "You shouldn't worry about shirts for me, though. You should be sewing for the baby."

"We were talking about that," Meris said.

"Rhexa gave me a bolt of lovely soft linen so I could sew for the baby. And she gave me a sewing box, with all the tools I'll need to cut and sew. So I will be, while we're on the road."

Owyn nodded. "It's something to do in the coach." He looked at her, then at his grandmother. "Would you teach me?" he asked. "I can mend, but not fancy sewing like you do. Will you show me?"

Aria looked at Meris and laughed. "Do you mean me or Grandmother?"

"Yes," Owyn answered. "Both." He looked around. "But not today. Steward's got that look, so we need to get going."

"What look?" Steward demanded. He'd clearly been close enough to hear Owyn. "I'm not sure what look you're talking about, but yes. Karse will be catching us up once he's finished here. And we've sent Trista back to Terraces with two guards. They'll either find the case, or find you and Alanar some other clothes, and they'll catch us up in the next day or two." He smiled. "Think you can manage without her for that long?"

Owyn snorted. "I like Trista, but I was dressing myself long before we had a servant to help," he said, getting to his feet. "Besides, it's not like I have anything to change into." He held his hands out to Aria and Meris. "Let's get you both ready. Aria, did you see that they sent Star for you?"

Aria's delighted smile made her look like a little girl. "They did? I haven't seen Star in months! Do you think she remembers me?"

Owyn helped her to her feet. "Come and find out."

Chapter Five

Del smiled, listening as Aria and Owyn sang together as they rode. He knew the song — it wasn't possible to live in Terraces for any length of time without hearing *The Stars Dance* at least once. He'd even heard Owyn sing it before, because when Owyn was happy and distracted by something repetitive, like prepping something for the pot or kneading bread dough, he would start singing, and it was always the first verse of *The Stars Dance*. But somehow, Del had missed that Owyn had learned the rest of the song, and he had no idea that Aria had learned it, too.

They finished the last verse, and both of them burst out laughing. Riding on their other side, Karse grinned.

"That was nice," he called. "You two sound good together."

"That did sound good. Aria, when did you learn that?" Owyn asked.

"I asked the children to teach me, before we left for the Palace," Aria admitted. "You told me it was a song, but I'd never heard it sung. I'd never heard you sing it."

Del guided Lady closer, and dropped her reins. "*You don't spend enough time with him in the kitchen in the mornings. He sings it when he makes bread.*"

Aria looked at him, then smiled. "That early in the morning? I prefer to be in my bed."

"Hey, you understood all of that!" Owyn crowed. "Good!"

Del grinned. "*That was very good!*"

"Thank you," Aria answered. "I think I'm starting to see the patterns in the signs. It helps that I see them so often." She smiled. "I should ask Aven to only speak to me in Water signs for a time, so I get better at them."

"That's not a bad idea," Owyn said. "Karse, you should try that."

Karse shook his head. "I don't know enough of them yet. Let me get a little more comfortable with it, then I'll try it. You going to?"

Owyn laughed. "I'm not sure it would help me, though. Not with me being able to hear what Aven is thinking." He grinned. "I'll ask Othi. I can't hear him."

"*Yet?*" Del whispered in his mind, and Owyn snorted. Aria looked at the both of them, then arched a brow.

"Del?" she asked slowly. "What did you say?"

Del shook his head, and Owyn laughed and answered, "He's wondering how long before I've got Othi in my head, too."

Aria blinked. "And...would you want that?" she asked slowly.

Owyn shrugged. "Well...I'm curious. And I asked him if he was just going to be with Treesi, or if he'd be open to any of us making an offer. He turned interesting colors. Said he hadn't thought about it."

"Which means that he either hadn't and is now thinking of nothing but, or he had and now thinks you caught him doing something he shouldn't have been doing," Karse said. "Either way, that wasn't the kindest thing to ask him, Owyn."

Owyn paled slightly. "It wasn't? I...was that something I wasn't supposed to ask?" He looked at Del, who shrugged.

"*I wouldn't know. That sort of thing makes no sense to me.*"

"And...yeah, if that's something I'm not supposed to ask, it's also something I never learned I'm not supposed to ask." Owyn frowned down at his reins. "Which means he's been sitting with that for days. I should apologize."

"I'm not sure he was as upset as you seem to think," Aria said. "Because you haven't heard anything about this from Treesi." She looked at Karse. "If Othi was upset, then Treesi would have taken it out of Owyn's hide. Don't you think?"

Karse looked at her, then at Owyn. "You know...you have a point."

"Treesi wouldn't do that!" Owyn protested. "I...would she?"

"*She would,*" Del signed. "*You know she would. She'd do the same if it was you, or any of us.*" He looked around. "*I haven't ridden this way before. We usually took the cutter to Forge. Are we close to Cliffside?*" he asked

Owyn looked and nodded. "I think so. I'll ride back, tell the settlers they're almost home." He looked down the road and grinned. "Is that Wren?"

"Yeah, it is," Karse said. He waved, and the guard waved back.

"Problem, Captain," he called as he reached them. "Camp is set, and we...ah...took care of cleaning up what scavengers didn't. But we diverted to Cliffside on the way, and there are people there."

Karse swore softly under his breath. "Where did they come from? Rhexa said there wasn't anyone here when she last sent out riders."

"*When was that?*" Del asked.

"A week ago," Karse answered once Owyn had translated. "Lovely. I need a herald." He turned his horse, raising one fist in the signal to stop the coaches. "Steward!" he shouted.

Steward rode toward them. "Why are we stopping?" he asked.

"Unexpected visitation," Karse answered. "Wren says there are people in Cliffside."

"Oh," Steward said. "Oh, that will be awkward." He frowned. "My Heir? How would you like to proceed?"

Aria frowned. "I think we should send advance riders to the town. Announce that we'll be stopping. And when we're there, we can see if these are people who have stopped for the night, or if they're intending to stay. If they are going to stay, then we can meet with whoever is in charge and make arrangements for our own settlers." She looked at Steward. "Who should we send?"

Steward looked thoughtful. "These are Earth tribal lands...and possibly Fire refugees. I think...perhaps Jehan, Lady Meris and Memfis? Representatives from both tribes. Should smooth over any ill-will."

"I don't like the idea of sending Grandmother into a possibly contentious meeting," Aria said. "I think perhaps she and Memfis should stay here?"

"You get to tell her that," Karse grumbled. "We need guards. I'm going. I'll leave Howl with the boys. Wren, you're with me."

"Yes." Steward nodded his agreement. "Hrm...we might want to send Alanar with Jehan."

"Wait, what?" Owyn sputtered. "Why?"

"Because he's Jehan's heir," Aria answered. "And because it will allow Jehan to speak to whoever is in charge while Alanar performs healer's duties."

Steward nodded. "A show of good faith."

"Are you sure Allie, though? Not Aven? I mean, Allie doesn't have boots, so he can't ride. That means we have to send a coach," Owyn said. "And...well, fuck. I don't want him going in without me. Not if it's...Aria, what did you call it?"

"A possibly contentious meeting?" Aria repeated.

Owyn nodded. "Yeah. That. A fight. If he's going into a fight, I'm going, too."

"No," Karse said. "Not with the target that's on your back. You're not going unguarded into a strange town."

"*I'll go with him,*" Del signed. Owyn twisted in his saddle to look at him.

"With Allie, or with me?" he asked.

"*With Alanar.*" Del looked over his shoulder toward Cliffside, then back at Owyn. "*Karse is right. You should stay here. Stay with Aria. I'll go with Alanar.*" Del looked around, saw Karse studying him. He waited until he was sure Karse was paying attention, and signed, "*Do you think I'm ready?*"

Karse narrowed his eyes. "I...yeah, I think you are," he said slowly. "I think you proved just how ready when you took down Lear in Terraces and didn't even blink after." He looked at Steward. "So you want to tell Jehan and Alanar they're taking a trip, or should I?"

THE COACH ROLLED TO a stop, and Jehan peered out the window. "There are definitely people here," he said, turning back to look at the others in the coach. "We've attracted a small crowd."

Del nodded and took Alanar's hand. Alanar smiled and squeezed Del's fingers. "Jehan, what do you see?"

"About twenty people," Jehan answered.

The coach slowed to a stop, and Jehan opened the door and stepped out. Del followed him, seeing Karse had already dismounted. Karse said something to Wren, who was acting as coachman, then went to join Jehan. Jehan spoke quietly to Karse while Del turned back to the coach and helped Alanar down. He stayed by Alanar's side, watching as Karse and Jehan walked toward the group. Del stepped closer to Alanar as the healer put his hand on Del's shoulder. To anyone watching, it would look as if Del was Alanar's guide.

"Who are you?" one of the men called.

"Senior Healer Jehan," Jehan answered. "We came ahead of the Heir's Progress. This is Guard Captain Karse." He looked around. "We were told that this village was abandoned. There's a group of settlers with us hoping to call this place home. Have you been here long?"

The man snorted. "Been here a few days. Not a bad place. Thought we might stay."

"You're Fire, aren't you?" Karse asked. "You're familiar. We've met, I think?"

The man shrugged. "I have that kind of face. But yeah, I'm Fire. And I don't think we met. Maybe?"

Del listened to them talk, watching as the men milled around. There was something odd...

Men. The group was all men. He didn't see a single woman anywhere.

"Is something wrong?" Alanar murmured. "You went tense."

Del swallowed and slowly said, "All...men."

"No women?" Alanar frowned. "That's odd. Any animals?"

Del looked around, then answered, "No."

"That's very strange," Alanar murmured. "Let's stay back until Jehan calls us." He tipped his head back. "Wren?"

"Healer?" Wren kept his voice low. "What is it?"

"Keep an eye. Del thinks there might be trouble."

Del nodded, then straightened as Karse looked back at him. Karse arched a brow, and Del signed, *No woman, no animals. Strange?*

Karse nodded, turning back to Jehan. "Senior Healer, we should let the healer make his rounds."

Jehan smiled. "We should. Healer Alanar, come meet..." He paused. "I didn't get your name, Headman."

The man smiled, and Del coughed. He *knew* this man. Chalen. That was his name. He'd been one of Fandor's men in Forge!

Del turned, taking Alanar's arm and pushing him back to the coach. Alanar resisted for a moment.

"Del?" he asked. "What is it?"

"C...c...coa...ch," Del forced the word out. He glanced over his shoulder, then pitched his voice low. "Trap."

Alanar stiffened. He reached out with his other hand, finding the coach door. He climbed back inside, and Del turned to see Karse staring at him. Del raised his hands and signed. "*Trap!*"

Karse's eyes widened. He glanced back at the man, then touched Jehan's arm. To Del's surprise, he repeated the Water signs. Jehan nodded.

"I have supplies in the coach," Jehan said. "I'll fetch them." He turned, and his eyes widened slightly. Del turned, seeing the armed man standing on the far side of the coach.

"I don't think you're going anywhere," Chalen said. "Bring them—"

Del snapped his hand down and threw the spike in one fluid movement, and the man closest to the coach fell.

"Del, go! Wren, drive!" Karse shouted. The coach lurched forward, speeding away.

Del drew another pair of spikes and ran after the coach, hearing the sounds of a fight behind him. Someone cried out in pain. Then a crossbow bolt pierced the ground in front of him as someone behind him shouted, "Hold! Hold or I'll kill them both!"

Del froze.

"Don't move," someone snapped. "Arms out to your sides. Drop what you're holding."

Del swallowed, then held his arms out and let the spikes fall. He heard footsteps behind him, and something sharp poked him in the back of the neck.

"Don't move." It was the same voice. Del stood still as someone ran their hands down his arms, then shoved his sleeves up and unbuckled his arm sheaths, letting them fall.

"Armed to the teeth, this one," another man said. He pulled Del's arms back and bound his wrists. "He's secure."

"Good." The sharp point moved away from Del's neck, and they turned him around. Chalen smirked at him. "I remember you. You're Mannon's little slave." He chuckled. "You used to be scared of your own shadow. Where'd you find a spine?" He looked over his shoulder. "How is he?" he shouted.

A man kneeling next to the man Del attacked answered, "Dead. He's dead."

"Dead?" Chalen looked at Del, his face smoothing into an expressionless mask. He said nothing.

Del never saw the backhand that threw him to the ground; it just felt as if the side of his face exploded. Then he was on the ground, gasping for breath. Through the roaring in his ears, he could hear Jehan shouting, but not the words. Something slammed into his side, hard enough that he felt himself leave the ground. He landed hard and tried to curl around himself, dimly remembering someone — Karse? Trey? — telling him that he had to protect his gut if he went down. He couldn't think, couldn't breathe.

The next blow brought darkness.

OWYN TIPPED HIS HEAD back against the side of the coach and grimaced, closing his eyes. Meris had decided they would pass the time discussing projecting, and they'd settled into one of the empty coaches. But Owyn didn't feel like he was learning anything, and now his head was pounding.

"What's wrong?" Memfis asked.

"Headache," Owyn answered. "Came out of nowhere." He opened his eyes. "I'm not sure I'm going to be good for much until I take care of this. Mind if I go find Aven?"

"Go on, darling," Meris said. "I think we all need a break. This is a very dry discussion. I'd like some tea. Do you think they've started a fire?"

Owyn climbed out of the coach, turning around to offer his hand to Meris. "If they haven't, we'll get them to light one. Who knows how long we're going to have to wait?" He helped Meris out of the coach, then offered his arm. "Think we'll make it to camp tonight?"

"Depends on how the talks are going in Cliffside," Memfis said. "There's Steward. And there's Aven."

Aven, Aria and Steward had gotten out some of the camp furnishings, and were sitting around a low table. There was a game board on the table, and Owyn smiled. Gambit. "Who's learning to play?" he asked.

Aven looked up and smiled. "We both are. But Aria is better at this than I am."

"We can play in the coach, if you want," Owyn said. "Aven, could you help me out?"

"What is it?" Aven stood up.

"Headache. Real strong, and it came out of nowhere. No buildup or anything. Just...like I got hit or something." Owyn closed his eyes as Aven touched his cheek, feeling the warmth under his skin that told him that Aven was using his healing gifts.

"That's...strange," Aven murmured. "There's nothing wrong. Nothing I can see that would be causing a headache." He slid his hand down to Owyn's shoulder. "Let's get Treesi...what's that?" Aven turned, looking toward the road. "Someone coming in fast. Owyn, get your blades. And my swords."

Owyn nodded, keeping his eyes on the cloud of dust that was growing larger. He stepped back to the coach, reaching in so he could pull out his smoke blades and Aven's hook swords.

"Steward," Aven said as he took his swords from Owyn. "Take Aria and go to the end of the line. Take Meris, Memfis and Afansa, and the boys. Send Othi and my mother up here, and any Water warriors in the guard. Tell Treesi to be ready."

"Aven, I'm not—"

Aven silenced Aria with a look. "Baby," he said. "You're not allowed to risk yourself or the baby."

Aria blinked. "Be careful," she murmured. "The both of you." She kissed Aven, then came around and kissed Owyn.

Once everyone else was gone, Aven licked his lips. He glanced at Owyn. "Just like old times?"

"Don't try something fuckheaded," Owyn grumbled back. "We don't have the time for it." He frowned as he looked back at the road. "That's a coach. That...that's one of our coaches!"

"Fuck!" Aven started running, and Owyn followed, his heart pounding. The coach was close enough that he could see Wren in the driver's seat, dragging back on the reins to slow the horses. By the time they reached the coach, it had stopped.

"Wren, what happened?" Aven shouted.

"It was a trap!" Wren jumped down to the ground and hurried to the coach door. He opened it, and Owyn almost cried in relief when he helped Alanar out of the coach. He pushed past Aven to get to his husband, hugging him tightly before he realized that Alanar was alone.

"Where are the others?" Owyn heard Aven ask. "Where are my father and Del?"

Wren leaned against the coach. "I couldn't get them all out," he panted. "I...they're back there. I thought Del got in. I really thought I had Alanar and Del." He closed his eyes. "Del caught it. I don't know what he saw, but he caught it was a trap. He got Alanar into the coach. The captain ordered me to drive." He shook his head. "I...I don't know if they're even still alive back there."

Owyn looked up at Alanar's pale face, and realized something. "They're alive. Del's alive, anyway," he said. "I'm sure of it." He turned and saw Othi and Aleia coming toward him, leading a crowd of Water warriors in Palace livery. "They're still alive. We can get them out."

"How can you be sure?" Aleia asked.

"Because Del has the worst headache right now, and I'm feeling it."

Chapter Six

E verything hurt, and something smelled strange.
Del could feel something digging into the corners of his mouth, into his arms. Into his wrists. The left side of his face hurt, and he couldn't open his left eye. He blinked his right eye and tried to focus. His head was spinning. There was blood on his torn shirt, and ropes crossing his chest. There were more ropes at his knees and ankles, and his boots were gone. He closed his eye again and tried to force himself to think.

A trap. It had been a trap.

Had Alanar gotten away? Where were Karse and Jehan? He opened his eye again and looked up, wincing as it set his head ringing.

A house? Or a barn? Some structure with four support pillars. Three of them had men tied to them. Across from Del was Jehan, bloody, and with his head slumped. To Jehan's right was Karse, awake, bootless and bound as Del was. He was grunting behind his gag as he struggled against the ropes. He turned his head, saw Del looking at him, and sagged slightly. Del looked around, then looked back at Karse. He nodded toward Jehan and cocked his head to the side. Karse shook his head in response.

Del closed his eye, trying to ignore the pounding in his head, the stabbing pain in his side. There had to be a way out of this.

He tugged against the ropes on his wrists, then looked down at himself.

His boots were gone, but had they searched him? Had they found all of his knives? There was one at the small of his back. If they'd missed it...if he could reach it....

He tugged against the ropes, trying to lean forward, then trying to shift his hips out so that he could get his bound hands up far enough to reach the sheath on his belt at the small of his back. His ribs screamed at him in protest, and his arms burned where the ropes dug in, but he managed to bring his hands up far enough to reach the small of his back.

There was nothing there.

He frowned, trying to think. Then he heard raised voices from outside the building.

"We're fucked. That's the Senior fucking Healer. And you heard him. He's on Progress with the Heir, and the coach got away." Del recognized Chalen's voice. "They're warned, and they're going to come looking. This entire operation is fucked. We need to cut our losses and get out."

"What about them?" someone asked.

"We'll take the slave," Chalen answered. "He won't begrudge us that, and it will maybe make up for what we lose on the weed. The rest? Well, we all wanted high-and-mighty Captain Karse to burn for years, didn't we?"

A bark of laughter. "You just want him bent over," someone hooted. "You always did. It isn't worth it. Let's just burn the whole thing."

Del looked at Karse, who had gone pale. He closed his eyes, then started pulling against the ropes again. Del tugged at his wrists and grimaced. Alanar and Wren had gotten away, so help would be coming. But if they didn't come soon...

———— ⚭ ————

THE SCOUT SLIPPED OUT from behind a tree and saluted Wren and Aleia.

"Report, Tayki," Wren said, keeping his voice low.

"I counted nineteen," Tayki said. "No signs of Karse, Del or Jehan, but there's one big building that looks like it's in much better repair than any other structure in that town. If they're anywhere, it's there."

Aleia nodded and turned to look at Aven and Owyn. "Thoughts?"

"We have to let them know we're out here," Owyn said. "Is there any way we can? Without giving us away?"

"Not easily." Aven shifted his swords in his hands. "And we don't know if there's anyone inside with them. Hostage situation...this isn't something we covered when you taught me to fight, Ama."

Aleia nodded and turned to look through the trees, frowning slightly. "Tayki, give me a map."

Tayki went to one knee and started sketching in the dirt. One large circle. Several smaller circles. A ring around them all.

"This is where I think they are," Tayki said, pointing to the large circle. "The smaller ones, these are houses, but they're all falling down. There's no cover past this point." He touched the ring. "Road runs up to this side of town, and out the other."

Aven looked down at the map, scowling. Owyn watched him for a moment, then turned to look at Aleia. She was wearing an identical scowl.

"I don't know tactics," Owyn said softly. "Not like this. But...can we get to the big building from the far side?" He crouched and ran his finger through the dirt to the side of the building facing away from the center of town. "Like this?"

Aleia nodded slowly. "A small group, yes. And the larger force to attack the front and divert them."

"Who goes?" Aven asked.

"You lead the small group," Aleia answered. "They might need you in there. Othi, Owyn. You're with him. Tayki, take them in." She looked at Wren. "Mind if an old woman takes command of the frontal assault?"

Wren grinned. "War Leader, it'll be an honor to learn from you."

She nodded. "Tayki, take them now. Aven, when you're in position, trill like you're calling Melody. That will be our signal to attack."

Aven nodded. "Good hunting, Ama."

For a moment, Owyn saw her mask slip, saw the worry in her eyes. Then it was gone. "You, too," she said. "Now move out."

Tayki led them through the underbrush, skirting around the town until they were behind the largest building. Once they were there, Owyn touched Aven's arm.

"How are we getting in there?" he whispered. "There's no door."

"We don't need a door," Othi said quietly from behind them. "Aven, those timbers down there, to the left? The dark ones. I can smell them from here. They're rotten, aren't they?"

Aven sniffed. "I smell it. The rot is bad if we can smell it this far. They should have been cut out and replaced a season or two ago, it looks like."

"Must have been something piled up against them that kept them wet." Othi grinned. "We don't need a door. We've got me. Tell me when?"

Aven looked up at his cousin. "Oh! You're sure?"

"Yeah, I think I can do it." Othi grinned. "You let Aunt Aleia know it's time, and I'll make a door."

"Make a door?" Owyn repeated. "Othi, what are you doing?"

No answer. Aven trilled, and the sound was answered by screaming on the far side of the building, followed by the sounds of fighting. Then Othi moved, running full speed toward the building and launching himself at the wall. He hit it, and the rotten timbers splintered around him, leaving an Othi-sized hole in the wall. Othi rolled out of sight inside, only to reappear a moment later.

"Aven, get in here!" he called.

Aven broke into a run, and Owyn followed, looking through the hole in time to see Aven drop to his knees next to Jehan. The Senior Healer was bound to a support post. He was too quiet. Too still.

"Othi, take my swords," Aven said. "Keep them out of here." He handed the swords to Othi, then drew his dagger and cut the ropes binding his father, gently laying him flat on the ground. Owyn felt a surge of near panic from Aven, but the healer gave no outward signs of it. He was quiet as he closed his eyes and rested his hands on his father's chest.

"Tayki, guard our backs," Owyn whispered. He ducked through the hole and entered the building. Something smelled strange, but he ignored it, staying close to the wall and keeping well clear of Othi, who was kneeling next to Karse. The captain was bound to another post, looking battered, but not badly hurt. Owyn ignored him, and went to the third post. To Del.

Owyn dropped to his knees. "How bad are you hurt?" he asked softly. At the sound of his voice, Del raised his head, revealing his bloody, bruised face. "Oh, fuck!"

Del's voice in his head sounded drunk. *"That bad?"*

"Love, you look like you've been dragged face down through the coal fields. Let me get you free." Owyn laid down one of his blades and took Del's chin in his hand, turning his head. Then he drew his dagger, cut the gag and started slicing ropes. "They beat the shit out of you. How do you feel?"

"*Dizzy. Broken ribs, maybe. Got kicked.*"

"If you can tell me which one, I'll kill him twice for you." Owyn looked over his shoulder at Aven, then over at Othi and Karse. Karse was standing, shaking his arms. "What happened to Jehan?"

"Not sure," Karse answered. "I went down first. When I woke up, we were all in here, and he was like that." He reached out and gently ruffled Del's hair. "This one...he caught the trap. Caught it before I did. He got Alanar out and killed a man to do it." Del smiled slightly and closed his eye. Karse looked back at the doors. "They were going to burn the place down around us. Kill us, hide the processing shit. This has to have been where Lear was getting the diceweed. I can smell it. We'll have to let Rhexa know."

"Then we have to get out of here. And before someone tries to use us for tinder." Owyn stood up. "We need to go," he called. "They're going to burn the place around our ears."

"I need a few minutes," Aven answered, sounding distant. "He's not stable. I need time."

Owyn leaned forward and kissed Del on his unmarked cheek, then picked up his smoke blades and went to join Othi. "What do you think?"

"Think I don't know enough," Othi answered. "Really hoping they don't try anything."

Owyn nodded. He went to the doors, trying to see through the gap between them. "Sounds like they're still fighting out there. Maybe—"

Something slammed against the door, making it rattle; Owyn darted back, and Othi put himself between the doors and the others. "Ven, we're out of time," he called.

"I can't move him yet!" Owyn looked back to see Aven shaking his head. He could feel the fear rolling off Aven, thick and toxic. "I need to focus."

"We have to hold them off," Owyn said softly. "We have to give him the time he needs."

Othi nodded. "Still have most of my marks," he murmured. "Still mostly a warrior." He looked at Owyn. "What do we do if they set a fire?" he asked.

"Get out the back and under cover," Owyn answered. "We won't have a choice. The whole place will go up like a torch. That tincture, that'll burn like inferno oil."

Othi grimaced. "I was trying not to think of that stuff, thank you."

"If they burn this place, whoever is downwind is going to be smashed off their arses for days." Owyn muttered. He went to crouch across from Aven. He didn't say anything, studying Jehan's pale face.

"I can't move him, Mouse," Aven whispered. He looked up, and Owyn was shocked to see clear terror in Aven's eyes. "I'm losing him."

"No, you're not!" Owyn protested. "You brought me back from the dead. You can do this. You're just...Aven, you're panicking. You need to stop. You have to stop thinking of him as your Fa, and be the fucking healer you are!"

Aven stared at him for a moment, then snapped, "I can't forget that he's my father! Maybe it'd be easy for you—"

"Aven!"

Othi's sharp voice stopped Aven, but the barb had already struck home. Owyn swallowed.

"Maybe it would be easy for me," he said softly. "But if you don't get your head together, you're going to find out what it's like real fucking fast. So remember who you are. The natural five healer who stole a dead man back from the Mother. That healer. You can do this." He swallowed again and got up, trying not to think too hard of what would happen if Aven went too deep trying to save his father. Trying not to let the words hurt. He stumbled back toward the hole and peered out, seeing Tayki on guard just outside.

"Report?" Tayki whispered. He glanced at Owyn, then went back to watching.

"Jehan's hurt bad," Owyn answered. "Del's hurt, but not as bad. We need to move."

"And the captain?"

"Mad enough to chew nails and spit tacks," Karse answered from behind Owyn. "Owyn—"

"Not doing this now, Karse," Owyn said without turning.

"He shouldn't have said that."

Owyn shook his head. "He's scared. This matters, and he's scared he's going to fuck it up. I get it."

Karse's hand settled on his shoulder. "You're a better man than me, Owyn. I'd have taken his head off."

"We need him," Owyn said. "Tayki, are we clear to move?"

Tayki slipped down the building and around the corner. He was back almost immediately.

"We're clear, but we need to move fast. They're still fighting up front."

Owyn nodded and turned to Karse. Karse just shook his head.

"You're doing fine, Owyn."

Owyn grimaced. "Don't feel like it," he muttered. He headed back inside and went to one knee next to Aven. "Healer, will moving him out of here hurt him worse?" he asked, and could have sworn that Aven flinched.

Aven frowned. He closed his eyes, then shook his head. "No."

"Right. We need to move now. Othi! Give the swords back to Aven," Owyn snapped. "You take Jehan. Karse, can you help Del?"

"Yeah, I've got him." Karse helped Del onto his feet while Othi handed Aven his swords and picked Jehan up. Owyn turned back to see Aven glaring at him. His temper snapped, and he pointed one smoke blade at Aven.

"Do not start with me," he snapped. "Not when I'm trying to save all our fucking lives." As he finished, something slammed into the doors, hard enough that they rattled. Owyn turned, smelling something acrid. A moment later, he smelled smoke. "Oh, fuck. Save it for later, Aven. Move it! Tayki, take the lead!"

"Follow me!" Tayki took off running, with Othi right behind him. Aven raced after his cousin, and Karse hesitated just a moment before dragging Del after them. Owyn followed, nearly running into Wren.

"What the fuck are you doing back here?" he gasped.

"Looking for you!" Wren panted. "We're pulling out. We've got them all, the War Leader thinks."

"Then who set the building on fire?"

Wren grimaced. "That was someone getting desperate. They must have thought we'd let them run off while we got the others out." He looked around. "Where are they?"

"They're heading back to the horses," Owyn answered. "Jehan is hurt. Hurt bad. They beat the shit out of him, and out of Del. Karse isn't as bad as they are." He looked around. "Let's get out of here."

They started toward the trail that would lead them back to the horses. Owyn heard someone shout, and had just enough time to see a man at the far corner of the building. He was raising a crossbow.

"Wren!"

Wren whirled, raising his own bow. He stepped in front of Owyn and fired, but not before the other man did; Wren fell backward, dropping his bow as he grabbed at his shoulder. Owyn caught him and dragged him along as he started to run.

"You're not going to die on me," he growled. "Not happening. I'm not losing another friend." He pulled Wren down behind some bushes, and tried to get a closer look at the wound. Wren batted him away.

"I'm not dying of this, Owyn," he croaked. "It hurts like fuck, but I've had worse." He smiled. "Thank you."

"Thank me if I get us out of this in one piece," Owyn said. He glanced at Wren. "One piece with no other holes in it."

Wren laughed. "You're crackpot."

"Yeah, I know." He peered through the bushes. "No one there. Let's go." He helped Wren up, steadying him, and they started off through the brush again. Every whisper of wind was someone behind them with a crossbow, and by the time they reached the others, Owyn was drenched with sweat. Karse met them as they entered the clearing.

"What happened?" he asked.

"One of them came around the building with a crossbow," Owyn answered. "Wren protected me."

"Good man," Karse said. "Can you ride?"

"Think so, yeah," Wren answered. "Where is everyone?"

"The War Leader and most of her folk went on ahead with Othi and Aven and Del. There's some in the town, making sure the fire don't spread. And here, it's just me, waiting for you lot." He looked over his shoulder. "I think Aria is going to have a word or two with the War Leader."

"Why?" Owyn asked. He left Wren and went to collect Freckles, who snorted and shied away. "It's all right, Freckles. It's just me."

"Yeah, and you stink of blood," Karse said. "And Aleia didn't take prisoners."

"So we get no answers?" Owyn asked. "We don't know why?"

"I think we know why," Karse answered. He rubbed one hand over his face and winced. "They were the last of Fandor's lot. They were processing diceweed in there. That was probably where Lear was getting it."

Owyn nodded. "Let's get back. I need..." He shook his head. "Hey, if Aven takes a swing at me, just let him, all right?"

"You don't want me to break his arms?" Wren asked.

Owyn chuckled. "He needs to put you back together first. Or Allie will. And if Aven takes a swing at me? Allie will be the one to break his arms."

Chapter Seven

I t seemed that the moment Owyn dismounted back at the coaches, everything started happening at once. He barely had any time to speak to his husband before Alanar and Treesi were bundled into a coach with the wounded, and sent on to the camp under a heavy guard led by Aleia and Othi. The settlers were told that they'd be escorted to Cliffside, but that the town would need to be searched before they could enter, something that Aria asked Steward to lead.

"I'll stay with the settlers," Aria said. "That way, we won't have to worry about a formal visit. I'll have already spent hours with them. Grandmother and Afansa said they'll stay with me. So has Memfis. We'll be fine. And we cannot have a formal visit anyway, with three of my Companions elsewhere."

Steward nodded. "That makes sense. I'll need to ride out and get this done. It's getting late, and if we don't get the settlers into Cliffside soon, we won't make the camp tonight."

"Aria, do you mind if I go with Steward?" Owyn asked. He shifted and looked away when Aria turned to him. "I just...I need to get away from all the noise. I need...to not be near anyone right now." He forced himself to look at her. To smile. To pretend he was really all right. "I'll see if I can find Del's things while I'm there."

"Owyn, what's wrong?" Aria asked.

"I..." Owyn paused. "Look...something...something happened, and I need to get my head around it. I need to work through it before I tell you. Or I'll tell it wrong, and you'll get upset. And since I can't go off alone to think, and there's nowhere here to be alone, I was thinking I could go with Steward. If you don't mind?"

"Owyn, if the point of you going is to not upset me, I'll have you know that it's already failing. This is not like you at all. What happened?"

Owyn closed his eyes and shook his head. "He...he didn't mean it, Aria. I know that. But...it's gonna bother me." He looked up. "Where can we be private? I don't want this getting out."

"The coach?" Steward suggested. "And am I allowed to hear this?"

"Only if you don't pester me about it on the way," Owyn answered. He headed to their coach and climbed in, sitting down and waiting for Aria and Steward to follow him. He clasped his hands in his lap. "Aven was panicking. I mean...I understand. That's his fa he's trying to save. But if he panicked, he'd fuck it up. So I told him that he needed to forget he was working on his father and focus on being a healer." He swallowed. "He was scared. And...he yelled at me. Told me that forgetting something like that might be easy for me—"

"He didn't!" Steward gasped.

"He didn't mean it," Owyn repeated. "I know he didn't mean it. It was like out on the canoes, when he was hurting. He don't mean to be mean. But...yeah, it still hurts. And...he's pissed at me now, because I bullied him out of being scared. And...I'm pissed at him. But he'll grovel, once he has a chance to think."

"And will you accept his apology?" Aria asked. "Because that wasn't just Aven being short tempered because he was in pain. That was cruel."

Owyn shrugged. "I don't know, Aria. I need to get my head around it. So I need some time alone in my head."

Aria nodded. "Go with Steward. I'll see you in camp, and you can tell me what you decide there. And I will have words with Aven when I see him."

"No, you won't." Owyn sat up. "This is between him and me. So let it be between him and me, yeah?"

Steward snorted. "I can almost guarantee that it won't stay between you and Aven," he said. "Who heard this? Was anyone else around?"

"Othi and Karse," Owyn answered. "And Wren knows there's a reason that Aven might take a swing at me, but not why."

Steward nodded. "First, I think Aven's sense of self-preservation is strong enough that he won't try to attack you. He knows Alanar will turn him inside out—"

"Steward, really!" Aria scoffed.

"He's not joking, Aria," Owyn said. "And that's what I told Wren. That if Aven takes a swing at me, Allie will break both his arms." He looked at Steward. "You said first. That implies a second. So?"

"So I don't think this will stay between you and Aven for any longer than it takes Othi to tell Aleia."

Owyn groaned. "I didn't tell him to keep his mouth shut, either. Mamaleia is going to tear Aven up one side and down the other."

"And perhaps he needs that," Aria said. "Now, you two should go. Steward, will you leave us a moment?"

Steward nodded. "Owyn, will you trust me to see to Freckles?"

"Yeah, Uncle. I trust you." Owyn forced a smile. "Thank you."

Steward squeezed his shoulder, then got out of the coach and closed the door. Once the coach stopped moving, Owyn looked across at Aria. She held her arms open.

"Come here, my Owyn," she said. Owyn crossed the coach, letting her pull him into an embrace. He rested his head on her shoulder and sighed.

"I shouldn't leave you alone," he murmured. "All the others are off—"

"I will be fine with my grandmother and Memfis, and I will visit with the settlers while we wait for you to come back and tell us it's time to move on," she said. "You need to clear your head and let your heart heal. Go with Steward." She kissed his cheek, and when he raised his head, kissed his lips. "I love you, my Owyn."

Owyn kissed her again before sitting up. "I love you, too, Aria. I'll see you in a bit."

OWYN RODE BESIDE STEWARD at the head of the long caravan of settlers. Steward was true to his word, not asking any questions that weren't about Cliffside and the state of things they might find there.

"I didn't see much," Owyn admitted. "Just the building where everything was."

"What's everything?" Steward asked.

"The diceweed processing. Vats and tincture, and there are probably plants growing nearby." Owyn looked at the buildings that were growing steadily closer. There was a plume of smoke rising, blowing out over the water. "Karse thinks that this is where Lear was getting his older plants. But that don't make sense. They've only been here a week! Someone would have found them if they'd been here long enough to grow older plants."

Steward nodded. "Unless they'd only just moved there from another ruin?" he suggested. "We'll discuss it with Karse. How badly was he hurt? I barely got to see him before they were gone again."

"Battered, but he came out of it the best of the three," Owyn answered. "Del said he thought he had broken ribs. Said someone kicked him."

"What? I...I didn't see him before they left. I had no idea he was hurt!"

"Yeah, might be a good thing you didn't see him," Owyn said. "I told him he looked like he'd been dragged face first through the coal fields."

"Suddenly I'm not as upset that Aleia killed them without letting us question them," Steward said, and Owyn could hear the anger.

"Yeah, I told Del that if he could tell me who did it, I'd kill them twice. So I'm not at all bothered by them already being dead." Owyn pointed. "Especially not since Karse said they were Fandor's people. Look, someone is waving."

The someone waving was Aven's tall side-cousin Fara, who tugged down the scarf she was wearing over her nose and mouth as Owyn brought Freckles to a stop next to her.

"Been quiet. The fire is still smoking, but doesn't seem to be spreading. And the smoke is going out to sea. War Leader said to try not to breathe it in." She tapped the scarf. "We thought this might help." She looked around. "The rest of the place is in shambles. The new folks, they better expect to sleep in tents for a while." She paused. "Steward, we've been talking. We thought...maybe some of us could stay? Help them rebuild? We all know our way around building canoes. How different is building a wall?"

Owyn dismounted, and looked around to see that Steward had done the same.

"How many are you thinking, Fara?" Steward asked. "I'm hesitant about leaving guards behind."

"Half of us, and only until we can get help from Terraces," Fara answered. She grinned. "Been thinking about it since the War Leader left us. This isn't the current we usually sail, so we might not be much help, but we're supposed to serve the Heir. To my mind, that means doing what we can to support all the tribes. So some of us will help get this place livable, and we'll send people back to Terraces to get help who know what they're doing." She cocked her head to the side. "Does that make sense?"

Steward nodded. "It does, and I like that way of thinking. Choose your team, and catch up to us as soon as you can." He looked around. "You wanted to search. Where should we start?"

Owyn led Freckles to the central well, and tethered him to a hitching post that looked like it was trying not to fall over. "You stay put, Freckles," he told the horse. Then he looked around. "They were processing in the big building. That means they weren't living in there. If they took Del's stuff to keep it, they'd have put it where they slept. So we need to figure out which houses were the ones they lived in. Fara?"

Fara pointed. "We searched most of them. They stink, but those three over there have bedrolls and clothes. And there's a stable back behind them. There are horses in there. And a cart."

Owyn nodded. "Let's start with the houses. Fara, you know what Del's bag looks like. See if it's in the stable? And...has anyone checked that well?"

"The water smells fine. And I'll check the stable, Fireborn," Fara said. She bowed her head slightly and trotted off between the houses. Owyn started walking toward the first of the three houses. Then he stopped and looked around. "Steward?" Then he stopped. "Fuck. I need to ask you something you're not supposed to know."

Steward joined him, studied him for a moment. "Ah. I see. Behind me, to my left. Your right. The one with the broken window and the door on one hinge."

"And the shutters that might have been red once?"

"Yes, that one."

Owyn looked up at him. "Well, then...we'll just...we'll just stay away from that one." He started walking again, stopping just outside the first house to make a face. "What is that smell?" he asked, and opened the door. "Oh. Oh, that's fucking awful, that is." He looked back at Steward. "I really hope we don't find Del's bag and his and Karse's boots in here. We'll never get the smell out."

Steward snorted. "We'll drag everything out into the open. Anything that can't be salvaged...well, we have a perfectly good fire burning."

"Yeah, some of this garbage might dampen the smell of the diceweed," Owyn muttered. "Let's get to it."

Working together, they dragged everything out into a pile, finding nothing of value. Before they started on the second house, Steward excused himself, coming back with two scarves.

"It might help," he said, handing one to Owyn. "This one smells worse."

"You know, there's a stream near where we're going to camp tonight," Owyn said as he tied the scarf over his mouth and nose. "I think once we get there, I'm going to go soak myself to get this stink off."

"I think what washes off me might kill anything downstream." Steward grumbled. When Owyn laughed, he smiled. "Good. That's the first time I've heard you laugh since you came back." He sighed and put his own scarf over his mouth and nose. "Let's get this done."

There was less trash inside the second house, but the smell was worse than the first. Owyn wasn't sure why until he found the body, neatly rolled in a bedroll. He yelped, and Steward was immediately at his elbow.

"Go outside," he ordered. Owyn stared, then ran outside, nearly running down Fara.

"Fireborn? What's wrong?"

"There's a body in there," Owyn stammered. Fara nodded and went inside. When she came out a few minutes later, Steward was with her.

"We'll deal with him before the settlers get here," she said. She shook her head. "Can't tell what killed him."

"Overdose, maybe," Owyn suggested. "Doesn't much matter now."

Fara nodded. "Truth. Are you done here?"

"Just one left," Steward said. "Then we'll sort through the trash and see what might be useful—"

"Let the settlers do that," Fara said. "They'll have a better idea of what they'll need. Go search. I didn't see Del's bag in the stable. So it has to be there."

"Or it was in where they were being held, and it's ash now," Owyn said. He headed into the last house. It was larger than the other two, with two rooms, and was spotlessly clean. Steward paused inside the door, and gestured to the inner room. Owyn headed for that door. Inside, he saw a narrow bed, two pairs of boots sitting side by side, and a pile of things sitting on top of the mattress. He stepped closer, and laughed out loud, seeing the collection of throwing knives spilling out of Del's bag.

"Found them!" he called. He reached for the bag, but stopped himself before he touched the cloth strap.

"What's wrong?" Steward asked.

"Just...being careful," Owyn answered. "I need a long stick."

"How about a long spoon?" Steward asked. He walked away, then came back carrying a wooden spoon as long as Owyn's arm. He handed it to Owyn, who turned it over in his hand. The piece was solid, made from heavy, beautifully-turned wood, and the bowl was expertly carved and smooth as glass.

"This is nice," he murmured. "This...this is quality work. Someone did a nice job with this." He heard Steward laugh and looked up. "What? I appreciate good tools!"

"I've just never heard anyone wax lyrical over a spoon before," Steward said. "What did you want it for?"

Owyn turned back to the bed, and carefully poked the pile of bag, knives, and sheaths. Nothing happened, so he crouched and poked the boots sitting next to the bed. Again, nothing happened. "Just wanted to be on the safe side," he said. "Since someone doesn't have a problem with putting snakes where I might find them."

"Good point." Steward joined him at the bed. "And?"

"And I think it's safe," Owyn said. He looked around. "So why is this place nice, when the other ones are bad enough that I wouldn't even keep pigs there? I mean...they didn't even notice a dead man!"

Steward folded his arms over his chest, tucking his chin as he frowned. "I wonder...you suggested that the dead man might have been an overdose. I suspect you're right. But the one in charge? This was where he lived. And he wasn't a dicehead."

"So he actually cared where he was laying down," Owyn said. "Make sense." He carefully packed the knives and the sheaths into Del's bag, then picked the bag up while Steward took the two pairs of boots. "We've got what we came for. Should we muck this place out, too? Drag everything out?"

"No, this one I think we can leave," Steward said. "Someone will find these things useful."

AVEN SHIFTED TO SIT on the ground and scrubbed one hand over his face, hearing voices outside the tent. He ignored them. He was tired to his bones, and felt more than a little ill. Tired because they'd just finished the final stages of healing on his father. Ill because he couldn't stop thinking about how he'd hurt Owyn.

"He'll be fine," Alanar said. "We'll keep a watch on him overnight, but you did very well on your own, Aven. We should be able to leave in the morning." He leaned forward in his chair, resting his elbows on his thighs. "I want to check with Treesi, see how she did with Wren and Del and Karse. I hated having to ask her to handle all three alone. She's bound to be exhausted now.. Will you stay with Jehan? You can have the chair."

Aven looked at his father. "I didn't do well," he said softly. "I panicked, Alanar." He closed his eyes. "And I hurt Owyn. I panicked, and he tried to help me, and I hurt him."

"Excuse me?" Alanar's voice was quiet, and cold as ice. "Explain yourself."

Aven took a deep breath. "He knew I was panicking. He told me I needed to forget I was working on my father, that I needed to focus. And..." He paused, then said, "I told him that doing that might be easy for him, but I couldn't."

The words hung between them, and a look of complete horror washed over Alanar's face.

"You didn't," Alanar breathed. "And you know how he feels about Memfis. You've known longer than I have! Aven—"

"I know," Aven said. "And I haven't had even a moment to talk to him, or try to apologize. To say anything. He almost took my head off when he thought I was going to say something—"

"Were you?" Alanar interrupted.

Aven sighed. "I don't even remember. But I deserved having my head taken off. I know I deserve it."

Alanar nodded. "You do. And...you're telling me this why? You have to know I'm not going to intercede for you. Not with this."

"I wasn't expecting you to," Aven admitted. "I wanted you to know why he was going to take my head off before he did it, so that you'd know it was my own fault and not give him a hard time over it."

Alanar grinned. "Well, that's thoughtful."

"Yeah." Aven took a deep breath and let it out. "Alanar, I panicked. I—"

"Reacted exactly the way anyone would have expected you to?" Alanar finished.

"Allie, I'm a warrior! And a healer. I—"

"And he's your father," Alanar interrupted again. "Come here." Aven got up and came around the bed to sit down at Alanar's feet. Alanar started combing his fingers through Aven's hair. "Healers aren't supposed to work on their own, Aven. We're too close to detach. When we worked on you, after Del stole you away from Risha and the Usurper? Your grandmother led that merge for just that reason. She wasn't as close to you. She could do what was necessary. Aven, you shouldn't have been in that position in the first place."

"But I was," Aven said. He closed his eyes and leaned into Alanar's leg. "I was the only one there, and I panicked."

"And will you the next time?" Alanar asked. "Or did Owyn force you to learn how to detach and do what you needed to do?"

Aven frowned. "I...I don't know."

"I think he did. Because your father is still alive," Alanar said. "You kept him stable and you controlled the brain bleeding until we were able to merge. And you ceded control of the merge when you realized you were out of your depth. You did a good job, Aven." He tightened his fingers in Aven's hair and shook him slightly. "At healing. You fucked up incredibly at relationships."

Aven winced. "Do you think I can fix it?"

"I think you need to speak to Owyn about that."

Chapter Eight

It was time for the Progress to move on. The sun was setting, and they were running the risk of not reaching the camp before dark. They needed to move out.

There was just one small issue...

"Get in the coach," Steward repeated. Owyn wasn't sure if it was the third or fourth time he'd said it.

"I really don't want to ride in the coach," Owyn answered for the third or fourth time. He pitched his voice lower and added, "I don't want Mem to get upset. Or Granna. They'll *notice*."

"And you're tired," Steward said. "I don't want you falling off your horse before we get to the campsite. We don't have a healer here. If you ride in the coach, you can sleep, and no one will bother you."

He was right. Owyn knew he was right. He couldn't hold the Progress up anymore. But he still didn't want to ride with his father and grandmother.

"I'll ride with the boys," he blurted. "You're riding with them, aren't you? I'll come with you, and I'll get to play with Howl, and we can go over the map. How's that? You'll be happy, and I...well, I won't make anyone upset."

Steward sighed. "Fine. Go get in the other coach. I'll fetch the map and tell Aria I need you to go over the route with me."

Owyn headed to the second coach. Aria was near the first coach, saying her goodbyes to the newly-appointed headwoman of Cliffside. Owyn couldn't remember her name, which only reinforced how tired he was.

"Owyn, are you coming in with us tonight?" Danir asked. He was sitting on the ground next to the coach wheel, and Howl was sitting in his lap.

"Yeah," Owyn said. He crouched and rumpled the wolf's ears. "Thought I might play with Howl a bit. And I need to work on the map with Steward. You can tell me about how you like the Progress so far."

Danir grinned. "As long as the ground doesn't shake, I like it just fine."

Owyn laughed and stood up. "Me, too, Danir," he said. "Let's get loaded. We'll be leaving in a few minutes." Danir scrambled up, and put Howl into the coach before climbing in. Owyn looked around. "Where's Copper?"

"Up here."

Owyn looked up and saw Copper looking down at him from the top of the coach. "What are you doing up there?"

"Watching," Copper said. "I like watching. If you're quiet, the birds will come sit up here. And I can see all the way back down the road." He pointed. "There are riders coming this way."

Owyn looked back the way they'd come. "I don't see anything yet. Can you see how many?"

"No," Copper answered. "Just the dust cloud."

"What dust cloud?" Steward asked as he came up behind Owyn.

"Copper says there are riders on the road. Maybe ours? Trista and the guards?"

"Maybe," Steward said. "But we're not going to wait. We're running late as it is. If they catch us up, fine. The first coach is ready. I have the map." He looked up. "Copper, you're a fantastic sentry. Come down now."

"Yes, sir," Copper said.

As the coach started rolling, Steward unfurled the map. "We'll work on this while we have light," he said. "Then you can play with the pup."

"Do you have charcoal?" Owyn asked. Steward offered him a box, and Owyn took a piece of charcoal out and studied the map. "Cliffside is here," he said. "There's a ruin near the coast. We hid there, the last time we were here."

Steward studied the map, then touched it. "This?"

Owyn frowned, trying to remember that night. "Not sure," he finally said. "It was dark, and we were trying to draw Risha's guards off so Aria and Memfis and Treesi could escape. They headed east from the camp, and Aven and I went west and north."

"And we're camping here," Steward said. "Near the stream. So those ruins make the most sense." He nodded slowly. "We'll send riders out in the morning, see if there's anyone there."

"Heavily armed riders, yeah?" Owyn asked. "Right, camp is here." He touched the map. "Tomorrow, we'll head south, maybe. Did Aunt Rhexa say there were settlers along this road?"

"None that she knew of, but her riders didn't venture far from the road," Steward answered. "We'll send riders out to scout and survey as we go south. If they find anyone, we'll arrange for a visit. If not, we'll move on to the next campsite."

Owyn nodded. "And once we get to the Eastern Trade Road, we'll figure out who goes Axia's Way, and who goes east, and where we'll meet up."

"I understand why, but I can't say that I like splitting the group that way," Steward said. He squinted, shifted the map, then rolled it up. "My eyes are old. I can't see anymore."

"You're not old," Owyn protested. "Not...not really. Not like Granna."

"Granny Meris is really old," Danir said, his voice a soft whisper. "Did she know Axia, do you think?"

Owyn snorted. "She's not that old, Danir. And Granny?"

"She said we could," Copper said. "She said we could call her Granny. We neither of us have grannies, so she said she'd be ours." He grinned. "That makes you our brother, doesn't it? Since she's your granny, too?"

Owyn leaned back in his seat and glanced at Steward. The older man was smiling. When he looked back at the boys, they were both watching him with a definite air of expectation.

"Yeah, I think it does," Owyn agreed. "I don't know anything about being a fa, but I can be a brother." He shifted, moving to sit on the opposite bench with the boys. "Let me have Howl. Tell me about how you like riding."

"THE COACHES!"

Aven jerked out of a doze and sat up. Someone outside the tent was shouting, heralding the approach of the rest of the Progress. Aven stumbled to the tent flap, looking out into the gloaming to see riders coming into the campsite.

"Aven." Aleia came through the shadows to join him. "How is he?"

"He'll be fine," he said. He went back in, resting his hand on his father's chest. "He's still in trance, but that should fade by morning. I don't think he'll even have a headache."

Aleia's smile was a brief flash of bright white in the dim light. "Good. Thank you." She came closer. "Othi told me—"

"I talked to Alanar about it," Aven said. "And I'll be apologizing to Owyn as soon as I see him. If he'll hear me. That was..." He shook his head. "Ama, I was horrible to him. And if he doesn't want to talk to me, I understand. I just hope he'll want to talk tomorrow."

"Or this will be a very long Progress." Aleia took his hand, and Aven leaned down to share breath with her. She smiled, and kissed his cheek before he had a chance to straighten. "Go see if you can put this right, healer. I'll stay with your father."

"Do you want a lamp?" Aven asked as he turned toward the tent flap.

"No."

Aven let himself out of the tent, walking toward the passage out of the campsite. He could smell something cooking, and his stomach rumbled. He heard footsteps, and turned to see Del and Alanar.

"How are you feeling?" Aven asked.

Del held his hand up and wiggled it, then tugged his other hand out of Alanar's and signed, "*Feeling a little disjointed. Allie says I should sleep, but I wanted to see Aria and Owyn before I did.*"

"You should sleep," Aven said. "I can take care of Alanar."

Del made a face. "*I want to see Aria and Owyn. And my fa.*"

"He's being very insistent," Alanar added. He smiled. "He told me so. Treesi will be along in a moment. She wanted to check on Wren's arm one more time. Karse is with her, to make sure that Wren does what he's told."

Aven nodded, and they passed through the rocks. The first coach had stopped, and Memfis was helping Afansa out. Then Meris. Then Aria, who looked around and saw them.

"Where's Owyn?"

Aven looked back to see Othi had followed them out. He arched a brow at his cousin, and signed, "*You told my mother?*"

Othi snorted. "*You expected me not to?*"

"*I expected you to let me tell her myself.*" Aven looked around, and saw Owyn getting out of the second coach, cradling a sleeping wolf in one arm. He went to Aria and said something. Then he went back to Danir and Copper, who took a place on either side of him as he walked toward Aven.

And walked past Aven to Alanar.

"Sorry I'm late, Allie," he said. "And I'll be a little later. I have two things to get squared away."

"I think I know one," Alanar said. "What's the other?"

"I need to deliver a wolf pup to his owner," he answered. "Where's Karse?"

"Captain!" Copper shouted, and ran toward the rocks, where Karse and Treesi had just appeared. Karse smiled and dropped to one knee, laughing as first Copper, then Danir hugged him.

"I'm fine," he assured them. "Healer Treesi set me right. Where's Howl?"

"I have him," Owyn called. He brought the puppy over to Karse. "We wore him out."

"Well, that won't last," Karse said, taking Howl from Owyn. "Come on, then. There's supper, and you all need to get some sleep."

Aven watched as Owyn went to Del, studied him for a moment, then kissed him. "We found your bag and your boots. Your fa has them," he said. "You don't look good." A long pause. "Yeah, I'll be all right," Owyn said. "You go with Allie. Eat something, and I'll come crawl in with you two when I'm done." Then, and only then, did he turn and meet Aven's eyes.

"Owyn," Aven breathed. "I—"

"We need to talk," Owyn interrupted. "Now. Come on. Let's go down to the stream. I need a wash."

Aven followed him blindly, feeling that same sick tightness in his chest that he'd felt before he'd told Alanar. He didn't say anything, didn't do anything but watch as Owyn stripped his shirt and boots off and splashed into the stream.

"Oh, fuck, this is cold!" he yelped. "But that place stunk." He knelt in the water and splashed himself, then ducked his head underneath, straightening up and shaking to spray water everywhere. "They were so smashed in there that they didn't notice a dead body in one of the houses."

"Oh, that's vile," Aven murmured.

"Yeah, if I had a change of clothes, I'd burn these." Owyn splashed up the bank and stood in front of Aven, water droplets gleaming like stars on his skin. "Who starts?"

"I'm sorry," Aven blurted. "Owyn, I was awful to you, and I'm sorry."

"Oh, you're starting?" Owyn said. "Fine." He frowned. "I know I made you mad. But I needed to make you stop panicking—"

"And you did," Aven said. "Fa is going to be fine, because you made me stop thinking like a son and start thinking like a healer." He looked down. "I'm just...I don't know how many times I can say I'm sorry. I should never have said that—"

"No, you shouldn't," Owyn agreed. "And it really fucking hurt, Aven. Mem is my fa. He's the only one I know, the only one I can remember. You know what it was like when we didn't know if he was alive or dead." He paused. "Both times. You were there when we threw my wedding to the four winds, because he was back and he was hurt bad. You saw all that. No, it wouldn't be easy for me to forget I was trying to save my father. If anything, it'd be harder, because I already know what it's like to lose one father. Losing a second one would be worse. So, for the record, if you ever say something like that to me again, you can take your own hook swords and fuck yourself with them." He folded his arms over his bare chest. "So...anything to add? Need to take a swing at me?"

"What?" Aven gasped. "Fuck, no! Alanar would murder me! Twice!"

Owyn grinned. "Glad to see you remember that."

Aven bit his lip. "Do you need to take a swing at me?"

Owyn looked startled, then snorted. "No! No, you know me. I don't hit. I walk away. But I can't walk away from you, Fishie. Not from any of you. I love you all too much." He paused, then shrugged. "Anyway, that's where my head is. Now that I'm thinking and not just reacting. I'm not angry. Hurt, but not angry. And hurts heal. So...we good?"

"You tell me," Aven asked. "Are we? I'm really sorry. I never meant to hurt you."

Owyn nodded. "I know. I know what you get like when you're crackpot in pain. Once I could think again, I figured...it's the same thing. Just...this time you were crackpot scared." He poked Aven in the chest with one finger. "I forgive you. And tomorrow, you get to apologize to Aria. She's not happy with you."

"I'll apologize to everyone when we get back to camp." Aven turned to look back the way they'd come. "I don't have to wait until tomorrow."

"Well..." Owyn drawled. "We could go back now, if you wanted."

Aven turned to look back at him, "You had something else in mind?"

Owyn stepped closer and grinned up at him. "Well...the last time we were here, you wanted to go and take a closer look at that stand of trees over there. Remember? We were very rudely interrupted by Risha's guards?" He gestured, and for a moment, he looked...nervous? Scared? It was nearly too dark for Aven to be sure. Whichever it was, he knew one thing. It was a look that shouldn't be on Owyn's face. He reached out, ran his hands up Owyn's still-damp arms, over his shoulders. Up the column of his neck to frame his face, holding him in place for a kiss that should have happened ages ago. Owyn's arms slid around him, and he knew he'd truly been forgiven.

"I remember," he murmured against Owyn's lips. "Let's go see what we find there."

ARIA SETTLED NEAR THE fire with Del on her left, and Treesi on her right. The lingering scents of their supper mingled with the woodsmoke and the distant, faint tang of the sea. Everyone else had gone to sleep, so it was only them at the fire. Del was holding her hand, and his head was resting on her shoulder. He'd insisted that he needed to stay up until Owyn and Aven returned, but Aria was fairly certain that he was asleep. His fingers were relaxed in hers, and his breathing was soft and regular. She turned her head and brushed her cheek against his hair.

"Treesi, how badly was he hurt?" she asked. "I don't remember if you told me."

Treesi took Aria's other hand. "I don't think I did. Three broken ribs, but not badly enough to do any damage to his internal organs. They broke his nose and his right cheekbone, and his brain was bruised." Treesi leaned forward to look at Del. "He should be in bed."

"No," Del's voice was quiet, but firm. Aria smiled and kissed the top of his head.

"I thought you were asleep," she said. "Have you been listening?"

He nodded and sat up, not letting go of her hand. He looked around "Wyn?"

"He and Aven have not yet come back," Aria said. "I think I know where they are."

"I was just about to go look for them." Aria tipped her head back to see that Othi had come up behind them. "I asked Steward, and he said that he didn't see them when he went to wash, but Owyn and Aven went down there first. They should be back by now." He frowned. "They've been gone too long."

Aria smiled. "They've not been gone long enough. I know what they're doing. There's a stand of trees near the stream. Owyn told me that Aven was taking him there the night we were surprised by Risha's guards. I think they may be thoroughly apologizing to each other."

"Is that where they went that night?" Treesi asked. "I remember them leaving, but I thought they were going to take care of Aven's horse!"

"They were going to take care of something," Othi muttered. "Still, they're out there without guards. I think I'm going to take a walk—" He turned and laughed. "Or not. They're back."

Aria heard footsteps, and Owyn came around to stand in front of Del. "What are you still doing awake?" he asked. "And where's Allie? He should have put you to bed."

Del glowered at him and raised his hands. *"I'm not a child to be put to bed. If anything, I put Allie to bed. He's worn out from healing. And I was waiting for you."*

"Oh," Owyn said. "I...sorry. Didn't think you'd wait up for me. I'm fine, Del."

"We're both fine," Aven added, coming around to stand with Owyn. "And...I need to apologize to all of you. I'm sorry. I was horrible. I panicked, and...I was horrible. I shouldn't have treated Owyn like that."

"Owyn?" Aria asked.

"Oh, I've forgiven him," Owyn said quickly. "I told you. I understood why once I had a chance to think. And getting away let things settle. And...well, I've already shown Aven I forgive him." He looked up at Aven and grinned.

"Then you're forgiven, my Water," Aria said. "Your supper is in the pot. Eat something and we'll go to bed."

"Wait," Owyn said. "Has Steward told you anything about what we found in there?"

"I've barely seen Steward since we ate. He said he would tell me tomorrow," Aria answered. "He wanted very much to go and wash."

Owyn nodded. "Yeah, it was...bad. And if he wants to save it until tomorrow, then fine." He looked at the fire. "I'm not sure I'm hungry—"

"You're going to eat," Aven interrupted. "And then we're putting you to bed."

"We're putting all of us to bed," Aria corrected. "Aven, would you serve?"

Chapter Nine

E ven as tired as he was, it was nearly impossible for Owyn to sleep past dawn. He woke up at the edge of a larger bed than normal — they'd pushed two of the large beds together, and Aven was buried somewhere in the middle of the pile. The only people not in the big bed were Treesi and Othi, who were asleep in the last bed. Aria had invited them, but Othi had demurred, his face flushing so dark that he'd gone nearly purple. Owyn reminded himself that he needed to apologize to Othi for asking inappropriate questions, and went to fetch his trousers. He shook them out and grimaced — he could smell them. But he didn't have a choice, so he put them on and left the tent.

There were already guards and servants moving around. Owyn waved across the camp to Wren, then headed for the fire to see if he could help with cooking. Afansa was standing near the fire, stirring the kettle, and talking to someone whose back was to Owyn. As he got closer, she turned, and he realized it was Trista.

"Good morning," he called in a low voice. "Wasn't expecting to see you this early. Did you ride all night?"

She looked up, and her eyes widened slightly. "We got to Cliffside late last night, and stayed there. Rode on as soon as we could see. And it looked like it's a good thing we did." She turned back to Afansa, taking a cup of tea from her. "We found the chest. It was right in your room, right where it had been when I packed it. But I know I sent it out with the porters. I'm certain of it."

"So they brought it back after we left." Owyn sat down next to her. "Made it look like it had been forgotten."

"Your aunt noticed it," Trista said. "She was going to send riders out with it." Trista paused, sniffing. "I...something smells awful."

"That would be me," Owyn said. "We had to muck out a couple of the houses in Cliffside yesterday. You missed...well, quite a lot. I'll tell you, but first you have to tell me where to find clean trousers. I think I need to burn these."

Trista smiled. "I'll get them clean, the first chance we get. And your clothes are at the coach. I'll go get you a change. A shirt, too? And socks?"

"Please on the shirt?" Owyn asked. "The socks can wait. And so can we. Eat something first."

"So we can enjoy the scenery?" Afansa murmured, and handed a cup of tea to Owyn. He laughed.

"You need to decide just who you're chasing, Afansa," he replied, his voice low.

"I'm not chasing anyone," Afansa said. "I'm just enjoying the scenery." She stirred the contents of the pot again, then started ladling porridge into bowls. Owyn looked past her and saw Karse come out of his tent. Like Owyn, he had yet to put on his shirt.

"Things just got more scenic," Trista said softly.

"Don't you start," Owyn muttered. Trista giggled. Afansa looked at them, then looked behind her.

"Oh." When Afansa turned back to the fire, her cheeks had darkened. She handed a bowl to Owyn, filled another for Trista, then filled a third and held it up for Karse to see. He smiled and waved, and came toward them.

"Good morning," he said, taking the bowl from Afansa. "Thank you. The boys and Howl are both still asleep."

"So is everyone in the Heir's tent," Owyn said. "And it looks like everyone else, too. Which means I have time to go scrub again, since Trista brought the box back."

"And you checked it?" Karse asked. Trista swallowed her mouthful of porridge and nodded.

"Unpacked it, shook everything out, checked every bit of the box, then refolded everything and repacked the case, and locked it." She smiled. "I asked Persis for a hasp and a lock. I have the keys for you, Owyn."

"You should keep them," Owyn said. He took another bite of porridge. "You're keeping us in clothes, after all." He scraped his spoon against the bottom of the bowl, then set it down and stood up. "I really need to wash. Anyone available to go to the stream with me? Is Wren on duty?"

"Wren's on light duty until we break camp tomorrow," Karse answered. "Which means he can escort you to try and get the stink off you. Which...why do you stink? What did I miss?"

"Well, to start with, a dead body that none of those diceheads seemed to notice was rotting in his bedroll," Owyn answered. Trista made a strained noise, and Owyn grimaced. "Sorry. We were trying to find your boots, Karse, and all of Del's stuff. When we did, it was in the only house that didn't smell."

"Oh, good." Karse looked up. "Afansa, is there soap anywhere?"

"I think so, yes."

"Good. We'll need approximately a bucket of it." He turned. "Wren! I have a job for you!"

Wren came trotting up. "Captain?"

"You're on escort duty," Karse said. "Take Owyn down to the stream and stay with him until he stops smelling like he's six days dead."

"If there's enough soap, I can clean those trousers," Trista added. "And your shirt? Does it stink, too?"

"Yeah, and I'll go get it," Owyn said. "And I should tell the others where I'll be, so no one worries. Be right back." He headed back to the tent and let himself inside. There was still no one moving in the cool dimness, so he went to the bed and leaned down to kiss Alanar. His husband hummed softly and turned. Then frowned.

"What am I smelling?" he whispered.

"Me," Owyn answered. "And I'm going down to the stream to wash. Trista is back, and has our clothes. So I'll be able to change. She says she can get this stuff clean."

"I doubt it," Alanar grumbled. "All right. Go get clean. I want you clean enough to be able to sneak up on me."

Owyn laughed and kissed Alanar again, then went to get his discarded shirt. Wren and Trista were waiting for him outside the tent, and they walked out of the camp to the coaches. Trista went through the baggage, then came back with several neat rolls of fabric and a basket.

"Shirt, trousers, and a towel," she announced. "And soap and a brush. Let's go."

The water seemed even colder once Owyn was naked. He dunked himself quickly, then started to scrub. Trista took his discarded clothes further downstream.

"What's she doing?" Owyn asked.

"Laundry?" Wren glanced at Owyn. "You don't know laundry? I thought you cooked? Captain said you cook really well."

"I do cook. But we had a laundry woman, and she never let me watch." Owyn scrubbed his fingers through his hair, then knelt down in the water to rinse the soap out. He shook his head, and continued, "And before that, I wasn't ever what you'd call clean. Never had the coin for the bathhouse."

Wren wrinkled his nose. "I can't imagine living like that. Like an animal."

Owyn nodded. "That's what I was before Mem. I was an animal. Mem made me people." He sat down in the stream, then laid back to let the water rush over him. When he stood up, he felt reasonably clean. "I'm going to miss hot baths," he grumbled, stepping out of the water and picking up the towel. "I got used to being really clean, once I had the chance." He dried off, then wrapped the towel around himself and sat down, tipping his head back to look at the wide blue sky and the high clouds. He sighed and shook his head. "It's still weird."

"What is?" Wren asked, sitting beside him.

Owyn grinned. "You're supposed to be guarding."

Wren laughed. "I can guard sitting," he said. "Not that there's anyone out here. So, what's weird?"

"How big the sky is," Owyn said. He looked up again. "Did you grow up in Forge?"

"Just outside," Wren answered. "Why?"

Owyn nodded. "I grew up in the streets. The only way I really saw the sky was between buildings. Maybe more if I was up on a roof. Being out here? The sky is big. Out on the deep? The sky is huge! I never realized how big it was before a year ago. So it's still really weird, seeing all of it." He looked at Wren. "We were two days outside Forge when I saw my first falling star. I thought those were made up. Just in stories."

"Did you make a wish?" Wren asked.

"What?" Owyn stared at him. "No. Why would I do that?"

"Because falling stars are wishing stars. You're supposed to make a wish when you see one." Wren laughed. "At least, that's what my grandfather told me."

Owyn looked up at the sky. "I've never heard that before," he said. "I like it. Are they falling because they're bringing the wishes to the Mother? Telling Her what you want?"

"Grandfather never said," Wren answered. "And it's just a story, really."

"Like *The Stars Dance,* or why the sea is salty." Owyn nodded.

"I don't know that one."

"It's a Water story. Othi told me when we were out on the canoes, after I got a mouthful of salt water while I was learning to swim." Owyn chuckled at the memory. "I think we all have stories like that. That explain things we couldn't. We had them in the streets, too. Do you know the Night Hunter?"

Wren frowned. "Wait. That sounds familiar. Creepy monster, hides in the shadows, steals street kids?"

"And they were never heard from again," Owyn intoned, making Wren laugh. "Yeah, that one. The reason a lot of the younger kids ran in packs, until they were old enough to hold their own. Or smart enough." He shrugged. "A lot of street kids vanished when I was small. Including Garci, the boy who took me in and named me. He just never showed up again. So...we explained it the best we could. There was something in the shadows hunting, don't go down those alleys, don't beg or steal on those streets. Stay in a pack, because the Hunter takes you when you're alone. Hide someplace small to sleep, or someplace up high where he can't reach you." He shook his head. "Haven't thought about those stories in years. Haven't wanted to."

"I learned them when I became a guard," Wren said. "The Captain told me. I don't think he thinks those were just stories."

Owyn coughed. "Really? There was really someone hunting street kids?"

Wren looked back over his shoulder. "You can ask him. Here he comes."

Owyn turned, and saw Karse coming down the slope, accompanied by two boys and a puppy. Behind them was Othi, and there was something different. Owyn hadn't seen anything different about Othi before, but he also had been very distracted. What was it…?

"Good morning," Karse called. "Thought we'd come down and let the puppies get some of their energy out before we got on the road."

His statement was met with indignant howls from the two boys. "We're not puppies!" Copper protested.

Wren laughed. "Sure you are. That's what he called all of us when we were new. We're puppies, and he's the pack leader. All the other guards called us the wolf pack." He looked up at Karse. "The fact that you've got a real wolf pup now? The rest of us laughed for hours!"

Owyn grinned. "Really? The wolf pack? How come I never heard that?"

"You weren't a guard," Karse answered, sitting down on his other side. "I'm not sure where it started, but I also don't mind. I like it."

"Widow Alaine, wasn't it?" Wren asked. "She used to call you a silver wolf, remember?"

Karse shook his head. "Started long before her," he said. "She picked it up from her man. He was a guard. And back then? This was more brown than silver." He ran one hand over his short hair. "Othi, come sit."

"Figured I'd keep watch," Othi answered. "You can't see from sitting. Do we want the boys to not get wet?"

"Nah, let them play," Karse said. "They'll dry." He glanced at Owyn. "You just wearing the towel?"

"I'll get into clean clothes in a minute," Owyn said. "Trista thinks she can save the ones I was wearing yesterday." He nudged Karse with his elbow. "How are you?"

"Fine," Karse answered. "Treesi set me right. Oh, and Jehan was by the fire when I came down. Looks a little pale, but otherwise fine." He paused. "Owyn—"

"Aven and I settled things between us," Owyn said. "It's over."

"Oh, so Alanar isn't going to break his arms?" Wren asked. "I'd have wanted to see that."

"No, you really don't want to see him angry," Owyn answered. "I saw him kill a man without touching him once. Do not get my man angry, Wren."

Wren blanched. "Healers can do that?"

"Alanar can do that," Owyn clarified. "Aven might be able to do it, if he tried. But I don't think he can get that angry." He reached out and picked up one of the rolls, shaking it out to reveal it was a shirt. He laid that down, then picked up the rolled trousers. "Right. Let me get dressed, and we can go back up." He stood up, walked down the slope toward the water, and let the towel fall so he could pull on his trousers.

"You're spending too much time with the Water folks," Karse called after him. "I don't remember you being this calm about being bare in company."

Othi snorted. "He hasn't spent enough time with us," he countered, folding his arms over his bare chest. "He turned his back. Skin's nothing to be ashamed of, Captain. We all have it."

"And some of us are much more decorated," Karse added. "And...a little less, maybe?"

Owyn looked at Othi. "That's it!" he crowed. "That's what I wasn't seeing! You were wearing a shirt with sleeves yesterday!"

He trotted up the slope to Othi and reached for his right hand. Othi held his arm out so that Owyn could see the unmarked skin from his wrist to his elbow. The skin looked a little swollen, and there was more pink to it than Owyn was used to seeing.

"It's tender," he said. "Treesi says it'll feel like I've been in the sun too long. But it worked. And we can get the rest as we go. When we're all done, all that will be left will be my family mark." He smiled. "It's strange, looking down and not seeing anything but skin. I'm not used to it."

"Another step on your road to the hammer?" Owyn asked. Othi nodded.

"One more step," Othi agreed. "You wanted to know about how things were different. Will you tell me how you would do a tattoo?"

Owyn nodded and went back to pick up his shirt. He pulled it on, settling it and tying the laces at his wrists. "While we ride," he answered. "And...yeah, I need to apologize to you, Othi."

Othi looked confused. "For what?"

Owyn grimaced. "I never really learned what I shouldn't say about sex, and about wanting people. I don't know how normal people talk about it. So I asked you something I shouldn't have asked you, and I think I embarrassed you. And I'm sorry."

Othi's frowned. "I don't...wait. Oh, I remember. You asked me when we were Terraces." He grinned. "Come and walk with me." He looked past Owyn. "We're going back to camp."

"We'll catch you up," Karse said, waving them off. Owyn picked up his towel, slung it over his shoulder, and joined Othi.

"You didn't embarrass me," Othi said. "If anything, you made me actually surface — I'd been swimming with those thoughts since before I left. I know Treesi can't only be with me. I understand that. And I can accept that. I just...didn't think anyone else would be interested in me."

"Why wouldn't we be?" Owyn asked. "I mean...yeah, I'm curious. But that's just me and not knowing how to act. You're pretty."

"I'm what?"

"Pretty," Owyn repeated. "And I like pretty." He grinned. "I said the same thing to your cousin. Feels like it was a hundred years ago." He looked up at Othi. "Do they not think you're pretty out on the deep?"

"Warriors aren't pretty," Othi grumbled. "And...what do you know about my mother?"

Owyn paused. "I...do you want to know?"

That drew a laugh from Othi. "Given you had to have learned it from Aven? That tells me all I need to know. Mother...she didn't want me to build a canoe with anyone, because then I'd have left our canoe and Neera. I needed to stay and be Neera's right arm. I don't think Mother thought Neera could be Clan Mother on her own." He paused. "So...before Treesi? I'd never had anyone allowed to be close enough to know if they thought of me as pretty."

"Oh, fuck, Othi," Owyn breathed. "I had no idea!"

Othi just nodded. "Why would you?" he asked. "After Mother and Grandmother died, I thought...maybe someone would ask me? But I think everyone was stuck in their own currents at that point. No one ever even looked at me. And, well, women set the course, so I couldn't ask...and Neera was so busy with bringing the canoes back into line. I just...yeah."

"So you're still trying to get your head around all of this," Owyn said. "All right. When you're ready, you can ask me anything. Nothing is off-limits."

"Nothing?" Othi repeated. "I...more than one person in a bed? How does that work?"

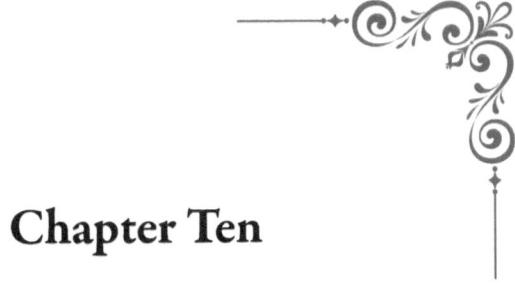

Chapter Ten

Before they left the camp near the stream, Steward sent out advance riders to look for settlers and carry news of the Heir's Progress. The riders returned to the Progress when they stopped at midday, reporting no signs of any settlers along the road. A second set of riders went out ahead of them, repeating the search, and with orders to meet them at sunset.

When the Progress reached the campsite, Owyn thought he recognized where they were. If this was the same place...he studied the sky as the others got out of the coach. "How long do we have before it gets dark, do you think?" he called.

Othi and Aven both looked up. "We made good time," Aven answered. "Maybe...two hours?" He looked around. "Oh. Is this...we're close, aren't we?"

"Yeah, I think so," Owyn answered. "Mem will know for certain. I'll ask him. If it is, I thought...let me see if Alanar is up for riding. See if Aria wants to go?"

They separated, and Owyn found Alanar with Aleia, Jehan and Memfis.

"I think you'll be back to normal by tomorrow," Alanar was saying. He paused, then turned slightly. "Owyn?"

"You doing anything now, love?" Owyn asked, slipping his hand into Alanar's.

"No. Why?"

"Because I was thinking we could take a ride. Mem, we're close to that cove, aren't we?"

"Yes." Memfis' brows rose. "You want to go there?"

"I thought it might...I dunno...be a good thing for Allie?" Owyn looked up at his husband. "If you wanted to go?"

"A cove?" Alanar asked. Then he blinked. "Oh. The cove where you found Virrik. Let's go get my boots."

Owyn squeezed his hand. "You'll ride double with me. I don't think it would be a good idea to take Meadowfoam on a leading rein on that trail. It's steep." He looked at Memfis. "Are you up for a ride? You're the one who knows where we're going."

Memfis nodded. "I'll get ready. Meet you by the coaches."

When Owyn and Alanar arrived back at the coaches, there was a small crowd dressed to ride, and the horses were ready. Steward was with Memfis, as were Karse and the boys.

"We're not all going, are we?" Owyn asked. "I wasn't thinking of this as a fun trip down to the beach."

"You're still not leaving without a guard," Karse answered. "The boys and Howl are going to stay, but I'm coming with."

"And I'm just here to find out what you're planning," Steward added. "I'm not going with you." Owyn could almost feel him asking to be invited, but he refused to take the bait.

"Aven says we'll have a couple of hours. Is that enough time to get there and back, Mem?"

"It should be," Memfis said. "It might be a short trip. We have no idea if the trail is still passable."

"We'll go, we'll bring Alanar to the place, then we'll come back," Aven said. "This is a very short trip. No spending time, no swimming. No fishing. Let's go."

It wasn't a long ride from their camp, and the trail was just as steep as Owyn remembered it. He spent the entire trip down murmuring encouragement to both his horse and his husband.

"Oh," Owyn heard Aria's voice from ahead of them, but whatever she was seeing was hidden from him by the last switchback. Then he rode out into the cove, and he could see the tumble of fallen rocks that had closed the passage to the sea.

"That's impressive," Owyn said. He dismounted, then helped Alanar down.

"What is?" Alanar asked.

"This cove used to be open to the sea at the end," Owyn answered. "You probably could have gotten a canoe onto the beach before. Now? Nothing is getting in."

"Or out," Aven added. "So definitely stay out of the water. We don't know what might be trapped in here."

Owyn looked around. They'd made camp there. The hammock had hung over there. And the spot where they'd found Virrik's body... "Right, I've got you, Allie. It's this way." He led Alanar slowly over the sand until they reached the cave. "Anyone else surprised it's still standing?" he called.

"I am," Aven answered. "I thought it would have collapsed in the tremors."

"So what is this place?" Othi asked. "If anyone said, I missed it."

"This is where we found Virrik," Aria answered.

Owyn led Alanar forward, and squeezed his hand. "This is it, love."

Alanar nodded. He let go of Owyn's hand and crouched down on his heels, reaching down to rest his hand on the ground, running his fingertips through the thin dusting of sand over rock. Then he shook his head.

"This isn't where you found me. This is just where you found my body," he said, his accent revealing that Virrik was the one in control. "It's not where I ended. That...that was back in that room in Terraces. That's where I died." He tipped his head back. "I wasn't ever here."

"I know," Owyn murmured. He rested his hand on Virrik's shoulder. To his surprise, Aven came up and put his hand on Virrik's other shoulder. He paused, then raised his voice, calling out a single word that bounced back off the rocks. Owyn didn't recognize it, but the sound made Virrik shudder. Aven called again, the same word. Another unrecognizable word. Then he started to sing, and Othi's voice joined his in spiraling harmony. The song was short, but by the time it was done, Virrik was sobbing.

Owyn dropped to his knees and hugged Virrik tightly, looking up at Aven. "What was that?"

"The final farewell," Aven answered. He knelt down and rubbed one hand over Virrik's back. "The last part of the Water ritual to honor the dead. I knew it then. I just...I didn't have the status to sing it."

"You did it well," Othi said. "You did it really well."

Aven nodded. "Vir?"

"Not him." Alanar sniffed and raised his head. "He went back. Thank you." He rubbed his hand over his face. "Thank you for bringing me down here. I...this was right."

"We'd better get back," Memfis called. "We still have to get back up the trail before dark."

They left the cove in silence, riding single file back up the trail. It wasn't until they were in sight of the camp that Treesi spoke, "What were those words? I didn't understand them."

Aven looked over at her. "I...That was Water."

"Wait. Wait," Owyn stammered. "Wait. Water has its own language? Other than water signs? How come I never heard it when I was with you?"

"Because it's sacred," Othi answered. "It's just for ritual. That may be the first time anyone outside the tribe has heard it."

"They're not out-tribe, Othi." Aven twisted in his saddle. "Aria is Heir. She's of all the tribes. The rest of the Companions were adopted by the tribe. Which means Alanar was, too, because he's married to Owyn."

"What about us?" Karse asked.

Aven looked at him and grinned. "And you and Mem can keep a secret."

IN THE TWELVE DAYS that it took them to travel from Cliffside to the border of Earth and Fire, they saw exactly one small settlement, who welcomed them with unbridled enthusiasm. They made camp on the night of the twelfth day at the crossroads where the Eastern Trade Road met the road that led to Forge. While they waited for their meal to cook, Steward brought out the map.

"There's a village here," he said, pointing. "Hearthstone. That's where we'll meet." He looked at Aria. "I know the lore, and I understand why you need to do this, but Aria, I do wish you would reconsider."

Aria smiled. "I know. But we can't take the chance. We have to follow the lore, and follow Axia's Way." She looked up at the standing stone that stood at the crossroads, then down the road toward Forge. "It won't be that long. We're close to Forge."

"I'm thinking you'll be gone two days," Steward said. "Perhaps three. It's only a day's ride to Forge from here, at an easy pace. But it's hard to say how rough the ground will be now, especially after the last tremor."

Aria nodded. "Then we'll leave at dawn, and we'll see you in a few days." She looked down the road again. "Owyn has a copy of this map?"

"He does," Steward answered. He looked down. "I should come with you—"

"Uncle," Aria sighed. They'd had the same discussion for three nights running. "The camp needs you. You will stay with the camp, and Grandmother and Memfis will make sure you stay safe until we meet up with you. And yes, I know it's not yourself you're worrying about." She stepped closer and stretched up to kiss his cheek. "I will have Aven and Owyn and Del with me. And Karse and Wren and Othi. We'll be perfectly safe."

"And I won't be there to take care of you," Steward grumbled. He sighed. "Promise me you'll be careful?"

Aria smiled. "I'll be careful, Uncle," she said. "I promise."

Steward nodded. "Then you should go and eat something, and get some sleep," he told her. "You have an early morning, and for all that you've been riding every day, the next three days will be hard. You need to rest."

Aria tried not to smile. "When you fuss at me like this, I wonder if this is what it would have been like."

"What?" Steward looked puzzled. "What would have been like?"

"Having a father," Aria answered. "My grandfather was there, but I don't think it was the same. And I see Jehan with Aven, and Memfis with Owyn, and I wonder...is this what it would have been like?" She looked back at Steward, and was shocked to see him in tears. "Steward?"

"And it's my fault," he said in a choked voice. "I...Aria, you should never have had to ask that question. I should..." He stopped and took a deep breath. "I know...it wasn't me...but...blast it all, it was! And it's my fault."

"And you're doing everything you can to atone for it," Aria told him, keeping her voice low. "You've done so much already—"

"Not enough," Steward interrupted. "It will never be enough."

"Perhaps? Perhaps not," Aria said. "You'll know at the end. For now? I know how hard you are trying. And for you to react this way? To feel this regret? No, Steward, it was not you. It was someone else." She hugged him, feeling his arms around her. He was shaking. "Steward, we'll be fine. And we'll see you in a few days."

DAWN WAS STILL A WISH on the horizon when the small party rode out the next morning, passing the standing stone as they followed the road south. They rode in formation, although Aven wasn't sure they'd discussed it. Karse led the way, which made sense. He knew where he was going. Aria rode behind him, with Aven on her left, and Owyn on her right. Del, Alanar, and Treesi were next, with Del taking the leading rein for Alanar's horse. At the very rear of the group were Othi and Wren, who was leading a packhorse. The only sounds on the road were the sounds of the horses' hooves, until the sun at last peeked over the horizon, and the air was abruptly filled with a cacophony of birdcalls.

Aven looked around and laughed. "I don't remember it being like this when we left Forge."

"How long will it take us to get there?" Treesi called from the rear. "I've lost track of where we are, and I've only done this ride once."

"From here?" Karse called. "If I was inclined to push, we could be at Forge by suppertime. But I'm not going to push. So we'll pass through the Ashen woods. You can see the trees up ahead." He looked around. "We should be out of the trees by late afternoon. Once we get on the far side of the woods, we'll have a good view of the land, and we can decide how the rest of the ride will go. Rhexa's riders didn't come this far, I don't think. Owyn?"

"They did. They went to the far side of the woods, then turned back." Owyn took his rolled map out of his saddle bag and unfurled it. "Yeah, the border of what we know is the far side of the forest. So anything we pass once we get out of the trees will be new."

"We'll see how far we can go once we get out of the trees," Aven said. "Do you have Axia's Way marked?"

"I don't really need to," Owyn answered. "It went to Forge."

"We will go as close as we safely can, and learn what we can," Aria said. "Then we will go east to Hearthstone."

The ride through the forest was peaceful, full of birdsong and butterflies. Twice they startled deer, and they saw rabbits and squirrels through the trees.

"It wasn't anything like this when we left," Owyn said when they stopped to rest at midday.

"It wasn't like this last spring either," Treesi said as she walked around the clearing. She closed her eyes and tipped her head back. "This is...nice. This is nice. It's restful."

"Except that your back hurts," Alanar said. "And I can feel it. Come here."

Treesi sniffed. "I haven't been riding as much as I should have. I'm still not used to it."

Alanar held his hand out. "Come here. There's no reason for you to be hurting."

Treesi went to sit with Alanar, who put his hand on the small of her back. He cocked his head to the side, then sat up straight.

"Treesi?" he said, his voice strained. "When...when did you have the block taken off?"

"What?" she asked. "Oh, blast it! I forgot! I should have had it reinforced before we left. Would you redo it? I know you know how now."

Alanar smiled. "I do, but it would be a very bad idea if I did, sweetheart," he said. "Congratulations."

"Congratulations?" Othi repeated. "What...wait...really?" He staggered to his feet. "Treesi?"

"What? Congra...you're saying I'm *pregnant*?" Treesi gasped. She stared at Alanar, then staggered to her feet and ran into Othi's arms, bursting into tears as he wrapped his arms around her.

Aria laughed, sounding delighted. "Treesi! How wonderful!"

Aven and Owyn both got to their feet. "Othi?" Aven said.

Othi looked up, and his smile was transcendent. "It is wonderful," he murmured. "I..." He shook his head and looked back down at Treesi.

"Othi, you're going to go away. You're going to apprentice. You'll be gone for a year!" Treesi sniffled as she looked up.

"It can wait," Othi said. "The ink and hammer will still be there when I'm ready." He wiped her tears away with his thumbs, cupping her face. "You're more important. This is more important." He kissed her, then rested his forehead against hers. "I know we didn't talk about this. I know we didn't plan it. But if you're happy, I'm happy. I mean...if this is what you want?"

"Yes!" Treesi threw her arms around his neck, and he laughed and picked her up off her feet.

"Oh, my little Treesi. I love you."

"I love you, too."

ONCE THE CELEBRATION was over, they mounted and continued riding. The trees slowly started to thin, the spaces between them growing wider and wider. There were trees at crazed angles, or dead on the ground. Then they passed an entire field of flattened trees at the edge of what had once been a flat plain. Now it was littered with stones, and looked like nothing Owyn had ever seen before. In the distance, dominating the hazy landscape, was a shattered stump of a mountain, still spouting smoke, still oozing red. Owyn blinked and shook his head.

"It...it don't look right," he blurted. "I mean...I know where we are. And...if you'd just plopped me down here, I'd swear I'd never been here before."

"I know," Karse called. He signaled for them to stop, then pointed. "There it is. I knew we were close. You see it?"

"I...what are you looking at, Karse?" Aven asked. "And...should the air be like this? Is it me, or is there a fog?"

"It's not just you," Owyn said. "It's...is that still ash in the air? It's been months! Shouldn't that all have settled?"

"I don't know," Karse admitted. "And what we're looking at is the Nerris stone."

"What's a Nerris stone?" Aria asked.

"Remember the standing stone at the crossroads?" Karse answered. "That's a Nerris stone. That one marked the edge of Fire lands, and the beginning of Earth. The one here marks the top of the ridge on the outskirts of Forge, and the edge of where the Guard were supposed to patrol. Not that anyone ever patrolled out this far. Not since I've been a guard, anyway."

Del looked at Owyn. "*I don't see a standing stone.*"

"I don't see one either," Owyn answered. "Karse?"

Karse started riding, heading out onto the plain. As they followed him, Othi coughed.

"What am I smelling?"

"The volcano," Treesi answered. "It smelled like this before it exploded, too. Lady Meris said that the air wasn't good for pregnant women. We shouldn't go too close, Aria."

"I don't think we're going any closer," Karse called back. He'd stopped again, near toppled rubble that Owyn realized was the remains of the Nerris stone. "We're heading east from here," he added. Owyn rode up next to him, and looked out from the top of the ridge.

There were no walls in the distance. He could see that even through the ashy air. There was no road below them. There were more rocks, fallen and blackened trees, and something that looked as if a careless cook had poured molten toffee randomly and let it harden.

"It's all gone," he breathed. "It's...there's nothing left. I've been saying this whole time that there's no Forge to go to. Not anymore. But this..." He looked out over the desolation. "It wasn't really real before."

Aven reached out and touched Owyn's arm. "Are you all right?"

"I..." Owyn frowned. "I don't know what I am." He looked at Aven, then back at Karse. "What do we do now? We can't go any farther south. The Mother knows we can't. So now what?"

"We head east, along the ridge," Karse answered. "Angle south, and pick up the road near the coal fields. That will take us toward Hearthstone and the others."

"Then let's go," Alanar said. "The smell here is making me ill."

They rode single file along the ridge, and Owyn kept looking to the south. To where Forge had been. He'd told the refugees back in Terraces that someday, they'd rebuild Forge. That someday, maybe they'd be able to dig down to the Forge that was, and find what had been left behind.

Was anything left behind?

"Do you think anything is left?" he asked no one in particular. "Under all that rock and ash? Do you think anything survived?"

"Maybe?" Othi answered. "Down deep, sometimes when things shifted, you'd find impressions in the rock of things that had been there and gotten buried. Sometimes we'd find shells that were like nothing we'd ever seen. My father told us that they were things that were old when the Mother took Her first steps."

Del frowned, and started signing. *"How could something be old when the Mother took Her first steps? Wasn't She here at the beginning?"*

"Owyn, what did he say?" Othi asked. "I can't see."

"He wanted to know how something could be old when Mother took Her first steps if things started with the Mother," Owyn answered. "Which...if something was old when She got here, that means that there was something here before Her. How?"

"Don't ask me!" Othi laughed. "I'm not that old!"

"Does it matter?" Wren asked. "We don't know. We can't know, because we weren't there. Why bother with something that happened that long ago?"

"If we don't pay attention to the past, then we'll make the same mistakes," Alanar countered.

Wren shrugged. "There's learning from the past, and there's maundering in the past. I don't think answering which came first, the Mother or the things that left shells behind is an important question. What's important is now. What we do now. And what we're going to do when the time is right."

They rode on, and Owyn gradually noticed that he'd been hearing an odd noise since they came out of the trees. It sounded like the waves on the beach near the Palace harbor, or Alanar's deep breathing when he was asleep. He couldn't tell where the sound was coming from.

"Does anyone else hear that?" he asked. "The breathing?"

"I thought it was just me," Alanar said. "I thought it was wind when I first heard it, but it isn't, is it?" He pointed to his right. "It's coming from that way, I think."

"He's right." Aven frowned, closing his eyes. "It's...is that the volcano? Is it...snoring?"

"Mother of us all," Karse muttered. "I...let's get moving. I don't want to be here when it wakes up again."

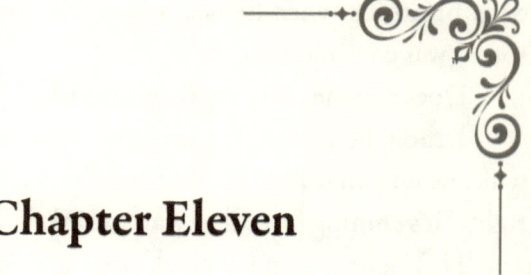

Chapter Eleven

They followed the ridge for what felt like hours, and the sounds of the breathing volcano accompanied them the entire time. Once they turned east, Karse called for a stop.

"The horses need to rest," he said. "We won't stop long."

"How long will we keep hearing that?" Treesi asked. "It's unnerving."

"It's getting fainter," Alanar said. "We'll probably be out of range by the time we stop for the night. Which...when will that be?"

Karse dismounted, walking back toward them. "If you all are able, I'm inclined to push," he said. "We'll have a full moon tonight, so the light will be good. I want as much distance between us and the mountain as possible. Treesi is right. That noise is unnerving."

"Karse, where are we?" Owyn asked. He dismounted, then helped Alanar down. "I'm lost. I never got out of Forge much, except to go to the coal-fields, but nothing here looks the way it should."

"We'll be coming up on Quarry Road soon. Once we're past the coal fields, I'll feel better about stopping for the night." Karse then pointed. "There's the road. See the marker?"

They rode on, passing a marker that was tilted at an odd angle. The road was crazed — buckling in places, cracked in others. Owyn watched the ground ahead of Freckles carefully for stones or cracks, trying to ignore the constant rise and fall of sound from the volcano.

The road forked, and they moved from broken pavement to dirt. Owyn realized he knew where he was. "That's the quarrymaster's hut!" he gasped. "It's still standing?"

"It's in the shadow of the ridge." Wren rode up next to him. "The blast probably went right over the top of it."

Owyn looked around. "It looks almost the same here as it did the last time I was here," he said. "This is...shouldn't there be rocks? Something?"

"*The blast went the other way,*" Del said in his mind. "*It went north and west, so probably most of the rocks and fire went north and west.*"

Owyn looked over his shoulder at Del, who was riding with Alanar. "It's just...everything else is gone. This looks like he just stepped out to go to his house for a drink."

"*Where was his house?*" Del asked. "*Do you think he's still here?*"

Owyn glanced back at him again, then raised his voice. "Karse! The quarrymaster's house is close. We should check and see if anyone is still here."

"We'll pass it on our way out of the fields," Karse called back. "We'll look."

"Did you come here a lot?" Wren asked. "Enough that you know where things are here? Back on the ridge, you were lost."

"I was here...every ten days, more or less?" Owyn answered. "It was the only place I could go outside the walls without Mem, and then only because he got special permission for me to do it. I had a tag I had to wear that told the guards I was allowed. Quarrymaster Hennick, he was nice. I hope he came out safely."

"If there's no one at the house, should we stay there for the night?" Othi asked. "It'll be easier to guard."

"Let me think on that," Karse answered. "Come on, now." He urged his horse into a faster walk.

Coming onto the house was a surprise. It always had been. It was tucked back into a corner of the rocks, hidden from view. You couldn't see it until you reached a certain point in the road, and even as often as Owyn had come here, it was still a surprise. Now, though, he was more surprised that it was still standing. The windows were broken, the door broken down. There was no smoke rising from the chimney, no signs of life of any kind.

Karse studied the building, then looked back over his shoulder. "Let's keep moving."

THE DISTANT BREATHING of the volcano was the only sound they heard for miles. They saw no animals or birds, and the bright greens that had painted the landscape on the far side of the Ashen Woods were jarringly absent. Even the air was still, and heavy with a haze of ash. No one seemed to want to talk, and singing just felt wrong. Aria watched as Owyn looked over his shoulder again. He'd been doing it every so often since they left the coal fields, and Aria wondered if he even realized that he was doing it.

"Owyn," Othi called from behind them. "Stop that. The mountain isn't going to do anything."

"How can you be sure?" Owyn asked. "I mean...are we far enough away if it did?"

Aria glanced over her shoulder. "We're at least as far away now as we were on the cutter when the mountain exploded. Nothing came that far out to sea that I remember. Treesi?"

"I remember seeing splashes, but nothing really close," Treesi agreed. "I think we're far enough to be safe."

"But we're still close enough to hear it," Karse called. "I'd like to keep going until we can't."

"How much longer will that be?" Aven asked. He looked around. "We can't keep going much longer. It'll be dark soon, and with the haze in the air, it might not matter how much of a moon there is. We won't be able to see."

Karse nodded. "There's a place up ahead where I think we'll be able to camp. Sort of sheltered, and there's a spring."

"Then let's go," Aria said. "I'm tired."

They rode on, and Aven reached out and touched Aria's arm. "Are you all right?"

She nodded. "Just tired," she answered. "And the air...I'm not used to the air feeling so wrong." She looked around. "It's...it's *heavy*. Air should not be heavy."

"I think the word you want is oppressive," Alanar called. "And it is. It's uncomfortable. And it may be what's making us all uneasy."

"That and the fucking snoring mountain," Owyn muttered, loud enough that they all heard him. Aria looked to see him turning around in his saddle again. "Hey...is it the mountain, or are we hearing Adavar?"

"Oh, now that is terrifying!" Othi turned and looked. "Hearing Father Adavar?"

"It's not Adavar," Aria said. "It's just air through the mountain. Owyn, you told me there are places in Terraces that sing."

"Yeah, down in the caves," Owyn agreed. "Wait...you think this is the same thing?" He cocked his head to the side, then nodded. "Yeah...yeah. That makes sense. There's more wind up high, too. Right? Topdrafts?"

"Updrafts," Aria corrected. "Yes. I think what we are hearing is the winds at that height blowing down through the mountain."

"And the eruption changed the sound and the pitch, like a flute," Karse added. "That makes a lot of sense, Aria. The spring is that way." He waved one arm. "See that big rock? We'll be passing that and turning south a bit. There's a copse."

The copse might have been a pretty place once, with trees that Aria thought might be willows. She wasn't entirely sure, because all of the trees were stunted and dead, and the water of the spring smelled strange. Karse dismounted and walked to the water's edge, then shook his head.

"We're not drinking this," he said over his shoulder. "We might not even want to stay here too long. I'm not liking this smell."

Del followed him to the edge, then stooped and picked up a stone. He lobbed it into the water, and watched the heavy ripples spread out.

"*It's full of ash,*" he signed, turning to face them.

"Then we definitely don't want to drink it." Aria shuddered. "It will burn."

"What?" Aven asked. "Why?"

"If you run water through ash, it turns to lye," Aria answered. "We would do it to make soap, but it's very dangerous. Lye can cause horrible burns."

Karse looked back at her. "That's useful to know," he said. "Right. We can't drink this. The horses can't drink this. Now what?"

"Is there perhaps a source of moving water?" Aria asked. "Something that would wash the ash downstream and might be safe?"

"The Quench," Owyn said. "Karse, how far are we from the Quench?"

"Few miles further south, and it runs down from the mountains, toward the sea. So it should be safe." Karse nodded. "It'll take us away from Hearthstone, though."

"Is it closer than Hearthstone?" Aven asked. "And is there a source of water between here and Hearthstone?"

Karse looked around. "Owyn, you've got a map, don't you?" He waited for Owyn to bring over his rolled map, and they studied it for a long moment.

"No running water between here and Hearthstone," Owyn said. "It's all springs. We never gave any thought to the springs being fucked."

"Here's hoping that the ones closer to Hearthstone are clear," Karse said. "Right. We'll head south to the Quench and camp by the river. Tomorrow, we'll head north and east to Hearthstone. We should be there...midday? Maybe a little later." He looked up. "Wren, what do you think?"

Wren looked at the map. "I...I might have a better idea," he said. He turned and looked at the spring, then up at the sky. "My grandparents lived not too far from here. The place...the house burned down a few years back. But there was a springhouse. If the spring is covered, it won't get filled with ash, will it? And the last time I was out this way, the barn was still standing. Mostly."

"Where is it?" Owyn asked, rooting around in his satchel. He took out a piece of charcoal and held it over the page. "Where are we going?"

Wren grimaced. "I'm not good with maps. Captain, mind if I lead?"

Wren led them away from the spring, and through the growing darkness. Aria tried to smother a yawn, but Aven saw her and grimaced.

"We'll stop soon," he said. "And you can ride with me if you get too tired."

"It's not far," Wren called. "We're almost...there it is!"

THE STRUCTURE THAT Wren led them to might have been a barn once, but now was barely more than walls held up by memories of what they had once been. But the water in the springhouse was cold and clear, and there was wood for a fire. By the time it was dark, the horses were tended to and Owyn was stirring a pot of something that smelled good. Aria sat down next to Aven, leaning into his warmth as the fire snapped and popped and made the night a little brighter.

"This must have been a nice place," Karse said, sitting down at the fire. "This barn was quality once."

"Grandfa was a merchant," Wren said. "He did well, before the Usurper. Enough that he could keep the place up. When I was young here, things were starting to fall apart, though. Not enough hands to keep things going." He shrugged. "Then Grandmother died, and Grandfa...well, he gave up. I'm not sure he even noticed when I left to join the guard."

"Did you come back?" Treesi asked. She was sitting next to Othi, curled in the shelter of his arm. Wren nodded without looking at her.

"I came back every Turning," he said. "And Grandfa...by the end, he wasn't all there. He thought I was a little kid, thought my mother was still alive, even though she died when I was a baby. He would go looking through the house for her." He paused. "That...that's what caused the fire, I think. He went looking for her, and brought a candle or a lamp someplace it shouldn't have been."

"Oh, Wren," Aria breathed. "How horrible!"

Wren looked down and shook his head. "Grandfa had a caretaker. Widow I paid to look after him. Make sure he ate, that sort of thing. She tried to get him out, but..." He stopped again. Then he took a deep breath. "One of the neighbors came to Forge and told me."

"Being here, this has to be torture for you," Owyn said, his voice gentle. "Wren—"

"It's worth it," Wren interrupted. "Look, we need to get back to the others. We need to keep the Progress moving. I...I can be uncomfortable for one night, to make sure that things happen the way they're supposed to happen." He looked at them, and gave a weak smile. "I'll just be the one on watch tonight. Owyn, how close is that stew to being done?"

Aria looked at Aven, who nodded and got to his feet, helping her up. She walked around the fire to where Wren was sitting; he scrambled up when he realized she was coming toward him.

"My Heir?"

Aria took his hands. "Wren, thank you," she said. "You didn't need to do this. You didn't need to cause yourself pain."

Wren shook his head. "It's worth it," he said. "Look. I'll be fine. It's not like this is new. It's been five years now since he died. It's scarred over now. It's...it's really strange being here, but it's not...it doesn't hurt anymore. If that makes sense?" He gently squeezed Aria's fingers, then tugged his hands out of hers. "And it's worth it, to see things happen the way they ought to happen."

Aria smiled. "I still appreciate this, Wren. We all do. And we won't forget." She returned to her place next to Aven, and rested her head on his shoulder. Owyn started serving, handing out bowls of stew. Aria ate slowly, trying not to fall asleep.

"From here, we should reach Hearthstone before midday," Karse said. "I think. Wren, do you know?"

"We didn't go to Hearthstone much," Wren replied, taking his own bowl from Owyn. "There was never the time or the money. I think we went...maybe once or twice? And I was small, so all I remember was a long ride in the wagon."

"But long is relative for a small child," Othi said. "An hour can be a long time."

"Right," Wren said with a nod. "So I'm not sure. Starting once we get something to eat...maybe?"

Karse nodded. "We'll find out tomorrow, then." He yawned. "Aria, do you think this satisfied the lore?"

"I certainly hope it did," Aria answered. "You said that the second stone marked the outermost border of Forge, did you not? The edge of the patrols?"

"Yeah."

"Then we reached Forge," Aria continued. "There is no city anymore, but we were within the Forge borders. I think that it satisfies the lore." She looked over at Othi and Alanar. "What do you think? Othi? Alanar, can you ask Virrik?"

"Vir would be a better person to ask," Othi said slowly. "I think you're right. I think reaching the border means you reached Forge."

Alanar sat up straighter in his place next to Owyn, and when he spoke, it was clear who was actually speaking. "How long was that boundary the boundary of Forge?" Virrik asked. "Captain, do you know?"

"*That's a good question,*" Del signed. "*If the borders of Forge were once closer to the city walls, then we didn't make it to Forge.*"

"Wait, the historic borders?" Owyn asked. "I...I've read about that. Let me think...was it the history of the tribes?" He frowned, then closed his eyes. Then he laughed. "Karse, you ever read *Nerris' Song*?"

Karse frowned. "I...I remember hearing it read, at Turning. I can't say I know it. Why?"

Wren burst out laughing. "*And by Axia's side, he walked the wide wealth of the lands that forged Fire. From east to west they walked, from the distant mountains to the sea. From north to south they walked—*"

"*From beyond the Ashen Woods, to the heart of the mountain's fire.*" Owyn finished. "When the lore says that Axia came to Forge, they meant the Fire tribal lands. The lands that forged Fire."

Virrik coughed. "I...are you sure, Owyn? That's not how I learned the story about Axia meeting her Companions."

"Did you learn the story told by Earth, or by Water?" Owyn asked.

"Ah...both, actually." Virrik frowned.

"And they say what about where Axia came in Fire?" Owyn grinned. "Because I'm willing to bet there's a lot of detail in the Water story about where she met Abin, and lots in the Earth story about where she met Mika, but the details are sparse in both about where she met the others. Right?"

Virrik looked thoughtful, then a slow smile slowly spread over his face. "You're right."

Owyn nodded and looked over at Del. "Del, am I remembering right? The city of Forge, that wasn't standing when Axia made her journey. There's no mention of it in the lore, and the Book of Silver marks it as being built...I'm not even sure. But it was after Nerris died."

Del frowned. Then he nodded. "*Forge was ordered built during the rule of Firstborn Anthais,*" he signed, and Owyn translated. "*He was the one who ordered a city built around the site of Nerris' forge. He was Nerris' and Axia's great-grandson.*"

"So the city wasn't there when Axia made her journey," Virrik said. "And the Fire lore speaks of Forge as being the land that forged Fire. So if we're within those borders, I'd say that the lore was satisfied."

"It sounds as if it was satisfied before we split off from the group, since we left them at that first stone," Othi said. "We didn't need to come this far."

"We did," Owyn answered. He turned to look at Othi. "We needed to see how things changed." He paused. "Othi, is Treesi asleep?"

Othi chuckled and looked down at the woman leaning against him. "She fell asleep a few minutes ago. Before Virrik came out, I think. She finished eating, and fell right to sleep."

"We should all get some sleep," Aria said. She put her bowl down. "Tomorrow, we have to go on to Hearthstone."

"You get some sleep," Owyn said. "I'll clean up. Who's keeping Wren company on watch?"

Chapter Twelve

The dawn light was weak and gray, and the air seemed even heavier than it had been the night before. It felt sick, the same way that the room underneath Terraces had felt sick, Aven shivered, even though morning wasn't particularly cold.

"What's wrong?"

Aven looked up to see Othi had come up behind him. He shook his head.

"Nothing. Me being fanciful," he said. They stood together and looked out over the land. "It just feels...wrong."

"The air, you mean?" Othi asked. "I know. It feels sick." He frowned. "So does Treesi."

"Treesi is sick?" Aven asked, turning.

"She woke up dizzy," Othi said. "Alanar is with her. I don't think it's this place. But I really want to get out of here." He looked around. "This place feels like it's trying to die."

"Or trying not to," Aven agreed. "Are we eating before we go?"

"Owyn said there will be something soon, and there's...I don't know. It looks like a brick. Sounds like a brick when you knock on it."

Aven grinned. "Hardtack?" he asked. "When I saw that first, I thought it was ballast." He looked around. "I was thinking...the feel of this place reminds me of the room underneath Terraces."

"What room...oh." Othi rested his hand on Aven's shoulder. "Are you all right?"

Aven shrugged. "It didn't kill me then. It won't kill me now. I wouldn't mind getting out of here, though."

"Come and eat, then."

They turned back toward the fire, and joined the others. Aven sat down next to Aria and asked, "Treesi, how are you?"

"A little dizzy," Treesi answered. "I feel like my legs are two different lengths. It's really strange." She smiled up at Othi. "Virrik says this is normal for pregnant women."

"I said it can be normal," Virrik corrected. "And not all pregnant women get dizzy."

"I did not," Aria said. "But I was horribly sick every morning for weeks."

"You were?" Aven turned to look at her. "You didn't tell me!"

"She didn't tell me either, and I was there," Owyn grumbled. "She hid it from all of us." He carried a bowl over to Aria and handed it to her. "But we understand. And that's all past now," he added, and leaned down to kiss the top of her head.

"When we get back to the Palace, I need to learn more about pregnancy. I didn't know any of that," Aven said. He took a bowl from Del, and reached into his carry-bag for his container of salt. He poured some into his porridge, then held the container up. "Othi, do you need salt?"

"I have some, thank you." Othi showed him a similar container. "Steward made sure I had some. We'll be leaving once we eat?"

"Yeah," Karse said. "We did what we needed to do. We need to catch up to the others and get moving." He frowned down at his own bowl. "From Hearthstone, stopping at the towns on the way like we've been doing, it'll take us two or three days to the mountains, where we head north."

"Really?" Treesi asked. "It took days and days from the mountains where I was born to get to the main healing complex."

Karse nodded. "The mountains curve west as you get farther south. Adavar is narrower here than it is up north. Going from Forge harbor to the mountains, you can ride the width of Fire in four or five days at a reasonable pace. If we rode hard? We could make it in two."

"We'll need to stay at Hearthstone for a day, to meet with them and let them know I hold the throne," Aria said. "And for the census."

Karse nodded. "Hearthstone should be pretty peaceful."

"I'm all in favor of peaceful." Owyn sat down next to Alanar. "You you now? Or are you him?"

Alanar burst out laughing. "That's the absolute worst grammar."

"Yeah, well, there's no grammar for people who are two people at once," Owyn grinned. "So?"

"I'm me. And Virrik is giggling. He thinks you're hilarious."

"Well, I am!" Owyn laughed. "Right. Let's eat so we can get moving."

They ate quickly, and Aven helped Owyn and Del clean up the camp and put out the fire. By the time the ashes were cold, the horses were saddled and ready. Wren stood off to one side, staring off at the ruins of the barn. Aven glanced at Karse, who nodded and walked over to stand with the younger guard.

"This has to be hard for him," Del signed. *"Coming here for him must have been like going to the tower for me. Too many memories."*

Aven nodded, and looked to his left as Aria joined them. She said, "I appreciate that he was willing to bring us here, even though it was hard."

"You understood?" Aven took her hand. "You're getting better."

She smiled. "Thank you. I have to put my mind to how Wren can be rewarded when we return to the Palace. If you have any ideas, I'd like to hear them." She looked over at Karse and Wren. "I don't know what would be appropriate. But he has risked his life for us, was injured to save Owyn, and caused himself pain to see that we could pass the night in comfort. He deserves...something. Some reward."

"We'll think of something," Aven said. "We can ask Karse, too. He would have a better idea." He let Aria's hand go as Karse and Wren started back toward them. "Time to go!"

THEY REACHED THE CAMP just before midday, and Aria could see the town beyond it. Hearthstone reminded her of Cliffside, only in much better condition. It was what Cliffside would be, she decided, and waved when she saw the welcoming party at the edge of camp. To her surprise, no one waved in reply, and it didn't appear that anyone was smiling.

"Something is wrong," she called.

"Yeah, I can see that," Karse said. "Let me ride ahead." He clicked to his horse, urging him on faster. Aria watched as he stopped near Steward, and heard him clearly when he gasped, "They what?" Then he rode back to meet them.

"What is it?" Aven asked.

"The Hearthstone headman has banned Jehan from the village. He doesn't believe that Jehan is Senior Healer, or that this is the Heir's Progress, or that there's really an Heir. They're waiting for us to go try again."

"Banning a healer?" Aven repeated. "That...I didn't think that was allowed."

"It's been a long time since there were last Earth healers in the Fire lands," Karse answered. "Come on. You need to get cleaned up so that we can go and meet with them."

Aria nodded. "This will be interesting," she murmured.

Steward was waiting for them as they dismounted. "How was it?" he asked. "What does Forge look like?"

"Forge is gone," Aria answered. "Completely. The Nerris stone on the far side of the Ashen Woods was as far as it was safe to travel, and...the Smoking Mountain now makes a sound very much like breathing. Or snoring."

"It does what?" Steward looked west. "And nothing untoward happened?"

"We were fine, Steward. Except that the sound is unnerving, and none of us wanted to be too near the mountain when it was time to stop. Now, tell me about Hearthstone." She started walking toward the Heir's tent. "What should I expect?"

"The headman is actively hostile," Steward answered. "Jehan is furious, and Aleia is worse than furious."

"And has my Grandmother spoken to him?" Aria asked. "Or Memfis? I'm sure they could put this right."

"Lady Meris was asleep when Jehan went to speak to the headman," Steward admitted. He sighed. "Memfis was reluctant to leave her. We none of us thought there would be this level of resistance. Not so close to Forge." He shook his head. "Once Jehan came back to camp, we decided to wait for you. We'll go back to town once you're ready, and Lady Meris will be ready to go with you. Oh, and the Water warriors who we left at Cliffside caught us up this morning."

"At least there's some good news. I'd best hurry to wash and make myself presentable," Aria said. She turned to see that all of her Companions had been following. "When we go to Hearthstone," she added. "We go armed. Is that understood?"

"That's highly irregular—" Steward began, only to be interrupted by Owyn's snort.

"Yeah, that describes everything about us," Owyn said. "Highly irregular. Because regular regular? That shit didn't work. Let's go be irregular at them." He looked around. "Once we wash up."

They went on foot, walking from the camp to Hearthstone, and Aria watched as people gathered at the edge of the town. When they were close enough that she could count the buttons on the headman's shirt, she stopped.

"I am Aria, daughter of Milon," she announced. "I am the Heir to the Firstborn, on Progress."

"We've heard that before," the headman called. "That last one, that Yana took our young folk and went off to die. We're not falling for that again."

Aria studied the man. He stood taller than she did, and the scowl seemed to be a permanent part of his face. "What is your name?" she asked.

"His name is Ancus, son of Dicus," Lady Meris called, coming to stand with Aria. "Son of Liga, son of Campai. Do I need to go back any further? Where is your village Smoke Dancer, Ancus?"

Ancus went pale. "I...Lady Meris?" he gasped. "Is...is that you?"

"It is, and you're wasting my time and that of the Heir, my great-granddaughter." She folded her arms. "Your Smoke Dancer?"

Ancus turned and shouted, and was shortly joined by a young woman. She looked at Aria, then turned on Ancus and snapped, "You idiot!"

"Grytha!"

"Grandfa, look at her!" Grytha waved one arm at Aria. "She's wearing the Diadem!" She shook her head and walked away from him, toward Aria. She stopped an arm's length away and bowed. "My Heir, welcome to Hearthstone. I apologize for my grandfather. He's an idiot."

Aria took a deep breath to keep from laughing. "He's still your grandfather," she murmured.

"And he's still an idiot," Grytha replied. "My mother used to say I got my brains from her side of the family." She grinned. "Welcome to Hearthstone. May I escort you into the town?"

Aria gave up trying to hide her amusement and smiled. "I'd like that. And if our healers might see to your people who have need?"

Grytha looked back over her shoulder. "What did he do?" she asked. "He stopped healers?"

"The Senior Healer is traveling with me," Aria answered. "And I'm told he was banned from entering—"

"Grandfa!" Grytha groaned. "Yes, of course." She bowed again, then offered her arm. "My Heir, may I show you around Hearthstone? It's not much, but it's home."

"Thank you, Grytha," Aria replied, and took her arm. "If you would first present me to your grandfather?"

"He isn't much, either," Grytha muttered under her breath. Behind her, Aria heard Owyn snort, and Grytha grinned.

"Are you always so disrespectful of him?" Aria asked.

"You don't know him the way I know him," Grytha replied. "He doesn't get any better than this. And if I had anywhere else in the world to go, I'd be there. But I don't, so I stay here and tell him he's an idiot. Regularly. And try to undo the damage he does. Regularly." She tugged on Aria's arm. "Come with me. I'll put on the kettle and we can talk. Grandfa will come join us when he stops growling, and I'll introduce you properly when he decides to be civil."

Aria nodded and turned. "Senior Healer?" she called.

"My Heir?" Jehan joined them and bowed.

"You and Alanar can start your rounds," Aria said. "Except I would like for Aven and Treesi to remain with me?"

Jehan nodded. "Once you're done with your meeting, send them on to me," he said. "If we're still in need."

"And take Wren with you," Aria added. "You'll find him very helpful."

Jehan arched a brow. Then he nodded. "Yes, My Heir." He bowed again, then went back through the group.

Aria looked around, then gestured to Steward. "Attend."

He came to her side at once. "My Heir?"

"If you'll organize the camp?" Aria said softly. "And...tell Karse I said that would be a good thing if his men drilled today while we are meeting."

Steward looked thoughtful, then signed, "*Are you expecting trouble?*"

Aria frowned, then shrugged one shoulder. Steward bowed again, then walked away. Aria turned back to Grytha.

"Shall we?" she asked, and let herself be led into the town. The layout was very similar to that of Cliffside — graveled streets lined with houses spread out from around a central well. Some of the houses facing the well had tables and awnings in front.

"How often do you have market day?" Aven asked. "Did we miss it?"

"Every ten days or so, and it's tomorrow," Grytha answered. She looked at Aven. "You're Water. How do you know about market day?" She giggled. "You don't have market day out on the water, do you? Do you have stalls underwater? What do you sell?"

"Shark teeth," Aven answered. "Shells. Pearls. Tapa cloth, which...we don't trade that outclan, so I don't think you'd know what that was. And we do trade, but we don't have a market like this. No, I was at the market in Cliffside, once. Near Terraces."

"I've heard of Terraces," Grytha said. "Not much, but I know it's there." She gestured to a long building. "This is the meeting house. Please, be welcome." She led them inside, then went and threw open shutters to flood with light a long room dominated by a plank table. There were rows of stools down either side of the table, and a high-backed chair at the head. Grytha frowned, then gestured to it. "That won't be comfortable for you, will it? With your wings? I can find something different."

"It will be fine," Aria said. She went and sat down, perching on the edge of the chair. Aven sat down on her left, and Owyn on her right. Del and Treesi took their places next to Aven and Owyn, and Lady Meris sat down next to Del.

"Shall we wait for your grandfather, or shall we begin?" Aria asked.

"Let me make some tea," Grytha said. "By the time the tea has steeped, he'll hopefully have gotten it through his head that he needs to join us."

"And if he doesn't?" Owyn asked.

"Then I'll make the decisions, and he'll have to live with them," Grytha answered. She set a burner on the table, arranged a rack and pot over it, then lit the burner. "It won't be the first time. Everyone in town knows I'll be headwoman when the time comes. They listen to me. Especially when he's being unreasonable. Which, if I'm being honest, is most of the time."

"Reminds me of my grandmother," Aven murmured. "Except no one would ever try to undermine her."

"In that case," Aria said. "Let's begin. We'll share news, and then I want to know what your people have need of."

KARSE WALKED THE LINE of drilling guards with Howl at his heels, stopping at the end. Neither of the last two 'guards' in the line came up to his shoulder, but they were just as serious at their swordplay as any of the others. It didn't seem to matter that they were only using wooden practice swords. He had to bite his lip to hide his grin — Tam had been right. Danir had clearly hit his growth, and his trousers were too short.

"Right!" Karse bellowed. "Take a break!" He nodded as he looked up and down the line. "Nice work. Get some water, walk it off."

The men and women broke ranks, laughing and talking. Karse started toward the boys, who were chattering at Fara. He only realized he'd lost his shadow when Howl started barking. He looked back at the puppy, who was barking furiously at the trees.

"What is it?" Karse asked, going to one knee. He studied the tree line, but couldn't see anything moving in the slight haze that still filled the air. He couldn't see movement, but somehow, he doubted it was a rabbit or a bird. If it had been, Howl would have been off after it. Therefore...

"Form ranks!" Karse shouted. "To arms! Form ranks!" He glanced back to see guards scrambling to recover weapons they'd laid aside, saw the boys both running back toward the camp, shouting the alarm. Then Karse turned to face the trees once more, just in time to see the first of the raiders burst into the open.

OWYN LOOKED DOWN AT his notes.

"So we'll be here two more days. Audience tomorrow, and we'll get the census done after," he said. "And once Senior Healer

Jehan is free, we'll discuss the logistics of setting up a healing center here."

"That might take a bit of time," Treesi added. "The more advanced trainees still have to be recognized as full healers, and then they need to spend time serving before they can be trusted to run a healing center alone. There just aren't that many full healers now."

"And three of them are part of the entourage," Grytha said. "Two Companions and...could we have Healer Alanar?"

"Not without a fight," Owyn said with a grin. He held his wrist up to show his pledge bracelet. "He's my husband."

Grytha sighed. "You're a lucky man, Fireborn. And he is. You both are." She drummed her fingers on the tabletop. "I'll keep an ear to the winds for word of that Risha. I don't know her name, but I've heard that poison about Air and Water from traders from the north and from the foothills. It's ridiculous."

"It's dangerous," Aria corrected. "It gives people who believe it permission to attack those who are not like them. And it's spread unchecked for too long."

"Well, I'm not letting it spread here," Grytha said. "If I can stop it here, I will."

"Thank you," Aria said. "Now, is there anything else your people need?"

Grytha looked thoughtful, then shook her head. "Nothing I can think of," she said. "For all that it's been a time since the mountain went, we're doing as well as can be expected. We don't have to worry about crops outside the kitchen gardens because we're not farmers. We're potters and we herd goats for milk and fiber. The ash has been good for the pottery, I'm told, but we're keeping the goats close. We have some trouble with raiders, but we're handling that."

"I remember someone saying that the ash would be good for the land for farming," Aria said. "But how would it be good for pottery?"

Grytha grinned. "I don't know," she admitted. "My mother is a weaver. Pottery isn't my trade, and I don't understand the esoterics of glazes."

"Afansa would be able to explain," Meris said. "She was a potter before she came to us."

"I might just ask her," Aria said. "I'm curious." She looked around the table. "Has anyone any other questions?"

Del sat straight up, but he didn't look at Aria. Instead, he looked toward the door.

"*Do you hear that?*"

Owyn frowned as Del spoke in his mind, then closed his eyes.

"Someone...shouting?" he said. "Grytha?"

Grytha blinked, then jumped out of her chair. "Blast it all! Raiders!"

Aven was out of his chair fast enough that it fell over, drawing his swords. "Owyn—"

Owyn pulled his whip-chain from his belt. "Coming. Del, stay with Aria and Treesi!" he called as he ran out of the meeting house after Aven. Outside, he could see Karse and several of the guards. Aleia, Memfis, Afansa and the boys. And three ragged men in chains.

"Captain, what happened?" Aven shouted. "Are we under attack?"

"We were," Karse answered. "At least, they thought they were attacking. This lot clearly have never faced a real fighter." He gestured toward the three prisoners. "These? They're the survivors."

Aven nodded. "Is it safe, then?" He looked back and smiled. Owyn looked and saw Aria standing in the doorway.

"Yeah, she can come out," Karse said with a laugh.

Chapter Thirteen

Owyn and Aven walked back to the meeting house, and Aven offered Aria his arm. She smiled at him, but shook her head and walked out alone, heading toward the crowd of guards. Aven arched a brow at Owyn.

"She needs to stand," Owyn whispered. "On her own. We can support her, but she needs to stand."

Aven nodded and fell in next to him as they followed Aria, staying out of range of her wings as she stopped and folded her arms over her chest.

"Headman Ancus?" she called. "Are bandits often a problem here?"

"They don't bother us," Ancus answered. "Your camp, on the other hand, is a target for a desperate man."

Aria arched a brow. "And yet they don't bother you," she said. "Why is that? Grytha?"

"Grandfa is being an idiot again. They do bother us. I told you that," Grytha answered, coming up next to Aven. "We keep the goats close, and the herders go out with dogs and bows. And when we go out to gather clay, it's in armed groups."

"That's some kind of not bothering," Owyn muttered.

Aria glanced over at Grytha, then at Ancus. "Desperate men, willing to prey on the weak. And yet...they attacked my camp. My armed guards, who were drilling this afternoon. They could see the Heir's banner at the camp. That's not desperation, that's suicide."

"That's ridding the world of another freak," one of the prisoners snarled. He spat on the ground at Aria's feet. "Fucking animal!"

"Mind your tongue!" Karse snapped. "Show some respect to the Heir!"

The prisoner laughed. "That ain't the Heir!" he protested. "That...that's blasphemy! Animal what thinks it's a woman, what thinks it's worthy of being the Heir. Lady Risha—"

"What?" Aven stalked forward. "You're one of hers? One of Risha's?"

The man smirked at him. "And you're a fish. I don't talk to animals."

Aven looked back at Aria, at the stony look on her face. He waited, and she nodded.

"You're going to talk to me," Aven said quietly. "You're going to tell me everything you know about Risha. Where she is. Where we can find her." He moved, bringing his swords down fast so that the hooks encircled the prisoner's neck. "You're going to tell me, and I might let you keep your head."

The prisoner tried to step back, and winced as the hooks cut into his skin. It was clear when he realized that he had no options — his eyes widened, his skin went ashy-pale. He moaned, and there was a sudden, acrid stink in the air.

"Ancus," he whined. "Ancus...do something!"

"Interesting," Karse murmured. "Why exactly should Ancus do something to help you?"

The man whimpered but refused to answer, only to yowl when Aven shifted his blades, pressing sharp metal against his skin. "Talk," Aven said. "Now."

"Ancus promised!" the prisoner shrilled. "He helps us wipe out the animals, and we share what we take, and he don't tell no one where we are!"

"Captain." Aria's voice was quiet, but Aven could hear her fury. "Take Ancus into custody. Grytha, I will be taking control of that meeting house until we can find the truth of this."

"Yes, my Heir," Grytha said, her voice shaking. "Mother of us all, I didn't know! I didn't know any of this!"

"We'll find the truth here," Aria said. "Captain, see them held someplace secure," Aria said. "Then join us. I want my Council in the meeting house immediately." Aven heard her coming closer, felt her hand on his arm. "Let him go, my Water."

"In one piece or two?" Aven asked. The prisoner moaned. Then he fainted, and Aven just managed to pull his swords free before the man slashed his own throat. Aria looked at him, then walked back toward the meeting house. Turning to follow her, Aven saw that most of the people around him looked horrified. Some looked frightened.

None of them would look him in the eye.

Inside the meeting house, Aven moved to a wall and leaned against it, tipping his head back.

"Fishie?" Owyn's voice was soft. "Come have some tea."

"I..." Aven swallowed. "I'm all right."

"Liar." Owyn leaned against the wall next to him. "We walked right into it. Again."

Aven nodded. "Let me go guard the door," he said. "Look around and see if there's another way in."

Owyn straightened, then turned. "Del says there's another door, but he barred it already. And the windows."

"Good," Aven said. "We're secure?"

Del nodded and signed, "*As secure as I could make it. What happened? Bandits?*"

"Yeah, and they were Risha's people," Owyn answered. "And the headman here was part of it. The raiders gave him up, and now they're all in custody. We're having Council as soon as everyone gets here."

Aven pushed off the wall and went to where Aria had taken a seat on one of the low stools. Treesi stood with her, her hands on Aria's shoulders.

"She's fine," Treesi said as Aven knelt in front of Aria.

"Now what do I do?" Aria asked softly.

"Now, we wait for the others, and we review the laws," Meris answered. "And you rule, my darling."

Aven went to guard the door, letting the Council in as they arrived. His father and Alanar. Aleia and Memfis. Steward, who arrived with Othi, Afansa and the boys.

"The camp is secure," Steward reported as Aven closed the door behind them. "What are we doing?"

"The headman of this town was in collusion with those raiders," Aria answered. "And they follow Risha. I think I remember this much of the law, but I need to be clear. If it's just him and the raiders, they pay for their crimes. If the entire town is conspiring against the Heir, the leaders are executed, and the town razed. Correct?" She looked at Meris. "Grandmother?"

"That is correct," Meris said. "And as the ranking member of the Council, not to mention the only remaining member of the Council, our laws allow me to act as tribal leader, if you wish to delegate."

"Thank you, but I need to show that I am Heir," Aria answered. "If there are only a few, then I will hand them over to you."

"And how do we know if it's really only a few, or if it's really the whole village?" Othi asked.

"Me," Alanar answered. "Let me truth-tell them." He looked around. "Owyn, is there a chair?"

Owyn went to Alanar's side and led him to one of the low stools. "Allie, I don't like the idea of you being out there alone..."

"Then you can stand next to me and glower at them," Alanar said, tipping his head back. "No one will dare do anything. They wouldn't even dare fart in the wrong key."

Shocked laughter rolled through the meeting house, and Aven watched Owyn relax.

"All right," he said. Then he chuckled. "Farting in the wrong key? That's a new one, love."

Alanar grinned. "I thought you'd like that."

"*I'll be there, too,*" Del signed.

Aven translated for Alanar, then sat down on the ground at Aria's feet. She ran her fingers through his hair, and he felt his shoulders loosen.

"Othi, would you tell Karse that he is to assemble the entire village near the well? And bring Grytha here? I want to know if she can be trusted before we begin."

Othi nodded. "I'll be right back." He bowed slightly and left.

"Did I hear Owyn correctly?" Steward asked. "Those raiders were Risha's people?"

"Or followers of the same teacher. And they don't know where she is," Aven answered. "I don't think he was lying."

"You made him piss himself," Owyn said. "He wasn't lying." He folded his arms over his chest and leaned back against the table. "And the headman, he's in on it. So now we need to find out if the whole town is. I hope not. I like Grytha."

Aria nodded. "I do, too. And she honestly seems to care for this town and these people. She'll do well as headwoman, if it comes to that." She turned and looked toward the door as someone knocked. Othi came back in, with Grytha by his side. The young woman looked like she'd been crying.

"My Heir, I didn't know!" she wailed. "I thought I've been taking care of things here, and I didn't know!"

"Now where have we heard that before?" Owyn murmured. Steward blushed slightly.

"*Stop that,*" Aven thought, and saw Owyn grin.

"I believe you, Grytha," Aria said. "But I want to be certain. I've trusted and been proved wrong before. Please come here, and talk to Healer Alanar."

Alanar smiled. "Grytha, come give me your hand," he said, and held out his own hand. "Have you heard of truth-telling?"

Grytha slipped her hand into his. "No. What is it?"

"It's something that some healers can do. Something I can do. I can tell if you're telling me the truth or if you're lying. So tell me, did you know about this? About any of this?"

"No!" Grytha blurted. "None of it! I've been the one making plans to keep the herds safe from the raiders, and arranging night watches and escorts out to the clay fields. I've been doing my best to keep this town safe from them, and now I find out that it's my own grandfather behind it? How could he do that?" She paused and bit her lip. "I'm sorry."

Alanar let her hand go. "Aria, she's true to the bone."

"I'd hoped you would say that," Aria said. "Grytha, come sit with me. We have plans to make."

Grytha dragged a stool over to sit next to Aria. "My Heir, I'm at your disposal. What do you need from me?"

KARSE ENTERED THE MEETING house. "My Heir, they're all assembled. And...am I keeping the prisoners locked away?"

"For now, Captain," Aria answered. "Thank you." She rose and held her hand out to Aven. "My Water, shall we?"

Aven nodded and held his own hand out, palm down. Aria rested her hand on top of his, and let him lead her out. She heard Owyn, Del and Treesi behind her. Behind them, she knew, was Alanar, Memfis, and Lady Meris, followed by Steward, who was escorting Grytha. The others would come as they pleased. For now, this was the processional.

Aven led Aria to a chair that had been set up near the well. She stood in front of it, but didn't sit.

"People of Hearthstone," she announced. "This proceeding is to determine if there are traitors among you, allies to the outlawed murderess Risha. The raiders are hers, as is your own headman. We would know if there are more." She looked around, but couldn't read anything in their faces. "First, I would have you know the charges against Risha herself. Steward, if you would read the listing of her crimes?"

Steward stepped forward, and Aria heard paper rustling. She closed her eyes and felt Aven's hand on her shoulder as Steward began to read aloud, listing events backwards. The murder of the Palace guard. The attack on the Palace. The attack on Aria, and the attempted murder of Aven. Virrik's murder, followed by a long list of missing, presumed murdered. Aria recognized none of the names, and she looked up at Aven.

"Rhexa, Pirit and Neera went through the records of all the Waterborn who vanished from Terraces to find the ones who were never accounted for," he answered in a soft voice. "These are the ones who never came home."

Aria moaned softly. "No one told me. Mother of us all, there are so many."

Aven squeezed her shoulder. "I know. She'll pay."

Steward paused, then cleared his throat. "The mutilation and attempted murder of six-year-old Del, son of Yana, now the Airborn Companion. And the murder of Yana, Heir to the Firstborn."

He fell silent, and horrified silence spread out over the crowd, finally broken by an older man who came forward. "Yana died in battle, we were told."

"Yana lived," Steward said. "She survived the last battle, but had the mind of a child for the rest of her days. She was cared for, and dearly loved. As her son was dearly loved, by the Usurper, whose name has been forgotten."

Aria saw movement, and Del stepped forward. He looked at Aven, who followed him, translating as Del started to sign.

"*I am Del, son of Yana. Son of Delandri—*"

"Delandri?" The older man came closer. "You're his son?" He frowned. "I...yes. You have him in you. His eyes." He smiled. "Delandri was my nephew, my sister's boy. Named for me, he was." He held his hand out. "It's a good thing, to meet family for the first time. I'm Andri."

Del looked stunned. Then he clasped the man's hand, smiled, and pulled free to sign, "*It is a good thing. We'll talk later. Please. I never knew him. I want to know about him.*"

Andri nodded once Aven had translated. "We'll have a good visit before you leave. And you can tell me what that is that you're doing." He took a deep breath and bowed to Aria. "So how will you tell if we're lying?" he asked.

"First, I give anyone involved the chance to confess," Aria answered. "If you come forward, then I will allow Lady Meris to set the penalties. I promise you that my grandmother will be merciful. I will not." She paused, and no one moved. "So?" She took a deep breath. "Then we do this a different way. Healer Alanar?"

Alanar walked forward and cocked his head to the side. "I met several of you today. For those who don't know, I am Healer Alanar. And I can truth-tell. I will demonstrate." He smiled. "Andri, we haven't met. Come here, please?"

"What can I do for you, Healer?" Andri asked.

Aven and Del walked back to stand on either side of Aria, and she took Del's hand. "Are you all right, my Air?"

Del nodded, not letting go of her hand, and Aria turned her attention back to Alanar.

"Andri, I want you to tell me three things. Two truths, and a lie. Make the lie something that everyone in this town will know is false, but someone who didn't know you would find it believable."

Andri was quiet for a moment, then said, "Three things? I'm a potter. My nephew Delandri was my apprentice, until he went off with Yana. And I'd have gone with him, if I didn't have a broken leg at the time."

Alanar smiled. "So what do you do, really? You're not a potter."

Laughter ran out, and Andri's was loudest. "I'm a weaver, Healer. And that's an impressive trick."

"And an effective one." Alanar gestured. "Andri, do you know anything of Risha?"

Andri frowned. "Just what you told us today."

"Thank you. If you'd go stand over there?" Once Andri was gone, Alanar spoke to the others. "Come to me one at a time. Tell me your name, and what you know of Risha. I'll tell you which way to go."

They came to him one at the time, and spoke to him, and he sent them to his left and to his right. By the time he was done, there was a large group on his right, and a group of six young men to his left. Alanar turned toward Aria and bowed.

"My Heir, these six are hiding something," he said. "The others? They're true to you."

"Thank you, Healer Alanar," Aria said. "Lady Meris? I told you that if it was only a few, I would hand them over to you for your judgment. Is six a few?"

Meris came forward. "Few enough," she said. "And still far too many." She turned to face the group. "You know who I am?"

The young men fidgeted and looked at each other, nudging one of them forward. He cleared his throat. "You're Lady Meris. You're on the Council."

Meris chuckled. "Young man, at the moment I am the Council. I am the ranking member of the Council. Until such time as the Council reconvenes, I speak for Fire." She drew herself up. "You have conspired against the Heir, and denied the Mother who dreamed us all. You have acted against your own people. You know the penalties for this. Your lives are forfeit." She paused. "Tell me what you know, and I will be merciful."

The six looked at each other, and drew closer together. None of them spoke, and Meris sighed.

"So, this is how it is?" she asked and turned away. "Aven, I hate to ask this of you—"

She never finished her question; the prisoners turned and tried to flee, knocking people over in their desperate attempt to escape. People rushed after then, and Meris was lost in the scramble. Aria heard Aven swear.

"Go!" she gasped, standing up. "Hurry!"

Aven dove into the fray, closely followed by Owyn. Del reached out and took Alanar's arm, then took Aria's hand. Someone touched her other arm, and she turned and saw Grytha.

"Come," Del said softly, and tugged her hand.

"We need to get you someplace safe," Grytha added. Aria nodded, starting to let them lead her back to the meeting house. Then someone wailed in the crowd, anguish and fear and pain all mingling in one horrifyingly familiar voice.

"Allie!"

Alanar whipped around. "Owyn!" he gasped. "Del, help me!"

It was Grytha who grabbed Alanar's arm. "Clear the way!" she shouted. "Let the healer through!"

The crowd parted as if it had been cut, revealing Owyn on his knees, holding a body that was too small. Too frail. Too still.

Aria went cold. "Grandmother?"

Chapter Fourteen

"Granna!" Owyn fought his way through the crowd. He caught a glimpse of the blue tunic that Meris had been wearing, then lost it again. He pushed past a taller man toward where he'd seen her, pushed past someone else, then tripped, catching a glimpse of blue as he fell. He twisted, and saw Meris on the ground. Her eyes were open and staring and empty.

"No," Owyn whispered. "No." He shoved himself up to his knees, pulled her limp body into his arms. There was something on her back, something warm that soaked through his sleeve. "No...Granna..." He touched her face, then threw his head back. "Allie!"

Almost immediately, he heard a shout. "Clear the way! Let the healer through!"

The crowd parted, and Grytha dragged Alanar toward them.

"What happened?" Alanar asked. "What is it?"

"Granna," Owyn choked. "Allie, she's dying."

Alanar held his arms out. "Give her to me."

Owyn shifted her into his husband's arms, and Alanar rested his hand on her chest and closed his eyes. Owyn wrapped his arms around his chest, trying to ignore the blood drying on his sleeve. He could feel the crowd around him, feel them staring. Then Aven dropped to his knees next to him, and reached out to put his hand over Alanar's. A heartbeat later, Jehan joined them, crowding in next to Owyn. Owyn didn't move. He couldn't move.

A hand on his shoulder, and he looked up to see Memfis standing over him with Wren at his side.

"What happened?" Memfis demanded.

Owyn shook his head. "I don't know," he whispered. "I...I don't know. I saw her. Then I lost her in the crowd. And...and when I went to find her, I tripped over her..." He choked, unable to say the word 'body.' "Mem, someone stabbed her. Someone stabbed her in the back!"

Memfis went to his knees behind Owyn, wrapping his arm around him from behind. "We'll find them."

"She's going to be so fucking mad," Owyn whispered. "She likes that tunic. It's ruined, and she likes it." He blinked as Jehan slowly drew his hand back. Then Aven shifted, moving to sit in the dirt. He scrubbed one hand over his face...and crumpled into tears.

"No!" Owyn moaned, and heard Memfis' hollow echo from behind him. He reached out to touch Meris' hand...and realized that Alanar's eyes were still closed, his hand still flat on Meris' chest. "Allie?" he called. "Allie, stop."

"I..." Alanar raised his head, tears streaking down his face. "I can't find her."

"Alanar, she's gone," Jehan said. He touched Alanar's hand. "She was gone before you even started."

"But..." Alanar looked broken. Lost. Then Aven crawled over to him and put his arms around the other healer; Alanar buried his face in Aven's shoulder.

Jehan sighed and looked up. "Aria..."

Owyn looked up, seeing Aria for the first time. Seeing the grief and fury in her face. "Who did this?" she demanded. "Who dared?" She turned, looking around. "Captain Karse!"

Karse came running, skidding to a stop. "Who started the fucking riot?" he snapped. "Prisoners went wild. Ancus broke his own fucking arm trying to get away. So what the fuck happened here..." His voice trailed off as he took in the scene. "Mother of us all..."

Aria swallowed and stood straight. "Someone murdered Lady Meris, Captain. I would know who."

"Yes, My Heir," Karse answered, his voice flat. Strained. He looked down again, and closed his eyes. "I...how the fuck am I going to tell Trey?" he murmured.

Aria ignored him, looking around at the people staring in horror. "Go to your homes," she ordered. "No one leaves the town. And I want those six men in chains. Immediately. Is that understood?"

Grytha nodded. "I'll see to it, my Heir," she said. "And...may I place my house at your disposal? So you don't have to go back to camp?" She rested a hand on Aria's arm. "Please? Let me help?"

Aria looked at Grytha, and Owyn saw the mask shift from fury to grief. He swallowed and looked to where Aven was still holding Alanar. Treesi had joined them, and it was clear that the healers were going to take care of their own. Which meant that Owyn needed to take care of his Heir. But there was someone else that needed to be cared for, too. "Jehan? Would...would you take care of Mem?"

Jehan turned, looked at him and past him, then nodded. "Come on, Old Man."

Memfis let Owyn go. "No," he croaked. "I need to see to my mother."

A ripple of whispers started through the crowd, and Grytha looked at Aria, then went to kneel next to Memfis and Jehan.

"I know what's needful," she said gently. "I'll take care of her like she was my own kin."

Memfis shook his head. "I have to do this for her." He blinked, then touched Grytha's hand. "But I'd appreciate the help."

Grytha stood up, starting to snap instructions. Owyn looked over his shoulder at Memfis. "Fa, I need to see to Aria," he said softly.

Memfis let Owyn go. "Go on."

"Do you want me to come back and help?" Owyn asked. "I—"

Memfis stopped him. "See to your Heir, Fireborn. This is mine to do."

Owyn swallowed. "Yes, Fa." He staggered to his feet and walked over to Aria. She looked at him as if she'd never seen him before, then blinked. He saw the flash of grief again, and bit his lip.

"Where am I going?" he asked. "Which is Grytha's house?"

"Fireborn?"

Owyn turned and saw Andri coming toward him. "I'll show you where to go. Del's gone off with that Steward, and the big Water warrior. I'll bring him if I see him. Come with me."

Owyn took Aria's hand, leading her past the people of Hearthstone. Every one of them looked the way Owyn felt. Numb. Horrified. Sick. He looked at Aria, saw the cracks in the facade, and shut the rest of the world out. The only person that mattered right now was his Heir. His Aria.

Andri opened the door of a neat little house with flowers in the windows. "This is Grytha's," he said. "You won't be bothered here." He paused, then added, "My Heir, what do you need?"

Aria looked at him. Then she shook her head. "Nothing but my own," she said. "I need to be alone right now."

"I'll make sure you're not disturbed," Andri said. He bowed slightly, and Owyn led Aria into the house. It was tidy and simple — a large room that was clearly an everything room, encompassing the kitchen and dining areas, and a workspace. There were herbs hanging from the ceiling in fragrant bundles, a spinning wheel near the fire, and a loom on the wall opposite the curtain. There was an inner door next to the fireplace, and there was a curtain along the left side of the room that probably hid the bed. The only thing that would mark this as something other than a weaver's house were the smoke blades that hung on the wall over the fireplace.

Owyn led Aria to the chair next to the fire, then knelt at her feet once she'd taken a seat. He took her hands in his, and waited.

And the facade shattered. Aria crumpled into tears, pulling her hands from Owyn's as she wrapped her arms around herself and wailed her grief. Owyn shifted to her side, wrapping his arms around her, letting her sob and scream into his shoulder, holding his own tears back so that she could vent hers. He'd mourn later, when she didn't need someone to keep her from breaking apart completely.

He heard the door open behind him, and glanced back to see the healers had come inside. He nodded toward the curtain, and Aven put his arm around Alanar and led him behind the barrier. Treesi came to kneel next to Owyn, resting one hand on Aria's knee. Aria raised her head and looked at Treesi, then frowned.

"Aven and Alanar are behind the curtain," Treesi answered.

"Are we all here?" Aria asked, her voice sounding choked and brittle. "I want all of my own here. I need you all here."

"Del's with Othi and Steward," Owyn answered. "Andri said he'd bring him if he saw him."

"I'll go tell him to go look," Treesi added. She stood up and kissed Aria's cheek, then leaned down and kissed Owyn before hurrying to the door. As she opened it, Andri drew back, clearly startled. His raised hand showed that he was about to knock.

"I...sorry to bother you. Grytha asked me to tell you there's two beds," he said. "There's the one behind the curtain, but there's another through the door. She usually hosted any village guests here, so that's the guest bed. She also said there's a good bottle of brandywine on the table, and you're welcome to it."

"Thank you," Treesi said. "Would you see if you can find Del? And Othi?"

"That's the big Water warrior?" Andri asked. "I'll find him. Won't have to look hard — you could probably see him from Forge."

Owyn snickered, looked at Aria to see her smiling slightly. She stood and went to the table, picking up the bottle.

"Brandywine," she said. "Treesi, is this something I can drink? Will it hurt the baby?"

Treesi closed the door, came over and took the bottle. She picked up a cup and filled it halfway. "That's all. Then you go and lay down."

Owyn came over and took the bottle from Treesi. He filled another cup, and took a long sip, letting the burn of the brandywine warm him from the center out.

"No getting drunk, Owyn," Treesi murmured.

"This isn't enough to make me drunk," Owyn answered, and took another sip. "It's good, but it won't light me."

"Light you?" Aria asked. She sipped from her own cup, then looked at it. "What is this?"

"Ah...fermented wine?" Owyn said. "I'm not really sure. Wine that's had something done to it. Makes it stronger."

"And light means drunk," Treesi said. "He means get drunk. And if I drink any, I will be. And I can't be." She looked at the curtain. "Owyn—"

"I'll put Aria to bed," Owyn said. "You go convince Allie that it wasn't his fault. And take the bottle. He'd like this." He drained his cup and set it aside.

Treesi nodded, then came closer. She kissed him, resting her hands on his chest. All at once, he heard her. *"You can hear me, can't you?"* He nodded slightly. *"Good. I can tell you're keeping a brave face for Aria. You can cry on me later."* She kissed him again, then took the bottle and disappeared behind the curtain. Aria put her cup of unfinished wine on the table.

"I don't think that I care for this," she said. "Owyn..." She paused. Frowned. Then she shook her head. "I...I don't know. I don't know anything. Not anymore. She knew. She had to have known. She knew that...why didn't she *warn* us?"

"If she had, we'd have tried to stop it. To save her." Owyn picked up Aria's discarded cup and drained it. "She couldn't tell us. That's something you'll learn. We know, but we can't...when the time comes, we can't warn others."

"Why not?" Aria demanded. "We know. Why can't we tell people? Why can't we warn them?" She wrapped her arms around herself, tucking her wings in close to her body. "If she'd warned us, would it hurt so much?"

Owyn put his arms around her. "Come with me," he said softly. "Come to bed. You can cry on me."

She sniffled. "Who are you crying on?" she asked. "She was your grandmother, too."

"Treesi," Owyn answered. "Tomorrow. Right now, you need me. I'll cry tomorrow."

Aria gave a wet, sobbing laugh. "My Owyn. My Mouse. You always take care of me." She touched his cheek. "I don't deserve you."

"The Mother says otherwise," Owyn said. He turned his head so he could kiss her palm. "Come on. Bed."

He led her through the inner door into a warm room that smelled of lavender and redbark. Aria sat down on the edge of the bed while Owyn went back out for a slip so that he could light a lamp. As he reached the fireplace, the door opened; Del and Othi slipped inside. Del's eyes were red, and Othi looked solemn.

"Aria's in the bedroom there," Owyn said, pointing. "And Allie is with Aven and Treesi over behind the curtain." He looked around. "Othi, why don't you go to Treesi? I think she can use your help."

"I'm not sure what help I'll be, but I'll go." Othi patted Del's shoulder, then went to the curtain. "Treesi?"

"Come in, Othi," Treesi called. Once he was gone, Owyn held his hand out to Del.

"*How's Aria?*" Del asked, taking Owyn's hand.

"Hurting," Owyn answered. "Come help me take care of her?"

Del frowned. "*Should I?*" he asked. "*Or should I give you privacy?*"

"Let's see what Aria wants," Owyn answered, and led Del to the bedroom. Aria had moved off the bed and was standing in the corner, looking at a woven tapestry. She glanced over, then looked again when she saw Owyn had brought Del.

"We're all here now?" she asked.

"Othi went to help Treesi," Owyn answered. "And Del came to help me, if you want him here."

"I...yes, please," Aria answered. "And he can help you, Owyn."

It took Owyn a moment to realize what Aria meant. "I...I'll be fine until I can spend some time with Treesi."

"She was your grandmother, too," Aria repeated. "You need to mourn as much as I do. More. You knew her longer." She held her hands out. "Let's go to bed."

OWYN DRIFTED IN AND out of a restless sleep punctuated by vague dreams. The weight on his chest anchored him, kept him from tossing and turning and keeping himself awake. Aria had cried herself to sleep in his arms. Once she'd fallen asleep, Del had held Owyn until he'd cried himself to sleep. Now...there was no more sleeping. He blinked, and realized that he wasn't the only one awake. Del was gone, and Aria was tracing abstract patterns on his chest with her nails.

"What do I do now?" Aria's voice was quiet and lost.

"We keep going," Owyn answered softly. "That's all she'd ask us to do."

Aria jerked, pushing herself up so that she could look at him. "*You heard me?*" she asked. Her mouth didn't move.

Owyn blinked. "I...Aria, I heard you!"

She blinked, then sniffled. "Her last gift?" she whispered. "We're finally whole?"

"We were already whole," Owyn said. "Just...now whatever was still in the way is gone. Whatever it was." He hugged her tightly to his side, and felt the baby kick.

Aria sighed. "She wanted to see the baby."

"I know." Owyn kissed the top of Aria's head. "I really hate that she won't. That she won't be there to see you wearing the Crown." He frowned. "Oh, fuck. I'm going to have to tell Milon."

"Oh." Aria sniffled again. "What do we do now?"

"The funeral pyre is probably already set," Owyn answered. "We need to dress. I...we'll need to get Trista to bring our clothes."

A soft knock on the door, and Trista looked inside. "I heard my name," she said. "The others are awake, and Steward had me bring your ritual wear. There's food, and he said they'll hold the ritual until you're ready." She bit her lip, then blurted, "My Heir, I'm so sorry!"

"Thank you, Trista." Aria sat up slowly and ran her fingers through her hair. "I'm not sure I can eat—"

"And Healer Aven said you might say that, and there is some spicy...something." Trista looked over her shoulder. "Moes?"

"Momo," Aven called from outside. "And if you want some, you have to come eat it before Alanar does."

Aria looked startled. "Who made momo?" She stood up. Owyn rolled off the other side of the bed, and they put their rumpled clothing to rights before walking out of the bedroom.

Owyn looked at the table, saw the bowl of momo, and a pot of porridge. "Who cooked?"

"Del made the porridge, and I made the momo," Steward said. "I...it was all I could think of to help. Aven told me you like them. And..." He frowned. Then he sighed. "We're all family here. I used to make them for Yana. I learned how, because she loved them."

Aria smiled slightly. "Thank you, Steward."

"You smiled. That almost makes it worth it," Steward said. "If you eat? That will make it worth it."

Aria sat down, and Owyn sat down next to her. They ate in silence, with Trista moving around behind them, filling cups and making sure that plates were full. On one pass, Alanar reached out and grabbed her wrist.

"Trista, sit," he said. "Eat with us."

"I...I couldn't!" she protested. "I'm...I can't!"

"We're not formal, Trista," Aven said. "And you're not going to be in trouble if we invite you. Sit. Have some momo."

"I've never tried them," Trista admitted. She sat down in the only empty chair, which put her next to Owyn. Her arm brushed his, and she blushed.

"Steward, we've done Earth funerals. What do we do for Fire?" Aven asked as they finished eating.

"Lady Meris' body is already laid out on the pyre. Memfis and Grytha and Jehan and I saw to her last night, and Karse and Wren have been standing sentry at the pyre—"

"Were you expecting trouble?" Alanar asked.

"No, that's part of the ritual," Steward answered. "The honor guard, to watch over the dead. They stand silent sentry to witness the dead leave this world and go on to the next. The sentries won't speak or stand down until the pyre burns out."

"Oh," Aria breathed. "Then we should do what's needful. What else?"

"Once you've eaten, dress and we'll go out. Memfis and Afansa are already out there." Steward paused. "He's refusing food. Said it's disrespectful to eat until she's properly burned."

"Is that part of the ritual?" Treesi asked.

"No, that's Mem not wanting to puke in front of everyone," Owyn answered. He looked down at his empty bowl. "Clothes are where, Trista?"

They dressed quickly — Aria and Del in white, Owyn in red, and the healers all in shades of brown. As they came out into the main room, Aven drew his knife and held it into the flame of the lamp.

"*Aven, can adoptees wear mourning stripes?*" Del signed.

Aven arched a brow. "You want them? You're not Water."

"*I was adopted into the canoe. Neera said so,*" Del insisted.

"I was, too," Owyn blurted. "Even though I haven't gotten the tattoo yet. If...if we're doing this, we should do it right."

Aven looked at him, then nodded slowly. "If you want. You are all of the family canoe." He carefully cut his own cheek, then ran the blade through the flame again. "Del? You're next."

Chapter Fifteen

Owyn's cheek stung and burned and itched, but it was a welcome distraction from the sick feeling in his stomach. He understood why Memfis was refusing to eat. On his left, Del squeezed his hand.

"*Are you going to be all right?*" Del whispered to him.

"No," Owyn answered. He looked at Del. "Not yet. Not anytime soon. But I'll live." He looked at Treesi on his other side. "Later?"

"Whenever you need me," Treesi said, and squeezed his hand tightly. Owyn looked forward again, toward the pyre. He could see Memfis and Afansa there. Jehan and Aleia. Copper and Danir, both of them holding on to Aleia's hands. Grytha was there, holding her smoke blades. How had she gotten those? And standing by two of the four torches that marked the corners of the pyre were Karse and Wren, both in Palace livery. Owyn tried not to look at the pyre itself, looking instead at the crowd surrounding it. The people of Hearthstone, all dressed in shades of red.

Memfis turned and looked at them, and his eyes widened, no doubt seeing the Water mourning stripes on all of the men's faces. He nodded slowly, then turned and whispered something to Jehan. When Jehan turned, Owyn could see the blood on his own face. He drew his knife, and carved a mourning stripe into Memfis' cheek.

"We've started a trend," Aven murmured. "Now what?"

"Memfis is recognized as Lady Meris' son by courtesy, and therefore is primary mourner," Steward answered. "He will lead the ritual. Mourners will speak for the dead, and the pyre will be lit."

They walked up next to Memfis, and Owyn let go of Del and Treesi, stepping forward to take Aria's hand. Aven stepped back, letting Meris' grandchildren stand at the front of the group.

"Mother of us all," Memfis began, his voice rolling out. "We surrender to Your arms a daughter of Fire. Meris, daughter of Armonia, daughter of Klea, daughter of Akayla, of the line of Nerris. Fire Companion to the Firstborn Riga. Smoke Dancer, and mother of Smoke Dancers." He paused. "We give her back to the fires that bore us, so that she may stand before You and Your judgment. May her blessings outweigh her faults, and may she be welcomed home to Fire." He closed his eyes. "Meris...was the closest person I had to a mother. The closest I remember. She was my first teacher, when I came to the Smoke. She took me in, gave me a home and a family. Sheltered me when my world fell apart, helped me rebuild. She kept me going when I would have given up, and didn't give up on me when I gave up on everything." He took a deep, shuddering breath. "I'm going to miss her." He bowed his head, a signal that he was done.

Owyn took a deep breath and stepped forward. "Meris let me call her Granna," he said. "I...I surprised her with it, the first time. It was right after Memfis adopted me. I hadn't realized that I thought of her that way. Not until I said it. But it was true. She was my grandmother in every way she could be but blood. She never looked at me like I was less, even though she knew every bit of my past. She helped teach me to be a person, instead of a wild thing. Let me play in her kitchen until I really learned to cook. She helped teach me to read, and to be a Smoke Dancer."

He reached up and touched the gem at his throat. "And when Aria gave me this, I don't think anyone could have been more proud." He glanced at Aria.

"I didn't know I had a grandmother...well, a great-grandmother, until we came to Forge," Aria said, her voice carrying. "I was...'frightened' seems not strong enough a word. When Memfis found us, I had no idea what I was doing. I had a Diadem and a few colored stones, and my Water, my Aven. Then I found my Fire, my Owyn, and I found my Grandmother." Aria paused, then nodded. "Meris was...safety. She was shelter, in a world where I didn't think I had shelter anymore. When everything fell apart, and I couldn't think clearly and felt I was alone and lost, the only place I thought I could turn was to her. I didn't have nearly enough time to know her, and I will treasure the time I did have forever."

She fell silent, lowering her head, and others stepped forward to add their words. Alanar. Treesi. Del, with Aven translating. Then Aven added his own words. Jehan. Aleia. Afansa, who burst into tears in the middle and couldn't finish. Danir and Copper both stepped forward, each of them speaking with unaccustomed solemnity before fleeing to Owyn for comfort. He wrapped his arms around the boys and looked up as Aven walked past him. He went to the pyre where Karse stood in silent sentry. He met Karse's eyes, nodded toward the group, then stood next to him and mimicked his stance. Karse looked at him, then must have realized what Aven was doing. He stepped out, turned to face Aven, and saluted. Then he walked to the group and turned to face the pyre once more.

"Thank you," he said. "Lady Meris. You...you don't realize sometimes how much someone means until they're gone. Meris, she had a way about her, a way of loving everyone. Even if you fucked up. She'd let you know you did, and make no mistake about it. But she'd also let you know she forgave you, and that she still loved you. Over the past couple of years...well, I'd have done anything she asked, and smiled doing it." He looked down at his hands, then wrapped his right hand around the pledge bracelet on his left wrist. "And if you were missing the obvious, she'd tell you that, too. She's the reason I finally saw the man who loves me. Who I love. And I honestly have no idea how I'm going to tell him she's gone." He bowed his head, then walked back to the pyre and his position. Before Aven could step out of the way, Karse hugged him. Then he resumed his position as sentry. Aven walked back to the group and took his place with the others, and Aria took his hand.

Memfis stepped forward. "Is there anyone else who will speak for the dead?" he called. Silence answered, and he nodded. "So be it. Let her return to fire, and in the fire return to the Mother who dreamed us all." He looked at Owyn and Aria. "Come with me."

Owyn hugged the boys to his sides, and followed Memfis, uncertain of what was happening. Until Memfis took down one of the four torches. He gestured, and Aria stared at him.

"We do this?" she whispered.

"This is for us to do," Memfis answered. "We have to light the pyre."

Aria shivered, her wings quivering violently. She walked past Karse and took down the torch at his side. Owyn followed, going around to the far side and taking one of those torches. "Who takes the last one?" he asked.

Memfis frowned, then looked back. "Grytha?"

"I would be honored." Grytha took the last torch, watching Memfis closely. Memfis nodded, and lowered his torch to the pyre. Owyn did the same, and watched as the flames caught and spread. He left the torch buried in the wood, stepping back and walking around to Aria's side. She had stepped well back from the pyre, and was watching the flames with a stony expression. But when she spoke, her voice shook.

"Memfis?" she called. "Attend."

Memfis looked startled. He turned from the pyre and came over to them, resting his hand over his heart. "My Heir?"

"My great-grandmother thought of you as her son," Aria said. "I think it is therefore fitting that you should be considered her heir. I ask you to take on the leadership of the Fire tribe, until the Council can be reconvened."

Memfis stared at her. "Aria! You...you want me to do *what*?"

"The Fire tribe needs a leader," Aria said. "I can think of no one better. Grandmother already called you her heir."

"I..."

"Say yes, Mem," Jehan said, coming up on Memfis' left. "She wanted this for you."

"And you'll do wonderfully," Aleia added, standing at Memfis' right. Memfis looked at Jehan, then down at Aleia. Then he turned back to Aria.

"Only until the Council reconvenes?"

Aria nodded. "As Grandmother intended, yes."

Memfis took a deep breath. "Then I accept. And...Aria, Lady Meris was going to rule on those prisoners. You ceded that to her. Do you want it back?"

Aria looked thoughtful. "No," she answered. "You may proceed."

"Then I want them here. All of them, right now." Memfis stepped back, gesturing to Jehan and Aleia. They formed a tight knot, and started speaking in low voices.

"Do you know what he's doing?" Owyn asked.

"No, but it is his to do," Aria answered. She rested her hand on his shoulder, and they went to join the others. Aven put his arms around them both, and they watched as the guards arrived, escorting the prisoners. There were nine of them — the six who had started the riot, the two raiders, and Ancus. All of them were battered and bruised, and Ancus' arm had been splinted and was in a sling. The guards arranged the men in a single line facing the pyre, and Memfis came to stand in front of them, his back to the pyre.

"Lady Meris is dead," he said, his voice carrying over the crackling of the flames. "I now stand as the leader of the Fire tribe, and it falls to me to deal with you." He paused, and looked up and down the line of men. From where he was standing, Owyn could see that one of the rioters was staring at the ground. Memfis went over to him and poked him in the chest.

"Look at her," he growled. "Look at what you've done." He waved his arm back toward the pyre. "Lady Meris ruled Forge for longer than you've been alive. She's been the Voice of the Council since I was a boy, and she led the tribe wisely and well. And you killed her. You might not have been the one who held the knife, but your actions, and your betrayal...those caused her death." He looked up and down the line again. "So tell me this. Was it worth it? Was your denial of the Mother's dreams worth this? Was your little tantrum over who you think is worthy to be called one of the Mother's children worth *this*?" He lowered his arm. "I have served the Mother my entire life. And that service...it has cost me almost everything. It cost me the man I love, my place in the world. My sobriety." He gestured to himself. "My *arm*. And now...it's cost me my mother." He let his hand fall. "All I have left is my son, my Heir, and my duty to this tribe. And I will not let you drag this tribe down, drag this world down. Do you know why the Smoking Mountain finally exploded? Because people like you think you can contradict the Mother's word. The Mother's patience is long, but Adavar is stirring, and if you go down to the Smoking Mountain, down to where Forge was, you can hear Him breathing."

"Did you tell him that?" Aven whispered.

"I didn't," Owyn answered. "I don't think. It don't matter. It's true."

"I told Steward," Aria said. "He must have told Memfis."

Memfis walked up and down the line of men. "The world is out of balance because of people like you. Adavar is rising, because of people like you. People who think that they can deny the Mother's will. But now...now that we have a chance of turning all of this around." He pointed at Aria. "We have a true Heir, and her true Companions. She has taken the Palace, and she has started the work to put things right. But you want to throw all of that away, because she doesn't look like you? Are you truly that selfish?" He stopped, tucking his thumb into his belt. "It's on me to deal with you. Now, my mother would probably have counseled me to be merciful. But I no longer have her guidance, and you no longer have the benefit of her tempering hand. So here is my judgment." He turned to Ancus and the two raiders. "You three. For your crimes against this town and these people, you are hereby sentenced to death." He turned back to the rioters. "And for you? You will stand here, under guard, for the next hour. At the end of that hour, you will be given a choice. Stand with the Heir..." He stopped and turned to face the pyre. "Or burn with the Lady Meris."

Then he turned and walked away.

AVEN STAYED AFTER THE others had left, watching the pyre. Watching the prisoners, who stood facing the pyre, still in a single line. One of the guards was Aven's cousin, Fara, and she walked over to him.

"What are you thinking?" she asked, standing next to him. "Aren't you on duty?

"I can see them from here," Fara answered. "So?"

Aven snorted. "Just thinking about how things were so much less complicated out on the deep."

"No, they weren't. It was just a different complicated," Fara answered. "Wait. You were off with your parents. You weren't with the family canoes. So maybe you did have things being less complicated. But this?" She shook her head. "This is really very similar to what it was like living near Grandmother for any length of time. You were lucky to be out of it."

"It didn't feel lucky," Aven admitted. "I always felt like I was never going to be a part of anything."

"And now, you're part of everything." Fara grinned and poked him in the shoulder. "So who wins?" She nodded toward the prisoners. "What do you think they're going to do?"

"I can't even guess, but I'd say you want to keep your blades sharp. Nine heads will dull your edges." Aven met her gaze. She nodded.

"The hour is almost up," she said. "Are you going to stay and watch, or go back to the Heir?"

"I'll go, but I'll be back. She'll want to witness this."

Fara nodded. Then she spat into the dirt. "Nasty business, this. Who murders a mother of the tribe? Who does that?" She frowned. "And which of them did it? Was it one of them, or did someone take advantage of the riot?"

Aven shook his head. "I don't know. I don't think we can know without having Alanar truth-tell them again. Which...I'll bring that to Aria." He took a deep breath. "Do you need anything, Fara?"

"When you come back, bring some salt water, will you?" Fara walked back to the line of prisoners, and Aven walked back to the meeting house. Aria was either there or in Grytha's house, and the meeting house was closer. He heard voices as he got close, and let himself inside, only to find that it wasn't Aria and the others.

It was Memfis, Steward and his parents, and they were arguing.

"You don't know which one did it!" Aleia insisted, and Aven got the impression she'd already said that at least twice.

"It doesn't matter," Memfis said. "If it wasn't for them, she'd still be alive. They have to face the consequences of their actions."

"So you're going to summarily execute nine people," Jehan

"Three," Memfis snapped. "The only ones who are being executed out of hand are the raiders who were preying on this town and the people, and Ancus for allowing it. The others...all they have to do to save themselves is swear loyalty to Aria."

"I won't have them near her without Alanar truth-telling them first," Aven said. "Have him ask them if they killed her."

From the stunned looks suddenly facing Aven, none of them had heard him come in.

"I..." Memfis stammered.

"You didn't think of that?" Aven asked. "Memfis, what are you thinking? Are you even thinking?"

"That's what we're trying to determine," Jehan said, his voice dry. Memfis scowled at him.

"Does it matter?" he asked. "If it wasn't for their riot, she'd still be alive."

Aven folded his arms over his chest. "I might not have done as much reading as you have, but I don't seem to remember death being a penalty for doing something that led to someone being killed. Only for being the one to kill them." He frowned. "Have I got that right, Steward?"

"You do," Steward said. "The laws in the Fire tribe are clear. And I know you're angry, Memfis, but we cannot go against the law. Not when things are so perilous."

"You're a fine one to talk," Memfis grumbled.

"Yes," Steward snapped back. "Yes, I am. I am the finest one to talk, because I can tell you exactly what happens when you go against the law. We would not be here today if I had abided by the law." He jabbed his finger toward the door. "What you intend to do out there goes against the law. It's not justice. It's revenge."

Memfis growled and stepped toward Steward, his hand balled into a fist. Steward glared at him, not moving; after a moment, Memfis sighed and backed down.

"You're right," he breathed. "You're right, and she'd be ashamed of me." He took a deep breath. "What do I do?"

"We find a way around it," Jehan said. He looked up. "Aven, I think we'll want you all to join us. This is going to be educational."

"Then why don't you come to the house," Aven suggested. "If we're going to learn a thing or six, we can at least be comfortable while we do it."

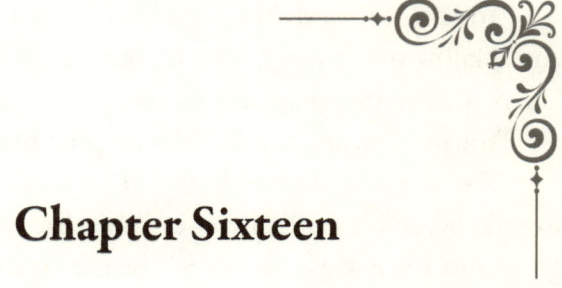

Chapter Sixteen

At the end of the hour, Memfis led the way out of Grytha's house. Behind him were Jehan and Aleia. Aria kept her Companions and Steward back until Memfis was halfway to the pyre, then allowed them to follow.

"The focus should be on Memfis," she explained as they waited. "This is for him to do."

"Now that he's got his head on straight," Owyn muttered in response.

Memfis stopped in front of the still-burning pyre and turned to face the line of prisoners. He gestured to the six rioters first. "The law says that death is the penalty for murder. And in my anger, and in my pain, I have condemned six for the crimes of one. That isn't right. So I vacate that decision. But I will still know which of you is the killer. So..." He gestured. "Healer Alanar, if you would?"

Alanar came forward, with Owyn at his elbow. "I will ask each of you one question," Alanar said. "You will answer." He stopped in front of the first rioter and held out his hand. The man rested his hand on Alanar's, and Alanar asked, "Did you kill Lady Meris, or attempt to harm her in any way?"

"No, Healer."

Alanar nodded, and moved to the next man in the line, repeating the question. When the last man had answered, Alanar turned to Memfis.

"None of them," he pronounced. "None of these men is the killer. Shall I ask the other prisoners?"

"They were locked up, and Karse was with them." Memfis rubbed his hand over his face. "If they didn't kill her, then who did?"

"I might be able to answer that," Grytha said. "There are two people missing, a pair of trouble-making brothers. I noticed they weren't at the ceremony, and we've been searching. They're not in town."

"But they were part of the group that wasn't hiding anything," Alanar protested. "They were true to Aria. I couldn't have missed something like that!"

"When we find them, you can ask them again," Grytha said.

"We might not be here—" Owyn started

"I'll hold them until you come again," Grytha interrupted. "Or send them to the Palace. Now, none of this lot are murderers. Idiots, but not murderers."

"And idiocy, while frustrating, isn't a crime." Memfis paused. "However, inciting a riot is a crime. One that is usually handled by the local authority."

"Who is awaiting execution," Grytha added.

"Are you?" Memfis asked. Aria bit her lip to keep from laughing at the stunned look on Grytha's face.

"Me? You're making me Headwoman?" she squeaked. "I..."

"You've been doing the work already. You told Aria that you've been serving in that capacity. And you're more than capable." He looked around. "Are there any objections?"

A buzz of conversation, then Andri stepped forward. "Not a one," he called.

"Then these men are yours to deal with, Headwoman," Memfis said.

Grytha frowned. She looked at the rioters, then at Memfis. "May I ask for guidance?"

"I would be honored." Memfis bowed slightly. Grytha grabbed his wrist, dragging him toward Aria.

"What do I do?" she whispered. "I..."

"What would you have done if you were making the decision for your grandfather?"

"The exact opposite of what he'd have done," Grytha answered. "He'd have made some excuse about boys being boys, and let them free without even a harsh word."

"And you'd have done...what?" Memfis asked.

Grytha looked back at the rioters, then nodded. "Clearing the goat pens and rebuilding them. Digging out new middens in a better place, and filling the old ones. Then building new kilns and breaking down the old ones. They're going to work their arses off, and maybe start thinking clearly when they're done. And if they don't do a good job, they do it again."

"Is that likely to be enough?" Aria asked.

"If it isn't, I'll find something else nasty for them to do," Grytha answered. She looked back at the prisoners. "And Grandfather and the raiders? They're still going to burn, aren't they?"

Aria looked thoughtful, then answered, "Perhaps not. Do you plead clemency?"

"Clemency," Grytha repeated. "That...oh. That...I don't like that either. Clemency for a death sentence means slavery. And they'd have to be slaves somewhere else. Where?"

Aria shook her head. "I don't know. But I don't know any other options. Have I missed anything? Memfis? Steward?"

"You haven't," Memfis said. He looked over at Owyn. "And I have a distinct distaste for slavery for some reason."

"I can't imagine why," Steward replied. He ran his finger down the bridge of his nose. "Grytha, if you plead clemency, the options are slavery or life in the mines. Which...neither actually is an option anymore." He frowned. "Are there options?"

"Roads?" Owyn asked. "We were talking about the roads on the way here, and how they need to be rebuilt. To do that, we need road crews."

"Which is something that we still need to organize," Steward said. "I like it, but what do we do with them in the meantime?"

"Send them to Cliffside to help them rebuild," Owyn said. "We should send a runner on to Aunt Rhexa about the roads. She might have some ideas. And if we're not ready to start the roads when the crew is done in Cliffside, maybe send them on to Terraces to help rebuild there."

"That seems to be a viable option," Memfis said. "But keep in mind that they have to accept clemency once it's offered. If they refuse, then there's no other option but execution."

They walked back to the pyre, and Memfis raised his voice. "The charge of murder has been vacated," he announced. "These six are remanded to the custody of Headwoman Grytha to face punishment for inciting a riot." He turned to the raiders and Ancus. "As for you, clemency has been pled—"

"I refuse!" Ancus snapped

"Grandfather, you don't even know what it is!" Grytha protested.

"I'm not spending the rest of my life as a slave," Ancus said. "Just kill me."

"For the record, clemency offers a sentence of rebuilding — first the town of Cliffside, then in Terraces, and then rebuilding the roads."

"I still refuse."

"So be it," Memfis looked at the two raiders. "And you? Do you accept clemency?"

The two raiders looked at each other. They whispered back and forth, a muffled, heated conversation that ended when one of them stepped away and said, "I do. Thank you."

"You're an idiot," the other snapped. "Not me. I won't do it."

"Taver, be reasonable!"

"I'm not living as a slave," Taver said. "That's my reason."

"So be it," Memfis repeated. "Ancus and Taver, you have refused clemency and accepted the sentence of death. And..." Memfis looked at the raider who had accepted clemency.

"My name is Cellan, Lord Memfis."

The addition of the title seemed to startle Memfis, and he hesitated before he continued, "Cellan, you'll be transported to Cliffside. We'll make the arrangements before we leave." He looked around. "Fara, would you see that the prisoners who are to be executed are held someplace secure? And the rioters should be held someplace else." He glanced at Cellan. "And leave this one."

Fara stepped forward and saluted. "And the execution?" she asked.

"Will be carried out at the discretion of the Heir," Memfis answered.

Fara bowed, then herded the prisoners away. Once she was gone, Memfis turned to Cellan.

"Do you have any questions?" he asked. "Anything to add?"

"I..." Cellan paused. "I'm to help rebuild, you said. That's...yeah, I can build most things. Fa was a carpenter. I know how to build. But..." He paused again, then blurted, "Can I come with you? When you go? Instead of going to Cliffside?"

"What?" Memfis gasped. "No, of—"

Aria raised one hand, and Memfis fell silent. Cellan looked at her, then went to one knee.

"Cellan, would you explain?" Aria asked.

"I...you want me to help rebuild," he said. "And...well, that's what you're doing. You're on this Progress, going all around, even to people who don't want you. Trying to rebuild what's broke. And...well, I can go help some people. A few people. Or...I can come with you to help you, and by helping you help everyone." He looked up. "May I?"

"Cellan, why were you with the raiders?" Aven asked, moving to Aria's side.

"And stand up," Aria added. Cellan looked at her, swallowed, and got to his feet, tucking his hands behind his back.

"I...my village was so small it didn't really have a name. We were near the mines, and my fa made tools for them, made cabinets and boxes and wagons. All sorts of things. If it could be made from wood, he could make it." He smiled. "He made instruments, too. Lap harps and viols and flutes. Made a lute once, and swore he'd never do it again." He took a deep breath. "The entire village got eaten by the mountain. I was out making a delivery for Fa, so I missed it. Came back to find the entire place gone. No signs of anyone. I...I went looking for someone...anyone, and Taver and his lot found me. I'm not really a fighter, though." He shrugged. "I'm a good carpenter. Good with my hands. I can build just about anything, and if you tell me to go to Cliffside, I will. But I'd rather come with you, if I might." He looked down. "Please."

Aria nodded. "Thank you, Cellan. We will discuss this and let you know what we decide. Grytha, where can he be held that is comfortable?"

"Are you going back to camp tonight, or staying at my house?" Grytha asked.

"I think perhaps we'll return to camp," Aria answered.

"Then come with me, Cellan," Grytha said. "You're staying with me tonight."

Cellan grinned. "Got any repairs that need doing? I can earn my keep."

THE SUN WAS PAST ITS zenith when Owyn headed out to search the village for Treesi. He found her with Othi, Copper, Danir, and a half-dozen of the village children, who were all laughing as Othi told them an animated story of some sort of sea monster. He stood at the back of the group for a moment, then caught Treesi's eyes.

"*Do you need me?*" she asked silently. He nodded, and she slipped away from the group and came around to join him. "What is it?"

"We're going to need you," he said. "And Afansa. Do you know where she is?"

"I'm not sure," Treesi answered. "Need me for what?"

"The pyre is almost out," Owyn said. "And Karse and Wren have been standing sentry out there since before it was lit. I was thinking, you and Afansa catch Karse, and Allie and me, we'll get Wren. Get some water into them, and some food. Get them taken care of."

Treesi nodded. "Let me tell Othi where I'll be. Then I'll help you find Afansa."

They finally found Afansa back at camp, with Aleia and Steward. Steward listened to Owyn's explanation, then started giving orders to have a cart prepared.

"I should have thought of this," Steward grumbled as the cart bumped and lurched into Hearthstone.

"So long as someone did, it don't matter," Owyn replied. "Stop there, and let me fetch Allie and Mem."

They approached the remains of the pyre, and Owyn studied the two men. Karse's jaw was locked, and he was clearly holding himself up through sheer force of will. Wren's olive skin looked more than a little pink, and he was gently swaying from one foot to the other. Neither of them so much as looked at the pairs that moved to stand in front of them — Afansa and Treesi to Karse, and Owyn and Alanar to Wren. Memfis walked a slow circle around the pyre. Once. Twice. Three times.

"There are no active flames," he pronounced. "The fires have claimed her."

Once the words were spoken, Karse slowly crumpled to his knees. Wren went down like a fallen tree; Owyn caught him before he hit the ground, then took a flask from Alanar.

"Here, drink this," he said, holding the flask to Wren's lips. "Slowly."

Wren sipped, then sputtered. "What is that?"

"Pickle brine," Alanar answered. "Terraces cure-all for dehydration. Drink it. Your body needs the salt and the water."

Wren took the flask from Owyn and sipped it again. Then he took a long pull before looking oddly at the flask. "I...I don't even like pickles!" he muttered.

"Let me have your hand," Alanar said. Wren rested his hand on top of Alanar's, and Alanar cocked his head to the side.

"Dehydration," he murmured. "Sunburn. The sugars in your blood are low. Are you dizzy?"

"A little, yeah." Wren drank more from the flask. "It just started."

"Finish that, and we'll get some food for you. Then a cool bath, and some more to eat. Then you're off-duty the rest of the night." Alanar let Wren's hand go. "Healer's orders."

Wren nodded, leaning more solidly into Owyn's body. He drank the last of the brine, and took a second flask from Owyn. "More pickles?"

"This is just water," Owyn said. He looked over at the other group. Karse was still on his knees, and Afansa had her arms around him. She was crying, and Owyn suspected Karse was, too. "We have food for you, if you think you can get up. Steward ordered a cart to take you and Allie back to camp."

"You're not going?" Wren asked.

"I have to be here for the census." Owyn looked around. "Me, Del, Steward and Mem, we're counting noses after the evening meal. And Grytha wants to go over the route, so we can be warned about problem villages. We're leaving tomorrow."

Wren nodded. "Wouldn't mind if you came back with me," he mumbled, and rested his head on Owyn's shoulder. "Wouldn't mind..."

"I'm taking you back," Alanar said. He looked at Owyn, and his internal mind was surprisingly clear, if a little echoey. "*If he needs it, I'll see to him. I think he's heat-drunk, though. I'm not sure he's coherent enough to consent.*"

Owyn stared at his husband, then laughed when he realized why he wasn't hearing jumbled noise. "You're talking in harmony now?" he whispered. Alanar grinned.

"We weren't sure that would work!" Alanar slowly got to his feet. "Help him up and to the cart, Owyn."

They loaded Wren into the cart, where he curled up with his head on Alanar's lap and seemed to fall asleep almost immediately. Then Afansa helped Karse into the back.

"I'm getting too old," Karse grumbled. He put his arm around Afansa as she settled next to him. "Fancy, you're getting yourself an old man."

Afansa sniffed, and for the first time in Owyn's hearing, didn't chide Karse for the use of the nickname. "I happen to like older men, Captain. Now hush and drink that. Healer's orders."

Treesi climbed into the cart, then nodded. "All right. We're off. See you back in camp, Owyn."

The cart rolled away, and Owyn yawned. He had a long night ahead of him, counting noses and taking notes.

THE PEOPLE OF HEARTHSTONE seemed to know exactly what was needed of them from the census — name, lineage, occupation. Owyn and Del both worked as scribes, each of them paired with their fathers to speed the lines along.

"Are you really stopping at every place where people live?" Grytha asked as the last person filed out. "Even the little places out in the hills, and the goatherders down south?"

"Are there still goatherders down south?" Steward asked.

Grytha shrugged. "The ones who used to come here to trade haven't, but they've been late before. They've come as late as midsummer, some years. So I don't know. If they do come, do you want me to count them and send the information to you?"

"Please?" Steward answered. "That would save us having to send someone. And I know we probably won't have an accurate counting, not between the nomads down south and the Wanderers in the mountains. There are some people that we're simply not going to be able to count because we don't know they're there."

Memfis yawned. "But we'll do the best we can," he added. "And try to make sure that people have what they need."

"I don't envy you the job," Grytha said. She sighed and shook her head. "Oh, Cellan will be here soon. He hasn't stood still all afternoon. He's been rebuilding sheds and fixing roofs as if it were playtime. When I saw him last, he was laughing over rebuilding a chicken coop." She smiled. "When you're done with him, send him back here, will you?"

Memfis chuckled. "You taken with him?"

"I could be," Grytha admitted. "But when I asked him if he wanted to stay, he told me he's committed to helping the Heir rebuild, and that's what he's going to do." She yawned. "You're leaving in the morning, aren't you? Did you bring the map?"

Owyn nodded and put away the census records, taking the rolled map out. As he unfurled it, there was a knock on the door. Cellan entered the meeting room and bowed.

"Sorry I'm late," he said. "The last board wasn't laying quite right."

"It's a chicken coop," Grytha said. "The hens won't mind."

"I mind," Cellan said. "And now it's a chicken coop that those hens' grandchildren will call home." He grinned. "Now, how can I serve?"

"I'm assuming that as a raider you knew this area?" Memfis asked.

Cellan nodded. "Knew it from before, too. Making deliveries for my father, finding the right wood for him. What can I tell you?"

Owyn gestured him over to the map and traced their route with one finger. "We're here," he said. "And we're taking this route to the mountains and north. What can we expect?"

Cellan frowned, studying the map. "I don't read well," he admitted. "You said this is Hearthstone?" When Owyn nodded, Cellan ran his finger over the road on the map. "Fireborn, this is Newmarket?"

"Yes."

"Right. There's good folk there." He touched the next marked town. "This one was deserted the last time we rode out that way. Nothing left to scavenge either. I think they all packed up and went north."

"Cellan, can I ask you something?" Owyn said. "Why were you with the raiders? You've got skills. You'd have been welcomed pretty much anywhere."

Cellan nodded. "That was my thinking. Once I started thinking again, I mean. But...Taver and his lot, they found me first. And once you were part of that group? The only way out was dead." He shrugged. "But I'm out now. I can start over. The roads aren't the only things being rebuilt now. Let's see." He frowned over the map, then tapped one marker in the foothills. "This is Wolf Ford, isn't it?"

Steward looked, and Owyn noticed that he appeared much more serious. "Yes."

"Avoid them, if you can. Grytha said you were trying to count everyone, but if you do, don't take the Heir in there. That's not a safe place for her."

Steward nodded. "That's not surprising." He looked at Owyn, and his next words confirmed Owyn's suspicions. "That's where Risha is from."

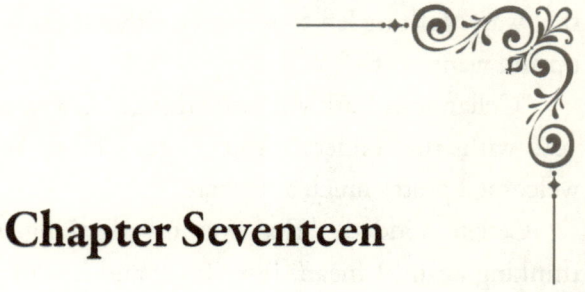

Chapter Seventeen

The executions were carried out at dawn, and Progress prepared to move on. Owyn helped Alanar into the coach with Aria, Aven and Del. It was the first time he'd seen his husband since Alanar had taken Wren back to the camp, and he waited until the coach was moving before asking, "So, how was he?"

Alanar snorted. "Patient confidentiality, love. I can't tell you that." He closed his eyes. "I will say that I'm tired. It was...a long night."

"And you're moving really stiff," Owyn said. A sick feeling settled in the pit of his stomach. "Allie...he didn't hurt you, did he?"

Across from them, Aven was suddenly alert. "Hand," he ordered, reaching across the coach. Alanar held his own hand out, and Owyn saw livid rope burns on his wrist. Aven took his hand, and his brows rose.

"And you didn't come to me immediately why?" he asked. Owyn sat up straight.

"Allie?"

Alanar rested his other hand on Owyn's leg. "It's all right," He was just...rougher than I'm used to. I wasn't expecting it. Not with how poorly he was yesterday." He smiled, but Owyn could see how forced it was.

"Allie..." Owyn lowered his voice, covering Alanar's hand with his own. "How bad was it?"

Alanar's smile faltered, and he sighed and shivered. "Bad. It...it was..." He shook his head. "I wasn't ready for it."

"I'll do more when we stop," Aven said as he let Alanar's hand go. The red marks on his wrists were already fading. "Let me know if you feel any discomfort. And if you want to talk, I'm right here. But you might want to wait and talk to my father, or to Treesi. They both have more experience than I do."

Alanar nodded. "I was planning on sleeping," he said. "I don't think I got much sleep, and I'm tired."

"*I can move,*" Del signed. "*Owyn, tell him?*"

"Del is offering to move so you can lay down," Owyn said. Alanar hesitated just long enough — Del smiled, kissed him on the cheek, then moved to sit next to Aria.

"Where's Treesi?" Alanar asked. "That you can shift. I just realized she isn't here, and I should have. She'd have fussed at me."

"She's with Othi," Aria answered. "She'll be in the coach later. Alanar, do we need to speak to Karse?"

"What?" Alanar looked shocked. "Because his guard took his grief out on me? Of course not! And besides, patient confidentiality—"

"Doesn't mean that a patient can assault their healer and get away with it," Aven said. "We'll talk to Fa when we stop and see what the right thing to do is."

"For now, lay down," Owyn added. He shifted over to the window so that Alanar could curl up on the bench, his head resting on Owyn's thigh. Owyn started petting his short hair, and waited until Alanar was limp and relaxed, his breathing soft and heavy.

"Aven, what did Wren do to him?" he asked softly.

Aven sighed. "Not without his permission, Mouse. When he wakes up, I'll ask him if I can tell you."

"Just tell me this much." Owyn looked down at his husband. He ran one finger over the corner of Alanar's mouth, and the tiny red mark on the skin there. "I already want to kick Wren's arse for this. Just...how many times will I have to do it before I feel better?"

Aria turned to Aven. "Was this very out of the ordinary, Aven?" she asked.

"I don't know," Aven answered. "I...I think so. I think...I need to ask my father. Owyn, when we stop, I'll take Allie and we'll go talk to Fa. Then I'll tell you what happened, how many times you can kick Wren's arse, and if I'm helping you do it."

Owyn closed his eyes. "I don't...he wanted me to go with them. I don't...I don't understand. Was this...was this what he wanted to do to me? Or was this because I didn't go with him?"

"Owyn, this is not your fault," Aven said. "This is one of the risks healers run. Alanar warned me about it himself."

"When did he do that?" Aria asked.

"After I got back," Aven answered. "He took over making sure I covered the parts of my training that I didn't finish, especially regarding the sexual parts of healer training. Fa..." he chuckled. "Fa was a little odd about talking about that part."

"If he knew..." Owyn looked down at Alanar again. "I'm not understanding."

"*He said he wasn't ready for it,*" Del signed, and Owyn heard him clearly. "*That might be why.*"

"Is everyone awake in there?" Jehan rode up alongside the coach and looked in the window.

"Fa," Aven said. Then he started signing, too fast for Owyn to follow, and his mind was a closed box. Owyn couldn't hear his thoughts at all. But there was no mistaking the shock on Jehan's face.

"I'll talk to him when we stop. He's asleep?"

Owyn nodded. "He said he didn't sleep last night."

"All right. We'll be to Newmarket well before midday, and I'll take him into our coach. Aven, will you come with us?" He frowned. "Owyn, I'll want privacy for this. I'm sorry."

"I understand," Owyn said. "He won't talk plain if I'm there. I know him. He knows I'll be upset that he got hurt, and he won't say anything."

Jehan nodded. "We'll talk after, you and I." He took a deep breath. "I'm going to ride ahead." He urged his horse on, and Owyn had the distinct feeling that Jehan was riding away before he said something he'd regret. Owyn rested his hand on Alanar's shoulder, where it met his neck, and felt him shiver in his sleep.

What had Wren done to him?

He closed his eyes and swallowed, pushing his worry down to keep his grief company. He couldn't fall apart now. Crying on Del the night before the funeral had helped, but...it hadn't been enough. Last night, Del had shared the bed with Aria and Aven, so Owyn had slept alone, and he'd slept badly. He desperately needed privacy and Alanar. But now...he couldn't. Not with Alanar like this. Treesi wasn't here. Aria couldn't carry her own grief and his, and Del and Aven were both helping her. She needed them. He needed...

To wait. He needed to wait. When they stopped for the night, he'd find someone he could talk to. Jehan would be busy, but maybe Mamaleia, or Mem...

The coach stopped. Aven shifted, looking out the window. He frowned, then reached down and slid one of his swords out from underneath the seat.

"What is it?" Aria asked.

"I don't know," Aven answered. He looked out the window again, then stood and opened the door, leaning out. "I don't hear anything. And there's no signs of anything up ahead." He ducked back in and closed the door. "The advance scouts must have come back."

"Do we wait until someone comes and tells us something?" Owyn asked. He looked down — Alanar hadn't moved. "Not that I'm going anywhere."

Aven nodded, but didn't put his sword away. He rested it hook down between his feet, scowling. "I'm not leaving you. But I don't like not knowing."

Owyn tipped his head back, then remembered something. "Copper says you can see a long way from the top of the coach. Would that work?"

"The top of the coach?" Aven stood up, opened the door, and looked out and up. "Yes, this would work." He jumped, making the coach shake as he clambered out and vanished onto the top of the coach. Del looked out the window. He whistled, and Aven's voice came from above.

"It's the advance riders, and there must be something wrong. If things were fine, we'd still be moving." The coach moved again, and Aven's feet appeared in the open doorway as he started to climb down. Owyn grinned as the hem of Aven's kilt caught on the top of the coach, leaving Aven bare from the waist down.

"Del, would you help Aven, please?" Aria's voice was choked with mirth. She looked at Owyn, and he laughed.

"Enjoying the view?" he teased. She blushed, then laughed as Del went to the door and helped Aven get untangled. He smoothed his kilt back into place and sat down next to Aria, putting his sword back under the seat.

"Karse is coming," he said. "I think we're about to have a report."

As he finished speaking, they heard the approaching horse, and the sound of Howl barking. Karse drew his horse in next to the coach and looked in the window.

"Advance riders are back," he said. "And Newmarket is empty. Looks like there hasn't been anyone there in weeks, they said."

"What did Cellan say?" Aria asked.

"That the last time the raiders came this way, the people here drove them off," Karse answered. "And that it was early spring."

"So quite a while," Aria murmured.

"Any signs of a fight?" Aven asked. "Or did they just pack up and leave?"

"The scouts say it looks like everyone packed up and moved on," Karse answered. "No signs of violence."

"Probably the same as the other town Cellan told us about," Owyn added. He ran his fingers through Alanar's hair, and looked up to see Karse looking at him.

"Is Alanar all right?" he asked.

"He spent the night with Wren last night, and he didn't sleep," Owyn answered. He looked at Aven, waiting. Aven sighed.

"Karse, we may need to speak to you later. Alanar and I need to talk to my father first. When we stop for the night."

"Which might be sooner than you think," Karse said. "Since we're not stopping at Newmarket, we'll be stopping for the night early, near that second abandoned town. And we can plan which way we go from there tomorrow."

"Meaning?" Aria asked.

"We can start north from there, or we can try Wolf's Ford."

Owyn shook his head. "I don't think we should go anywhere near Risha's people."

Aria looked thoughtful, then nodded. "I agree. But they still need to know. So when we make camp, send riders out. Tell them that if they wish to see their Heir, they should come to me tomorrow."

Karse grinned. "As you wish, my Heir." He bowed his head slightly, making Aria laugh.

THE REST OF THE RIDE was quiet. They stopped for a quick midday meal, and Treesi traded places with Aven, who went out to ride with Othi. Alanar didn't wake, and Owyn dozed off and on, waking at last when the coach stopped again.

"Are we here?" he yawned.

"I think so." Treesi stretched. "Aria, were you tired all the time during the beginning of your pregnancy?"

"I could have slept for days," Aria answered, laughing as she set down the sewing she'd been working on. "I can still fall asleep without warning."

"Speaking of sleeping, Allie isn't going to sleep tonight if I don't get him awake now." Owyn ran his fingertips over Alanar's cheek. "Allie? Wake up, love."

Alanar jerked, then flailed, tumbling off the bench. Owyn lunged to catch him, and caught an elbow in the chest that made him yelp. Del dove off the opposite bench, knocking Alanar away from Owyn and setting the coach rocking wildly.

"Allie!" Owyn shouted. "Allie, stop it!"

Alanar went still, his face pale. "I...Owyn? Owyn?" His voice cracked, and he crumpled, burying his face in his hands. Owyn crawled over to him and wrapped his arms around him, rocking him gently.

"It's fine, Allie," he murmured. "It's fine. It was an accident. You didn't mean it." He looked up to see Treesi and Aria staring at him.

"*Are you hurt?*" Aria whispered in his mind. He shook his head.

"What just happened?" Treesi asked. Before anyone could answer, the coach door jerked open. Aven stared inside, and Owyn could see Jehan behind him.

"What happened?" Aven asked. "We could see the coach rocking."

"Allie woke up rough," Owyn answered. "I think you need to take him to talk. Right now."

"Oh, fuck," Jehan breathed. He brushed past Aven. "Alanar, come with me. I'll take care of you."

Alanar sat up slowly, his face red and streaked with tears. "I...yes. Owyn, I—"

"You don't have to apologize, love," Owyn said. He kissed Alanar, then let him go. "You go on. Let them help."

Alanar nodded, and slid along the floor to the door, standing up outside. Jehan put his arm around Alanar and let him away. Aven frowned, then looked inside. "Treesi, see if Owyn needs healing, then come join us? I think we'll need you."

Treesi blinked. "What did I miss?" she demanded.

"I'm fine," Owyn said. "Maybe a bruise. It can wait. Go help." He swallowed. "I'm...I'm going to go find my fa."

Treesi narrowed her eyes at him, then nodded and went with Aven. Aria held her hand out to Owyn, and he sat down on the bench next to her.

"You're not fine," she said.

"No, I'm not," Owyn agreed. "But Allie needs them more than I do." He took a deep breath. "I'm going to go find Mem. Will you be all right?"

"I...um...here," Del said slowly.

Owyn tugged Del up off the floor and into his arms. "Thank you," he murmured. "For trying to help."

Del smiled and kissed him, then shifted off Owyn's lap. "Go."

Owyn nodded and slipped out of the coach, heading toward the head of the line and the camp. It was easy to find Memfis, but harder to get his attention — he was in the middle of bossing people around. Owyn knew from experience that getting his father to stop in the middle of something like this was asking for failure, so he went and stood at Memfis' elbow and waited.

"...and make sure that the Heir's tent is set and ready," Memfis finished. Then he turned and smiled. "Was wondering when I'd see you today."

"Fa, do you...can we go off and talk?" Owyn asked, trying to keep his voice level. "I...I really need to talk."

Memfis immediately turned serious. "Of course," he said. "Where's Alanar?"

"That's part of it," Owyn said. "He's with Jehan and the healers. But...come on."

Memfis nodded and looked around, then raised his voice. "Steward, I'm taking my boy for a walk. We'll be back when we're back."

Owyn looked to see Steward wave at them. Memfis put his hand on Owyn's arm, and they started walking, leaving the camp and heading out into the trees on the far side of the road. They walked side by side until Owyn thought they were far enough from camp.

"Fa," he said softly. It felt wrong to say the words out loud. "I...Alanar put Wren to bed last night. And...I think something went wrong." He swallowed. "Wren did something...he hurt Allie. And...I don't know."

"Mother of us all," Memfis breathed. "Is Alanar all right?"

"No. He was hurt when he got in the coach this morning, and when he woke up, he woke up swinging. Aven and Jehan and Treesi took him off, and they'll get the story out of him. I hope I'm wrong. I really hope I'm wrong." He swallowed. "That...that isn't why I wanted to talk with you. But you asked about Allie, so...yeah. I needed to talk—"

"About Meris," Memfis said. "I was wondering if you would. I think we both need to talk." He shook his head. "I can't believe she's gone. And...and like that."

"And it weren't any of those rioters," Owyn breathed. "It wasn't...we don't know who, and we don't know why, and...and it's not right!" He felt the tears starting to rise, scalding and painful. "She was supposed to be there to see the baby!"

Memfis nodded. "I know. And...I wonder what it was like for her, going into that town, knowing she wasn't going to leave. She knew."

"Aria asked me why she didn't warn us." Owyn scrubbed at his face. "I told her what you told me. That if we warn people, it makes it worse. I don't know if I believe that."

"It does make it worse," Memfis said, his voice solemn. "It makes it so much worse. I knew your first vision, Mouse. I knew you were going to drown. Knowing you were somewhere out on a ship? Owyn, I knew you were going to die out there, and there was nothing settled between us. I'd never apologized. I never got the chance to make things right—"

"That's over, Fa," Owyn said. He took Memfis' hand. "I forgave you a long time ago." He looked up at the trees. "Fa, I know she'd tell us we have to keep going. But it hurts, and I want to know why. She never hurt no one. She loved everybody. And someone killed her and I want to know why!" His voice broke; Memfis wrapped his arm around Owyn's shoulder, and Owyn buried his face in his father's chest and cried.

So he never saw the attackers that closed on them from all sides.

SITTING IN HIS PARENTS' tent, Aven glanced at where Alanar was sitting on the bed. "How are you feeling?"

"Numb," Alanar answered. "I...Pirit warned us, but it's nothing you think will ever happen to you." He turned. "How long has it been?"

Aven shook his head. "Not long. Steward told me that Owyn went for a walk with Memfis."

Alanar nodded. "Good. I don't think he's really faced his grief. I can tell. But I haven't been able to do anything because...well, because." He sighed. "Do we have to wait in here?"

"Steward said he wanted you out of sight until they'd brought Wren in and secured him." He rubbed one hand over his face. "I don't understand why he'd have hurt you like that."

"Power," Alanar answered. "It's about the power he has over someone else." He let his head hang. "He wanted Owyn there. I can't...what would he have done to Owyn?" All at once, he sat up. "Where is Owyn?"

"With Memfis," Aven repeated. "And Karse already had that thought. He went after Owyn himself. But I don't think he thought there was too much of a threat. He took the boys with him."

Someone scratched the tent flap, and Aria, Treesi and Del came in. Del had Howl in his arms, and set the puppy down once the flap was closed. Howl ran over to Alanar, and put both front paws on his knee. Alanar smiled slightly and ruffled the puppy's ears, then picked him up and wrapped his arms around him while Howl licked his face. Del came and sat on his left, while Treesi moved to his right. Aria stopped in front of him, leaning down to kiss the top of his head before sitting with Aven.

"He was going to be promoted," she said. "Karse told me that he was going to announce it tonight. He was an exceptional guard, and Owyn thought of him as a friend."

"We all did," Treesi said. She shook her head. "I don't understand what he was thinking..."

"Hello the tent!" Steward called from outside. He came in, and Aven sat upright when he saw the expression on the older man's face.

"What is it?"

Steward scowled. "Wren is missing. And so are four of the other guards."

Chapter Eighteen

"**I** thought you'd be something special. I really did. You're stubborn, I'll give you that. You just will not roll over and fucking die, no matter what. But that don't make you special."

The voice was familiar. The position was also familiar, albeit not as recent. Uncomfortable, in a way that made his stomach churn. Something was digging into his throat, into his jaw...

All at once, Owyn remembered where he'd felt something like this before. Panic hit like a thrown rock, and he thrashed against the straps that bound his wrists and ran the length of his back before he remembered that fighting only made it worse. Only made it that much harder to breathe. But there wasn't a gag this time. He could breathe. He could talk. He could scream. If he could find his voice. He opened his eyes and saw he was still in the clearing.

"Mem," Owyn breathed. He tried to move, and realized that his ankles and knees were bound as well. He wasn't going anywhere. Neither was Memfis — his father was bound and gagged, and there was blood on his face. He was breathing, though.

"Mem?" Owyn called.

"If I were you, I'd be more worried about myself, slave" the familiar voice said. This time, Owyn knew who it was.

"Wren?" He tried to turn, to see who was behind him. He heard rustling. Shuffling. It wasn't just one person behind him. Then Wren came around to crouch in front of Owyn.

"He always said you were something special," Wren repeated. "Now, I never did see it. But he was so taken with you. He was going to have you for his own, no matter what it cost him." He snorted. "Then it cost him everything. Cost us everything."

He...Owyn went cold. "You...you're talking about Fandor." He shifted, hearing the leather binding creak. "But...you're one of Karse's men. He trusted you. We all trusted you."

"That was the point," Wren said. "Get in, get close. Get information. Help my father—"

"What?" Owyn yelped. "No! Fandor...he never had any kids. His wife disappeared!"

"She did," Wren agreed. "And he wasn't my real father. He adopted me. Nor formal. Not like you. He just took care of me like one. Told me I was like his own boy. And I was, too. Just no one could know about it, seeing as I was a guard. But you're not telling anyone, and I want you to know why you're dying. I want you to understand." He paused, looking over at Memfis. "Fandor made sure I understood what I needed. Made sure I'd be ready to take over when it was my turn. Made sure I knew how to run his businesses, and I made sure he knew what was going on in the guard. We looked after each other, just like a real family." He snorted. "But you, and Fisher, and Karse and that bitch Meris went on and spoiled everything we were working for. All of the holdings, all of the businesses. Everything gone. And then you all spoiled my new operations in Cliffside." He stood up and walked over to Memfis, nudging him with the toe of his boot. "I didn't think I hit him that hard. Wonder if he'll wake up? I want him to. I want him to know why he's dying before I kill him."

"I...I don't understand," Owyn stammered. "I...you hurt Allie. Why? He never did anything to you. He didn't even know you until you came to the Palace."

"Because you're mine, and he put his hands on you," Wren answered. "Did you know that Fandor said you were for me? He let me have you once. He had his special boy one night when I came to see him, and he let me take a turn." Wren leered at Owyn, who felt his stomach twist. "He had you in a blindfold, so I don't think you even noticed it wasn't him. He told me you'd be mine, too. Wanted me to have a taste. He wanted you so much it made him stupid. It got him killed, and I still don't get it. Maybe you can convince me." He shrugged and looked past Owyn. "Well?"

"Wren, I don't like this." Tayki came into view. "They're going to come after us. He's the Fire Companion. They'll come after him."

"And they'll never find him. They'll never find any of them," Wren answered. "You're finished? Where are Arc and Keel?"

"Yeah, we're done. They're coming. Wren—"

"Are you going to turn on me, Tay?" Wren asked. "All we have to do is be smart. Follow the plan. We spent a lot of time on this—"

"This? This wasn't the plan, Wren! You said we were just going to kill him. You didn't say shit about Lady Meris, or Memfis, or Karse or kids! Just him!" Tayki looked at Owyn, his face pale. "Look...I know we owe you, but...but Karse was good to us. He's always been good to his pack. You know that. And...I don't know. I don't like killing that boy. He's a terror, but he's just a kid. We could take both of them—"

"A boy?" Owyn repeated. "Wren, what are you doing? You leave those boys alone!" He struggled against the wrist straps, twisting, trying to find some slack. Behind him, he heard a whimper, then something heavy landed on him — Danir. The boy was gagged, and his wrists tied in front of him. He looked terrified. Owyn stared at him, then twisted to look at Wren "Where's Copper?"

"I already told you that you shouldn't bother worrying about anyone but yourself, slave." He came over and crouched again, drawing a dagger from his boot. He reached out and tapped Owyn's cheek with the point, then dragged the blade over his jawline. Owyn felt the pain as the blade passed, felt the blood starting to run down his face, and tried not to react. It would only get worse if he reacted. "You get one chance to prove to me why I should keep you alive," he said softly. "Maybe I missed it the first time."

"Fuck you," Owyn spat.

Wren just laughed. He grabbed the Fire gem and sliced the cord, throwing the gem off into the woods. Then he walked away, snapping orders. Owyn heard something about a cart, but ignored him, trying not to be sick as he turned his attention back to Danir. Wren was lying. He had to be lying.

"Are Copper and Karse alive?" he asked. Danir looked away, then shrugged. Owyn swallowed, then tried to look around. He couldn't see much, couldn't see behind him. "Is there anyone watching us?" he whispered. Danir shook his head. Owyn nodded and looked across at Memfis. They had one chance. "Did they tie your ankles?" Danir shook his head again, and Owyn swallowed. "You need to run, Danir. Find help."

Danir whimpered and looked around. Then he bolted, vanishing into the trees like a rabbit. Owyn heard a shout and someone ran past him. Then they came back.

"He's gone," Tayki snapped. "He'll bring them all down on us."

"Then get the cart ready. We need to move." Wren dropped to one knee next to Owyn and pulled something out of a pouch. He held up a gag, and a blindfold. "Saved your things for you, slave."

"THEY SHOULD HAVE BEEN back ages ago," Alanar said. "Something's wrong."

Aven nodded. "Karse and the boys should have been back, too. Alanar, I don't like this."

"When are we going to go look?" Othi asked as he joined them. Howl paced at his heels, whining softly. Othi stroked the wolf's head, then straightened. "We know what direction they went. Do you think Howl could find them?"

"Maybe. Probably. Let's get Fa and—" Aven stopped, hearing crashing in the brush, coming closer. Howl yipped and ran off. Othi started to follow, then swore and broke into a run.

"Danir!"

Aven reached Othi as the big man dropped to his knees, pulling his knife and slicing the ropes tying Danir's hands.

"Easy," Othi crooned. "Easy. I've got you. You're safe." Gently, he untied the gag and tossed it away. "What happened?"

"Wren," Danir wailed. "Wren and Tayki and Arco and Keelan. They jumped us, and they hurt the Captain. They put him in a box and Copper bit Wren so they hit him and tied him up and put him with Karse and buried the box! And they've got Owyn and Memfis and they're going to take them away and kill them!"

"Danir, can you show us where?" Aven asked. He turned. "Alanar, get my parents!"

Alanar spun and headed back into the camp, shouting for Jehan and Aleia. Aven turned back to Danir, who was clinging to Othi.

"Can you find them?" Othi repeated.

"I...I think so." Danir let go of Othi and straightened up. "I need to find them. They need me. Copper needs me. And...Howl." He looked at the wolf. "Howl can find them."

"Wait," Aven said. "We need weapons!" He heard someone running, and turned to see Del racing toward him, carrying the harness and Aven's hook swords. Behind him were Jehan, Aleia and Steward.

"What's going on?" Jehan demanded.

"The missing guards," Aven said, talking fast as he took his swords from Del. "They've taken Owyn and Memfis, and if we don't find Karse and Copper, they're dead. We're going." He tossed Othi one of the swords. "Use it well, cousin. Don't kill them. Aria will want them."

Othi grinned. "Then let's go break some skulls. Howl, find Karse!"

The wolf took off running, and Othi and Danir ran after. Aven followed, and realized quickly that he was doing something he hadn't really tried since his hip had been rebuilt.

Running.

"Oh, we're going to have a grand time settling that hip again," he heard his father call.

"My hip is the least of our worries right now!" he called back.

Movement, from the corner of his eye, and Del drew up next to him. He had a crossbow slung over his back, leaving his hands free. And a moment later, Aven heard hoofbeats — Steward rode up next to him. He reined in his horse and held out his hand.

"They're going to need you," he said. "Jehan, help him up."

Jehan held out his cupped hands. "Don't argue. Move."

"Wasn't going to," Aven answered. He put his foot into his father's hands, and let himself be hoisted behind Steward. He barely had time to grab onto Steward's belt before they were moving again.

"Buried in a box, Danir said," Steward shouted over his shoulder. "That means we have a chance."

Aven looked over Steward's shoulder, trying to see Howl. He saw a flash of movement, and resisted the urge to point. "To your left!"

"I see him," Steward called. "Aven!"

"I see them, too!"

There were two people in the clearing, digging frantically at the ground, throwing dirt everywhere. As Steward rode into the clearing, Aven saw Howl was digging, too.

Steward swung his leg up and over Alabaster's head, sliding to the ground. He helped Aven down, then hurried to help, digging into the recently-turned dirt with both hands.

"How deep?" he snapped. "Do you know?"

"Deep enough that the Earth that bore us can bring us home," one of the men answered. He glanced up. "You en't Earth. About the length of an ell of cloth."

Steward blinked. He looked up at Aven. "About from your fingertip to the tip of your nose," he said. "More or less. We'll never reach them in time. We need a shovel."

"Hain't got one," the man snapped. "Dig, man."

Aven turned to see the others had reached the clearing. "There's no room without getting in each other's way. Othi, Fa, look around. See if they left the tools. They wouldn't need them, so they might have just left them. Ama, take Alabaster. Go back to camp and bring guards, and a litter. Two litters. Or one of the baggage carts. Tell Alanar and Treesi we'll need them ready. And bring shovels, if we have them." He looked around until he found

Danir. "Danir, go back to camp with my mother. Go to Treesi and stay with her."

"I can't stay?" Danir asked. He looked at the diggers. "I...I should stay." He drew himself up. "I'm staying."

Aven nodded. "Then go help Othi and my father."

Del tapped him on the arm. "Me?" he asked.

"Can you figure out which way they took Owyn and Memfis?" Aven asked. "Find the trail?"

Del nodded, and Aven turned back to watch the men digging. The hole was deeper, but not by much. He knelt and closed his eyes, reaching...

"They're still alive," he whispered. "I can feel them."

"Healer?"

Aven opened his eyes to see one of the men looking at him. "Yes."

"Seer told us you'd find us. Waterborn healer, Heart of the Sea." He grunted as he tossed a handful of dirt and rocks to the side. "Don't you worry. He's gone after the Twiceborn himself."

"He sent you?"

The man nodded, tossing another handful away. "Woke us all up this morning yelling, saying that the traitors were moving, that today was the first crossroad. We all live or die, depending on how this day ends. Sent us here, told us to find the grave and save the Protector of Now and the Protector to Come. Said he'd go after the Twiceborn his own self, it's that important." He looked up. "Shovels!"

"Aven, you were right," Othi said. "We found them in the woods."

"Make way," the digger shouted. "Give me one. It'll go faster. Mind the dog."

Othi tossed a shovel to the man, then went to Aven. "I'm going with Del. I don't like him alone out there." He trotted off after Del.

Aven stepped back, bumping into his father. "They're alive down there," Aven said, watching the men dig. Two shovels, and Steward leaning into the growing hole to scoop dirt out with his hands. "I can feel them. But I can't tell how much longer they have. Fa, how long can a man live without air?"

"When they're panicking?" Jehan answered. "Not as long as you think." He shook his head. "We can't lose them. Not so soon after losing Meris."

"We won't," Aven growled. "We won't lose them." He knelt at the edge of the hole again. If he reached down, it would span from his fingertips to his elbow. "Karse! Copper!" he shouted. "We're coming!" He felt a surge from deep in the hole, and heard muffled sounds from below. Howl started barking, and Aven looked at his father. "Someone heard me."

"They can't be that much deeper, then," one of the men muttered, thrusting his shovel into the dirt. It hit something, making a hollow sound. "Got it! Out of the hole!"

Steward joined Aven and Jehan, brushing dirt from his hands and his clothes. "Mother help us," he murmured. "If She hears me at all—"

The rest of what he said was lost in shouting, as the men tossed shovels aside and did something in the hole. Howl raced around them, barking, as one of the men shouted, "Healer! We need you!"

Aven and Jehan both ran forward; Jehan reached them first, dropping to his knees and reaching down to take a struggling, screaming Copper from the men. The boy was bound and gagged, and there was blood on his face and on his clothes.

"Steward, help me!" Jehan called. Steward ran over, and they moved Copper away from the hole. Aven knelt down and looked into the hole, seeing the box, and the men. And Karse, bound and gagged, pale and still. Howl whined softly.

"I don't think he's breathing, Healer," one of the men said.

"Get him up here," Aven said. "Let me see him."

The two of them lifted Karse up, laying him on the ground next to the hole. One of them drew a knife, slicing the ropes that bound Karse's hands behind him. Aven touched his throat, and felt a faint pulse.

"He's not dead!" he whispered, and rested one hand on Karse's chest, forcing healing power into his lungs. He reached up and tugged the gag out of his mouth, then leaned over him, pinching Karse's nose closed and breathing into his mouth. He wasn't sure how long he breathed for them both before Karse coughed and started breathing on his own. Howl whined again and licked Karse's face, and Aven sat back and took a deep breath, feeling like the forest was spinning gently around him.

"What are your names?" he asked. "Now that we have the time for me to ask that."

"Lestra, Healer," answered the first man. "And he's Ulla."

Aven nodded. "My name is Aven," he said. He held his hand out to Ulla, who was still in the hole. "Here. Let me help."

"I'm fine, Healer," Ulla said. He lifted himself out and sat down on the ground next to Karse. "Thought he was dead. He weren't breathing."

"The rest of him hadn't figured that out yet," Aven said. He rested his hand on Karse's chest again, examining him.

"How is he?" Jehan asked.

"His skull is cracked," Aven answered. "They hit him pretty hard. I've set the bones to heal, and Alanar can reinforce it when we get him back to camp." He looked up at his father. "How's Copper?"

Jehan scowled. "Hurt. Traumatized. Steward and Danir are with him. Steward...well, he knows how to help traumatized little boys. I'll take care of him once he's calm."

Aven looked across the clearing, where Steward sat on the ground. He was holding Copper in his arms, rocking gently as the boy cried. Danir sat next to them, one hand on Copper's bare ankle.

"Fa—"

Karse coughed and groaned, then gasped, struggling to sit up. Aven grabbed his arms and pushed him down.

"Karse!" he shouted. "It's over! You're safe."

Karse blinked, clearly not recognizing Aven. Then he blinked again and croaked, "Copper? Where's Copper?" He pushed against Aven's hands, and Aven helped him to sit up.

From behind him, Aven heard scrambling, and Copper's voice, "Captain!"

The boy pushed past Aven and threw himself into Karse's arms, joined a moment later by Danir. Karse hugged them both tightly as Howl danced around them, barking.

"We're safe," Aven heard Karse murmur. "I've got you." He looked up. "Where are the others?"

"Othi and Del are tracking Owyn and Memfis," Aven answered. "Danir told us what happened."

Karse nodded. "I'm—"

"Going back to camp," Aven finished. "You've got a cracked skull, Karse. You're in no condition to fight. You and Copper and Danir are going back as soon as Ama gets back with help."

"Which, I think they're coming," Jehan added. Aven looked back the way they'd come, and saw people coming toward them.

His mother, still mounted on Steward's horse. And a cart, being driven by Afansa.

"Think you can stand?" Aven asked.

Copper and Danir shifted off of Karse, and Aven helped him to his feet, steadying him when he swayed. They started walking toward where Afansa had drawn the cart to a stop, but before they reached it, Afansa was running toward them. She threw her arms around Karse's neck and burst into tears. Karse wrapped his arms around her. "It's all right, Fancy. I'm fine."

Aven stepped back to give them a moment of privacy, then turned when Jehan touched his arm.

"Othi and Del are back," he said. "They've got a trail."

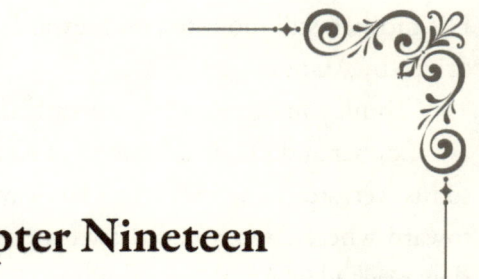

Chapter Nineteen

Del studied the ground of the clearing, but the signs weren't changing. He got to his feet and dusted off his knees, turning to see Othi bringing Aven and Jehan back with him.

"They're both alive," Othi said. "They're on their way back to camp. Show them what you showed me."

Del held out his hand. The Fire gem rested on his palm. Aven took it from him, running the cord through his fingers. Then he raised the cord and sniffed it.

"Blood," he murmured. "The cord was cut, and it has blood on it."

Del nodded. "*I found it near the trees,*" he signed. "*I nearly stepped on it. There's more blood here, and the signs of a struggle.*" He pointed across the clearing. "*And more blood there. And there are wheel marks going that way.*"

"I don't understand why," Othi said. "Owyn said he was friends with all the guards. And Karse thought of them as his own sons."

"Well, when we find them, we'll ask them." Aven looked in the direction Del pointed. "We're going to need horses. We can't follow them on foot. Not and have any hope of catching them."

"And we'll need more men," Jehan said. "Aleia is going to want to come, too."

"She had the same thought," Steward called as he joined them. "She's taken Alabaster back to camp, guarding the cart.

She'll be coming after us with horses and men, and more weapons. I sent the Seer's men back to camp with them. They said they'll bring us to the Seer tomorrow. He's expecting us." He frowned. "I'll wait for Aleia here, and we'll follow you. Which way?"

Del pointed. *"I'll leave a trail, just like you taught me."*

Steward nodded. "Be careful."

Del started following the cart tracks, moving in an easy, loping pace that he hoped wouldn't put too much stress on Aven's hip. He glanced back to see the complete lack of expression on Aven's face. He'd only seen that stony look once before — when Aven had found out that Owyn was a prisoner on Risha's ship.

Today wasn't going to end with Owyn dying.

THE GAG WAS TIGHT. It made it hard to breathe, and the blindfold was tight enough to hurt. But he could feel that the cart had stopped moving. He wasn't sure what was happening.

The cart bounced and shook. He recognized the thump of heavy boots before someone put their hands on his arms, pulling him up to seated. They fumbled at the blindfold, tugging it off and taking some hair with it. It was Tayki, and he reached for the gag straps next.

"We don't have a lot of time," he whispered as he unfastened the gag. "Wren went off to scout ahead. He'll be back soon, but we're not going to be here when he gets here." As if his words caused it, the cart started moving. Tayki let the gag fall. "Listen. Owyn, I'm sorry. Wren...well, it don't matter what he's got on us. We were wrong. And Keel and I, we're out. We're not doing this. We're getting you and Memfis out of here, and we'll face whatever we're going to face for what we did."

Owyn swallowed. "Get this fucking thing off me," he whispered, and looked around. The cart was the sort of rolling house that the Wanderers used, with two benches along the sides that doubled as beds. Memfis was lying across from him, and didn't look as if he'd moved or awakened. "Where's Arco?"

Tayki shook his head. "Dead. Wren killed him. Said he was finishing off Fandor's loose ends. Lean forward." He started working at the buckle on the collar. "I think that's why he killed Lyka, too, even though he said it was an accident when it happened. They were both Fandor's boys. Like you."

The collar fell loose, and Owyn shook his head. "Did you know he was working for Fandor?"

"Not until he told you," Tayki answered. "He just told us he had a score to settle, and we owed him a debt. Which...yeah, we did. We've been through a lot, and...well, you understand the family you make, right? I thought he was family. Family takes care of each other." He shook his head. "I had no idea he was using us until today."

The cart stopped, hard enough that Tayki stumbled. He caught himself and raised his voice. "Keelan! What's going on?"

No answer. He turned to the door.

"Tay, get these off me!" Owyn hissed. "Don't leave me like this."

"Just a moment," Tayki said over his shoulder. "Let me see what's going on." He opened the door, and Owyn heard a snap; Tayki fell backward, stretching his length on the cart floor as he fumbled at the crossbow bolt that had nearly pierced him through. Wren stood outside the cart, shaking his head as he lowered his crossbow.

"Idiots," he sniffed. "The pair of them. Should have known they'd betray me." He looked at Owyn. "Well. Change of plans, I suppose." Then he slammed the door and Owyn heard a bolt shooting closed. A moment later, the cart was moving again. A moment after that, Tayki stopped moving.

Owyn closed his eyes, trying not to panic. He needed to wait to fall apart until he was safe. He needed to think. He wasn't strangling anymore because of the collar. That meant that he could get out of this. He could get free. He just needed to get his hands out. And...yeah, maybe having nearly starved to death hadn't been all that bad — his wrists and hands were thinner than they'd been. He could slip the cuffs. Tayki had a knife on his belt, so he could cut the ropes and be ready when Wren opened the door again. He could get out of this. He could stop Wren. Get Memfis back to the camp.

Then he could fall apart.

He twisted his wrists and started to pull, feeling the cuffs sliding over his skin and catching on the base of his thumbs. He tucked his thumbs into his palms and tried again, and got a little farther; he pulled harder and nearly tipped over when the cart stopped again.

"No," he whispered, and tried tugging again. It didn't work. He couldn't get his hands free, and he was out of time. He heard thumping, coming from overhead. Then he saw something that didn't make sense. There was a window in the door, and something was sheeting off the top of the cart roof, splashing in through the openings.

He didn't think it was water.

The door swung open, and Owyn saw Wren outside, holding...

A bucket?

He drew back, and Owyn twisted, just in time to avoid being hit in the face with the warm, oily liquid. The bucket clattered into the wagon, and a second wave of liquid washed over Memfis. Owyn looked back to see Wren toss the second bucket into the cart, then take off his gloves. He threw them at Owyn before reaching into his pouch and pulling out a flint and steel.

"I'm going to enjoy hearing you scream, slave." He laughed, and Owyn realized what had been in the buckets. What was currently soaking into his clothes, coating his skin...

Inferno oil.

Wren held up the steel. "You know what's going to happen, don't you?" he asked. "Good." He brought the steel down on the flint, and Owyn saw a spark...

A meaty thump, and Wren jerked forward, howling in pain and turning. Owyn saw a long arrow in the back of his shoulder. Another thump, and a second arrow blossomed from his chest. He fell backward, and Owyn heard a man giving orders.

"Move him and secure him. I'll get them out. Make sure you strip off anything that poison touches."

Two men grabbed Wren and dragged him away from the cart, and a third man appeared in the doorway. He was solid and tall, possibly taller than Alanar. His dark hair was graying at the temples, and his eyes were calm and crystalline blue. He had a knife in his hand, and he ducked his head as he climbed into the cart, kneeling to slice the ropes binding Owyn's legs.

"Are you hurt, Twiceborn?" he asked.

"No," Owyn answered. "Mem is hurt, though. He's hurt bad. He needs a healer."

The man nodded. "Turn, and let me free your wrists. We'll take him to our camp, to our healer. She'll hold him until the Heart of the Sea arrives."

All at once, Owyn knew who this was. "You're the Seer."

The Seer smiled. "My name is Frayim. Yes, I am the Seer. Now, let's get you out of this firetrap." He quickly unfastened the cuffs from Owyn's wrists, then turned to Memfis and cut the ropes binding him. "We have a cart, but we'll need to get these clothes off the both of you."

Owyn started to unfasten the lacings on his shirt. "I...tell me you have soap? A lot of soap?"

Frayim nodded. "We've baths waiting for both of you." He glanced at Memfis. "Well, it will be waiting for when he wakes. We'll clean him as best we can. Help me get him out of the cart now."

Owyn nodded, and helped Frayim shift Memfis toward the door, where another man was waiting to help. They took Memfis and carried him clear, laying him down on a blanket spread on the ground.

"Felix, bring a blanket, then go fetch the cart," Frayim said. "Twiceborn—"

"You saved my life," Owyn interrupted. "You get to call me Owyn."

Frayim smiled. "Owyn, the Twiceborn Son of Smoke. I know your name."

"You're allowed to use it." Owyn tugged his shirt over his head, then looked down at himself. "I liked these boots," he grumbled, and sat down to tug them off. "What are you going to do with Wren?"

Frayim looked over at where Wren was laying on his side, glaring at the guard standing over him. "We'll take him back to camp," he said. "And hold him for the blesséd Mother's judgment. Mauri, keep a careful eye on him."

Owyn nodded. "Oh, that's going to be interesting. Especially when she finds out he killed our grandmother. She might just kill him herself."

Frayim shrugged. "It will be as she wills. We should burn this, and give the two who have died peace."

"Can I help with that?" Owyn asked.

"You've had a trial, Twiceborn—"

"Owyn."

Frayim continued as if Owyn hadn't said anything. "Take off the rest of those ruined things. Once we have the cart, you can rest while we do what's needful."

"What about Mem?" Owyn asked, getting back to his feet.

"I'll take care of him." The other man came up, holding a folded blanket. "I'm Felix. Here." He shook it out and held it wide. "In case you want some privacy," he added.

"Thank you," Owyn said. He started to unfasten his belt, then heard a shout and a thump, followed by Wren's voice, near incomprehensible with rage.

"I'll fucking kill you all!"

Owyn reacted, grabbing the pouch at his belt and the whip-chain, pulling it free as he shouted, "Felix, duck!"

Felix sprawled in the dirt, taking the blanket with him, and Owyn let the whip-chain sing. There was a brief pang of regret – he'd put the ball in place after the blade had sliced a hole in the pouch. But he dismissed the thought as quickly as it had come.

The ball would leave Wren alive for Aria.

Wren howled as the ball slammed into his ribs, and Owyn thought he heard the crunch of bone. He brought the chain around again, and wrapped it around Wren's legs, bringing him down to the dirt. He kicked the chain free and ran at Owyn, who stepped to the side and grabbed Wren, using the other man's own momentum to throw him bodily into the back of the oil-soaked cart. Then he darted forward and slammed the door, shooting the bolt home.

"Twiceborn?" Frayim said softly. "Are you hurt?"

"Me?" Owyn panted. "No. I'm fine. I think we need to leave him there, though. Maybe...I dunno. What do we do with him now?"

"We leave him," Frayim answered. "We'll take the horse with us. Felix will stay and watch, and the Mother knows."

Owyn glanced at him. "You...mean the Mother Mother, right? Not Aria?"

Frayim broke into giggles. "Yes, I mean the Mother of us all. Mauri, are you hurt?"

"Just my pride, Fray."

"Then go and see to Memfis. Felix, bring the cart closer." Frayim picked up the blanket, shook leaves and twigs from it, then held it wide while Owyn stripped.

"Just realized something," Owyn said as he wrapped the blanket around himself. "You didn't have a fancy name for Mem."

Frayim walked over to the edge of the road. He picked up a longbow and a quiver of arrows, and came back toward Owyn. "He is the Father of Smoke, the Reforger of Forges. But you seem to prefer plain names to fancy ones."

"Reforger of Forges, hm?" Owyn nodded. "He'll like that." He pulled the blanket more closely around him, watching as Mauri gently cut Memfis' clothes away and bundled him into another blanket. Behind them, the cart shook and bounced on its wheels, and they could hear Wren swearing, nearly drowning out the sound of a second cart as it rumbled into view. It was a heavy thing drawn by a pair of oxen. "An ox-cart?" Owyn looked at Frayim. "I've never seen one before. Read about them, but I've never seen one. We didn't use them in Forge."

"And folk around here don't use horses to plow or draw. The ground here is too heavy for horses to draw a plow, and the roads too steep for a heavy load for either horse or mule. An ore-horse might do, but they eat too much. Oxen suit us just fine," Mauri answered. He stooped, and picked up Owyn's whip-chain. "I'll find a new pouch for this when we get back to camp."

"Thank you." Owyn draped the chain around his shoulders, watching as Mauri and Felix moved Memfis to the back of the cart.

"Felix, you stay and keep watch on this," Frayim said as the men came back. "Unhitch the horse and keep it here with you, and you can lead the healers back to camp."

Felix walked around to the front of the cart, and Owyn heard him crooning softly to the horse.

"Is Keelan up there?" Owyn called.

"Is that his name?" Felix called back. "Yes. We'll make sure he's named when he goes back to the Mother."

"And Tayki is inside, with Wren," Owyn added. He frowned. "I'm not sure where Wren killed Arco, but Tay said he did."

"I'll send people out to find him," Frayim said gently. "We won't leave him to be lost. Is he Fire as well? Will he need to be burned, or buried?"

"Burned," Owyn answered. He closed his eyes as the weight of everything settled into his bones. He felt ten thousand years old, and as fragile as glass.

"Come to the cart, Owyn," Frayim said, and his hand on Owyn's shoulder was warm and solid and comforting. "We'll go back to camp. You can clean up, and we'll—"

The noise behind them sounded like a quiet cough. It was hardly enough to register as a sound. It could even have been a gust of wind, if it hadn't been for the screaming that followed. Owyn turned, and everything seemed to freeze.

The cart was engulfed in flames.

"What the fuck?" Owyn gasped, and started to run toward the cart. He stopped short when Frayim grabbed him.

"No!" He pulled Owyn back, away from the fire. "You can't. You're still covered in that poison."

Owyn froze. Frayim was right. He couldn't go any closer. He couldn't do anything. "Inferno oil," he murmured. "It's...it's inferno oil. And he knew. He had to know what would happen. I...he did that on purpose." He looked up at Frayim. "He...he picked a horrible way to die."

"And the Mother will deal with him now," Frayim said. He raised his voice. "Felix?"

"I'm fine. Blossom here is a bit scared, but I told her I won't let it hurt her." Felix skirted wide around the fire, leading the surprisingly-docile horse.

"You talk to horses?" Owyn asked.

"Talk to most animals. How'd you know?"

"Got a friend back at the Palace who talks to birds."

Felix laughed. "That's not much of a conversation. Birds...they don't know much." He glanced at the growing fire. "What do you want me to do, Fray?"

"Keep watch on it," Frayim answered. "It's a good thing it's not on the grass, or we'd have to worry about it spreading. Let it burn, and wait for the healers." He looked up, studying the sky. "They'll be here in an hour or two. The Heart of the Sea, the Healer, the Forgotten and the Silent One. Look for them when the skies start to pink, and bring them to camp. We'll need them."

Felix nodded and led Blossom to the grassy edge of the road, stripping off her bridle so that she could graze. Frayim put his arm around Owyn's shoulders and turned him back toward the cart.

"Let's go back to camp."

"THE SMELL IS GETTING stronger," Othi said. "Do we need to worry about fires, with all these trees?"

Aven looked around. "Fa?"

"I don't think that's a forest fire," Jehan said. He drew his horse in and closed his eyes. "No. There's birdsong. If there was a forest fire near, the animals would have run from it."

"It's not just wood, either," Steward added. "There's something else to it. The smoke...it's wrong."

Del snapped his fingers, and signed, "*It smells like the smoke outside Shadow Cove. Memfis said they were burning bodies.*" He pointed up. Aven turned and saw what Del had seen over the trees — the high shreds of a smoke plume.

"We need to go easy," Aleia said. "There might be anyone waiting there."

Aven knew she was right. He knew they needed to be careful. That rushing ahead might get them in trouble, might get Owyn killed.

Then Del growled and spat, "Fuck." He glared back at the others, then kicked his horse into a gallop.

"Del!" Steward shouted.

Aven stared after Del, then looked at Othi.

"I agree with him. Fuck that," Othi repeated. "Come on, Mountain!" Othi took off after Del.

Aven followed, quickly outpacing Othi and his slower horse to catch up with Del and Lady. They rounded the curve of the road together, and saw ahead of them the still-burning pile near the edge of the road. There was a man watching the blaze, and he turned toward Aven and Del as they slowed their horses.

"You," he called, pointing at Aven. "You're the Healer, the Heart of the Sea, aren't you?" He didn't wait for an answer before adding, "He's safe. The Twiceborn is safe." He grinned. "He's never wrong, the Seer isn't. Ah, there's the other healer. We can go. I'm Felix, and I'll take you to him."

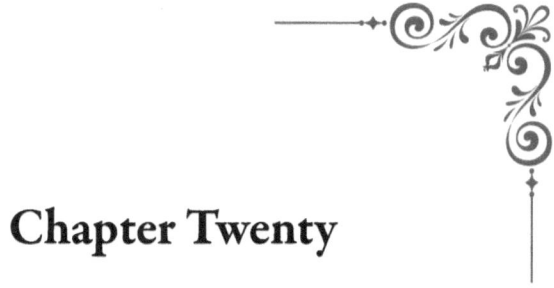

Chapter Twenty

"You're with the Seer?" Jehan called. "Where are Owyn and Memfis?"

"Yes, Healer," Felix answered. "The Twiceborn is safe. The Reforger is hurt. Our healer will be keeping him comfortable, but he needs you and the Heart of the Sea."

"And what happened here?" Steward asked. "That...was that a Wanderer's cart?"

Felix nodded. "It was. And that's how that one was going to kill them both. He doused them in...something. Fire oil?"

"Inferno oil?" Aven asked.

"That was it," Felix said. "Frayim — that's the Seer's name — he shot the false one, and we got the Twiceborn out, and the Reforger, but that false one, he attacked again. Twiceborn beat him, locked him in the cart to wait for the blesséd Mother. False one, he had other ideas." Felix shook his head. "Screaming...that stopped a while ago."

"Mother of us all," Jehan breathed.

"At least he sent the two Fireborn guards he murdered back to the Mother when he made himself Her problem." Felix sniffed. "I'll take you back to camp now."

"What about that?" Steward asked, nodding toward the fire. "We can't just leave it. The flames might spread."

Felix shook his head. "I know, but there wasn't anyone else to come down, and Mauri went back to help care for the Reforger. I'll come back directly—"

"I'll stay," Steward interrupted. "I'll keep watch on this, and you can come back for me in the morning. Or I'll come with the rest of the Heir's Progress, when your other men bring them."

Felix looked startled. "It'll be a cold camp, and a lonely one. Dangerous—"

"I'll stay with him," Othi volunteered. Del nodded and dismounted, clearly indicating that he would stay as well.

"Go on," Steward said. "Memfis needs you. Go and see to him."

"If we get back before sunset, I can come back down, bring a bit of comfort," Felix offered. "But we have to leave now."

Aven didn't wait for his parents to say anything. He met Del's eyes and nodded, then turned to Felix. "Lead on."

OWYN GRIMACED AND SCRUBBED his fingers through his hair again, feeling the oil coating his skin. "It's not coming out," he called. "That's four times I've washed my hair, and the oil is still there. I'll still go up like a torch if I get too close to the fire."

Frayim peered through the curtain of the tiny bath hut. "I hate to have to offer, but I'll shear you if you want."

Owyn looked at him, feeling the sick twist in his stomach. "I...I told my husband I wasn't going to cut it."

"I think the Healers will understand," Frayim said. Owyn stared at him.

"You...you mean Allie? You know...what am I saying? Of course you know." He took a deep breath. "All right. Where do you want me?"

"Out here, while we still have the light."

Owyn wrapped a blanket around his waist and followed Frayim out of the hut. Frayim led him to a stump and gestured for him to sit.

"Once we do this, then you'll bathe again," Frayim said, taking his knife from his belt. "We've found clothes that I think will fit you. And your hair will grow back."

Owyn sat down, tipping his head forward and closing his eyes. "I...I probably won't grow it long again," he murmured, feeling Frayim's hands in his hair, the chill of the knife against his skin, the slight tug, and the feathery touches as hair started to fall down his back and over his arms. "I...my grandmother, she was going to teach me how to twist it when it was longer. But Wren killed her."

Frayim sighed softly, and his breath was warm on the back of Owyn's neck. "I would have liked to have met the Mother of Forge. I dreamed of her."

"She'd have liked you," Owyn said. "And she'd have loved to know more about you."

"I imagine I confused her?"

"Oh, completely!" Owyn watched as the hair gathered in his blanket-covered lap. "A non-Fire seer? She wasn't sure what to think about that!"

"No one has ever known what to think about me," Frayim said. "My clan took me to the Smoke Dancers, and they didn't know what to do with me."

"Wait." Owyn fought the urge to turn around. "What Smoke Dancers?"

"I don't remember which town," Frayim answered. "But my clan brought me there when I started seeing visions. I took ill when I was seventeen, and they thought I'd lost my mind. Then

I started seeing visions, and they brought me to the Smoke Dancers. I confused them, too."

"I don't think that ever got back to Granna Meris. She'd never heard of an Earthborn Seer before...what was his name?" Owyn frowned, feeling the cold creeping over the top of his head as his hair floated down like dark snowflakes. "You sent him to start a town, near the Palace."

"Torri," Frayim answered. "He'll be a good headman. He takes care of his people."

"That's where we heard of you first," Owyn said. "How much more?"

"I'm nearly done. Then you can bathe again, and you should be clean."

Owyn took a deep breath. The chill on his scalp told him that his hair was again as short as it had been the day he'd been put on the block. It felt strange. Wrong. He hadn't had his hair this short since Memfis had bought him, brought him back to the forge and told him that he didn't have to be shorn anymore if he didn't want to be.

"Frayim, what did the healer say?" he asked. "About Mem?"

"That the other healers can't get here soon enough," Frayim answered. "She's good, but she's not a strong healer. Not like the Heart of the Sea, or his father. Or your Healers."

Owyn swallowed. "Is he going to die, Frayim? Am I losing him, too?"

"No, Owyn," Frayim said. "His road is a long one. I've seen him as old and as grizzled as an old bear. His road doesn't end here."

"And everyone says you're never wrong. Don't you start now."

"I am not wrong, Owyn. He'll live a long time. He'll see your children. All of them."

"But...Granna won't. She wanted to see Aria's baby, and now she won't. She won't see my Jaxsyn, either." Owyn closed his eyes, and felt something wet hit the back of his hand. He took a shuddering breath, then shattered as arms closed around him from behind, as he finally gave in fully to his grief.

When he could breathe again, he ran one hand over his shorn scalp. "I'm going to grow it out," he croaked. "And learn to twist it. Just...just because she wanted to see me do it."

"I think that's a fine thing," Frayim said. "Now, let's get you through a bath once more. By the time you're done, the others will be here."

IT TOOK TWO MORE FULL baths before Owyn finally felt clean enough to put on the clothes that had been left for him — loose, baggy trousers and a long tunic. He was tying a woven belt around his waist when he heard the commotion.

"Owyn?" Frayim called from the other side of the curtain. "They're here."

Owyn headed out into the gloaming, and Frayim gestured toward the other side of the camp. Toward the noise.

Then Aven's voice rang out, both in Owyn's mind and through the din, "*Owyn!*"

Owyn had a moment of sheer elation as he saw Aven run. Then he was in Aven's arms, and he felt the warmth of Aven's healing creeping over his skin like sunlight.

"Mouse," Aven whispered. "Mother of us all...your hair..."

"It'll grow back," Owyn mumbled, his face pressed against Aven's chest. "I'm fine, Fishie. I'm fine."

"Heart of the Sea," Frayim said. "I hate to interrupt, but the Reforger needs you."

Aven's arms loosened. "I just need to do one thing first." His hands ran up Owyn's arms, up the sides of his neck, and leaned down to kiss him. Owyn could feel the vestiges of Aven's fear, and his relief. And when he pulled back, it was only far enough that they could breathe together.

"I'm fine," Owyn repeated. "You have to go to work, Healer."

"I know," Aven murmured. "I'll be back as soon as I can." He stepped back, then turned to Frayim. "Where am I going?"

Frayim bowed. "This way, Healer." He led Aven and Jehan away, and Aleia took Aven's place, pulling Owyn into a tight embrace.

"Are you sure you're all right?" she asked.

"I'm fine, Mama," Owyn answered. "Karse? And the boys?"

"We found them in time," Aleia said. "Karse has a broken skull. Alanar and Treesi will put him right, and they'll be here tomorrow."

Owyn ran his hand over his shorn head. "Allie's going to be angry. I promised him I wouldn't cut this."

Aleia took his hand and pulled it away from his head. "He won't be," she assured him. "He'll be too happy you're safe. And it will grow back. I heard you just tell Aven that."

Owyn sniffed. "Had to tell him something," he said. "He frets." He looked around. "It's just you?"

"The wagon was still burning when we reached it. Steward, Del and Othi stayed behind to make sure the fire didn't spread, and Felix is going back to help them make camp. They'll be here tomorrow with the others." She drew him over to the fire circle. "What happened, Owyn? Why did he do it?"

"Do I have to tell it all now?" Owyn asked.

"A grain of it?"

"A grain of it, and that leads to a landslide," he murmured, then took a deep breath. "He said he was Fandor's man. Wren.

He was Fandor's heir, and he was out to kill me, and Fa. And it was him that killed Granna."

Aleia's face went slack. "Owyn—"

"And he went crackpot at the end there," Owyn added. "I mean, he had to have. He knew what he'd thrown on me and Mem. He had to have known what would happen if he struck a spark." He rubbed his hands up and down his legs. "He killed himself."

"Pretty horribly, too." Aleia looked into the fire. "Felix says that he's the Mother's problem now."

"I just...I would have wanted to ask him why," Owyn said. "Why bother? I mean...he killed Lyka, and Granna, and he killed all his friends who were in it with him. He hurt Allie. Why?" He shook his head. "There don't seem to be any point to it."

Aleia put her arm around his shoulders and hugged him to her side. "Maybe he wasn't just crackpot at the end?"

Owyn shrugged. "He said he had me. Once. He said Fandor let him have a turn, and I didn't notice. And...I don't know. Maybe." He stared into the fire. "If Wren hated me because I killed Fandor, that's one thing. But he said he wanted me dead because Fandor promised me to him, so that made me his, and that's why he hurt Allie and...it don't make sense." He finally made himself look at Aleia. "I don't understand why."

Aleia shook her head. "I wish I could answer that, Owyn," she said.

Owyn looked down at the ground. "Frayim says that Fa will be all right. Now that Aven and Jehan are here, I know he'll be all right. I...I should go see him, shouldn't I?"

"You should eat first," Frayim said as he came back, carrying a tray. "The healers are working. He will sleep until very late. Eat, and I'll take you to him when you're done." He lowered himself down to sit on the ground between them, never once tipping the tray. "Eat."

There were two bowls on the tray, and Owyn picked them up and handed one to Aleia. "Mamaleia, this is Frayim, the Seer."

Aleia turned, giving Frayim her full attention. "We've heard quite a bit about you," she said. "And not nearly enough."

Frayim laughed. "I imagine so," he said. "It's a pleasure to meet you, War Leader."

Aleia smiled and looked down at her bowl. "What am I eating?"

"Pulse and venison stew," Frayim answered. "One of my people is an excellent cook."

Owyn took a bite, and closed his eyes as the rich broth filled his mouth. He chewed and swallowed. "I want this recipe. This is wonderful."

Frayim nodded. "I'll bring you to meet him. Now eat." He picked up a heavy-looking metal teapot and filled three cups, then cradled one in his hands. "The blue wagon next to the hut where you changed is yours, Owyn. War Leader—"

"You can call me Aleia, Frayim," Aleia said, and took a bite of her stew. Her brows rose. "This is very good. I'm not usually fond of pulse, but this is lovely."

Frayim smiled. "I am glad. Huris will be glad to hear it."

Owyn choked on his tea. "What?" he sputtered when he could breathe again.

Frayim looked at him, frowning slightly. "Is something wrong?"

"Your cook...you said your cook...his name is *Huris*?" Owyn put his bowl down. "I need to meet him. Now. Right now. Can we meet him now?"

"Owyn, what is it?" Aleia asked. "I...oh!"

"Yeah, you remembered," Owyn said. He stood up and ran his hands over his chest. "Please?"

Frayim smiled and unfolded up from the ground. Any other time, Owyn would have been fascinated to watch a tall man moving like he had no bones. But now...he could barely sit still.

"You're going to hear me say something I rarely say," Frayim said. "I'm not sure what you're talking about. I think the Mother has kept something from me. This way."

"Mamaleia?" Owyn looked at her, seeing that she'd gotten up. "Come with me? Please?"

"It might not be him," Aleia said softly. "Fire reuses names."

"I know," Owyn whispered back. "I know. And if it isn't...then I might cry on you."

Aleia took his hand, and they followed Frayim through the camp. On the far side of the camp, Owyn could see a large canopy. As they got closer, he started smelling something savory. Then he saw a fire pit, one that boasted a large tripod and a metal grating for roasting meat. There was a dark-skinned man standing near the grating, turning long skewers that had been threaded with chunks of meat. His left arm was curled oddly at his side, and when he looked up, the left side of his face hung slack.

"These will be ready soon," he called, and Owyn stopped in his tracks.

He *knew* that voice. Even slurred, he knew that voice.

"Owyn?" Aleia said his name softly as he tugged his hand out of hers. He staggered toward the fire, and the man looked up at him.

"You..." Owyn's voice caught in his throat. He coughed, then tried again. "You...you're Huris? Huris the...the Smoke Dancer? You...your wife is Dyneh, the healer?"

Huris straightened, proving to be no taller than Owyn himself. "I'm not a dancer anymore. Not since...well, I'm not. But yes. I'm Huris. Why?" He frowned. Then his jaw dropped. "No. No...you...you can't be. But...you look just like her. But you can't be. You died." He came around the firepit. "Jax?"

Owyn shivered. He knew that voice in his bones, even though he couldn't remember the man. "Is...is that what you called me?" he asked. "I don't remember. I...I barely remember you! But I knew your voice." He swallowed. "I...they called me Owyn, and...I use that name. I use both. Owyn Jaxis. Son of Memfis, son of Huris, son of Dyneh."

"Fireborn Companion to the Heir," Aleia added.

Huris blinked. "I...Frayim, did you see this? Did you know?"

Frayim shook his head. "The Mother hid this one from me. I'd have told you your son lived if I knew."

Huris licked his top lip and stepped closer. "You...you're really here. I...I can't believe it. I can't believe you're here. You're alive. And...we need to go tell your mother. Frayim, will you watch the skewers?"

"She's here?" Owyn gasped. "She's alive?"

Frayim smiled. "She's our healer."

Owyn looked back at Aleia. "Then...she's been working on Mem." He looked back at Huris. "Just...just so you know? The man she's working on right now? Is my adoptive father."

Huris smiled, the right side of his mouth curving upward. "I look forward to meeting him. I imagine we have a lot to talk about. I want to know everything. I want to know you." He started to hold his hand out, then froze. "What do I call you? Jax? Or...what was it? Owyn?"

Owyn smiled. "Aunt Rhexa tried to call me Jaxis, and I kept forgetting to answer. I'm still getting used to having two names."

"Rhexa is still alive?" Huris laughed. "And you know her? She found you?"

"It's a long story," Owyn said, suddenly worried. When he told them...would they still want him? A warm hand settled on his back, and he looked over his shoulder at Aleia.

"Go meet your mother," she said softly. "Frayim and I will keep an eye on supper."

Chapter Twenty-One

Owyn followed Huris as he limped through the camp, trying to force his mind around what was happening.

His parents were alive.

And they'd thought *he* was dead. That was why they never came back for him. Not because they didn't want him, but because they didn't know he was alive.

He swallowed. Aven was busy, and none of the others would be here until morning, but Owyn wanted them so badly he ached. He needed his husband. He needed Del. He needed Aria, and Treesi.

He was facing this alone, and it was terrifying.

"I...it's weird," he said. "I should be calling you Fa, but..."

"Ease into it," Huris said. "This is...unreal. I never thought..." He stopped and turned around. "I need to say this. I don't know what you're thinking, what you thought about what happened, but we didn't abandon you. We didn't leave you behind. Mother of us all, Jax...I can't even imagine what it was like. How you survived. You were a baby! You were just past two. We were trying to save the money to get out of Forge and go back to Terraces. Forge...it was getting worse, and we wanted to get away. But that cost coin we didn't have. So Dyneh was taking extra shifts at the healing center, and I was working in Mastersmith Durna's forge—"

"You're a smith, too?" Owyn interrupted. "I'm a smith."

Huris grinned. "I was a journeyman." He paused. "There was a woman who minded babies in our District. Granna Felina, she and her daughter took care of all the little ones in our District, and we'd left you with her. But those were bad days. It wasn't long after the Heir came through, and there were tempers. You know what I mean?"

Owyn nodded. "I understand."

"Tempers were high that day. We'd just gotten the news about Yana. I don't know what happened, why it started, but there was a riot. Durna sent me out, told me to get Dyneh and get you and get home." Huris snorted. "Never saw her again. I ran off for the healing center, and...well, I never made it." He gestured to himself. "Someone tried to stove my brains in with a brick. Friend found me, dragged me off to Dyneh. She saved my life, but she couldn't put things right." He tapped his left cheek with his right hand. "Can't see out of this eye. Can't feel much. Arm...well, that's pretty useless, and the leg is weak." He shook his head. "We didn't get back to Felina's until the next day. And...it was gone. The place was gone. Burned to the ground. We searched. We..." He stopped. "We thought we found you. Your...your body."

"What?" Owyn stared at him. "I...how did you know?"

Huris nodded his head. "I'll show you." He started walking away, and Owyn hurried to follow him into a wagon. Huris gestured with one arm.

"This is ours. Yours now, too." He went to a cabinet and pulled out a small woven basket. "Why did we think we found you? The body...well, the poor baby we found...we couldn't recognize them. But this was with the body. Your mother gave it to you for your naming day, and you wouldn't ever let it out of your sight." He took something out of the basket and held it out to Owyn. A stuffed fire mouse. Owyn took it, turning it over in his hands. It was familiar, in a way that felt uncomfortably real. But it wasn't right. It was...

"It's so small," he said, his throat feeling tight. "It...it's not supposed to be this small." He turned it over again, looking at the bright, button eyes in the soot-stained flame-colored fabric. He swallowed, hugged it tightly to his chest, and burst into tears. A strong arm closed around him, and Owyn smelled woodsmoke and the scent of roasting meat.

"It's all right, Jax," Huris said gently. "It's all right."

Owyn shook his head. "No, it isn't," he gasped. He looked down at the stuffed mouse. "It's not fair. I remember this. But I don't remember you! Or...or Mama." He sniffled and looked up. "Can we go see her?"

"If we go with you looking like this, we'll upset her." Huris took the fire mouse from Owyn. "Basin is in the corner. Go wash your face."

Owyn sniffled and did as he was told. He was drying off when he heard someone calling from outside the wagon. "Huris?" The wagon bounced slightly, the door opened, and a woman looked in from the outside. Her resemblance to Rhexa was strong, except that she barely came up to Owyn's shoulder. "Frayim said you were coming to see me, but..." She stopped. "Why did you take Trinket out of the basket?"

Huris pointed to Owyn, who set the towel down and stepped into view. Dyneh looked at him for a moment, then turned back to Huris.

"Hur?"

"You look just like Aunt Rhexa," Owyn said, and she whipped around to look at him again. "I met her. She knew me. She...she told me a lot about you. She thinks you died. She thinks you're both dead. So...the past year it's been her and me. And...I have a fire mouse now. A real one. Her name is Trinket. I guess...I remembered that, too?" He swallowed. "It's not fair that I remember the stuffed toy, and not you. Except...who sang to me? Who sang *The Stars Dance*?"

"Mother of us all." Dyneh stepped into the wagon. "Jaxis? It...Jax?"

"I...I go by Owyn now," Owyn said. "I...I'm late. I'm sorry."

Dyneh moaned. Then she threw herself at Owyn and hugged him, crying and laughing all at once. Owyn hugged her back, trying not to cry again. Failing, when Huris came and wrapped his good arm around Owyn's shoulders.

"I did," Dyneh finally answered, her voice thick with tears. "I sang to you. We both did, really, but I sang *The Stars Dance*. You remember that?"

"I only remembered part of the first verse, and it was all I remembered for years. And it's how I found Aunt Rhexa." Owyn sniffled and straightened. "I have...so much to tell you. Not all of it good. I...yeah, there's a lot you won't like."

"You're here," Dyneh said. "You're alive. I don't care about the rest." She looked down at his arms. "And you're married?"

Owyn looked down at his arms, at his pledge bracelet. "My husband will be here tomorrow," he said. "He's with the Heir—" He stopped. "That's the first thing to tell you. I'm the Fireborn Companion. We're on Progress, and...well, shit happened, and they'll be coming here tomorrow to get me back."

"Get you back?" Huris repeated. "What happened?"

"Fa, it's a long story. And I need to ask about Memfis. About my other fa." He turned to Dyneh. "Memfis—"

"The man I was just working on, yes," Dyneh said. "He'll be fine. The young healer said he'd come to find you."

"I'd better go find him, then. Aven worries." Owyn smiled. "Will you come with me? You need to meet him proper, since...well, I'm not married to him, but everyone tells me the

Companion bond is like being married so I sort of am? Which means I'm married to a lot of people and you are in for a bunch of grandchildren."

Dyneh sniffled as she laughed. "Hur, he even rambles like you do!" She stepped back. "Let's go out. It's crowded in here."

"It's a good crowded in here," Huris grumbled. But he followed Dyneh and Owyn out into the air. Owyn looked around, trying to see Aven.

"The young healer might still be at the healing tent," Dyneh said. "We can go that way." She held her hand out. Owyn stared for a moment, then took his mother's hand, letting her lead him away from the wagon and through the camp.

"Mouse!"

Owyn turned, seeing Aven running across the camp. He smiled and waved.

"Aven, I'm here!"

Aven ran up to him, pulling him into his arms and kissing him. "Mouse," he breathed in Owyn's ear. "First things first. Mem will be fine. Fa is with him. He'll sleep until morning, so if you want to see him now, you won't see much."

Owyn clung to Aven, needing the solidity, the anchor that Aven promised. He nodded, feeling his cheek scratching against Aven's shirt. "I know," he said. "I know. I...Aven, you need to meet them."

Aven let him go and stepped back. "Meet..." he paused, looking at Dyneh. "I met Healer Dy—" His voice trailed off, and Owyn heard his thoughts. "*Oh, it can't be!*"

"It is," Owyn said, grinning. "Aven, this is Dyneh, and this is Huris." He smiled, broad enough that his cheeks started to hurt. "My parents."

Aven bowed formally to Dyneh and Huris. "It's an honor."

"Stop that," Dyneh chided. She tipped her head back to smile at Aven. "I understand that you're sort of married to our son? He says so. That means you're my son, too."

Aven's formal smile faded to a crooked grin. "I suppose it does," he agreed. "It's nice to meet you, Mama Dyneh. I never thought I would. And when they told me your name at the healing tent, I didn't make the connection. We thought you were dead."

"Dyneh, we need to feed these boys," Huris said. "Let's go back to the cooking tent. There wasn't much cooking left to do. Let's hope Frayim didn't burn those skewers."

"Your mother was at the cooking tent with Frayim, Fishie," Owyn said. "And I have a wagon where we can bed down tonight." He looked around. "I...you'll stay with me?"

Aven seemed to understand what Owyn was asking. He put his arm around Owyn's shoulders and hugged him to his side. "Of course."

AT THE COOKING TENT, Aven left them and went to speak to his mother. Owyn sat down with his parents, with one of them on either side of him.

"I want the recipe for that venison pulse stew," he blurted. "I want to make that for my Allie."

"Allie?" Dyneh repeated. "That's your husband?"

"It's short for Alanar," Owyn said. He looked down at his pledge bracelet. "He's a healer, and he's Senior Healer Jehan's heir. And...umm...he's Air and Earth, and he's blind."

"Oh! The Blind Healers!" Dyneh gasped. "Frayim told us about him. Is he really two people in one body?"

"Yeah, and no one knows why," Owyn answered. "And...Frayim knew about him? But he didn't know to tell you about me?"

"The Mother needed us to be here when you got here," Huris said. "If we'd known there was even a chance that you were alive? We'd have been out looking for you."

"Which means you wouldn't have been here when you were needed," Aleia said as she and Aven came to join them. "You'd never have found Owyn, and Memfis would have died." She sat down next to Dyneh, and Aven sat on the ground at Owyn's feet.

Huris shook his head. "Living with Frayim over the years, you learn that things happen for a reason. We were where we needed to be." He looked at Owyn and smiled. "And now we know the reason."

Owyn felt his face grow warm. He looked down at Aven, who frowned slightly. Then he reached out and rested his hand on Owyn's foot. The contact was enough. Owyn nodded.

"I should tell you," he said softly. "I should tell you all of it. If you come with us, you'll hear it. I'd rather you heard it from me, and not from someone trying to use my past as a weapon."

"Oh," Dyneh murmured. "Oh, Jax..."

"And...ah...don't interrupt me?" Owyn forced himself to smile. From the horrified look on her face, he failed miserably. "If I stop, I might not be able to start again."

"Go ahead," Huris said. He rested his hand on Owyn's arm. "But before you start, I want you to know that no matter what, you're still our Jax."

Owyn closed his eyes. "Older boy named Garci, he picked me up, named me Owyn. Took care of me. Taught me to steal. Which, just so you know, I'm lousy at." He took a deep breath. "I was a lousy thief. I was a better whore."

Aven's hand, warm against his skin, was the anchor he needed. It kept him in place, kept him from running from his past. Offered him the strength he needed to tell his parents everything.

"And that's it, I think," he finally said. "That...that's me. Slave, whore, thief. Smith, Smoke Dancer, Fireborn." He took another deep breath and opened his eyes. He could feel them there, one on each side. They hadn't run. But he was afraid to look at them.

Then a strong arm encircled his shoulder, hugging him tightly. More arms, from his other side, wrapping around him.

"You survived," he heard Dyneh say. "You survived so much. And you came back to us. We missed you so much."

THE EVENTS OF THE PAST few days caught up with Owyn before he'd finished eating, and he fell asleep leaning against Huris' shoulder. He didn't remember going back to the wagon at all, but he woke up there. He could see faint light outside the window, and hear birdsong. And he couldn't move, because Aven's weight was pinning him to the bed. He closed his eyes, feeling Aven's breath warm the back of his neck. Alanar would be here soon.

Owyn couldn't wait to introduce his husband to his parents.

He closed his eyes. More sleep would be good...

Someone knocked on the wagon door. They knocked again, and he heard Aleia's voice, "Anyone awake in there?"

Aven jerked, his arm tightening around Owyn. "What?" he mumbled. He looked around, then looked down at Owyn. "Oh. Am I squashing you?"

"I like it when you squash me," Owyn answered. He nodded toward the door. "Your mother is outside."

"And your father is wanting to see you," Aleia called. "And that goes for both of you. Get dressed. Memfis is awake. There's breakfast, and Frayim has his people breaking camp."

"What?" Owyn shifted, and Aven sat up. Owyn found his borrowed trousers on the floor and pulled them on before going to the door. "They're leaving?"

Aleia tipped her head back to look up at him. "Frayim hasn't said, but I think they're coming with us." She smiled. "Get dressed and come out. I'm sure that the others will be here soon." She walked away, and Owyn closed the door. Aven stood up, but couldn't stand up straight without hitting his head.

"Allie isn't going to like this." Owyn reached up and touched the ceiling. Then he laughed. "I never thought being short would be a good thing."

"I have no complaints about how tall you're not, Mouse," Aven said. "And I'm not complaining about the low ceiling, because you're here and you're safe." It only took him one long step before he was pulling Owyn into his arms, holding him tightly. "Owyn, I don't understand why."

"Can I tell it all at once?" Owyn asked. He wrapped his arms around Aven, and felt Aven's gem against his head. "I...did you find my gem?"

"Del found it," Aven said. "You'll have it back today." He kissed Owyn. "Now, let me find my kilt so we can get moving." He grinned. "Just to prove I love you? I rode a horse to come after you."

"You...rode a horse...in a kilt?" Owyn stared at him. "I should be taking a closer look, make sure you didn't damage yourself."

Aven laughed. "As much as I'd enjoy that? Our parents are waiting." He bent, picked up his kilt, and wrapped it around his waist. "Where's my shirt?"

"Aven, I don't remember getting undressed. I couldn't tell you where my shirt is!" Owyn looked around and rubbed his hand over his too-short hair. He snorted. "There's not enough floor in here to hide a pair of shirts."

"That's because there are a pair of shirts out here."

Owyn turned toward the door. "Good morning, Frayim!" he called. He opened the door to see the Seer standing outside, holding a shirt in each hand. He handed one to Owyn, then looked past him, and his face lit up.

"Oh," he breathed. "Heart of the Sea, may I look more closely?"

"You can call me Aven, and yes. Let me come out," Aven answered. He followed Owyn out of the wagon and stood still while Frayim walked around him.

"I haven't seen a Water warrior in their pride before," Frayim said as he handed Aven his shirt. "Not with my eyes, I mean. It is impressive." He tugged down the high collar of his tunic to reveal a small tattoo of his own, an intricately stylized tree at the base of his throat. "I dreamed this one," he said. "My first dream."

Owyn looked closer. "That's pretty."

"Thank you," Frayim resettled his collar. "I'll come with you to the healing tent. Then I need to oversee the rest of the preparations."

"Ama said you were coming with us," Aven said as they started walking.

Frayim nodded. "We've been waiting here for you to arrive. Now, we'll come with you. Some of us. Some will go on to Terraces." He tipped his head back. "You have time to speak to people, and to eat. She won't be here until after midday," he added.

"You mean Aria and the others?"

Frayim nodded without looking at them. "The blesséd Mother." He closed his eyes slightly. "The village they were not expecting welcomed them. Their emissaries arrived at dawn. They are...still speaking. She does well, but misses having you by her side."

Aven looked at Owyn, then back at Frayim. "Who is with her?"

"The Peace Bringer," Frayim answered. "The Protector of Now. The Blind Healers."

"Peace Bringer is Treesi," Owyn said. "Torri called her that. Blind Healers is Alanar. Protector of Now?"

"Karse," Aven answered. "One of the men who helped us save him called him that." He turned to Frayim. "Thank you for sending them."

Frayim smiled. "You're welcome. Now, I have to go. The healing tent—"

"Is right there," Aven finished. "I know. Thank you, Frayim." He held his hand out to Owyn as Frayim walked away. "Come on. Mem is waiting."

They walked into the tent, and the first person Owyn saw was Dyneh. She smiled at him. "Good morning. Did you sleep well?"

"I don't remember being put to bed," Owyn answered. "Does that count?"

She laughed. "I think it might." She drew back a curtain, revealing the two men on the other side. It was clear that neither Jehan nor Memfis had heard them — they were both occupied with each other. Dyneh let the curtain fall back.

"We'll give them a moment," she murmured, and led them outside. Once there, she cleared her throat and said, "It's a lovely morning, don't you think?"

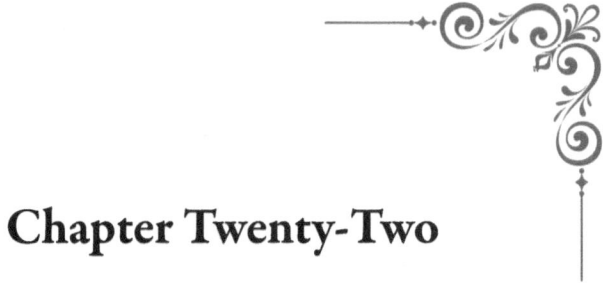

Chapter Twenty-Two

The meetings were finally over, and the camp was being packed. Aria touched the empty pouch at her belt and walked toward the man sitting with his back to her. He stiffened when he heard her footsteps.

"It's still empty," she called, and watched him relax. She wrapped her arms around his shoulders. "And we're leaving. He's alive, and he's safe, and we're going after him."

Alanar wrapped one hand around her forearm. "I know. I just...Aria, I wasn't there for him. I...I should have been there for him."

"Alanar, don't you start that," Treesi said as she joined them. "You were attacked. You were assaulted. You needed to be cared for."

"Which might have been Wren's plan all along," Alanar said. He took a deep breath and let it out slowly. "Hurt me enough that I need a healer. That separates us. Where does Owyn go?"

"To his father," Aria murmured. "It may have been. I don't understand why."

"And we won't, until Owyn tells us." Alanar squeezed Aria's forearm. "Thank you. For letting me share your bed last night. For being here for me."

Aria kissed his cheek. "You're one of mine, as much as Owyn is. I love you. I don't like seeing you in pain." She straightened, and rested one hand on her back. "I should not lean like that."

Alanar turned. "Back hurting?"

"Only a little, and once I start moving, I'll be fine. The coach is ready."

"Or we can ride," Karse said as he and Afansa came to the fire. "I was coming to tell you. I was talking to the Seer's men. They don't think the coach will get up the trail to their camp. So I was thinking we'd ride out, and the rest of the Progress will follow and set a camp at the base of the trail."

Aria nodded. "That makes sense. Alanar, will you trust us to ride with us?"

"Will it get me to my Owyn faster?" Alanar asked. "Will one of you help me with my boots?"

To Aria's amusement, Karse kissed Afansa goodbye before the riders left the camp. At the fore of the group, leading the way, were the Seer's men, Ulla and Lestra. Behind them was Karse, and then Aria rode with Treesi, Alanar, Copper and Danir. Both boys had stubbornly insisted that they were coming with Karse. Aria guided Star up to ride alongside Karse's big gelding

"The boys aren't going to let you out of their sight ever again," Aria murmured.

"I know," Karse answered with a nod. "I know. I didn't know how much of a father I'd become to them both, until yesterday. Now...yeah, they're my boys, and I'll talk to Lexi about it when we get home. I know she was thinking that Marek and Esai were going to adopt Copper, but I think we suit each other better."

"And what about Afansa, Captain?" Aria asked.

He grinned. "I knew someone was going to ask. Thought it would be Owyn or Mem, actually. Yes. We're going to wait to make anything formal until we have Trey back. But he asked me about her before he was taken. Because he likes her, and he thought she'd be good with us. I've been pushing back because I wanted to wait for him. But...I came closer to dying yesterday than I ever have, Aria. And I realized that I can't wait. I might not get another chance."

He shook his head. "Never expected to come out of this with a family. Well, a normal family. My guard..." He stopped, took a deep breath in through his nose. "I thought they were my family. Wren and Keel and Arc and Tay? They were my puppies. My pack. I thought that meant something."

"Have you talked to Leist?" Aria asked. "He's the last of them, isn't he? The last of your guard from Forge?"

Karse nodded. "The last of my puppies, yeah. And he's as lost as I am over this. All he kept saying was that Wren was completely awful at cards. He couldn't keep a straight face if he tried. He has no idea how they kept this from him."

"What do cards have to do with this?" Treesi called from behind them. Karse turned in his saddle.

"I didn't know you could hear me back there," he said, and slowed his horse enough that they were all riding abreast. "When you're gambling, if you've got a really good hand, or a really shitty hand? You have to keep your expression neutral, so you don't give it away. Wren was horrible at it. Couldn't keep it secret." He shook his head. "I knew his tells. How he gave away what he was thinking. So did Leist. And we never saw them. Any of them."

"Was it an act, then?" Alanar asked. "He let you see what he wanted you to see?" He snorted. "Let all of us see what he wanted us to see. He's been manipulating us the entire time."

"And now he's going to pay," Aria said. "I'll have to consider what the proper punishment is. Consult with Del and Steward."

"Why proper?" Alanar asked. "Can we just do something...I don't know...very improper? I mean..." He took a deep breath. "Never mind me. I'm bloodthirsty."

"You want revenge," Karse said. "And I understand that. And I've been warned about your temper, Healer Alanar." He smiled when Alanar laughed. "Right. I'm not sure how long of a ride we've got. Ulla?"

"Midday, if we pick up the pace," Ulla said.

"Can we do that? Pick up the pace?" Alanar asked. "I'll manage. But I need to move, and at this point, I might get off and run."

Aria looked at Ulla. "If you please, set the pace that would get us there as soon as we can, without having to stop?"

"As you wish, my Heir."

DEL HEARD THE HORSES long before they appeared around the curve in the road. He shaded his eyes, then looked over his shoulder as Othi and Steward joined him.

"Is that them?" Othi asked. He narrowed his eyes, then grinned. "Yeah, it is. I see Treesi."

"They must have come ahead of the rest of the Progress," Steward said.

"*Do you blame them?*" Del signed. "*Honestly, I'm surprised that Alanar didn't show up alone and on foot hours ago.*"

"I'm surprised that they didn't all show up hours ago. They're later than I expected them to be," Steward said. "I wonder what happened?"

"We'll find out soon," Othi said.

The riders were close enough that Del could hear them when Othi's patience ran out — he trotted out to meet them, then walked back with one hand on the neck of Treesi's horse. Once they stopped, he lifted Treesi down from the saddle, kissed her soundly, then helped Aria to the ground before he went to stand at Alanar's stirrup.

"Can I help you down, Alanar?"

Alanar nodded. "Please. Unless...is this it? Is Owyn here?"

"The Twiceborn is up in camp," Felix answered, coming over to take Meadowfoam's reins. "There's a good lad. Meadowfoam, hm? A good name. Had a nice run, did you?"

"Not really," Alanar answered. "I'm not the best rider. You've the Earth sense to talk to horses? And who are you?"

"I talk to most animals, Healers," Felix answered. "And the Twiceborn, he told me about your friend that talks to birds. Now, I'm Felix, and I apologize. I should have led with that. Frayim told me, and I forgot."

"Did...did you call me Healers?" Alanar asked. "Did you mean me? Or me and Treesi?" He turned. "Treesi?"

"I meant you, Healers," Felix answered. "Frayim calls you the Blind Healers. So I meant you and the other healer in your head. Seemed rude to not include him when I was talking to you both."

Alanar laughed. "You've amused Virrik. And he says thank you."

"This Frayim seems to know an awful lot about us," Karse said as he swung down from his horse. He lifted Howl out of his saddlebag and put him down, then pointed a finger at the puppy. "No running off," he added. Then he laughed as Steward engulfed him in a tight embrace. "I'm fine!"

"You almost weren't," Steward said. "And I'm glad to see that you are. How are you? Really?"

"Fine," Karse repeated. "Copper, Danir? Keep an eye on Howl. We might be leaving soon. I'm fine," he said again. "And I'm wanting answers. Where are the traitors?"

"If it's answers you want, then you'll have to wait to speak to Owyn," Steward said. "The guards are all dead. They were dead before we got here."

Karse blinked. "What?"

"That one, that Wren?" Felix waited for Karse to nod. "He killed the others. Two here, one down the road a bit. Then he killed himself when he figured out he was beat." He gestured to a pile of burned timbers and twisted metal. "It weren't pretty."

Karse stared at the wreckage, then gasped, "The fuck was that?"

"Wanderer's cart," Felix answered. "Dunno where they got it." He frowned. "Now, we saw to the guards that Wren killed. They went back to the Mother proper. I'm thinking that Frayim will be sending a few of us back down the road south to find the poor sods that the cart belonged to and send them back as well."

"My Heir?" Ulla called. "I'll wait here for your folks, and Felix will take you on. Felix, come meet the Heir properly."

Felix walked over to Aria and went to one knee. "My Heir. We've been waiting for you a long time now. It's good you've finally come."

"Thank you, Felix." Aria smiled and offered her hand. Felix took it and pressed her fingers to his forehead. "Now, if you'll take us on?"

"To be sure," Felix said. He got to his feet. "Ulla, where do we meet when we come down?"

"Ah..." Ulla looked up the road toward the north. "Meadow near Mirror Lake? Fodder for the beasts, enough room to spread out. Sounds good?"

"Sounds good to me," Felix said with a nod.

"Who's arranging the camp?" Steward asked.

"Afansa," Karse answered. "She's been bossing them around. She's been paying attention to you, Steward."

Steward smiled. "Glad to know someone is. Ulla, I'll go to set the camp with you, if you don't mind the company?"

Ulla grinned. "You'll be good company, Steward, and I'll be glad of it. Lestra, tell Berry I'll see her in a few hours?"

Lestra nodded. "I'll tell her. Now, we should get moving. Who's going and who's staying?"

In the end, It was only Ulla and Steward who stayed behind — Felix and Lestra took the lead up the winding trail.

"Can a cart make it down this trail?" Karse called. "Or is there another way?"

"Our carts have a narrower axle than your coaches," Lestra answered. "Wanderers, we know the ways in and out of these hills. These trails? Some of them date back to our grandmother's grandmother."

"When I first heard about the Wanderers, I thought that your folk were like mine. Like Water on land. That your carts were like our canoes," Othi said. "Do you follow the stars?"

Felix nodded. "Stars. Wind. There are signs on the trees and the rocks that you can read if you know how." He glanced back at Othi. "So, we distant cousins, then?"

Othi laughed. "Maybe. But aren't we all? We're all the children of the Mother's dreams. That makes us all cousins."

"Felix, how long is the ride to camp?" Aria asked.

"Not too long, my Heir. Not too long."

OWYN VOLUNTEERED TO help Huris cook, but it was hard to focus — he kept looking across the fire to where Memfis sat with Dyneh.

"You can join them if you want," Huris said softly. "I'll be joining them myself now that this spit is ready. Take that end?"

Owyn took the spit that bore a half-dozen birds, helping Huris move it over the bed of hot coals. "Who stands and turns it?" he asked.

"No one." Huris clamped something around one end of the spit, then looped a long leather thong over it. The other end went around a gear on a mill-wheel in miniature. The wheel stood underneath a large funnel, and when Huris pulled a stopper out of the funnel, a stream of sand started to flow out, turning the wheel, which made the spit start to turn. Owyn stared at it, then laughed.

"That's brilliant!" He went to kneel next to the contraption. "How do you change the rate of flow?"

"That knob there on the side. I'll slow it down in a bit. And we have to refill the sand, but won't need to for an hour or so." He wiped his hands, then smiled. "You like it?"

"This is fantastic. Fa, did you design this?" Owyn looked up to see Huris' crooked smile, and it took him a moment to understand why.

"Oh, I'm going to remember this forever," Huris murmured. "You didn't talk, you know. Before. You were late talking, so you never called me Fa. That's the first time I've ever heard it."

Owyn smiled. "Sorry it took me so long," he said, and got to his feet. He looked up at the sky. "It's late. Frayim said after midday. That's..."

"Soon. They'll be here soon." Huris rested his hand on Owyn's shoulder. "Still trying to figure out what to call you."

"You can keep calling me Jax," Owyn said. "I'll get used to it."

"Maybe we should blend it," Dyneh said as they came to sit with her and Memfis. Owyn sat on the ground so that he could look up at all three of them.

"Blend it?" Owyn repeated.

"Combine Jaxis and Owyn?" Huris nodded slowly. "Jaxsyn?"

Owyn coughed, felt his face warm, and heard Memfis snort.

"We've missed something?" Dyneh said.

"I...yeah. No way you could know," Owyn answered. "I...I saw in the smoke...I'll have a son, someday. And his name will be Jaxsyn."

Huris looked startled. "Your visions are that specific? Mine were never that strong." He looked at Dyneh. "Maybe if they had been, we'd have known..." He stopped when Memfis shook his head.

"You know it doesn't work that way, Huris. We can't change the visions," Memfis said. "You were where you needed to be. And for good or ill, it happened the way it needed to happen."

Huris sighed and nodded. "I know. It just...we lost so much time!" He sniffed, then looked at Owyn. "A grandson?"

"At least one from me," Owyn answered. "And...well, two by this time next year who aren't from me."

"Two?" Memfis repeated. "Have I missed something?"

"We didn't tell you?" Owyn grinned. "Treesi's pregnant. We found out when we went south to Forge and you all went east."

"You certainly did not tell me!" Memfis laughed. "Othi?"

"Yeah, it's Othi's, and he's giddy about it. He's going to wait to go back out to the deep until after the baby comes, he says. And I'll let him tell you the rest, so act surprised."

Dyneh leaned against Huris' arm. "I can't wait to meet the rest of your family, Jax," she said. "Even if I will have to make a list to keep them all straight." She sat up. "Senior Healer!"

"I told you, Dyneh," Jehan said as he came up to stand behind Memfis, resting his hands on Memfis' shoulders. "You can call me Jehan. The healing tent is packed. Will we have time to eat those birds before we need to leave?"

"Frayim says we'll have time for the meal once they get here. Then we'll roll. The kitchen tent is mostly packed." Huris looked over at the boxes and bundles. "This is the longest we've been in one place for...what? Two years, Dy?"

Dyneh nodded. "I was starting to wonder when Frayim was going to start to itch," she answered.

"How specific are his visions?" Memfis asked. He tipped his head back. "You don't have to fuss over me, Jehan."

"I want to fuss over you," Jehan answered. He leaned down and kissed Memfis, then straightened. "You're lucky Aleia is off doing something, or she'd be fussing, too."

"Where is she, anyway?" Owyn asked. "And Aven?"

Jehan looked as if he was about to answer, but was distracted by a commotion. He turned. Then he smiled.

"I think they've been acting as lookouts," he answered. "And I think if you don't get yourself over there in the next five seconds, there's going to be shouting."

"Over..." Owyn jumped to his feet, trying to see across the camp. He couldn't see anything, but he heard a familiar voice.

"Owyn!"

"Allie!" He broke into a run, toward the voice. Toward the commotion.

Toward his heart.

Alanar had clearly just dismounted, and was standing between his horse and Del. He had one hand on Del's shoulder, and was turning his head this way and that, an expectant look on his face.

"Allie!"

"Owyn!" Alanar turned. "Del, where is he?"

Del started forward, then stopped as Owyn reached them, almost knocking them both over as he threw himself at Alanar. Alanar's arms closed around him. Then Del's. Then others, and Owyn didn't care who — they were all here. His whole heart, his whole family. He lost track of who was kissing him, whose arms were around him.

Until Othi kissed him, which surprised him enough to start paying attention. He blinked, and laughed as Othi blushed.

Then he looked around again, seeing Aria in front of him. She opened her arms, and he walked into her embrace.

"I'm sorry I scared you all," he murmured.

"It was never your fault, my Fire," she answered. "I have something that belongs to you." She smiled. "Or rather, Del has it. Del?"

Del came up next to Owyn and held his hand out. The Fire gem rested on his open palm, and Owyn breathed a sigh of relief.

"You found it."

Del nodded. He smiled as Aria took the gem from him, then looked puzzled, reaching out to touch the dangling cord. Aria looped the cord over her fingers and let the stone hang.

"Del, did you replace this?" Del shook his head, and Aria took a deep breath. "Well, that is...interesting." She took the cord in her hands, and gently lowered it over Owyn's head, letting the gem come to rest at his throat. She touched it with her fingertips, then kissed him.

"Welcome back, my Fire."

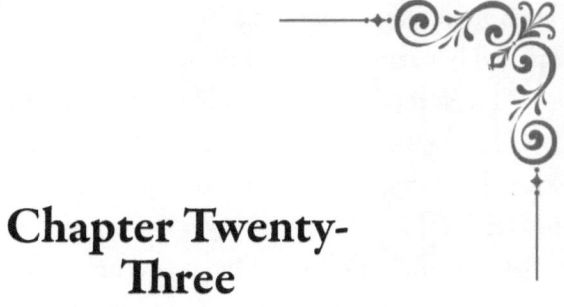

Chapter Twenty-Three

Aria smiled, watching Owyn resting in the circle of Alanar's arms. His shorn hair was startling, and Aria still wasn't entirely certain how it had happened, but she didn't care. Hair would grow back. Owyn was safe, and he was back with them. They were whole again.

"There's the whole weight of the world off your wings, isn't it?" Karse murmured from behind her. She turned to look at him, and saw the small group standing off to the side. Jehan and Aleia and Memfis standing with a tall man she didn't know. Karse followed her gaze and laughed.

"Mem!" he called, and started toward the group. Aria watched him go, then turned to see Owyn leading Alanar and Del toward her.

"Aria, there are people you need to meet. That all of you need to meet." He looked around. "And then we need to talk. I need to tell you all what I learned. Not that it will change anything, with Wren being dead. But he told me shit."

"When you are ready to tell us, we're all ready to listen," Aria said. "Who do we need to meet?"

Owyn nodded toward the group, where Karse had just let Memfis go after hugging him, and was now talking with Jehan and Aleia. The tall man was nodding.

"Him," Owyn said. "He's first. Then..." He looked around. "I don't see them."

"They're probably at the kitchen tent," Aven said. "Do you want me to go see?"

"Would you?" Owyn asked. Aven leaned over Owyn's shoulder to kiss him, then walked away. Owyn started walking again. "There'll be food before we leave. And I'll tell you everything while we eat." He grinned. "It's not all bad. I promise it's not all bad."

"It can't be all bad," Alanar said. "You're alive, and he's dead."

"Truth," Treesi agreed. She hugged Owyn from behind. "I can't get over your hair, though."

"It'll grow back," Owyn said. "And I'm going to. I'm going to grow it out long enough to twist, because Granna was going to teach me to do it. I just...need to learn how to twist it. But I have time to learn. Now, come meet Fray."

They started walking, and the tall man looked over at them. He met Aria's eyes for a brief moment, then turned bright red and looked away.

Aria stopped and looked at Owyn. "Is something wrong?"

"No," Owyn answered. "He just realized he might be about to make an arse out of himself." Owyn answered. "Fray, she won't bite you! Now come over here. You've only been waiting for this for..." He stopped. "Wait, you never told me. How long?"

The tall man laughed. "Fourteen years? I think?" He narrowed his eyes for a moment, then nodded. "Yes, I think that's right. I keep having to remind myself that I am seeing this with my real eyes."

"Oh," Aria breathed as she realized who he was. "You're the Seer."

His smile was radiant as he came forward and sank to his knees in front of her. "And you are the blesséd Mother, come to set things right and bring balance and hope back to Adavar. I am Frayim, and I am honored to serve."

Aria held her hands out to him. He put his hands into hers, and got back to his feet, towering over her. She had to go on her toes to kiss his cheek. "Thank you," she said. "For saving my Fire and my family."

He raised her hands to his lips and kissed her fingers. "My Heir, my life and my gifts are yours. And I am truly, deeply sorry for your loss. I would have liked to have met the Mother of Forge."

Aria swallowed. "Thank you," she murmured, her voice feeling suddenly thick. "She would have liked you, I think."

"So the Twiceborn tells me." He squeezed her hands, then let them go. "Twiceborn—"

"Owyn."

Frayim smiled. "Owyn, have you...?"

"They're next," Owyn answered. "Aven went to see if they're at the kitchen tent. I thought they might be."

"They are," Aleia said as she, Jehan and Memfis joined them. Aria smiled and embraced Memfis.

"I'm fine," he said as he hugged her as tightly as he could. "Jehan and Aven got to me in time. I'm fine." He laughed as the others came forward, surrounding him in a crowd of affection. Owyn hung back, and Aria went to his side.

"Who are we meeting?" she asked. He looked at her, then smiled.

"You wouldn't believe me if I told you," he said. "So you get to meet them first. And...I'm not sure if I should be introducing you first, or Allie?"

"Why not at the same time?" Alanar said as Del brought him back. "I want to take my boots off. Do we have time?"

"Yeah, we have time." Owyn took Alanar's arm and led him to one of the houses on wheels. "Come sit. Here, there's a stump. Careful now. I'll help." He knelt and tugged Alanar's boots off. He set them side by side next to the steps. "Better?"

"Much." Alanar stood up. "I'll carry them."

"No, we can leave them here. No one will touch them," Owyn said. He took Alanar's hand and looked around, bouncing slightly on the balls of his feet. He was, Aria thought, so excited he couldn't stand still.

"Owyn, who are we meeting?" Aria repeated.

"Come on," Owyn answered. "I'll show you." He started walking, and Aria looked at Del. Del shrugged, and they followed Owyn through the camp. Aria could smell something good long before they reached the fire where spits ladened with roasting birds turned lazily over glowing coals. Aven was there, talking with a couple — a woman and man. The woman reminded her of someone, but she couldn't think who. The man looked as if he'd been injured, or had suffered a brainstorm — his left side seemed slumped. But he turned to the woman on his left, and Aria saw his profile as he smiled....

"Oh," she murmured softly, and looked around. Treesi was closest. "Treesi? Look at that man. The one standing by Aven."

Treesi nodded. "Next to the woman...she looks a lot like Rhexa, doesn't she?"

Aria blinked and caught her breath. "Oh. Oh, that's it! I couldn't place who she looked like! And...look at him! He looks like—"

"He looks like Owyn!" Karse said from behind them.

Owyn turned to face them, holding his hand out to Aria. She came closer, and he led her and Alanar to the couple. The woman smiled broadly.

"Aria? Alanar?" Owyn glanced back. "Everyone? I...I want you to meet Huris and Dyneh—"

"What?" Karse gasped.

"My parents," Owyn finished. "Fa? Mama? This...this is Aria, the Heir. And this is..."

"Alanar," Dyneh finished. "Our other son. Jax, you certainly do like them tall!"

Alanar looked startled. "You're not dead?"

"And neither is Jax," Huris said. "We thought he was. He thought we were."

"And Frayim wasn't allowed to see that the Twiceborn was our son," Dyneh added. "Because we'd have left to go after him, to find him. And that would have made a mess of everything, because there wouldn't have been a healer here when one was needed."

Aria blinked. Blinked again. "Allowed to see?"

"Like when the Mother threw you out of the vision, Owyn?" Alanar asked. "Before we left Terraces?"

"Yeah, just like that," Owyn agreed. "There are things we can't know, because it will change what we do. This was one of them. But now..." He smiled and looked around. "I want you all to meet them. They're going to be coming with us when we go."

"A number of us will be coming with you when we go," Frayim said. "But for now, we should sit and eat, and Owyn has things to tell you of what happened and why."

"Oh, I can't wait to hear this," Karse growled.

They found places to sit around the fire, and Owyn went to help Huris serve. Aria sat next to Aven, and looked at him.

"They really are?" she asked in a soft voice.

"Yes," he answered, just as quiet. "Fa confirmed it. And they're very nice. I like them." He smiled. "Owyn told them that he's sort of married to all of us, and Mama Dyneh is really taken with that idea. She's excited that she has the chance to mother us, and to be a grandmother to all of the children we're likely to have."

Aria swallowed. "I...I would have liked to be consulted about that."

"She's looking forward to getting to know you," Aven said. He kissed her cheek. "I like her very much. She's a good healer, and she's very kind. She took excellent care of Memfis. You'll like her."

Aria leaned into his shoulder, and looked up as Huris stopped in front of them. He had two plates balanced on his arm.

"Aven, take these before I drop them, will you?" he said. "I want to be sure you both are fed."

Aria smiled up at the man as Aven took the plates. "Owyn cooks. Did he tell you?"

"He did," Huris said, his face lighting up with a crooked smile. "And I've been getting to know his other father this morning." He looked around. "We know he hasn't had the best time of it. Jax was sort of insistent that we know. Said he didn't want someone to turn his past into a weapon to hurt us. So he told us."

"And?" Aria asked.

"And I don't give two shits about what he had to do to survive," Huris answered. "He survived. He's here now. My son is alive, and I'm hearing him call me Fa for the first time in his life. I don't care about anything else."

Owyn came over with another plate. "Fa, I think we've got everyone. Did you get something?"

Huris laughed. "See? I have my boy calling me Fa. Nothing else matters." He turned slightly. "I have a plate, Jax. Do you?"

"I'll eat after I tell," Owyn said. He took a deep breath. "If I think I can keep it down. Go sit, and I'll talk."

"Owyn, you don't have to make yourself sick for this," Aria said. "It can wait."

"No, it can't," Owyn insisted. He swallowed and looked down. "He killed Granna, Aria. It was Wren. And he's been the one trying to kill me the whole time."

"I figured that part," Karse said. "When he took you. But why kill Lady Meris? That makes no sense."

Owyn nodded. "Karse, tell me about Fandor. About his operation."

"Fandor?" Huris spat into the dirt. "That piece of filth?"

"Is why I was a slave," Owyn said. "And maybe why this all happened. Karse?"

Karse looked thoughtful, pulling a piece of meat off the bone to feed to Howl. "Fandor's operations. He had a finger in every dirty pie in Forge, but he was canny about keeping it hidden. We didn't know the extent of it until he was dead, and there were things in there that we never could understand how he kept hidden, or how he kept ahead of us. There was shit in there that would have had us pitching him into the Smoking Mountain years ago if we'd known."

"Yeah, about that. The reason you didn't know? He had men in the guard."

"Knew that," Karse said as he took a bite of meat. "Knew some of them—"

"Wren was one of them."

Karse coughed, swallowed, and coughed again. "What?"

"He was feeding Fandor information about the guard, and about you. That's why he was always one step ahead of you." Owyn paused, then took a deep breath. "He told me he was Fandor's heir. That all the operations were going to be his.

That...that I was supposed to be his. He wanted you dead, and Mem and Granna Meris, for revenge because he lost everything and because of Cliffside—"

"That was his operation?" Karse blinked. "And here I was thinking Chalen was going out on his own."

"Wren was behind that," Owyn repeated. "And...he hurt Allie because he said I was his, and he needed to teach Allie a lesson. And he killed the others. Lyka and Arco and Keelan and Tayki. They were helping him, until he tried to kill you. Then Tay and Keelan tried to stop him and he killed them. But Tay said that Wren called killing Arco cleaning up loose ends. And he said that Lyka was one of Fandor's other boys." Owyn moved over to sit down next to Alanar. Alanar put his arm around Owyn, who leaned into his side. "That's all, I think."

Karse teased more meat off the bones to feed to Howl, then shook his head. "Wren. I...I don't know how I missed this."

"Karse, it isn't your fault," Jehan said gently. "He had us all fooled."

Karse shook his head. "Nah, it's my fault. I brought him in. He was one of my puppies. I trained him. I practically raised him from the time he was seventeen. I knew him better than anyone, and I never once noticed he was a traitor, and that he was a threat to the people around me." He looked down at the puppy. "To people I cared about. It got Meris killed, and Lyka and Arc and Tay and Keel. It almost got Owyn and Mem and Copper killed." He let out a long breath. "Anything else to lay at my feet, Owyn?"

Owyn shook his head. "I don't think so, no." He frowned. "Karse, I don't blame you. And you left yourself off that list. He almost killed you, too."

"If we'd been a heartbeat later getting you out of that pit, he would have," Aven said. "You weren't breathing when we got you out."

"You might not blame me. But I blame myself," Karse answered. "I'm supposed to be better than that. I wasn't. I didn't see what I should have seen, and people died. I need..." He stood up, then stopped. "Not sure what I need."

"Space?" Dyneh asked. "Time to think? An ear?" She kissed Huris on the cheek, then stood up and walked over to Karse, offering her hand. "Come walk with me."

Karse stared at her. "I almost got your boy killed!"

"And he's sitting right there with his man. Healthy and...well, I don't think he's all that happy at the moment, but he's alive." Dyneh looked around. "We've all of us almost ended up in disaster one way or another. But we're all still here. We survived. And we can't punish ourselves for our mistakes. Or for surviving our mistakes. We can regret what happened. We can mourn. But punish ourselves? You might as well spit on a fish for all the good it will do." She offered her hand again. "Come walk with me. Tell me."

Karse looked blank for a moment, then took her hand. They walked away from the fire, and Howl trailed after them. Copper trotted after them, coming back with an armful of squirming puppy.

"Good thinking, Copper," Jehan said. He looked after Karse and Dyneh. "He needs to get the weight off of his shoulders. She'll be able to help him?"

"She'll help," Huris assured them. He picked up Dyneh's empty plate, stacked it on his own, and stood up. "She's not the strongest healer of bodies, but what she does, she does well."

"Dyneh heals hearts better than anyone," Frayim added. "She'll be able to help the Protector of Now let his guilt go."

"She's a mind healer." Jehan smiled as he looked off in the direction they'd gone. "Good. We need someone who can teach those skills." He turned toward Treesi. "Treesi—"

"I'll talk to her once we're on the road." She frowned. "She is coming with us, isn't you? Aren't you?"

"We'll talk to her, and I'd like to know that, too." Jehan put his plate down and turned to Frayim, who was feeding bits of meat to Howl. "What's the plan?"

"We will leave once we finish packing the last of the camp," Frayim answered. "I've already sent many of our wagons on to your camp near Mirror Lake."

"How did you know that's where the camp will be?" Othi asked. "No, wait. Silly question. You're the Seer."

Frayim laughed, taking Howl into his lap. "I knew that because Felix told me," he admitted. "I don't know everything. I don't know your name yet, for example—"

"Me? I'm Othi."

Frayim nodded. "Othi. It's good to meet you. And I don't know why the Waterborn looks as if he's trying not to explode like the mountain over Forge."

Aria turned to look at Aven, who had a strangled expression on his face and tears in his eyes.

"What's wrong?" she demanded.

"Nothing." Aven practically squeaked. "I...just...spit on a *fish*?" He barely got the last word out before he collapsed into giggles. His mirth was infectious, and laughter quickly swelled and rolled around the fire, and even Owyn was smiling when it was done.

"So all of that..." His voice trailed off, and he didn't say anything while Huris walked away, coming back with a laden plate that he handed to Owyn. Owyn picked at the food, then looked up. "I don't think he was hiding anything at the farm. When he told us about his grandfather. I think that was real."

"We can ask Karse when he comes back," Treesi said. "Remember, he said he'd met Wren's grandfather. He'll know how much of that was true."

"Considering that he heard all of what Wren told us? Most of it was probably true," Othi said. "Something I don't understand. I liked them. Tay and Arc and Keel. And Lyka. Wren convinced them to help him. That's...how does that happen?"

"Wren had something on them, I think," Owyn said. "Dunno what. Tay didn't say. Just that he and Keelan were going to face up to it when they got me and Mem out."

"But—"

"Some people can do that," Aleia answered. "Some people have that...power of personality. They can convince you to sail into a storm. Your grandmother was like that."

Othi nodded. "I remember. I remember how many people came to Neera after Grandmother and Mother died, and said they never really liked how Grandmother ruled the canoes. They all swore they never wanted to cut off the canoes that sailed closer to shore. But they did. We did." He shook his head again. "I don't understand why no one stood up."

"Because that takes a person with a stronger will, and even stronger support. They have to stand against the storm, and stand for what's right." Jehan shook his head. "My mother is like that. There were others like that. From what I'm told, Yana was like that." He smiled. "Aria is like that."

Aria met his smile and nodded. "And if I'm to stand fully, we're going to need to keep moving. What needs to be done while Owyn eats?"

Chapter Twenty-Four

"What do you want to show me?" Alanar asked as Owyn led him away from the fire. Owyn held his hand tightly.

"Well, my parents have been living with the Wanderers, and...well, they gave me a wagon. It's ours. There's a bed, and a place for our things. And it'll be more comfortable for you, I think." He looked around. "And I wanted to get you alone. Because I never had a chance to talk with you after you talked with Jehan. Allie—?"

"Yes," Alanar said softly. "Senior Healer said that what happened to me was well beyond what was acceptable. And Wren was going to be arrested, but he'd already disappeared." His hand in Owyn's shook slightly. "You said he did it to teach me a lesson, but I was thinking that he did it deliberately. I think he did it so that I'd be with the healers, and everyone would be worried about me, and not paying attention to you when you went off to talk with Memfis. He knew us well enough to know how we'd react. He knew you well enough to know that you'd need to talk it out."

"Allie, I'm sorry." Owyn stopped outside the wagon. "We're here. This is where I left your boots, by the way. That's why I knew no one would touch them."

"I was wondering. All right. Show me."

"There are four steps," Owyn said, and opened the door. "And it's short inside. Aven can't stand up straight." He led Alanar inside, and to the bed. "It's nice. It's cozy."

"It smells good," Alanar said. "Are there herbs hanging in here?"

"There might have been, but there aren't now." Owyn looked around. "There's a table that folds down on the wall across from you, and baskets and drawers. I'm not sure how we'd keep it warm in the winter—"

"Braziers," Dyneh said from the doorway. "And did you ask about herbs? There was lavender and mint hanging in here." She smiled. "May I come in?"

"Please," Alanar said, sliding over on the bed. "Come and sit."

Dyneh sat down next to Alanar. "You do like tall men, don't you, Jax? Between Alanar and Aven, you never have to stand on a box to reach a high shelf."

"I'm useful like that," Alanar said, sounding amused.

Dyneh laughed. "Tell me about yourself, Alanar. I want to know all about you."

Alanar shrugged. "I'm a Healer, but you knew that. I have another healer in my head, but it sounds like you already knew that, too. Felix called me the Blind Healers."

Dyneh smiled. "Because Frayim calls you that, yes. I don't think he knew your name until Jax told him." She hummed softly. "It's interesting. He knows so much, but there are things he doesn't see, or isn't allowed to see. I don't remember Huris' visions being so specific, and at the same time so vague, but it's been a long time since he last danced."

"You really can't compare one dancer to another," Owyn said, coming to sit on the floor at their feet, facing them. "My visions are really specific, and really...what's the word?"

"Visceral?" Alanar suggested. "From everything you've told me, the word is visceral."

"Yeah, that's a good word. But I'm really sensitive, especially since I came back." He reached up to scratch the back of his neck, and noticed Dyneh was looking at him in shock.

"Came back?" she repeated. "Jax, he calls you Twiceborn. But...came back from where?"

"You didn't know." Owyn took a deep breath. "I...died. I drowned. And Aven brought me back. That's why people call me Twiceborn. Frayim didn't know that?"

"If he knows, he didn't tell us," Dyneh said softly. "Which...he didn't know you were ours, so saving us from that...that doesn't make any sense. You truly died?"

"Aven said I was dead for nearly a minute."

Dyneh swallowed. "And...you're still a dancer? You still dance the smoke?"

"I had a new waking vision and everything," Owyn grinned. "Remember? There's a grandson in your future?"

She nodded. "You did tell us that. You...we almost lost you before we ever knew you were still alive?"

Owyn took her hand. "Mama, I'm here now. I'm fine."

She squeezed his fingers. "I know. I'm still trying to convince myself it's real." She smiled. "Sensitive how?"

"Heart visions," Owyn answered. "Do you know what those are?"

Dyneh frowned slightly. "Huris let me read his books. I know he wasn't supposed to, but I was curious. I think I remember something—" She closed her eyes, then blinked. "You hear people's thoughts?"

"Mama!" Owyn gasped. "You do know!"

"That's better than Lady Meris and Memfis did," Alanar said. "They couldn't find anything in the Palace library."

"I don't hear everyone. A deep emotional bond, Granna said. I never heard her, and I don't hear Mem. But Allie and all of the Companions. And Trey. That's Karse's man. I'll tell you about Trey later," Owyn said. "I should ask Fa which book it was."

"I don't know that they'd have had access to it," Dyneh said. "It was in one of his grandmother's journals. We took it with us when we left Forge. One of the few things we did take." She smiled. "Did you tell Alanar about Trinket?"

Alanar arched a brow. "I know about Trinket. She likes to get into my shirt."

"No," Owyn said with a laugh. "Not the real one. There's a toy fire mouse that was mine when I was little, and that I lost when...well, Fa said that the place where I was when they were working burned down in a riot in Forge. They found the toy, but not me."

"And that's why they thought you were dead?"

"That's why," Dyneh said.

Owyn nodded. "But I remembered the toy enough to name Trinket after it. And I remembered it when Fa showed it to me yesterday." He frowned. "Which feels like it was ten years ago."

Dyneh laughed. "You've had a very busy few days," she agreed. She squeezed his hand again. "Now, I want to know more about my other son. Alanar, your family?"

"My father's name was Dantris—"

"You're Dan's son?" Dyneh gasped. "I trained with him! He went north, to the healing center near the Solstice village, and came back with a wife. Alane was darling." She paused, then laughed. "Oh. Oh! I do remember you! You couldn't have been more than three or four when Hur and Jax and I left Terraces."

Alanar smiled "You're doing better than I am. I don't remember you at all!"

"You were so small when I last saw you," Dyneh said. She paused again, frowned slightly, then cocked her head to the side. "And...how did it happen, may I ask?"

Alanar blinked. "My wings, you mean?"

"I remember you learning to fly right before we left. And...well, sitting this close? The scar tissue is making my back itch. And there are burn scars." She shook her head. "Old ones. You were how young?"

"I was ten when it happened," Alanar said. He shook his head. "Mama died when I was six. Fa took a position as a village healer in an Earth village to the east of Terraces. There was a fire. Fa got me out, but he didn't make it." He raised his hand to wave it in front of his face. "Lost my wings, lost my sight. The village headman brought me to the main healing center, and Pirit raised me after that." He chuckled softly. "It's funny to think you knew me when I was still a fledgling, and now I'm married to your son."

"It's funnier than that," Dyneh said. "I know Dan and Alane were at Jax's naming celebration, so I'm fairly certain you were there, too."

"No!" Owyn burst out laughing. "Really? Allie, you've known me my whole life?"

Alanar smiled. "I wonder if that's why you felt so comfortable when we first met. I remembered you without even remembering."

Someone knocked on the door, and Owyn heard Del's voice in his head. "*Owyn? May I come in?*"

"Come inside, Del!" he called, and held his hand out as Del came into the wagon. Del looked around and smiled, settling on the floor next to Owyn and leaning into his side.

"*I like this! It reminds me of my old room in Terraces.*" Del dug his tablet out of his bag and wrote something, then handed it to Dyneh. She looked puzzled, then looked down and read the tablet.

"I don't think we have," she said, handing the tablet back. "It's nice to meet you, Del."

Owyn tipped his head to read the tablet — *We haven't been really introduced. I'm Del.* He groaned. "Del, I'm sorry! I...well, I never did introduce anyone properly. Mama, Del is our Air—"

"The Broken Feather of the Vision of the Dove," Dyneh interjected. "And Frayim calls you the Silent One. Do you talk?"

Owyn saw Del lick his lips. "Del?"

Del nodded. "Ah...kin...spek...some..." He took a deep breath, wiped his tablet, and wrote again. "*This is faster. Or speaking to Owyn and having him tell you.*"

Dyneh read the tablet and chuckled. "You can take your time and tell me anything, Del. Or you can write it if you're in a rush."

Owyn looked at Del, then leaned close and asked, "Do you want me to tell her about your parents?"

"*All of them?*" Del asked silently. When Owyn nodded, he smiled. "*Please?*"

"Mama, you should know this. Del is Yana's son, by her Fire, Delandri."

Dyneh's jaw dropped. "Truly? She lived? The riot...the one that separated us...we all thought she was dead."

Del shivered slightly, and Owyn hugged him close. "No, Mama. Yana survived the battle where everyone thought she died. Her Fire didn't. And she was hurt. When we met the Usurper, he told us that she'd had a head wound, and when she woke up, she had the mind of a child. He took care of her until she died." He paused, glanced at Del. "Until she was murdered."

"What?" Dyneh's shrill gasp made Del wince, and Owyn hugged him more tightly.

"Was Risha one of the healers you trained with, Dyneh?" Alanar asked.

"Oh, she was..." Dyneh paused, then shook her head, a sour expression on her face. "I knew Risha. And I wish Pirit had sent her away. She was vile. Why?"

"Because after Yana woke up, she didn't remember how to fly. So...she couldn't teach Del. The Usurper—"

"You don't have to keep calling him that. I know he's with you, and loyal to Aria," Dyneh said gently. "Frayim told us."

"We call him Steward," Owyn said. "And...he wasn't in the Palace. Risha brought Yana and Del up to the top of the Heir's Tower, and she pushed Del out the window. Then...I'm not clear if she pushed Yana, or if Yana went out after Del, but it don't matter. Yana died, and Del lost his wings and his voice. And the Usurper didn't know for years what had really happened. Not until Del learned to use Water signs." He took a deep breath. "Risha...she's been condemned to death, once we catch her. She's been...well, she's been turning people against Water and Air, telling folks they're not human, that they're not really the Mother's children."

"I've heard that before. Here, in the hills," Dyneh said. "Risha says it, too?"

"And people are believing her," Owyn answered. "And it's been bad. We might eventually have an accounting of how many Airborn lost their wings to her, but we may never really know how many Waterborn she killed." He glanced at Del again, who shook his head gently.

"*We need to ask Aria before we tell them more*," Del murmured.

"There's more," Owyn said, nodding. "And things I'm not sure we can tell you. Except...the Usurper...Steward, he was Yana's

Air. She recognized him when she woke up. He loved her, Mama. And he's Del's adoptive father."

"And we'll meet him later today, won't we?" Dyneh asked. "We'll be leaving once they finish breaking camp." She looked around. "We have a mule for this wagon. I'll bring him."

"Del and I have horses," Alanar said.

"You want to ride?" Owyn asked. "To put boots on?"

"Not if I have a choice," Alanar answered with a grin. He closed his eyes and tipped his head back. "I like this, even though I really can't tell where I am. It's a little like being on the cutter."

"It's not big enough in here to get lost."

"Wyn," Del said aloud. He reached out and touched Owyn's shorn head, then arched a brow. Owyn sighed.

"Do you know what happened? You met Felix on the road. He tell you?"

Del nodded. *"I know, but Alanar didn't hear, I don't think."*

"Ah. Then I need to tell Allie, too." Owyn swallowed. "We were in a cart like this one, and Keelan and Tayki, they were going to get me and Mem out of there. Tay was untying me when Wren killed him." He took another deep breath. "Then he poured inferno oil on Mem, and on me. And he was going to light it when Frayim got there. They got me out, and we locked Wren in the cart. He lit the cart on fire himself, from the inside."

"Felix told us that they were dead, but...no one told me the details." Alanar let out a shuddering breath. "And...is that why your hair is so short now? I noticed, but I never had the chance to ask and I got distracted."

"Yeah. Because we couldn't get the inferno oil out," Owyn said. "I...I'm sorry. I know I told you I was going to let it grow, but...I'm starting over. And I'm still going to learn to twist it, just like Granna wanted." He sniffed, and wiped his face. "I...I think that's all. I think I told you everything else." He frowned. "How's

Karse? We talked, but I never asked him...and I saw Copper. I didn't ask how they came out of it."

"Physically, he's fine," Alanar answered. "He had a broken skull, but it healed clean. Copper will be fine, too."

"He's heart-wounded," Dyneh added. "He does still blame himself for not seeing through this Wren. But he's receptive, so he'll heal." Dyneh smiled softly and held her hand out. "Come up here, Jax. I'll move over so you all can sit together." Del got to his feet first, and went to sit on Alanar's other side. Dyneh laughed. "All right. I won't move, then." She waited until Owyn was sitting between her and Alanar, then leaned into him and put her arm around his shoulders. "Changing the subject?"

He smiled, feeling brittle. "A little, yeah."

"Hur does that," Dyneh said. "I tell him he still dances. It's just now he dances around topics he doesn't want to talk about."

Alanar laughed. "Owyn does that, too. Will someone tell me why Huris' voice sounds crooked?"

"Brain injury, during the riot when we lost Jax," Dyneh answered. "His entire left side is crippled." She paused. "Do you think...I mean, you're a much stronger healer than I am—"

"After twenty-odd years?" Alanar frowned slightly. "Maybe in merge? I'll talk to the Senior Healer. I don't know if there's anything that can be done. But we can see." He shook his head. "Some things are beyond a healer's power. Nerves are one of them." He put his arms around Owyn and Del. "As much as I'd like to see the men I love, it's not going to happen. It's frustrating, sometimes."

Someone knocked on the side of the wagon, and the door opened to reveal Frayim. He smiled gently. "Dyneh, Huris is ready for you. I've brought the horses."

"We'll need to get Bossy and get him harnessed," Dyneh said.

"Felix is bringing him," Frayim said. "You know Bossy doesn't do anything for anyone but Felix."

"Sounds like our Stubborn, back in Forge," Owyn said. "How different is this from driving a coal cart?"

Frayim frowned slightly. "I've never driven a coal cart," he admitted. "Dyneh?"

"I don't find it very different from driving an open wagon," she said. "But it's taller, so you have to slow down for turns. We can have Felix drive down the trail, if you don't want to try yet. Then you can get used to driving on the roads."

"*That makes sense,*" Del murmured in Owyn's mind. Owyn nodded.

"Can we do that?" he asked. "Just...I've had enough excitement. I'd like some boring now."

Frayim looked at him. "Boring won't come for you for a while, Twiceborn. It will come, though."

THE LONG PROCESSION of wagons and carts rolled slowly out of the camp and down the trails. Owyn sat in the driver's seat with Felix, talking about how to handle the steep trail, while Alanar and Del made commentary from behind him, through a small window set in the wall behind the driver. Then the trail leveled out, and Owyn saw the charred remains of the wagon..

"Did anyone go back and look?" he asked Felix. "Wren had to have gotten the wagon from somewhere."

"They didn't need to," Alanar said. "Wolf's Ford sent their people out this morning to meet Aria. They repudiated Risha, swore loyalty to Aria, and told us about some strange goings on over the past day. There was a small camp attacked in the woods. The people got away, and they're in Wolf's Ford. They're safe."

"Oh, thank the Mother," Felix breathed. "I was busy with the beasts, and I assumed Frayim had sent someone else out to search."

"*He did send someone,*" Del added. "*To bring them an empty wagon.*"

"Del says Frayim sent someone off with an empty wagon for them," Owyn translated. Felix grinned.

"I should learn not to ask why Frayim does what he does. He always has a reason," he said. "So if he wanted a pair of fully kitted out wagons just laying empty, there's going to be someone who needs them. One was this one."

"And the other went to the people Wren attacked." Owyn nodded. "That's good. Now, can I try driving?"

ARIA SAW THE CAMP, and saw the man standing at the edge. She waved, and saw him waving back. Then she heard his distant bellow, "They're here!"

"He'll raise the entire camp," Aven laughed.

"They're all eager to see that Owyn and Memfis are safe," Aria answered. She looked over at Frayim. "Frayim, what do you know of my steward?"

"He's the Forgotten," Frayim answered. "And that is all." He shrugged. "Sometimes, the information I need is best learned when I need it, and not before."

"Like with Owyn being Jaxis," Aven said.

"Just so," Frayim agreed. "I'm very curious about the Forgotten. His role in this was the spark to start the blaze, and yet I know nothing. I don't even know his face."

Aria glanced at Aven. "Is that unusual?" she asked.

"Very," Frayim laughed. "It's very unusual. I'm very much looking forward to meeting him and finding out why!"

There was a crowd waiting for them as the wagons came to a stop, and Steward hurried over to Aria.

"I was starting to worry," he said. "Let me help you down." He reached up, looked past Aria, and froze, a look of startled shock on his face. When Aria looked to see, Frayim wore a similar expression.

"Steward?" she murmured gently. He jerked, looked up at her, and blinked. "When I'm down, I'll introduce you."

He nodded, not saying anything, and helped her to dismount. Aven joined her, and they walked over to where Frayim had gotten down from his wagon.

"Steward, this is Frayim," Aria said. "We know him as the Seer."

"I...Aria," Steward stopped. Swallowed. Then turned to look at her. "Aria, I swear I have never seen this man before in my life—"

"And I know you as if I was born knowing you," Frayim finished. "No wonder the Mother hid your face from me. I'd have walked barefoot over coals to find you." He held his hand out. "Steward, I think I've been waiting my entire life to know you. And it is good to finally meet you."

Chapter Twenty-Five

"And I am more than ready for my own trousers," Owyn grumbled as they walked toward the Heir's tent. Del laughed, and Owyn grinned at him before adding, "And boots! I had to burn my boots." He frowned. "Do I even have another pair of boots?"

"You're going to have to ask Trista," Treesi said. "And...has anyone told Owyn?"

"Told me what?" Owyn asked. He stopped walking. "What happened? Is Trista all right? Wren didn't try anything, did he?"

"No. She's fine," Alanar said quickly. "She's just...distracted." He slung his arm over Owyn's shoulder. "We're going to have to discuss this habit of yours—"

Owyn jabbed his husband with his elbow. "I keep telling you. It's not my idea that people keep trying to kill me!"

Alanar burst out laughing. "No, not that habit. The turning peoples' heads habit."

Del snickered, and Owyn looked at him. "Whose head? What are you talking about?"

"Trista," Aria said. "Owyn, she's very fond of you."

"I like her, too," Owyn stammered. "She's a friend. And..." he paused, then groaned. "Wait, are you telling me she fell in love? With me?"

"Or in lust," Alanar agreed. "I don't think it matters which. She's young, and you're nice to her."

"We saw it with Gathi, too. Remember? We might be the first ones to treat her nicely. Servants don't usually have people treat them like...people. They don't expect that," Del's quiet voice murmured in his mind, and Owyn stared at him.

"What do you mean, they don't expect to be treated like people?" he demanded. Then he stopped and shook his head, remembering when he had been on the other side. "Oh. Oh, I get it. I understand." He sighed. "Yeah, I understand. I just...I never thought about it like that."

"Like what?" Aven asked.

"That servants have the same issue whores do. Just...maybe not as bad?" He turned and looked at Del. "Tell me it's not as bad?"

Del shrugged. *"Maybe not as bad in the Palace, I don't think. I don't know,"* he signed.

Owyn shook his head. "Sometimes, I think I don't know nearly as much as I should. Aria, can we...I dunno...make it a law that people can't treat servants and whores like things?"

"You want to legislate...that people treat other people the way they ought to be treated?" Treesi asked. "I don't think we can do that."

"I think that's already in the laws," Aven added. "That's why we have laws. So people treat other people the way they should be treated. But we can't make people...not look down on others. And I think we all know what that's like." He looked around the circle. "I was the Mudblood. Owyn, you were the slave. Del can't speak, Alanar is blind, and Treesi gets lost walking a straight line. We were all treated as...less." He looked at Aria. "I never asked you."

"Fatherless girls among the Air flocks are automatically less," Aria answered. "Even though we knew who my father was. My mother and grandfather tried to counter that. Which...may have been why I was such a handful when we first met."

Aven grinned. "Spoiled, you mean?"

"I would not have said it..." She paused, then laughed. "Yes. I was spoiled. And you were right to push me into the water."

Aven grinned and put his arm around Aria's shoulders. "We've done all right, for being the ones that people thought of as less. And we'll keep doing all right, because we know what it's like. Now...let's go put Trista out of her misery."

They started walking again, and Aven held the tent flap open so that they could file in. Owyn saw Trista standing next to the bed, folding and rolling clothes. She glanced over her shoulder, and dropped the shirt she was holding as she whirled to face them. "You're here!" she gasped. "You're back!" She hesitated, then finished, "Your hair..."

Owyn laughed. "It'll grow back," he said. "I'm sorry I worried you."

Trista bit her lip. "I...thank you. I know it wasn't your doing. I..." She paused, looked him up and down, then blurted, "Owyn, who in the Mother's name dressed you?"

Owyn looked down at himself — the baggy tunic and long, loose trousers. He laughed. "Yeah, I need my own clothes. Please."

She smiled and turned to a chest, opening it and taking out rolls of cloth. "What happened?" she asked as she laid them on the bed. "And...you are all right, aren't you?"

Owyn nodded. "Yeah. I'm fine. Well, fine enough. And what happened to my hair was that I had inferno oil thrown on me. It wouldn't come out of my hair, so we had to cut it."

Trista covered her mouth with both hands, and her voice was muffled when she squeaked, "Inferno oil?"

"I'm fine," Owyn repeated. "And I really want my own clothes."

She blushed. "I'll go. I'm so glad to see you safe, Owyn." She bowed slightly. "If you need anything—"

"Trista." Owyn stopped her before she ran out of the tent. He held his hand out to her. "Look, I want you to know that I don't think of you as a servant. You're my friend. My friend with better taste in clothes than I have."

She giggled and took his hand, letting him pull her into a hug. "Thank you," she murmured against his ear. "I..." She stepped back and kissed his cheek. "Thank you." Her blush deepened, and she fled the tent.

Aven chuckled as the tent flap fell closed. "Alanar is right. You really need to break this habit."

DEL EXCUSED HIMSELF while Owyn changed clothes, heading out into the camp and wandering through the neat rows of tents and wagons. It was impressive organization, and Del made a note to ask his father if this was Afansa's work. If it was, he was going to suggest that Steward think about making her his assistant. He walked up one row and back down the next, smelling smoke as he reached the end. There was a kitchen being set up there, under the supervision of Steward, Afansa and Huris. And, standing close enough to see them, but not so close as to be obvious, was Frayim. Del smiled and went to him first, taking out his tablet.

"*Are you all right?*" he wrote, and handed it to Frayim. Frayim frowned, and his lips moved as he read the words. Then he looked up and smiled.

"I'm fine, thank you." He handed the tablet back to Del, and looked past him. "Confused. I don't understand why he was hidden from me until now." Del shrugged, and Frayim chuckled. "I don't know either," he said. "He's your father. Do you mind..." He paused, then laughed. "I don't even know what I'm asking."

Huris turned and saw them, then waved them closer. "Fray, come look at the cooking set up. We're combining our supplies with theirs and...what's wrong?" He turned fully toward them. "Fray, what is it?"

Frayim shook his head. "Nothing, Huris." He glanced at Steward, and Del saw a faint hint of color creeping up his throat. He cleared his throat and turned to Afansa. "We haven't met. I'm Frayim."

"The Seer. Karse told me," Afansa said. "It's good to meet you." She looked up at Steward. "Now, are we staying here very long?"

"I'll want to consult with Aria," Steward answered. "I'm not sure if she'll want to leave immediately tomorrow morning, or stay here for another day so that people can become acclimated. And we have a long way to go."

"But not all of us will go that far," Frayim said. "At least, not all of my people. When the road branches to the west, most of my people will leave. But we'll be gathering more as we go north."

Steward stared at him. "Gathering more?"

Frayim nodded. "The blessèd Mother will draw people to her as we travel. My people, other people who have hoped and dreamed of her for their entire lives. And those who have waited for the coming of the Child. Those will come last, but they will come, and they will follow."

"The Child? You're going to have to explain that. But later. Right now, we need to worry about logistics." Steward frowned. "More people. How are we going to feed them all?" He turned to Afansa and Huris. "If we have too many people, forward progress will slow to a crawl. How can we manage?"

"We'll be fine," Frayim said. "Trust in this. We will be fine."

Del could see how skeptical his father was. But Steward just nodded. "I'm going to have to learn to trust you, aren't I? Huris says you're never wrong."

Frayim chuckled. "It goes against your nature to trust blindly. I understand." He cocked his head to the side. "Do you trust the Smoke Dancers?"

"Yes, but I've known them for longer than a day," Steward answered. "Give me time." He smiled. "Frayim, I can feel in my bones that I can trust you. But I've known that feeling before, and I've been betrayed. A little time is all I ask."

Frayim bowed deeply. "And you will have it. Now, is there anything I can do to help?"

Afansa looked thoughtful. "Everyone is settled. Or at least, they're settling. Huris is taking over cooking, and your people know what needs doing here. And...no, I don't think so, Frayim. I think we're as settled as we can get," Afansa said. "I wanted to go and see Owyn, Karse told me that he's fine, but I wanted to see for myself."

"And I need to meet with Aria, and find out the details of the meeting with Wolf Ford," Steward said. "Huris, if you need any help—"

"I'll shout," Huris said, waving one hand. "But we know how a kitchen goes together, and how to feed people. Go on. You're busy people. Go...do busy-people things." He shooed them off, and turned to the kitchen tent. Del laughed and waved back, then fell in next to his father. Steward smiled.

"I imagine Owyn is getting into his own clothes?" he asked. "I can't see Trista letting him look so unkempt."

Del grinned. "*The first thing she asked about was his hair. The second was who dressed him. She does take our appearance personally.*" Steward laughed, and Del continued. "*Fa, how are you?*"

Steward nodded and signed, "*Confused. I know I've never met him before, but the last time someone looked at me that way? It was your mother. It's unnerving.*" He shrugged. "Worried, a little, about how the Progress will continue. Trying to remember the lore. The first day sets the tone of the Progress. But there was something about the path to the hinge, and the path after. Do you remember it?"

Del frowned, thinking back on his reading. "*No, but Virrik might know. His father was a Loremaster.*"

"Then I'll talk to Alanar and Virrik. There was something about a hinge..."

"Forge was the Hinge, where the Progress turned," Frayim said from behind them. "The path to the hinge mirrors the path of the past — the blesséd Mother's journey to the Diadem. From here to the end, the path of the Progress will show the path of the future, and show what form our blesséd Mother's rule will take."

Del turned and arched a brow, and Frayim blushed. "Should I not be listening? Was it a private conversation?"

"I doubt you understood the actual private parts of the conversation," Steward said. "Unless you understand Water signs?"

"No, I do not," Frayim said. "I know it is how our Water brothers and sisters speak when they surrender their voices. But I don't know what the movements mean."

"Well, at some point, if you want to learn, we can have Aven or Othi or Aleia teach you," Steward said.

Frayim nodded. "I should learn. And I should practice my reading. I do read, but not well."

"We can learn that together." Afansa stepped up next to Frayim. "Lady Meris was teaching me to read, but I'm still learning. Now, Steward, you wanted to speak to Aria?" She pointed. "She just came out of the tent."

Del turned and saw that Aria, Aven, Treesi and Othi had come out into the air. He waved, and they came toward him.

"Owyn wanted some privacy with Alanar," Aria said. "So we agreed to leave them alone."

Del nodded. *"I don't think they had much time to talk in camp,"* he signed. *"When I found them, Healer Dyneh was with them."*

"We should make sure she knows that they need to be left alone," Aven said. "Where is she? At the kitchen?"

"No, we set up a healer's tent," Steward said. "I'll show you where."

"You wanted to talk to Aria," Afansa reminded him.

Aria looked up at Steward. "What do you need to discuss?"

"First, are we staying here a day so that we can...well, get to know Frayim and his people?" Steward asked. "See how we all fit together?"

Aria nodded. "And to give anyone we may have missed a chance to meet with us," she added. "Was there another reason?"

"You met with Wolf Ford," Steward said. "How was that?"

She smiled. "Surprisingly pleasant. And Copper writes with a very clear hand." She looked around. "Where are the boys?"

"With Karse, working with the guards," Afansa answered. "Honestly, between the boys and the wolf, Karse has had barely a moment alone since he came out of the healing trance."

Othi snickered. "Between them and the wolf," he repeated. "Just them and the wolf?"

Afansa blushed. "Well, someone has to watch him when they're asleep," she murmured. "The man needs watching." She laughed. "And I'm going to go watch him drill the guards, since Owyn is busy. I'll see him later. I'll take Aven to the Healer's tent. Treesi, do you want to come, too?" She led the healers away, toward the other end of camp.

"I'm not going to be much help," Othi said slowly. "And Treesi is busy. Steward, do you need me anywhere?"

"Not if you want to go drill," Steward answered. "Go catch Afansa." As Othi left, he turned to Aria. "We've set up a canopy for meetings, so that you and the Companions aren't sitting out in the sun as it gets warmer. Shall we go there?"

"Yes, please," Aria agreed. She took Steward's arm, and let him lead her toward the center of camp. Del followed, with Frayim falling in next to him. The tall seer had his hands clasped behind his back, and his eyes on Steward.

OWYN LED ALANAR BACK to his wagon, and they both sat on the bed. It was quiet. Peaceful. And he didn't have a single idea of what to say. He couldn't bring himself to touch his husband.

"Allie..." His voice trailed off. "I...I'm sorry." He looked up. "It was my fault. He hurt you because of me."

"It's not your fault. And I'm frankly terrified to even think of what he'd have done if you had said yes and come with us." Alanar turned toward Owyn. "It was bad, but it could have been worse. It could have been so much worse. Would have been, if you'd been there. Because he'd have hurt the both of us." He frowned. "Killed me, in front of you."

Owyn shuddered as Alanar took his hand. "Probably. I...he hurt you."

Alanar nodded. "And hurts mend," he said. "I...I think I blacked out for part of it. I don't..." His voice trailed off. "I...Owyn, I don't remember parts of it," he said slowly. "I remember the beginning, when I realized that things were getting much rougher than they should have been. I got scared, and I was going to stop him. Then...I remember the end, in the morning. When I woke up, I could feel that he'd hurt me. When he untied me—"

"He left you tied all night?"

Alanar snorted. "Honestly? That was the least of it. He was laughing and telling me how much I'd helped him." He frowned deeply. "I hurt...and I know what he did to cause some of it...but not all of it. I don't remember all of it."

Owyn ran his thumb over the back of Alanar's hand. "You...you blacked out. It happens. Or..." He sat up straight as realization dawned. "Virrik, what did you do?"

Alanar twisted. "What?" He blinked, shook his head, then laughed softly. "You're quick," he said in Virrik's voice.

"Virrik?" Owyn repeated the question. "What did you do?"

"I underestimated how fast you'd figure it out," Virrik said. "I promise you, I was going to tell him. He's much more fragile than he's letting you see, and I was waiting until he was more stable to tell him." He raised Owyn's hand to his lips and kissed his knuckles. "I took his place. When I realized how bad it was, how much worse it was going to get...I changed places. Pulled Alanar so deep that he didn't know what was happening. So...in a way, I suppose you can say he did black out." Virrik closed his eyes. "He's angry at me. But I would do it again in a heartbeat. I knew his body would heal. He'd hurt, until Jehan or Aven took away the pain. But his mind and his heart? He didn't experience it. He'll wonder what happened. Why he hurts. I can let him know if he needs to know. But even then, it's removed. It happened to someone else. He'll be horrified that it happened, but it didn't happen to him."

Owyn nodded slowly. "And...if it was that bad...Virrik, what about you?" he asked.

Virrik smiled slightly. "As silly as it is to say? I can live with it. I can live with knowing I protected our Alanar from that." He closed his eyes. "Yes, I do still love you, you silly bird. I never stopped loving you."

"You called him a silly bird?" Owyn bit his lip to keep from giggling.

"Only when he was being one." Virrik shrugged. "I'll get out of the way now. But that's your answer. He won't remember what happened because he wasn't there. And...yeah, guessing won't do either of you any good. I really doubt your imaginations are that...twisted."

"Oh, fuck," Owyn breathed. He squeezed Virrik's hand a little tighter. "I...Virrik...thank you."

Virrik shook his head. "If I could have done more, I would have."

"Why didn't you hurt him?" Owyn asked. "I mean...he was touching you! You could have...Allie broke Teva's arms. And he killed someone, without even touching them."

Virrik's eyes widened. "I knew about Teva. But...Allie *killed* someone? Without touching them? He did that?" He shook his head. "Owyn, that honestly never occurred to me. I took over when I realized that what was happening was..." He paused. "If I'd let Allie stay forward...it might have saved you both a lot of grief." He cocked his head to the side. "Allie says no. It might have been worse. Because then he'd have been a healer who misused his power to harm a patient, and you and Jehan would have had to deal with that. Wren really thought this through, didn't he?"

"What's the penalty?" Owyn asked. "I mean, I know I'll find out when we catch Risha, but what might have happened?"

A long pause. "I'll ask Jehan to explain," Alanar answered in his own voice. "We should tell him this. All of this."

"Later," Owyn said. He turned and tugged Alanar into his arms. "Right now, we're safe, we're private, and you're all mine. And...look, I'm still sorry."

"It still wasn't your fault, and I accept your apology." Alanar shifted so that he was resting in Owyn's arms, his head on Owyn's shoulder. He sighed, a contented sound, and Owyn felt him relaxing. "We're safe, and private and...what are we going to do about that?"

Owyn smiled and turned his head to kiss Alanar on the forehead. "I'm leaving it up to you, love."

Chapter Twenty-Six

The canopy faced the lake. It was wide, and Aria thought that they'd set it up to combine features of both the Hall and the Little Council room — there were five low-backed chairs set near the center of the canopy, with a carpet on the ground before them, and small tables between the chairs. Behind the chairs was a long trestle table, ringed with stools, and on which Aria could see the map that Owyn had been working on through the beginning of the Progress.

"Steward, have we had this the entire time?" Aria asked, resting her hand on the back of one of the chairs. "I don't recognize any of this furniture."

"No," Steward answered. "Well, we had the canopy, but the furnishings came from Frayim's people." He looked at the Seer, who smiled. "From what I understand, Owyn isn't the only one who had a wagon waiting for him."

Aria blinked. "A wagon? One of the houses on wheels? Frayim, I don't think I would fit in one—"

"Yours is a storage wagon, not a living one," Frayim said. "These furnishings, a few other things. Things we'll need as we go north." He smiled. "We've been preparing for you for a long time, Aria."

"Now, I took the liberty of fetching Owyn's map from the coach," Steward said, gesturing to the table. "We need to update it, and I want to hear about Wolf Ford. Aria, you said that Copper wrote with a good hand. Do you have his notes?"

"In my writing desk," Aria answered as they sat down at the table. "The meeting was very pleasant. It was their headman and their village elders. The headman is quite young to be in the position, but he told us that his mother died last winter, and he was named headman then. He hasn't had an easy time of it. Wolf Ford was hard hit with the tremors when the Smoking Mountain exploded. Then they were attacked by the raiders, and Hearthstone...well, we know why Hearthstone sent no aid when they called for assistance. I encouraged him to reach out to Grytha. I think they'll get on well together." She paused, thinking. "Rodic. That's his name. He told us that his mother was distantly related to Risha's father, but Risha's mother wasn't from Wolf's Ford, and Rodic wasn't sure where she did come from. They both died quite some years ago, and Risha has no immediate family left in the area. At least, that he knows of. All of this is in the notes. I want to compare it to what Pirit knows. From what I remember being told in Terraces, it seems that what Risha told Pirit about her family history was entirely fabricated." She paused again. "There are good people in Wolf Ford. They've sheltered people from Newmarket—"

"What happened there?" Steward interrupted. "I'm assuming they know?"

"They were taken by an ague, Rodic said. After the tremors. He thinks something may have fouled their well. The survivors left, and some of them are in Wolf Ford now. Including Rodic's new bride. They've settled in nicely, as have some Wanderers who had need. Rodic told me that they heard we were coming from the Wanderers." She paused again as Frayim chuckled. "He was quite curious about us, and about what is happening in the rest of the world. When we told him what had happened, and what

Risha has done, he was horrified. He declared right there that Risha is barred from ever returning to Wolf Ford, and that they'll have none of her. The elders supported him in that."

"Surprising," Steward murmured. "Pirit was very...emphatic about how...backwards she considered the thinking in the border villages. I wonder if she ever verified any of Risha's claims."

"It appears not," Aria said. "And I will say that Cellan was as surprised as you are. He said that he warned you?"

Steward nodded. "He did. Said that it wouldn't be safe to bring you there. So I'm very surprised at the positive reception you received." He frowned and looked down at the table, and at the map that had been rolled out and weighed down on the surface. "We'll have to update this."

"Once Owyn is available," Aria said. "Where is Cellan?"

"Cellan is...let me think." Steward looked thoughtful. Then he nodded. "Oh, of course. One of the wagons broke an axle. He's working on repairs. That's out near where the guards are drilling. We'll speak to him later." He looked around. "And speaking of people I should speak to, has anyone seen Memfis? I haven't seen him since you got here."

Aria looked at Del, who shrugged and signed, *"He was with Jehan and Aleia when we got here. Is he still with them?"*

Steward frowned. "Possibly. I'll go and see once we're done. Frayim, how badly was he hurt?"

Frayim looked startled at being asked. "I would have to ask the healers for specifics, but I think there was bone pressing on his brain, and bleeding inside. And I think he is perhaps feeling somewhat fragile."

"Understandable," Steward said. "Thank you. And I wonder at how he's feeling with everyone making a fuss over Owyn. He may be feeling neglected."

"Memfis?" Aria asked. "Oh. I hadn't thought of that. We'll go once we're done here." She looked down at the map. "I think perhaps we will stay here a day. Give everyone a chance to know each other, and all of us need to learn how to proceed." She rested both hands on the table. "We've had no time to..." She paused, then closed her eyes. "No time to mourn. Memfis especially." She looked up. "When was the last time Owyn danced?"

Steward blinked. "I...I don't remember. When he projected, I think. It feels as if it's been a thousand years since, doesn't it?"

"It does. I will ask him if he will. If he can..." She stopped and straightened. "Frayim, what do you know?"

"Many things," Frayim answered. "And occasionally nothing at all. About what?"

Aria couldn't help it — she laughed, and he smiled in response. "You did that on purpose?" she asked.

"I did." He leaned down to look closely at the map. "This is lovely work. I know all of these places. But there are some places I know that aren't on the map."

"You'll have to sit down with Owyn as we go, then," Steward said. "Now, Aria?"

"Frayim, what do you know about my father?"

Frayim looked up. "The Firstborn who was," he answered. "And who, if we succeed, will be again. What of him?"

Aria smiled. "You know he's alive." When Frayim nodded, she continued. "Owyn can reach him when he dances. It may help Memfis to hear from my father."

"It may." Frayim smiled broadly. "I've never seen a Smoke Dancer dance. I would like to."

"We will talk to Owyn later, then." Aria turned back to Steward. "What else was there that we needed to discuss? And

Frayim, are there settlements or towns near here? While we're camped here, we should reach out to them."

"IT'S A LITTLE HEALING center in here," Aven said as he finished his examination of the healing tent — a long tent like the Heir's tent, but separated with curtains into one larger area and four private examination spaces. "This is nice. We...we didn't have this before, did we?"

"We had the tent, but it was apparently Afansa's idea to set it up like this, so that we can see to people who need a healer while we're camped." Jehan looked around. "I like this arrangement. We'll make this standard for healers when we're traveling. Which I think we'll be doing a lot of, until we get our numbers back where they should be." He looked around again. "Right. When we're camped, we'll set up a rotation to man the tent, the same as we would in the healing center in the Palace."

"There are candidates among the Wanderers," Dyneh said. "We were going to send them on to Terraces, but Frayim said we should wait for you to come to us." She smiled when the other healers turned to look at her. "I'm not a very good teacher. I can show the very basics of healing, but I can't assess, and once we're past the basics, I'm out of my depths. All of the potentials are physical healers, not mind-healers. Which reminds me. You wanted me to speak to someone?"

Jehan nodded slowly. "Introduce me," he said. "And I'll start their lessons as soon as I know what we're doing. And I wanted you to speak to Treesi." He turned. "Treesi, what do you...where did she go?"

Aven looked around. "She was right here. And...Memfis?" He walked over and moved the curtain to look into one of the examination spaces. "Mem is gone, too."

"You're looking for Treesi and Memfis?" Aleia asked as she came into the tent. She went to Jehan's side and shared breath with him, then stayed next to him, holding his hand. "I just saw them. They're walking down by the lake."

Jehan frowned. "Mem has been feeling...off. Ever since he woke up. I was going to examine him again, make sure we didn't miss anything."

"Fa, we didn't miss anything," Aven said. "He's healthy—"

"And heart-sick," Dyneh said. "His arm...that's recent, isn't it? It felt recent."

"A few months now," Aven answered.

"I think he's feeling the lack," Dyneh said. She glanced back at the tent-flap. "I'm thinking that he's telling himself that if he'd had both arms, he'd have been able to protect himself and his son, and possibly several other impossible things."

Aleia looked quizzically at her. "How do you know they'd be impossible?"

"Because the same guards who attacked Owyn and Memfis also attacked and took down that very capable-looking guard captain," Dyneh answered. "He looks like he could beat a bear before breakfast. If they could take him down, then Memfis didn't have much of a chance."

Jehan nodded. "You have a point. Several points. And someone tell Karse that he beats bears before breakfast. I want to see his face." He sighed. "Treesi noticed he was hurting, and she took him off. That..."

"That is Treesi in a nutshell," Aleia finished. "She'll be very good once she's fully trained, if this is how she works on instinct."

Jehan nodded. "Truth. However, since she's not fully trained, I think one of us should go and support her."

"I'll go," Aven offered. "Unless you want to...examine him privately?"

To Aven's surprise, his father blushed. Aleia laughed.

"Go on, Ven. If Memfis needs more, we'll claim him later." She took Jehan's arm. "Let's go watch the guards drill. I might join them."

"Really?" Jehan sounded skeptical. "Woman, I don't want to have to put you back together."

Aven headed for the tent flap, hearing footsteps behind him. He turned to see Dyneh,

"You limp, very slightly," she said, falling in next to him.

"I hadn't realized that I was," Aven admitted. "I must have strained it. My hip was...well, absolutely destroyed would be putting it mildly. It took four healers in merge over two days to rebuild it." He shrugged. "It'll never be the same, but it's much better than it was."

Dyneh didn't say anything, and Aven looked at her to see an expression that was tantalizingly familiar. He chuckled. "Owyn makes the same face."

"What?" Dyneh looked at him. "What face?"

"The 'I want to ask a question but I don't want to be rude' face." He smiled. "You want to know what happened."

Dyneh blushed slightly. "I do, but not if it will upset you."

"Risha happened," Aven said. "She's been murdering Waterborn, trying to break the cycle of the change. And I survived, somehow. She'd love to get her hands on me again to figure out how."

"Break the cycle of the change?" Dyneh frowned. "I...why?"

"Because she thinks it will make us human, instead of animals," Aven answered. "It's how Virrik died."

"And how he ended up in Alanar's head?" Dyneh shook her head. "That's horrible. And...Jax said that we'll never know how many she killed. That's monstrous."

"We'll find her, and she'll pay," Aven said. "And once I'm done helping Treesi, I should go and dance. If I'm limping, I need to."

"Dance?"

Aven smiled. "Come with me to the drilling ground when we're done. I'll show you how Water dances." He looked down the gentle slope toward the lake, where he could see Memfis, throwing a stone at the water. Treesi was standing next to him. As he watched, she picked up a stone, then threw it. She threw it oddly, slightly sideways, and a series of rippling rings in the water showed the path of the stone as it skipped across the surface.

"Now you do it. Try again," Aven heard her say.

"How did you do that?" Aven called. She turned and grinned.

"You've never skipped stones?" she asked. "I learned this when I was little. The healing center where I grew up was on a lake, and my brother taught me. And I was teaching Memfis, because he doesn't know either." She picked up another rock, turning it over in her hands. "Eli said that when you had heavy things bothering you, to put them in the stone, and see how many times you can get it to skip." She threw it, and Aven counted five rings before the stone sank. Treesi made a face. "Only five."

"How many have you gotten?" Dyneh asked.

"My best is twelve," Treesi answered. "But Eli got twenty once. You need the right stone, and a nice, smooth lake." She stooped, picking up another stone. "Memfis, try again."

Memfis took the stone from her, and mimicked her sideways throw. And laughed out loud as three rings appeared, one after the other. "I did it!" He turned, smiling. "All right. It's not impossible."

"And you'll get better, if you practice," Treesi said. She handed him another rock. "It's like anything. If you practice, you get good at it. And if you give up...you don't."

Memfis looked down at the stone in his hand, then back at Treesi. "Is that what I'm doing? Giving up?"

"Without barely trying," Treesi said. She threw another stone; it danced across the surface, leaving nine circles trailing behind it. "You've got yourself convinced you can't. But you haven't really tried. And...well, we're partly to blame. All of us. We've been coddling you." She looked over at Memfis. "You don't need coddling. Not anymore. You need to practice doing."

Memfis frowned. He threw the stone he was holding, and it vanished beneath the surface. He growled, then muttered, "I couldn't protect my mother. Or my boy—"

"Against four fully trained guards? Who were capable of taking down Karse?" Aven said. "Dyneh, what did you say?"

"That Karse looks as if he could beat bears before breakfast," Dyneh said, and Aven watched Memfis' lips twitch.

"Anyone tell him that?" he asked, sounding as if he was trying not to laugh.

"Not yet," Aven answered. "Fa wants to see his face."

"So do I," Memfis said. "All right. Point made. Even when I had both arms, I couldn't have taken them. I'm twenty-five years out of practice. But it's still galling that they took me down so easily."

Treesi nodded. "I understand. And the only way to change that is to see what you can do now."

Memfis looked at him. He nodded slowly, then looked out at the water. He held his hand out. "Let me have another one of those. I want to try again. Then...maybe we'll go talk to Karse and see what else I need to practice."

OWYN YAWNED AND LOOKED over his shoulder. Alanar's eyes were closed. "You asleep?"

Alanar smiled slightly, but didn't open his eyes. "Yes."

Owyn laughed and turned in the circle of Alanar's arms. "Talking in your sleep, then? Or is that Virrik?"

"No, it's me," Alanar answered, and opened his eyes. "I like this. It's comfortable. And there's just enough room."

"Not enough room if we want Del in here," Owyn pointed out. He slid one hand up Alanar's side, and his husband hummed happily and closed his eyes. "Or anyone else."

"We have the bigger bed in the tent if we want company," Alanar said. He yawned and pulled Owyn closer. "Oh. Speaking of company..."

"Del?"

"No," Alanar paused, then smiled. "Remember I said that if I could have a child, I would?"

"If you're going to tell me you figured out how to get pregnant—"

Alanar burst out laughing, hard enough that the wagon rocked gently. "No!" he gasped. "No, I started thinking more about it. And about how among the Earth tribes, sometimes women will volunteer to carry a child for married men who want a family."

Owyn nodded slowly. "You told me about that. I remember. Why...wait. You had someone volunteer? Who?" He mentally ran down a list of Earthborn women in the Progress. Not Treesi. She was already pregnant. Who else...

"You're talking about Trista, aren't you?" he asked.

"She's already besotted with you, love. And with me." Alanar blushed at the admittance. "I…"

"Allie, did you sleep with her?" Owyn asked.

"No," Alanar admitted. "But she offered. She was trying to help. I was scared, and…Trista offered. I said no. I spent that night with Aria and Treesi." He rolled onto his back. "Trista loves all of us. And is terrified that she'll be dismissed if she tells anyone."

"We wouldn't do that!" Owyn propped himself up on his elbow. "Let me guess. Nestor would have?"

"I think so." Alanar closed his eyes. "We should get up. Get dressed. And think more about this. Then we can talk to her and see what she thinks. We have time to think this through."

Owyn nodded. He sat up and twisted to face Alanar. "If we do this, I think it should be you and Trista."

Alanar frowned. "Why?"

"Because Aria wants a baby with me, and I think Treesi does, too. I'll have two. At least two. So there will be little Owyns running around. I want one of our children to be a little you."

Alanar blinked. Then he smiled. "I like that. All right. We'll discuss this more, and then we'll talk to Trista." He tipped his head to the side. "And…keeping this to ourselves?"

"Until we're decided, and Trista says yes? Yes." Owyn ran his hand down Alanar's chest. "Just for us. For now."

Chapter Twenty-Seven

They heard shouting and cheering as they walked through the camp, and Owyn looked around.

"That sounds like people are having a lot of fun," he said. "Are they having a party without us?"

"That's not fair," Alanar said. "Sounds like it's coming from that direction." He pointed. "What's that way?"

"No idea." Owyn took his hand and they made their way down the row of tents to where the noise was coming from. A crowd had gathered around an area enclosed by cords, and inside, Owyn could see Karse, armed with a wooden practice sword. And to Owyn's shock, his opponent was Memfis.

"Mother of us all!" he breathed. "Mem?"

"What's he doing?" Alanar asked.

"Fighting!" Owyn pulled him along a little faster. "Against Karse!"

"What?" Alanar gasped. "He can fight? What's he fighting with? He doesn't have smoke blades."

"A sword." Owyn couldn't look away from his adoptive father. "I've never seen him fight with a sword before. I didn't know he could!" He saw Aven in the crowd and headed for him, tugging Alanar along with him. "Fishie, what is this?" he asked as they reached him.

"Memfis is testing his limits," Aven answered, not looking away from the fight. "Treesi is an excellent healer."

Owyn frowned, not sure what one had to do with the other. He looked past Aven, and saw Aria and Treesi sitting in chairs on his other side. Dyneh was standing on Treesi's far side, and Del was sitting on the ground at Aria's feet.

"So...this is a good thing?" Alanar asked.

"It's a very good thing," Aven answered. He glanced at Owyn and smiled. "And I'm glad you're here to see it. Mem is feeling...fragile. And useless. He thinks he should have been able to protect you."

"Against four guards?" Owyn looked out at the fighters. "I've never seen him fight like that. Ever. I didn't know he could."

"He and Milon had a swordmaster when they were both in Forge," Jehan said as he came up behind Owyn. "Mem practiced with Milon at the Palace, but he told us he hasn't touched a sword in years, because he had to be Fisher, and Fisher didn't know how. But he was good back then. Milon fought well, too. It's why he wanted to learn from Aleia. It was a style he didn't know."

Aria looked up. "I didn't know that," she said. "My mother never told me that."

Jehan smiled. "I'll tell you all kinds of stories, if you want." He nodded toward the fighters. "Watch."

Owyn saw a flash of movement, and looked back at the fighters in time to see Aleia come out of nowhere and attack. Memfis laughed, stepping back and blocking her strike. Karse moved in...and a moment later, Memfis was on his back in the grass.

Laughing.

Karse tucked his practice sword under his arm and went to offer Memfis his hand. "Satisfied?"

"I'm out of practice!" Memfis protested, letting Karse help him up. Aleia came up behind him and dusted grass and dirt off his back.

"We can work on that," she said, hugging Memfis. "But honestly, Mem, it'll take time for you to get back to the point of taking on two opponents again. We'll have to work on it."

"Again?" Owyn squeaked. Memfis turned toward him, and his smile grew even wider.

"Didn't realize we had this large an audience," he said. He turned back to Karse. "Thank you for humoring me."

"Thanks for the workout," Karse said, wiping his face. "Been a while since I got run through my paces like that. Tomorrow?"

Memfis nodded. "If I can move tomorrow," he agreed. He handed the practice sword to Karse and put his arm around Aleia's shoulders as they walked off the field. He stopped in front of them and grinned at Owyn. "Surprise?"

"You never told me you could fight," Owyn said. "Not with a sword."

"Fisher couldn't," Memfis said. "I didn't even own a sword when we were in Forge. The last time I did was..." He paused and looked down at Aleia. "We practiced the morning before, didn't we? You, me and Milon?"

Aleia frowned. Then she nodded. "Yes, we did. Mem, how do you remember that?"

Memfis shrugged. "I remember when we were happy. I think I want to swim. And maybe throw more rocks."

"Throw...throw rocks?" Owyn repeated. "Mem...did my mother put your brains back sideways or something? You're not making sense."

Memfis laughed. "No, I'm fine. I'm fine. And Treesi...Treesi, where are you?" He turned and saw her sitting next to Aria. "You haven't taught them?"

"Not yet," Treesi answered. "Owyn, do you know how to skip stones?"

Owyn blinked. "I...maybe it's my brains that are sideways. Stones skip?"

Treesi got out of her chair. "Come on. We'll go down to the lake and swim, then I'll show you."

"Before we go, I promised Mama Dyneh I'd show her how Water dances," Aven said. "Where's Othi?" He turned. "Othi! Come dance?"

Othi cut across the empty field. "Sword?"

"No, just for show." Aven turned to his mother. "Come dance with us?"

"Which one?" Aleia asked.

Aven frowned. "Ah...Tapa?"

Aleia nodded. "That's a good one for showing off. All right. You lead." She and Aven walked away, meeting Othi in the field. They spoke for a moment, then stood in a line, facing the chairs. Aven shouted, something that Owyn didn't understand, and they all three started moving in unison. It was more explosive than the sword dance, and louder — they were shouting, slapping chest and legs and arms as they stamped and moved in unison. Where the sword dance was dangerous and fluid, this was threat and challenge. Owyn glanced at Jehan, and saw his lips moving.

"Why aren't you out there with them?" he murmured. Jehan looked at him and shook his head.

"Not my place. I know the dance, but it's not my place to be out there."

Dyneh came over to join them, putting her hand on Owyn's shoulder. "And this dance is for...what?"

Jehan grinned. "Weddings. This is what a man faces when he joins his wife's canoe. All her male relatives challenge him, and he'd better not flinch. There's a response to the challenge, and he dances that part, letting them know that he's willing to fight for the right to take his place at her side. When he's done, they all dance together, the bride included." He smiled slightly. Sadly. "It's amazing to see."

"And you didn't get that," Aria said, looking up at them. "You were never recognized by Aleia's mother."

"No, but I have been recognized by Neera. I'm part of the canoe now. I just...never got the dance. Because it didn't feel right to claim it after twenty-five years. And...well, I'm not Water."

"You are." Owyn jumped at the sound of Steward's voice behind him. Steward chuckled. "Sorry to sneak up on you, Owyn. Jehan, if Elcam was right about you being his son, then you're part Water through your grandmother. You could claim that." He nodded toward the field. "Go challenge them, Jehan."

Jehan looked at Steward, then back out at the dancers. "I...should probably not spring that on Aleia. Let me talk to her. Then...we can do it when we get back, if Neera agrees."

"In front of all the canoes," Aria said. "The way it should have been."

Jehan smiled. "Don't start planning the feast just yet, Aria. Let me talk to Aleia."

On the field, the explosive dance ended, and Othi burst out laughing.

"Never thought I'd get to do that one!" he declared.

Treesi immediately turned in her chair, her eyes wide. "Aria? Do you think...?"

Aria nodded slowly. "It will have to wait until we get back to the Palace," Aria said. "I want to talk to Neera and see if it is appropriate."

Treesi jumped up and kissed Aria, making Del roll out of the way to keep from being stepped on. "Thank you!" Then she looked down at Del, sprawled on the ground and laughing. "Oh, I'm sorry!"

Del waved one hand and got to his feet, dusting his trousers off. *"We're going swimming now?"* he signed.

"I think that sounds lovely," Aria said.

"And when you're done, I'd like to update the map, and discuss our plans for the rest of the Progress," Steward added. "We'll need to confer with Frayim and his people over the route and what to expect."

Aria nodded and stood up. "We'll do that over the evening meal."

THE MEETING ENDED UP happening after the evening meal. Once everyone had been fed and the kitchen area cleaned, Huris and Dyneh excused themselves, taking Afansa off to talk about something to do with the camp, while Aleia joined Karse for a review of the guards. Aria and the Companions gathered around the table under the canopy. They were joined by Alanar, Othi, Steward, Frayim, Jehan and Memfis. Aria sat at the head of the table, her chin propped on one hand, watching as Owyn went over the map one more time, tracing their route so far with one finger, then laying aside his pen.

"I think that's everything," he said. "Once we're back to the Palace, I'll want to send people to double check the new boundaries around Forge to make sure I've got them right. But I think we're up to date now." He looked across the table, to where Steward was standing. "Will this be enough to get the work started on the roads?"

"It's enough to start the process," Steward said. "We'll need to find people who know how to do the work, but that's what the census is for. And I'm hoping that when we get back to the

Palace, we'll have an accurate accounting of everyone who settled in Terraces from Forge. That's where we'll find our surveyors, I think, and the specialists." He looked around. "Frayim, did you take in any Forge refugees?"

Frayim was sitting on the ground, his back against a tent pole, and looked up at the sound of his name. Howl was in his lap, snoring audibly as Frayim petted him. "We took in several," he answered. "But they went on with the groups that went to Terraces. Our ways...well, people who are used to living in one place sometimes don't adapt well to Wanderers' ways. They want a house that doesn't move. But you'll find the people you need."

"Is that prophecy?" Aven asked, turning in his chair at Aria's right.

Frayim smiled. "No, that's faith." He shifted the sleeping puppy to the crook of his arm and got to his feet, unfolding himself effortlessly from the ground and coming around the table to stand next to Owyn. "This is a beautiful piece of work. I've never seen all of Adavar depicted on a page like this."

"There's stuff missing, though," Owyn said, looking up at him. "You know this area. What are we missing?"

Frayim frowned, then reached down and tapped the map. "We're here, yes? This is Mirror Lake?" He ran his finger over the road, heading north. "There are small settlements all along this road. Places where refugees stopped and stayed. There was a healing center here—" He looked across the table at Treesi. "Where you began, I think."

"We're that close?" Treesi leaned forward. "That's...how many days, Owyn?"

Owyn frowned, measuring the map with his finger. "Two weeks? Maybe? Maybe more. Hard to say. I'm not sure how fast we'll be moving once we get started again." He nodded. "Call it two weeks."

"There was nothing there when last we ranged that far north. The Western Road is here," Frayim continued, tapping the map. "And this is where many of my folk will leave us. There are more settlements along that road, and we may wish to stay a day or two at the crossroads there, to give them a chance to come and see." He paused, and frowned. "And from that point, my vision is clouded. There are too many things that may happen for me to see clearly. I do know that this area past the Western Road is dangerous." He touched the map north of the Western Road. "We've had to stop going to the Solstice village because of the wolves that live between the crossroads and the mountains."

"Wolves?" Karse said as he and Aleia arrived. "What about wolves?" He grinned. "Not my wolf, I'm guessing. He likes you. He only sleeps like that on people he likes."

Frayim looked down at the puppy. "I like him. And no, not your wolf. Human wolves, preying on travelers. On Wanderers. We couldn't fight them, so we stayed to the south of the crossroads, and let them have the north." He shrugged and straightened. "They may not attack a caravan as large as this one, but once we reach the crossroads, we will have to be very careful."

Karse nodded. "Understood." He frowned. "Frayim, how many of your people do you think would be willing to train with my guards?"

Frayim cocked his head to the side. "There will be some. Felix and Ulla will both be interested, I think. And they'll bring others."

"I haven't heard anything about raiders or bandits in that area," Steward said. "Nothing ever was reported to the Palace. How long has it been happening?"

Frayim shrugged. "It's been growing for years. Their forces reached the point where we began avoiding them..." He paused, frowning. "Three years? Two? I have trouble keeping time straight. Huris would know."

Steward nodded, looking down at the map. "I'll ask him. Something should have been done about this before now."

Aria looked at the map, and reached out to touch the spot on the map where the healing center had been. "Treesi, you never speak of your family. I didn't even know your mother's name until I asked you at the Palace." She paused. "I don't know anything else about your family. Did they survive when the healing center was razed? Will we meet them?"

"I..." Treesi looked startled. "I...don't know that I would want you to meet them." She paused, clasping her hands in her lap. "I...Jehan? I...I haven't been entirely truthful. When I went to Terraces. I wasn't sent. I...I escaped." She looked down at her hands. "What Pirit said, about the border villages being backwards? That was my healing center. Backwards. Completely."

"You said something about that, in the coach," Aria said. "That they'd have believed the spindrift. Remember?"

"I remember," Treesi said. "My parents were healers. But they were...closed minded. Like Risha, a bit. Different was bad, and...well, they didn't want me to be a healer. Not more than the basics. I didn't need it, they told me, because I was a girl, and I didn't see right, so it was wasted on me."

"They said what?" Jehan asked. He came over to crouch next to Treesi's chair. "Sweetheart, you're a fine healer."

Treesi didn't look up. "They didn't think so. And they told me that they had someone who wanted a woman to bear his children, and he wanted me. But I didn't want that, so I ran away. I joined the caravan heading west, and I went to the healing center and I told Pirit that I was sent for more training, and she believed me. I never thought I'd come back here. And...well, when the healing center fell, and they never came to Terraces, I...I was relieved. Because I didn't have to worry about them finding me anymore." She shook her head. "I'm sorry."

"You did what you had to do," Othi said. He rested his hand on her arm. "Treesi, you didn't do anything wrong."

She looked at him, her face so pale her freckles stood out in stark contrast. Othi smiled and put his arms around her, holding her as she started sobbing into his chest. Aria sat up straighter and looked around the table.

"I wonder," she murmured. "Rodic didn't know where Risha's mother came from. I wonder if perhaps we were looking in the wrong place. If the source of this twisted belief wasn't Fire at all, but Earth." She touched the map, tapping her finger near where the healing center had been. "This place...it's so isolated. How often would someone from the Palace have come here? Someone from the main healing center? How often would they have heard from someone outside their own ranks?"

Jehan didn't stand up. He shook his head. "I don't know. That's a question for Mother, or for Rhexa. I haven't been Senior Healer long enough. I'm guessing not often. Not once travel was constrained. The poison there had a chance to take root."

"Weeds, Aunt Rhexa called it," Owyn said. "Pull the weeds. Looks like this is where it was coming from? This area, I mean?"

"And this was why it was so easy for you to believe the lies," Alanar added. "Because you grew up being fed that poison. Trees, why didn't you tell us?"

Treesi's voice was muffled. "I didn't tell anyone. I couldn't tell anyone, or I'd be sent back." She sniffled and raised her head, wiping her face. "I couldn't go back."

Jehan rested his hand on her shoulder. "Treesi, you're not going back. And I don't blame you." He got back to his feet.

"Trees, when you got to us, you already had a good grounding," Alanar said. "You were good. If they didn't want you to learn—"

"I have three brothers. Had three brothers," Treesi said. "They were all healers. Astur taught me. He's my twin. He's older than me by five minutes. As he learned, he taught me." She looked at Othi, then back at Alanar. "That was the hardest thing I had to do. I had to leave him behind. He told me to go, and helped me get out, but he wouldn't come with me." She sniffed. "That's my big regret. That he never knew that I did it. That I'm a Healer." She looked at Othi again, reaching out to take his hand. "That I have all of you, and I'm happy."

Aven reached past his father and rested his hand on Treesi's shoulder. "He knew, Treesi. I'm sure he knew. He knew you'd do amazing things. That's why he told you to go."

"And you did do amazing things," Othi added. "And you'll keep doing amazing things. Because you are amazing." He put his arm around Treesi. "And I love you. We love you." He gestured around the table. "All of us. We all love you."

Chapter Twenty-Eight

They lingered over the table until it was dark enough that Steward lit lanterns. Conversations turned to plans and travel, and discussions of how to organize all of the wagons. It was during a lull in the conversation that Owyn heard music.

"What's that?" he asked, looking around. "Where's the music coming from?"

Frayim sat up straight in his chair. "Is it that late?" he asked. "Is it moonrise?"

"Yes," Steward said. "Why?"

Frayim smiled and stood up. "Because it's time to sing the moon," he answered. "It...come with me. It's easier to show you." He walked out from under the canopy. Aria stood, so Owyn wiped his pen and corked his ink bottle before standing up and taking Alanar's hand. They followed Frayim toward the music.

"This is our way," Frayim called over his shoulder as he walked. "Most nights, we sing the moon. We didn't last night, because there were clouds. But if we can see the moon, we sing." He led the way back to the kitchen tent, where Owyn could see a crowd gathered around the fire.

"Frayim, there you are!" Dyneh called as she came toward them. "I was just coming to find you. We can't start without you."

"I hadn't realized it was so late," Frayim answered. "I'm here now." He kissed Dyneh's cheek, passed her and was almost immediately surrounded by children, all clamoring for a story. Dyneh laughed, and joined Owyn and the others.

"Did he explain?" she asked.

"Not much," Aria answered. "Singing the moon?"

Dyneh nodded. "It's a Wanderer tradition. When the sky is clear and the moon rises, they sing the moon. It's not just singing, though. There are stories and dancing, and just being together. It's time for family. When we first came to the Wanderers, we needed that." She took Owyn's free hand. "Come and sing with us."

They joined the circle of people, and Owyn saw Frayim sitting near the fire, surrounded by children, Copper and Danir among them. Frayim smiled and looked at the children.

"What story?" he asked.

An immediate cacophony of voices as all of the children shouted their choices. Frayim held up one hand, and the sound faded away.

"Let's have our new friends choose," he said. "Danir? Copper? Would you pick?"

Danir looked at Copper, and the two boys whispered together for a moment before Copper said, "The first story."

Frayim smiled. "Very good." He leaned forward, resting one elbow on his knee and waving his left arm in a wide circle. "Worlds begin. Worlds end. Worlds begin again..."

Dyneh hugged Owyn's arm and guided him over to where Huris was sitting. "He's an excellent storyteller," she murmured. "Come sit with us."

Owyn guided Alanar down to sit with his parents, and watched as the others found places around them. Del came and sat down on the ground, leaning back against Owyn's legs. Owyn smiled and ran his fingers through Del's hair.

"*It's good to have you back,*" Del murmured in his mind.

Owyn leaned into Alanar's side and listened to Frayim telling the first story, the story of the Mother and Axia, the first Firstborn.

"He is very good," Steward said from somewhere behind Owyn.

Dyneh nodded. "He is. And the children love him."

Frayim's story ended, and people laughed and clapped until someone started singing. The children scattered as Frayim got to his feet, running off to their families. Danir and Copper went to sit with Karse and Afansa, who sat side by side near the edge of the group. Owyn closed his eyes and sighed as Alanar put his arm around him. Then someone tapped him on the shoulder.

"Shall we sing?" Aria asked.

"Like we did on the road?" Owyn asked, turning to look at her. She nodded, and he laughed. "Yeah, let's do that."

The singer finished, to more applause and appreciative laughter. As the sound fell away, Owyn started, hearing his mother's delighted laugh as he began, "*The sun is sinking in the west, the moon will soon be high. The stars have come to dance, the midnight festival is nigh.*" Aria's voice rose in sweet harmony, and a solid, deep voice joined as well, one that Owyn felt in his bones and knew at the very core of his being.

His father.

He looked to the side, and saw Huris wink at him. He grinned, and closed his eyes to better fall into the music. The song went on forever, and not nearly long enough, and the applause as they finished was almost as rewarding as Dyneh tugging him to his feet so she could hug him.

"That was wonderful!" she cried, her voice ever so slightly choked. "You sound so good together!"

"You do sound wonderful together," Frayim said as he came around the fire. "Thank you, for honoring us." He smiled broadly as he reached them. Then he blinked and turned, looking away from the fire into the shadows beyond the circle. "Who's there?"

Aven and Othi both jumped to their feet, moving to stand on either side of Frayim. Frayim shook his head. "No, it's not a threat," he murmured. Then he raised his voice. "Come out. You're welcome here." Something snapped out in the darkness, and darker shadows moved into the light, revealing themselves to be a man, a woman, and two small children. All of them were dirty and thin, their clothes ragged. Frayim smiled and walked toward them, holding his hands out. "You're welcome here. You're safe here. Come to the fire. Huris, find our new friends something to eat?"

"Jax, help me?" Huris said. Owyn followed Huris to the kitchen tent. By the time they came back, carrying a basket with bread and cheese and bowls of stew from their supper, the newcomers had been wrapped in blankets and seated near the fire. The woman was crying softly, and Aria was sitting with her, holding her hands.

"You're safe here," Aria said.

"You're here," the woman hiccupped. "You're real. We thought...we thought it was just a story. That what we were hearing was another lie. But you're really here. You're going to make everything good again."

BY THE TIME ARIA CRAWLED out of a delightfully overcrowded bed the next morning, there were five more families who had come into the camp overnight, looking for safety and sanctuary and following the rumors of the Heir. She and Aven met with all of them over breakfast, listening to them and learning their stories. Two of the families had come from Newmarket, and confirmed Rodic's report of fouled wells and sickness. Two families were from Forge, and hadn't yet found a place to settle and call home. And the last family — an older woman, a younger woman, and four small boys — had come from the north.

"T'aint safe north," the older woman said with a sniff, resting her hands on the tabletop.. "My son, Teek, he tried to stop them. Tried to protect me and his woman and his boys, you understand?" She took a deep breath and shook her head. "He didn't stand a chance. But we got away from them. And now...we're safe? But you're still going north?"

"You don't have to go north with us. At least, not all the way. When we reach the Western Road, there will be a group going west to Terraces," Aria said.

Aven rested his elbows on the table and laced his fingers together. "Mother, if you stay with us, we'll keep you safe. But if you'd rather not, we'll send people to protect you when you go west."

"Never been west. Never been anywhere but where I was born." She sniffed, then reached across the table and patted Aven's hands. "He's a good, solid one, this one." Aven grinned, then laughed out loud when the woman turned to Aria. "Good at the plowing?"

"Mama!" the younger woman gasped.

Aria bit back a laugh, glanced at a clearly-amused Aven, then rested her hand on the curve of her belly and answered, "I'd say yes."

The woman cackled, then patted Aria on the hand. "You'll do, my Heir," she said, nodding. "My name's Idaya." She gestured to the now-blushing woman sitting at her side. "Marzi is my heart daughter, and the boys are Telo, Fasa, Ricart and Mizah." She pointed to each child. None of the boys looked up — they were all focused on the porridge in their bowls.

"There are a dozen or more children their age in the camp," Aven said. "They'll be welcome."

"That's a good thing," Idaya said. "They haven't had much chance to be boys these past few months. Had to do a man's work, helping keep us going. It'll be good for them to be boys again."

Aria nodded. "I'll have my pages come and fetch them, so that they can introduce them to the others." She rested her hand on Idaya's arm. "You're safe here, Mother," she repeated. "And we'll get you all settled once we're done eating." She smiled as Owyn, Alanar and Del came to join them. "Good morning."

"Good morning," Owyn said. He leaned down to kiss her, then bowed to Idaya. "I...we haven't met, have we?"

"Owyn, Mother Idaya and her family joined us overnight," Aven answered. "We have five new families in the camp."

"Then it's a good thing we're staying here today, so everyone can get settled in together." Owyn led Alanar to a seat, then filled a bowl of porridge for him. "Where's my fa? Either of them?"

"Memfis is with Karse at the practice field," Huris said as he came up behind Owyn. "And I'm right behind you."

Owyn laughed. "Good morning! What are we planning today?"

"We'll be touring the camp today," Aria said. "So that we can meet our new traveling companions. Then I was hoping that you might feel well enough to dance?"

"Oh, you want me to see if there's anything?" Owyn served his own bowl of porridge and sat down next to Alanar. "I can do that. Later, when the practice field is empty. I think it's flat enough."

"You're going to dance for visions?" Huris took a deep breath. "Jax...I...will it bother you if I don't come to see you?"

Owyn looked startled. "You don't want to watch?" He stopped, turning to look past Alanar at Del. "Oh. Oh, I didn't think of that." He turned back to Huris. "When you're ready, Fa. I'm not going anywhere. I'll be here."

Huris smiled. "Now tell me what Del said," he said. "Your mother told me about the heart visions."

Del laughed, and Owyn nodded. "He said that you coming to watch me dance might not be a good thing for your head, because you can't dance anymore. And...since you haven't been around Smoke Dancers, you haven't dealt with not being able to. So we shouldn't force you to deal with it all at once."

Huris let out a short huff of breath. "He said all that? In that short a time?"

Owyn looked at Del and smiled, then back at his father. "He told me not to push because it would hurt you. I figured the rest on my own."

Huris nodded. "Thank you, Del. He's got a good head on his shoulders. And so do you." He looked around. "I need to go get some work done. We need to get the newcomers settled. And I need to see if Dyneh is available to help me, or find someone else. Do you need anything else?"

"Fa, I know how a kitchen works," Owyn said with a laugh. "You go do what you need to do."

Huris laughed and limped away, and Owyn turned to Del.

"Thanks," he said. "I didn't think of that. I mean...I should have. Mem did the same thing. He was a dancer. Now he's not. That's got to hurt."

"He'll see you dance when he's ready," Aven said. "There's time. And we can help him if he needs it."

"What happened to him?" Idaya asked. "If I might ask?"

"Head wound," Owyn answered. "In a riot in Forge. Someone hit him with a brick."

Idaya shook her head. "Lucky to be alive, then. And he knows it. You can see it in him." She looked at her daughter. "Marzi, you write with a good hand. When you're done, go see if you can help him. I'll mind the boys until they go off to meet the others."

"Yes, Mama." Marzi looked after Huris. "If I can find him." She looked back down at her bowl. "He's your father, Fireborn?"

"Yes," Owyn answered. "My mother is around here somewhere, too. I'll introduce you—

" To Aria's surprise, Marzi's shoulders slumped slightly. Owyn looked surprised, and stammered, "I...oh. Oh."

"He's not the only man in the camp, Marzi. You'll find someone," Idaya said gently. "Teek wouldn't want you to be lonely the rest of your days."

"I miss him," Marzi murmured. "And...I'm sorry, Fireborn—"

"You can call me Owyn." He looked in the direction his father had gone. "Really? My fa?"

"He has a kind eye." Marzi answered. "A good laugh, and a nice smile." She chuckled. "I need someone to be a good father to my boys. A kind man. Their father was kind."

"If you don't find someone to your liking here, then there are plenty of good people in Terraces," Aria said. She looked around. "Where is Treesi? Is she not having breakfast this morning?"

"Treesi was having a touch of vertigo this morning, and she and Othi were going to join us later. They both said that they didn't need me," Alanar said. "Trista is with them, and said that she'd come and get me if anything."

"Vertigo?" Aria asked. "She hasn't had that since the morning before we reached Hearthstone. Or has she, and I just didn't notice?"

"It's not as if you haven't been distracted," Alanar said. He shook his head. "Today was stronger than usual, she says. Once she gets her legs under her, she'll come and eat. Or try to."

"Is this Treesi pregnant? Is this Trista another healer?" Marzi asked. "Or a midwife?"

"She's our..." Owyn paused. "Well, I'm not sure what she is exactly, other than a friend."

"Trista is our valet," Alanar said. "And she's our friend."

"Do you have a midwife?" Marzi asked. "Or just healers?"

Aven chuckled. "I've never been called just a healer before," he said slowly. "And we did have a midwife, but she stayed behind in Terraces, and was going back to the Palace. After the last quake, she decided that the Progress was too much for her."

Marzi nodded. "You have a midwife again," she said. "I was our village midwife."

Aven smiled. "Good! I'll introduce you to my father when we're done here. He's the Senior Healer, and I'm sure he'll be glad to meet you." He nodded toward her bowl. "Once you finish your breakfast."

The boy sitting next to Marzi leaned forward. "May I ask a question?" he asked in a small voice.

"Of course," Aven answered. "Telo, right?" The boy nodded. "What do you want to know, Telo?"

"You're Water," Telo said. "What's it like? To breathe underwater?"

Aven grinned and looked at Owyn. "You asked me that once."

"And you told me it felt normal," Owyn answered. "Remember? It feels like it was years ago."

Aria laughed. "It was a year ago. Not even a year, and so much has changed."

Aven nodded. "It's normal for me, Telo. Being underwater, making the change? That's as normal to me as putting on trousers is for you. And breathing underwater for me is the same as breathing on land. It's just breathing."

Telo frowned slightly. Then he nodded. "It's the way you are," he said slowly. "And you've got nothing to compare it to?"

"Exactly. So it's a hard question to answer."

"Who drew on you?" the smallest boy blurted out. "Someone drew all over you. In ink. Mama got mad at me when I drew all over myself in ink."

Telo added, "It was days before it all came off."

"My ink isn't on my skin. It's part of my skin." Aven dipped his finger into his water cup, and drew it over his forearm. "It won't come off. It won't wash off."

"Really?"

"Really," Aven said with a nod. "It takes a long time, and it's done with a hammer and a special tool. It hurts, but not for long." He tapped his shoulder. "This one tells people what canoe my family is from. The rest of my arm and my chest are warrior marks." He held his hand up so that the back faced the boys, who were all staring in amazement. "This one marks me as a navigator."

Telo nodded. "Waterborn...can I be a warrior, too? Can I learn how?" He looked at Marzi. "I want to be a warrior. I want to be able to stand up to bad people, like my Fa did." He sat up a little straighter. "Fa was a warrior, wasn't he, Mama?"

"From what I've heard of him, your father stood up against the people who would have razed your village. He saved your lives," Aria said, looking at Idaya to see the older woman nodding. "That means that he was indeed a warrior."

"And our pages are learning to fight with the guard," Aven added. "Perhaps you can learn with them?"

Telo turned to his mother. "Mama, may I?"

"Before she says yes, we should talk to Karse," Owyn warned. "Just in case. We want him to say yes before your mother does. Just in case Karse says you're not old enough yet. We'll go see him after breakfast, and we'll talk to him." He looked past them. "Treesi!"

Aven stood up and let Othi settle Treesi into his chair. Aria poured some tea and put it in front of her, then filled a cup with salted fruit juice and passed it to Othi.

"How are you feeling?" she asked. "Owyn, would you fill a bowl?"

"Dizzy," Treesi said with a grimace. She took the bowl of porridge from Owyn, took a bite, then waited a moment. "That's going to stay, I think. Aria, were you this dizzy?"

"Every woman is different," Marzi said. "How far along are you?"

"I..." Treesi looked around.

"Marzi is a midwife," Aria explained. "She and her family joined us last night."

"Oh!" Treesi smiled. "I should know this, but there's a difference between reading about being pregnant and actually being pregnant. And I'm not entirely sure." She paused, looking at Othi. "I forgot to have my contraceptive block renewed before we left the Palace. I'd been forgetting for probably a week or two at that point. I was...distracted."

"I'm sorry," Othi murmured.

"I know. And I'm not complaining," Treesi said, then laughed. "Except when it feels like my legs are two different lengths. A month? Maybe? About a month, maybe a little more."

Marzi frowned slightly. "And it started when?"

"A few days ago," Othi answered. "Three?" He frowned. "Is it only three days? It can't be."

Owyn started counting on his fingers. "It started the morning we got to Hearthstone. That night was when Granna was killed. The next day was the funeral. The next day we headed for Newmarket and...well, things happened. The day after that was when you came up to the camp. And then today. Five days." He snorted. "That's a lot for five days."

"And it tells me that you're more than a month along," Marzi said. "Morning sickness starts midway through the second month, usually."

Othi hummed softly. Then he blushed. "That...that's about right," he murmured. "That...yeah." He turned to Treesi and smiled. "The first night out."

She giggled and leaned into his arm, and he put his arm around her. "So...a winter baby," she said. "We'll be back to the Palace by then."

"And everything will be fine," Othi added.

Alanar nodded. "From your mouth to the Mother's ears."

Chapter Twenty-Nine

"**I** didn't think that touring the camp was going to take all morning," Owyn said as they walked back to the Heir's tent. "I didn't realize how many people there are here."

"I don't think we saw enough of it to know that the Wanderer camp was a small town all by itself," Treesi agreed. "I don't think I've ever drunk that much tea. Ever."

Walking behind them, Frayim chuckled. "It's our way," he said. "When you come to visit a wagon or a tent, you are welcomed to their fire as part of their family."

"It's not all that different from the way they welcome people to one of the Water and Earth villages on the coast. At least, they did it in Serenity," Owyn said. "Mother Danzi was good at it, too. But in Shadow, they didn't do it. Barsis said it was old-fashioned."

"Is it similar?" Frayim asked. "I've never been to the coast. Or seen the sea." He looked thoughtful. "Perhaps one day."

"You don't know?" Aven asked, turning to look over his shoulder. "But you see so much—"

"I see all roads but mine," Frayim replied. "I see all the little streams, and how they come together to form a river. But after a point? They all blend into one, and I cannot see anything. I may see the sea someday. I'd like to." He smiled. "I don't see the way you do, Owyn. I don't have to dance to catch glimpses through the veil of time. I see...time. Constantly." He shrugged.

"Except for where and when I don't. The Mother doesn't show me everything. Just what I need to see. And if there's too much, too many threads? Then I can't see anything at all."

Owyn nodded. "Like when the Mother doesn't want me to change what I'm planning. She'll push me out of a vision." He stopped near the tent. "Let me get my blades, and I'll meet you at the practice field. It should be empty." The others walked on, and he ducked into the tent, grinning when he saw Trista. She turned, looking startled.

"Owyn!" she gasped.

"Didn't mean to scare you," Owyn said. "I came in for my blades and my book."

Trista blinked and looked around. "I...oh...the book..."

"Is in the traveling chest," Owyn said. "Thank you, by the way. For taking care of Treesi this morning."

Trista looked down slightly. "I like Treesi. I'm sorry she wasn't feeling well."

"Well, we have a midwife again, so she and Aria will have someone to ask questi—"

"Midwife?" Trista blurted. "Is Treesi pregnant?"

Owyn stared at her. "They didn't tell you?" he asked. "Yeah, we've known a couple of days. She and Othi are really happy about it."

Trista smiled. "Someday," she murmured. Then she blushed. "I'm sorry. I..."

"Friends, remember?" Owyn went to the travel trunk and took out the bag that held his book and drawing supplies, then picked up his blades. "Are you busy in here?"

Trista shook her head. "I was just tidying. Everything is done. I should go and see if anyone needs help."

"My fa does, and I'm not sure that my mother is available. Maybe you can help him? He's getting people settled in the camp." Owyn gestured toward the tent flap with his blades, and Trista followed him out. "The others are waiting at the practice field. Frayim is with them, and he'll probably be able to tell you where Huris is." He grinned. "So, you want a family?"

Trista blushed again. "Someday," she said softly. "When I find someone who looks at me the way you look at Alanar."

Owyn nodded. "I never thought I'd have that. Never thought anyone would want me the way he does." He nudged her arm. "You'll have that. You'll find someone."

She nudged him back. "Is that a vision, Smoke Dancer?"

Owyn burst out laughing. "I'm not dancing, so no. But I'm still certain there's someone for you."

"You're a romantic, Owyn."

"Do you blame me?" Owyn nodded toward where he could see Alanar standing with Aria and the Companions. "I mean...look at what I have. Look at who wants me in their lives, even knowing who I was. Why shouldn't I believe in romance? In love?" He stopped and looked at Trista. "There's someone for you. And they'll find you. And in the meantime...you've got us."

She smiled, then kissed his cheek. "Alanar is very lucky," she murmured. "I've never seen you dance. May I watch?"

"Come on," Owyn answered. "You can stand with Alanar." He led her to the others, smiling as Alanar turned toward him.

"You're not alone?"

"No, Trista wanted to watch," Owyn said, looking around. Karse and Afansa and the boys were standing with Dyneh and Aleia on the far side of the field; Dyneh waved when she saw him looking. "Little audience," he said. "Allie, will you hold my bag?"

Alanar took the bag from him, leaning down to kiss him. "Be careful, love," he said. Then he frowned. "Who has the food for when Owyn is done?"

Del held up a basket, and Owyn nodded. "Del has it. Right. I'll be done when I'm done." He slipped under the rope and walked to the middle of the field, studying the turf. Practice hadn't churned it up too much, and there was a nearly untouched area that looked perfect. He stopped there, closing his eyes and taking a deep breath. Another. A third, and he started to move, flowing through the forms.

Until he ran out of forms. Confused, Owyn lowered the blades and looked around.

"What's wrong?" Aven called.

"Nothing," Owyn answered. "I just...there wasn't a vision. I'm going to try again."

"Be careful," Alanar warned. "The last time you pushed, She pushed back."

Owyn laughed. "If She pushes back, I'll take the hint." He looked around once more, and saw that Memfis had joined the group watching him. He raised his blade in salute, then set himself and started again. This time, the vision came, gently, almost like a dream.

A man. Long hair, but in the dim light it was hard to see the color. What Owyn could see was that his clothes looked ragged, and he was sitting along in what looked like a Wanderer's wagon. Owyn heard shouting, and the man jerked and looked up, and even in the dim light, Owyn could see that he had incredible blue eyes.

An older man, with long white hair, and white wings banded with gray. He was standing and talking with someone, but Owyn couldn't see who, other than the fact that the other person had no wings.

Ruins. He knew these ruins. He'd seen them before. He was there with Aven and Del, all of them armed. He didn't see Aria or Treesi. But he could hear a baby crying.

The visions fell away, and he found himself kneeling in the middle of the field. He sat back on his heels and croaked, "I need my book!"

Del came running with the battered bag. Owyn pulled out his book and a piece of charcoal, opened to a clean page, and started sketching.

The man first, alone in his wagon. As the picture grew on the page, Owyn realized something that he'd missed.

The man was chained. He was a prisoner in the wagon.

He finished, turned the page, and started on the Air man. That one went relatively quickly — the elder had been in profile, and the most distinctive thing about him had been his wings. The other person had been hidden by the Air elder's position and by his wings, and Owyn wasn't even sure if they were a man or a woman.

He turned the page again...and stopped. He didn't need to draw the ruins again. There was a drawing identical to what he'd seen already in the book. He looked up, and saw that the others had come to surround him.

"What did you see?" Aria asked.

"Food first." Aven sat down next to Owyn and opened the basket, passing a roll and some dried apple to Owyn. Owyn took a bite of the roll and looked up.

"Normal visions today," he said. "I didn't get anything from up north. I can try again tomorrow, after we stop."

Aria nodded. "What did you see?" she asked again.

"Show you in a few minutes." He tore into the roll again, and grinned when Aven offered him the basket. Inside was a flask and a cloth-wrapped bundle that opened to reveal a piece of cheese.

"It's not going to bite you," Owyn said as he picked up the cheese and took a bite. "Just touching it won't hurt you." He frowned. "Will it?"

"I don't want to find out," Aven answered. He shifted, setting the basket down. "So it was just like on the beach?"

"It didn't even hit me that hard," Owyn answered between bites. "This...I might as well have been dreaming. It was...it was nice." He grinned as Howl came sniffing around his side, sticking his head into the basket, then turning his attention to Owyn and the cheese in his hand.

"Good," Karse muttered from over Owyn's head. "We could do with some nice. Howl, let him be! That's not for you."

"Dogs can eat cheese. So wolves should be able to, right?" Owyn asked. "Because I'll share." He broke off a piece and offered it to the puppy, who sniffed it, then gobbled it up and climbed into Owyn's lap looking for more.

"Now you've done it," Karse said. "Before he decides to eat you, what did you see?"

"Two new visions, and an old one." Owyn gave Howl the rest of the cheese, wiped his hands, and picked up his book, flipping it open to the first new picture. "I don't know who this is, but he's in trouble."

Aven took the book and studied the image. "That's a wagon like yours, isn't it?" he asked. "I don't know him, but...is he familiar?" He looked up and handed the book to Aria. "Doesn't he look familiar?"

Aria took the book and nodded. "He does. I..." She paused, then looked past Del to Treesi. "Treesi, look at this." There was a hint of alarm in her voice, and Owyn blinked.

"Oh, fuck," he breathed. "You're right. I didn't...he does, don't he?"

Treesi took the book, and nearly dropped it. "Astur," she gasped. "This is Astur!" She looked up. "He's alive?"

"And in trouble," Othi added, looking over Treesi's shoulder. He rested his hands on her arms. "We'll find him."

"Fray, take a look," Owyn said, getting to his feet. "Any ideas?"

Frayim came to stand next to Othi, looking at the drawing. He frowned, then closed his eyes. "I...north," he murmured. "But not as north as north is."

"Not as...what?" Karse demanded.

"He's on the way to the Solstice village," Owyn said. "He's north of us, but not as north as where we're going."

"Glad you understood that," Karse muttered.

Aria took the book from Frayim. "We'll find him, Treesi," she said. "Owyn wouldn't have seen him if we weren't going to find him."

Treesi nodded. "I...I thought he was dead," she said, leaning back into Othi. "When he never came to Terraces, I...I just assumed he was dead. I...if I'd known...."

"There's nothing you could have done, Treesi," Alanar said gently. "He's alive, and we'll find him."

Aria turned to Owyn and handed him the book back. "What else did you see?"

Owyn turned the page and showed her the drawing. "Who is this?"

Aria laughed. "That's my grandfather!" she said. "Who is he talking to?"

"I never saw them," Owyn said. "Those were the two new visions. The old one...I saw the ruins again. Me and Aven and Del, and a baby crying. Only...now it might not be yours, right?"

"*How long was your hair in the vision?*" Del asked.

"What?" Owyn turned and looked at Del, who lowered his hands. "What do you...oh. Yeah. I get it."

"What?" Aria asked.

Del started signing again, "*If Owyn has short hair in his vision, then it has to be soon.*"

Aria nodded. "I'm fairly certain that we won't still be at the Mother's Womb in the heart of winter, either," she added. "Unless...was it cold?"

Owyn shook his head. "No. No, it wasn't."

"Then it must be soon." She rested her hand on her stomach. "I'm losing track of time, but I know that Midsummer is growing closer by the day."

Aven looked startled. He coughed. "I...yes, it is."

THE HEALERS WENT OFF to the healing tent, and Aria sat down with Owyn, Steward, Memfis, Huris, Frayim, and Karse at the large table, looking over the map. They planned out the route over the next several days, making notes as to where they thought they might be able to stop, and starting a list of who would be going to Terraces when they reached the Western Road.

"With this many people, it makes no sense to send advance scouts to set the camp," Steward said. "Not until we know what the pace will actually be. Advance runners to settlements, yes. But we'll set camp when we get to a good stopping point. Owyn, I think your two weeks to the healing center and the Western Road may be optimistic."

"Maybe, but what happens when we get there?" Karse asked. He touched the list of people who would be going west. "We don't have enough guards to send a proper escort with this many people. I could send all the Water warriors, get them back to the sea. It won't be good for them to head into the mountains. It's too dry. But even if I send all of them, that's barely half the number I'd want to send with them, not with what we're hearing about raiders."

"We have two weeks," Owyn said. He ran his finger over the map. "Maybe a little more, like Steward says. Can you give some of the ones who'll be going west a...a quick and dirty how to survive class? How to help the guards so that everyone stays alive for the..." He frowned, studying the map. "Eight...or maybe ten days it'll take to get from the crossroads to Terraces?"

"We're going to have to," Karse snorted. "Felix and Ulla already said they wanted training. I'll send them, too. And we'll see who else. Because I can't send more than the Water warriors without leaving the Progress nearly unprotected. And I can't do that. Not with whatever it is north of the Western Road. We've already had one disaster and far too many near-disasters. I'm not courting anymore." He looked at the list of names. "Huris, you're going west?"

"What?" Huris took the list from Karse. He studied it, then looked up. "My name is on here. Dyneh's name is on here. Not her writing, and I don't write anymore. Who put us down?" He looked across the table. "Jax? Did you put our names on this list?"

Owyn turned pink. "I...yeah, I did." He looked down at his hands. "Fa, I only just found you again. I want you safe. And where we're going...it's not safe."

"I could say the same," Huris said. "I want you safe. I understand why you did it, Jax, but you could have talked to me first. You, me, your mother, and your other father." He looked at Memfis. "You're going?"

Memfis nodded. "I have to see this through. The end of this road..." He turned to Aria. "Do they know?"

"I have not told them. Frayim knows, but I don't know if Huris knows." She took a deep breath. "Risha is somewhere in the north, Huris, and she has my father."

"Your father...Milon? The Firstborn?" Huris coughed. "He's alive?"

"And I've been talking to him in visions for months, Fa," Owyn said. "That's why I danced today. To see if I could reach him." He took a deep breath. "I just...I want you safe. Because I barely know you, and I want to. And...yeah, I know I'm coming out of this. I know that. So I know we'll have a chance, but you and Mama have to go west."

Huris sighed. "Jax, I can't argue, but I still want to see you safe." He looked at Frayim. "I could say the same about you, Fray."

Frayim shook his head. "You need to go west, Huris." He rested his hand on Huris' hand. "I will miss you both, but your road is west."

Huris nodded slightly. "I don't like it," he grumbled. "I don't have to like it. And you get to tell Dyneh."

Frayim laughed. "I will talk to her." He rested his elbows on the table. "My people going west will be safe. That much I know. So your plans for guarding them will be fine."

Karse nodded. "And for us?"

Frayim shook his head. "I can't see that yet."

Huris sniffed. "Memfis, you'll keep an eye on our boy?"

Memfis smiled. "Both of them. And he has the rest of the Companions, too."

"Not the same," Huris said. "They're not his father. That's on us." He smiled. "So we're going to Terraces? Rhexa is going to drop when she sees us." He sighed and looked up. "It's getting late. Come on, Jax. Your punishment for not talking to me about this is you have to help me cook."

"Who says that's a punishment?" Owyn asked, getting to his feet.

Chapter Thirty

The rest of the evening was quiet, and the Progress moved on early the next morning. Wanderer wagons and coaches, horses and guards and families on foot, all making their slow way north. Their pace was hampered not only by the sheer number of people now traveling together, but by the fact that every mile they covered was met with another group waiting to see the Heir. Meet the Heir. Join the Heir on her Progress. By the time they stopped to make camp, they'd acquired four more wagons, and seven more families traveling on foot.

The second day was the same. On the third day, they were met by a dozen Wanderer families who called Frayim by name, and who asked if they could join their journey to the Progress. By sunset on the fourth day, they finally made it to the site where they had planned to camp the day before.

Aven tried to project how long it would take them to get to the Western road. How long it would take them to get to the Solstice village. Then he looked at the sky, at the angle of the sun, and shifted in his saddle. The parade of wagons and people continued on — he couldn't see the end of the line, and it bothered him. Just that morning, over their morning meal, Steward had mentioned his concerns over keeping this many people supplied. How were they going to feed everyone?

It was a concern, but it was the least of Aven's worries. He looked at the sky again, but the answer was the same.

They were running out of time.

He turned his horse toward the north and started following the caravan, waving at people that he didn't know who called him by name. Then he heard another voice calling him, and his father rode out of the crowd to join him.

"I didn't see you this morning," Aven said as they rode. "Did you eat?"

"I ate in the saddle," Jehan answered. "Steward made sure I had something. And we had a birth overnight, so Marzi and I were busy. A little girl. Both the mother and the baby are doing well, but I wanted to be sure they were ready before we moved out." He nodded toward the distant front of the line. "They're in the spare coach with Marzi." He looked back. "Mark me on this, Ven. We're going to double our numbers before we reach the Western Road."

"At least," Aven agreed. "Fa...we're taking too long. At this rate, we'll be a month before we see the Western Road."

Jehan nodded. "Given the way the first days have gone, I think you're right."

"We can't feed this many people for that long." Aven looked over his shoulder. "Even if we pick up the pace once we're past the Western Road, we're not going to get to the Solstice village until close to Midsummer."

"And that's what is really bothering you, isn't it?" Jehan asked. "That we won't be back in the Palace before the baby comes."

Aven swallowed. "Fa...I'm not ready."

"There's not a first-time parent in the world who's ready, Ven," Jehan said. "I certainly wasn't. But you'll learn. And you'll be a wonderful father." He chuckled. "I had much the same conversation with my mother, right before you were born, you know."

"You did?" Aven asked. They rode on in silence while Aven thought about his grandmother. About what he knew, and what he'd heard. What he'd been told. "Fa? Grandmother said something to me in Terraces about not wanting you to leave, and about wanting to know me. I was born on land?"

"You spent your first six months on land, I think," Jehan answered. "At the main healing center."

"Was that planned?"

Jehan let out a low whistle. "Yes and no," he answered. "Yes, it was planned. No, it wasn't the original plan. We were still in hiding, but we were going to go back to the canoes once the furor had died down after the attacks. We had a canoe, and we had all our supplies. We thought that you'd be born at the family canoes. But...well, your mother got sick. She didn't have an easy pregnancy. We told you that." He paused. "Maybe I shouldn't be telling you this now."

"I want to know, Fa."

Jehan nodded. "You were a big baby, Ven. And you know your mother is small. There were complications and...well, that's why you have no siblings. Because if Aleia ever got pregnant again, it might kill her. Especially without a full team of skilled healers. So..." He paused again. "You don't need to worry about Aria. She is much better suited for pregnancy than your mother was. And the baby isn't too large for her."

"Which is good, because she's going to give birth before we get back to the Palace." Aven looked down the line, saw Idaya wave at him. He smiled and waved back. "What do you think of Marzi?"

"I wish I could convince her to stay with us when we go north," Jehan answered. "I talked to her about it yesterday, and she's set on going west."

"I can't blame her," Aven said. "If it was an option, and she'd allow it, I'd take Aria back to the Palace today. But we're none of us safe until we find Risha. Not Water or Air, or the people that are different or disabled. Not until we stop her."

Jehan spat. "Truth. And I hate that she's using my work to justify her hate."

Aven listened to the creaking wheels and the steady percussion of hooves on the road. "Treesi's family thought that way. Do you think Risha heard it from someone up in that healing center?"

"Aria said that Risha's mother came from somewhere outside Wolf Ford," Jehan pointed out. "It's not too farfetched to think that people who are spouting the same poison learned it from the same source."

"The same...Fa, Treesi said that her mother claimed Wanderer blood, but she wasn't sure if it was true."

"When was that?" Jehan asked. "I missed it."

"I don't think you were there," Aven said, and frowned. "No, you weren't. It was right after we found out about the Wanderers. In Terraces." He glanced at his father. "I think we need to ask Frayim more about the Wanderers."

"His wagon is further up the line, I think," Jehan said. He urged his horse forward, and Aven followed him. They found Frayim's wagon, and Aven was surprised to see Steward riding alongside. He nodded at them as they approached.

"You're on a mission," he said. "What is it?"

Frayim just smiled. "Good morning," he called, and waved one arm at the rolling fields to their left. "Have you ever seen such green?"

"Green?" Aven looked out at the bright greens of fresh growth. "Is this unusual?"

"I've driven these roads my entire life," Frayim said. "I have never seen such green. The land renews as the blesséd Mother passes. Balance is being restored." He laughed and shook his head. "It's a marvel to see it. Truly see it. Now, you have a question?"

"Frayim, how many other groups of Wanderers are there?" Aven asked. "And...are your folk typical Wanderers?"

Frayim immediately sobered, his smile vanishing. "Why do you ask?"

"Because things aren't adding up," Aven answered. "Because Risha's mother had to come from somewhere, but no one knows where. And the only other place we've heard about that has people saying the same sorts of things as Risha is the healing center where Treesi is from, and Treesi says that her mother claimed Wanderer blood. So are they the unusual ones, or are your followers the ones rebelling?"

Frayim took a deep breath. "I see. Yes...it's my followers who are going against Wanderer beliefs. It's why the Wanderers exist — they want nothing to do with the tainted tribes, as they call them. When I learned to see, when I started seeing with more than my eyes, I started to speak against that. I was cast out. But others heard the truth, and came to follow me. We do not stay in the hills and hide. The others? They tell themselves that they are the true children of the Mother, that the rest of us are...fallen. Flawed."

"Different. And wrong."

Frayim nodded as Jehan spoke. "Just so. They say that the lowlanders are evil, and that the Mother will cast them out. That the Usurper was the beginning of that end."

"Frayim, why didn't you tell us any of this?" Steward asked. "Why didn't you tell me?"

"And you would have done what?" Frayim asked. "There's nothing that can be done. To try to force them to change their minds would only convince them that they are correct. They will not change." He paused, and looked at Aven. "The ones in the hills wait for The Child to deliver them. They believe that Axia will come again, in the form of a child of all the tribes. That The Child will wipe the tainted tribes from the world and that they will once more live in peace."

Aven went cold, dizzy, and grabbed into his saddle horn before he could fall off Pewter's back. "Is that why Risha didn't set the block like we asked?" he stammered. "She wanted Aria pregnant, because our child would be of all four tribes?" He looked around, saw Jehan looking at Steward.

"You said it," Jehan said. "That a child of all four tribes would bring balance. Did you know?"

"I've never heard any of this before," Steward said. "No... no, wait. I have. Once. Risha swore by the Child to come. Back in Terraces, when she thought she'd broken the cycle of the change. It's...this is terrifying."

Aven nodded. "We can't tell Aria this. We can't." He swallowed. "Owyn's vision. Me, him and Del in the Temple ruins. A baby crying. Risha wants my daughter. And she gets her."

"Daughter?" Steward breathed.

"You didn't hear that," Jehan muttered. "Aria doesn't want it known."

"I heard nothing."

"Fa," Aven sputtered, then turned to Jehan. "It happens. She...she...what do I do? How do I stop this?"

"Do nothing," Frayim said. "The vision shows it happens. To try and change it now is to court disaster. You are there in the vision. What happens after is in your hands. Focus on that."

"And what does happen after?" Aven demanded. "You're the Seer. Tell me. What happens after?"

Frayim looked distant. He frowned slightly. Then he shook his head.

"Too many paths. Too many choices between here and there. Between then and now. It's too soon to tell which ones we will take." He sighed. "I am sorry. I wish I could see more."

"Ven, he's right," Jehan said. "Right now, all we can do is what we're doing. We're going forward and fulfilling the lore. We'll have a better idea of what to do as we get closer. For now? What do you want to bet that the human wolves that Frayim mentioned are the same as those Wanderers? That they're getting bolder because Risha is out there and telling them to rise?"

Aven blanched. "She has an army?"

"A fractured, disorganized army," Steward offered. "But that's still a dangerous thing, and we have to pass through their territory. I'll speak to Karse, tell him what we've learned." He picked up the reins that had been lying slack in his lap, then turned to Frayim. "Any idea how soon?"

Frayim shook his head. "Ask me again when we part from the others," he said. "It will be after that. That much I can tell."

THE DAYS FLOWED ONE into the other as the Progress continued north. Every day, the entourage grew a little larger, and every day, Aria spent time speaking with each and every newcomer personally. She learned their names, and their histories. Where they came from and why they were on the road. And every evening at the shared evening meal, Owyn heard the whispers about the Heir, the blesséd Mother of prophecy. The Dove, come to bring life back to the land and set everything to rights.

"You know, back in Shadow Cove, I asked them if they thought Aria was going to make everything all puppies and kittens and double-yolked eggs," he said to Aven as they washed up after the meal one night. "I was joking. But...the folks here aren't. They think that."

Aven nodded, lifting a heavy pot and moving it. "They're not wrong, either," he said. "And even someone who has never lived on land before can tell. When we rode north from Forge last year, everything was dead and brown. Now...now that Frayim pointed it out, even I can see the land is waking up. And...we were at the top of a rise this morning. Did you look north?"

Owyn frowned and shook his head. "Not really, no. Why?"

"Because the land we haven't crossed yet is still brown. It's all green behind us. Ahead of us is still brown and dead." Aven shook his head. "It's turning green where we've passed. And only where we've passed." He grinned. "She's obviously fertile, and she's bringing that to the land."

Owyn licked his lips. "So...the land is pregnant, because she is?" he asked. "That's what you mean?" When Aven nodded, Owyn grinned. "Did you tell Aria that?"

"No," Aven answered. "Why?"

"Because if the land is echoing Aria, then..." Owyn shook his head. "No, that's silly."

"Mouse, tell me," Aven said. "What is it?"

Owyn licked his lips. "If the land is waking up because she's pregnant and passing through, what would it do if we all went out into the middle of a field and had sex?" he asked.

Aven blinked. He opened his mouth to answer, then stopped and looked puzzled for a moment. Then he chuckled. "I'm not telling her that," he said finally. "Because she'd do it. She'll have all of us naked in the middle of a field in a heartbeat if she thought it would help."

Owyn burst out laughing. "Oh, why not!" he teased. "I mean...it would mean the best harvest in *years*!"

Aven stared at him, then started to giggle, hard enough that he had to hold on to the edge of the table to keep his balance. When he finally stopped laughing and regained his balance, he snorted. "You first," he muttered. He glanced at Owyn, and they both started laughing again.

"What's so funny?" Huris asked as he came into the tent. "I didn't think pots were that funny."

"The pots are hilarious," Aven said, surreptitiously nudging Owyn with his elbow. "*Do I even need to say don't tell your father what we were talking about?*"

Owyn snorted and looked up at Aven. He winked, then looked back at his father. "We're done here, Fa." He wiped his hands on a towel. "Fishie, are you doing anything before moonrise?"

"Fa is having lessons tonight, and he asked the rest of the healers to sit in. Today we had four healers-in-training join the Progress. Three girls and a boy."

"Four?" Owyn repeated. "And given where we are...from Treesi's old healing center?"

"Maybe," Aven answered. "But if they were, they would have been on their own for a while. And I don't think they were. None of them are more than eighteen years old. And they're all at least a few years into their training. They won't say who trained them, but Fa thinks it was one of Treesi's brothers. He told her, and she's hoping he's right. But they don't trust us yet to tell us who taught them or where to find them. What we do know is that something happened to whoever it was, and now they're here." He took a deep breath. "I think Fa wants me there so that they can see me. Which means I'm going to be getting stared at until moonrise."

"Only if their teacher told them the same garbage about the Water tribe that you all were telling us about," Huris said. "He might want you there because you're one of his best students."

Aven smiled. "Thank you," he said. Then he looked up. "I should go. Owyn, I'll bring Alanar to meet you at moonrise." He kissed Owyn, then headed away from the kitchen area, toward the healing tent. Owyn watched him go, then turned to his father.

"Mama will be with the healers, too," he said. "So what are we going to do?"

Huris looked thoughtful, then took a deep breath. "I wouldn't mind seeing you dance," he said softly. "If you're willing."

"Fa!" Owyn wasn't sure which was stronger — the shock or the excitement. "Really?"

"Dyneh was...disappointed," Huris admitted. "That I didn't come see you when you danced at Mirror Lake. And I've been letting it simmer since then. What was really bothering me. Why I didn't want to see my son follow in my footsteps. Why I wouldn't be proud to watch you."

"I just thought...you lost it, and it's hard to know you've lost that." Owyn rubbed the back of his neck. "Saw that with Mem, since he lost his arm. He was a smith, and he was a dancer. Now...he's danced twice. Caught a vision once."

"Well, if you're willing, I'd like to see you. It doesn't need to be for visions."

"They tend to sneak up on me," Owyn said. "Let me grab something to eat, just in case. Then we'll go to the practice field. My blades are in the Heir's tent."

"Go get your blades," Huris said. "I'll bring the food and meet you there."

Owyn nodded and trotted away toward the Heir's tent, passing the meeting tent as he went. He waved when he saw Aria, Memfis, Frayim and Steward sitting at the table, and slowed down to join them.

"Where are you running off to?" Memfis asked.

"Fa Huris asked me to dance for him," Owyn answered. "So I'm going to get my blades."

Memfis nodded. "Mind company? And are you going to the practice grounds? I think Aleia is working with Del."

"I don't mind company, and we'll see when we get there," Owyn said. "I want to dance before it gets too dark." He went and ducked into the tent, finding his blades among the baggage. When he came out, everyone was standing.

At the practice field, it was clear that Del and Aleia were just finishing whatever practice they'd been doing. Karse was standing with them, flanked by Danir and Copper, and with Howl sitting on his feet.

"Now, do you see what she did?" Karse was saying. "How she came up under his guard? That's something we'll practice tomorrow. It's a good move for someone who's smaller than their opponent."

Del laughed. "I...wan...t'...lee...learn...too," he said slowly. Then smiled when Aleia nodded.

"That was very good," she said. "Very clear. Have you been practicing?"

"No...no...muck." Del scowled. "Muck...much," he spat.

"Take your time," Karse said. "You get better every day."

Del shook his head. "*I'm trying,*" he signed. "*But there are too many people I don't know now. I don't want people...*" He shrugged.

"We can practice on the road, or in the coach," Aleia said. "And you can practice with Owyn." She pointed, and Del turned and smiled broadly.

"You did sound good," Owyn said, coming over to stand at Del's side. "You could practice with Allie. He'll love it. And he can't hear you thinking."

Aleia cocked her head to the side. "Does that get in the way of hearing what he says?"

Owyn grinned at Del. "Not really," he said. "But sometimes we just get lazy. It's not as much work for either of us."

"*And it's very private,*" Del whispered in his mind, a soft warmth. Owyn shifted his blades to his right hand so he could put his left arm around Del.

"And it's private," he repeated. "With all the new people around, sometimes private is good."

Aleia nodded. "You have your blades. Are you dancing?"

"Fa wanted to see me," Owyn said. He smiled. "He asked to see me. So I'm going to see if I can without catching a vision."

"*Do you have food?*" Del asked, signing and thinking the words at the same time.

"Fa has it," Owyn answered. He turned to look back over his shoulder, seeing Huris coming toward them. "Can I use the field?"

Karse nodded. "I should get these boys off to bed so they don't fall asleep before the first story is over again—"

Immediately, both boys started to protest.

"That was just one time!"

"Captain, we want to sing the moon!"

"We'll be good!"

"And we'll stay awake!"

Karse chuckled. "You're getting too tall for me to carry, Danir," he said. "And Fancy can't lift either of you. So you stay awake, or there's no singing for you tomorrow. Understood?"

"Yes, Captain!" Both boys chorused, then raced off the field, followed by a barking puppy who was clearly overjoyed at the chase. Karse sighed theatrically.

"Trey's going to be shocked. We've got a wife and children," he said.

"He'll love it and you know it," Owyn corrected.

"He will," Karse agreed. "All right. If you're going to dance while you have the light, you should get on with it."

Owyn nodded, and waited until the others walked off the field. He looked around, saw Huris watching him, and took the first deep breath.

No vision this time, he told himself. Just for show.

And of course, he didn't listen.

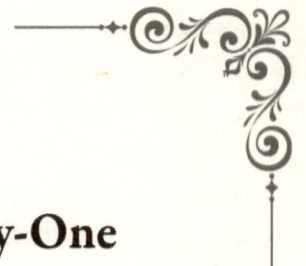

Chapter Thirty-One

The dark cellar where Milon and Trey were being held was so familiar at this point that Owyn knew it before he'd even opened his eyes. He recognized the earthy, musty smell of it. He opened his eyes and looked around. There was still sunlight coming in through the little, high window, which lit the room just enough that he could see that the chair where Milon usually sat was empty.

"Milon?" he whispered. "Where are you?"

He heard a moan from behind him, and a voice he'd know anywhere slipped into his mind.

"*Wyn?*"

He turned, searching the shadows. "Trey?" he called, and started toward the far wall, where he'd heard chains one of the other times he'd been here. "Trey, I'm here."

He heard movement ahead of him, and more behind as the door opened, the hinges creaking and screaming. Someone swore, loudly, and someone else shouted, "Who's that?"

Fuck! He wasn't just here, he was *here*! He'd projected again. Owyn turned, saw two guards carrying Milon between them, then closed his eyes and willed himself back to his own body.

He felt himself hit the ground, and opened his eyes to the glowing pinks and purples of twilight clouds. There was no one standing over him, which told him that it hadn't been very long. He sat up slowly, seeing Aria, Del and Huris just inside the barriers. Memfis was right behind them. Steward and Frayim were on the far side of the barrier, with Aleia, Karse and the boys.

"Owyn?" Aria called.

"I caught a vision, and I projected again," he called back. "North again. I went back north. And this time, some of Risha's men saw me. They really saw me." He rubbed his hand over his face, lowering his voice as they came closer. "If it had been one, maybe he'd have thought he was seeing things. But two? I may have just fucked things up beyond recognition."

Del sat down in the dirt next to Owyn, offering him a wrapped bundle. Inside were nuts, dried fruit and a wedge of cheese. Owyn started eating.

"What else did you see?" Aria asked. Owyn closed his eyes, thinking.

"They had your Fa outside the room. They were bringing him back when they saw me. And...Trey heard me. And I heard Trey. He knew me." He looked past the others to see Karse. "He's alive, Karse. And he knew me."

"There's still hope, then," Karse said softly. "Thank you."

"He'll tell, won't he?" Huris murmured. "If they question him—"

"Trey wouldn't give me up," Owyn insisted around a mouthful of cheese. He swallowed, taking the bottle that Del offered him. "I'm sure of that. Not Trey." He uncorked the bottle and took a long drink of water. "Anyway, I don't know if Milon ever knew I was there."

Aria nodded. "We're going to have to be careful," she said. "I don't think you should dance again, Owyn. Risha may set watchers to try and catch you."

"And if she does, what happens?" Memfis asked. "What happens if you're caught there while projecting? I don't think we know what would happen, but you'd be solid enough that they could hurt you."

Huris nodded. "At the very least."

Memfis turned to him. "You know about projecting? Between Meris and I, we didn't know very much. What do you know?"

Huris scowled, looking ferocious. "Projecting is a lost art, and a dangerous one. Not surprised you don't know much. There hasn't been anyone who could do it in generations. Now, from what I know, you can get hurt when you're separated from your body. Trapped between the worlds. Even lost there, if something happens to break the link between here and there."

"You can?" Memfis sounded horrified. "Meris said nothing about that! And there wasn't anything in the references we could find in Terraces!"

Huris nodded. "You probably wouldn't find it anywhere outside the Dancers archives," he said. "And maybe not even then." He shrugged one shoulder. "They didn't have copies of my family journals."

"Fantrada the Wise," Owyn said. "My...what did Granna say, Mem? Fifth great-grandmother?"

Huris laughed. "How do you know that? Yes, she was the last Smoke Dancer we know of who could project. I have fair copies of her journals. I'll show you."

"We'll need to make copies of those for the archives," Memfis said. "If you'll allow it? The Dancer archives...those were lost."

Huris' jaw dropped. "All of them?" he sputtered. "I...yes, of course. Dyneh copies with a good hand. We'll have it done in Terraces, once we're settled."

Memfis nodded. "Thank you. Perhaps someday, we'll be able to go back, to dig down and find the archives, see if they survived."

"That's something for our children to think of, I think," Aria said. "We saw what Forge looks like now, Memfis. I do not think we'll be able to dig down to Forge-that-was anytime soon. We have to rebuild first."

Memfis nodded. He looked toward the south. "Maybe one day, I'll ride south and see it for myself. I should have gone with you."

"It's better that you didn't, Mem," Owyn said. He slowly got to his feet, bending and picked up his blades. "That wasn't something you needed to see. Not now. Later, once the mountain stops...snoring."

Huris coughed. "The mountain is doing what?"

"Snoring," Owyn repeated. "Aria, we thought it was wind through the hollow places, right? Like a flute?"

"It was Karse who compared it to a flute, but yes," Aria said. "And you thought it was Father Adavar snoring."

Owyn smiled. "Because that's what it sounded like, and it's honestly not the strangest thing we've come across in the past year."

"Would I be the strangest thing you've come across?" Frayim asked, grinning. Steward snorted, clearly trying not to laugh. Aria just looked at him, then at Owyn.

"In the top five, I think?" she asked. Frayim laughed, sounding delighted.

"Top three," Owyn answered, setting Frayim off into another peal of laughter. "Definitely top three. No, the strangest thing is the snoring mountain."

"Should I attempt to be stranger, or more normal?" Frayim asked, wiping his eyes. Aria took his hand.

"I want you to be nothing other than yourself, Frayim," she said. He smiled and raised her hand to his lips, kissing her fingers.

"Your will is my life, blesséd Mother."

THEY WALKED SLOWLY back to the Heir's tent, and Owyn put away his blades. When he came out, he could see a crowd at the meeting tent. Alanar and Aven stood out among them, so he went to join them. Standing with Jehan were four strangers — a young man with dark olive skin and dark brown hair, and three young women. One was dark haired, another had hair as pale as Alanar's, and the third was as small and brown as a sparrow. They stood close together, looking nervously around.

"How were the lessons?" Owyn asked, coming up next to Alanar and taking his hand. Alanar smiled at him, pulling him close and putting his arm around him.

"We have four very gifted healers-in-training who will be heading west to Pirit, love," he said. "And...you'll have to introduce yourselves. I'm not sure what order you all are standing in. I'll point at the wrong person."

Aven chuckled. "Owyn, from left to right—"

"Whose left?" Owyn interrupted, and saw a hint of a smile on the sparrow girl's face. "My left or their left?"

"Your left, Mouse," Aven answered and pointed in turn at sparrow girl, the boy, pale hair and dark hair. "Selsi, Arjin, Jesta and Pallas." Then he waved his hand at Owyn. "This is Owyn, our Fire."

"It's nice to meet you all," Owyn added. He smiled. "You've probably heard this at least once from every healer in camp, but you're safe here."

They all looked at each other, then Arjin shook his head. "Everyone has told us that, but...it's not. Not if we keep going north. So we're going to go west when the group splits."

Owyn nodded. "Which is fine. Now, when you get to Terraces, you'll meet Healer Pirit. She only looks like she chews nails and spits tacks, and eats healers-in-training for breakfast. She's really not that bad."

Pallas coughed. "She isn't?"

"Nah, she gave up on nails," Owyn drawled. "Said they had too many tacks."

Pallas looked startled, but Arjin snorted. It seemed to be the signal they needed — all four started laughing. Owyn grinned.

"Better," he said. "You were all stretched too tight. We're singing to the moon soon. You can come sit with us." He leaned into Alanar's side. "And have you all eaten? We can go find something—"

"You're going to sit down before you fall down," Memfis grumbled. "You need to rest, or you'll be the one falling asleep before the end of the first story."

"Why are you falling asleep?" Alanar asked.

"Fa asked me if he could see me dance," Owyn answered. "And a vision caught me."

Alanar blinked. "Are you all right?"

"I'm fine. Just tired. So I won't stay up too late." He looked around. "Where's Treesi? And Othi? I haven't seen them for a while."

"They're sitting down with Marzi," Jehan answered. "Treesi had questions I thought it best to ask a midwife. So I excused her from the lessons." He smiled and nodded. "There they are. She should come meet the new trainees."

Owyn turned and saw Treesi and Othi walking toward the tent. As he did, he heard a gasp.

"That's Treesi?"

Owyn turned to see Pallas had covered her hand with her mouth, and the other three trainees were looking at her.

"Pallas!"

"We promised!"

"I know!" Pallas whimpered. "But..."

"And that answers the question we all had. Somewhat. So which of Treesi's brothers taught you?" Aven asked gently. "She's been hoping that it might have been one of them."

The four of them looked at each other, and Arjin swallowed and put his arm around Pallas' shoulders. "We promised we wouldn't say. Because...because we were in hiding. They—" He stopped, looking stricken.

"They?" Jehan repeated.

"Candle is already burning, Jin. We can't unburn it," Selsi murmured. "Tell them. Tell her. Let her know."

"And then we'll see what we can do to find them," Aven added. "But we can't do anything if we don't know what's happened."

"You'd do that? For us?" Arjin asked.

Aria closed the distance between them and took his hand. "You're part of us now," she said. "Yes, we'll help you."

Arjin looked at Pallas, then nodded. "I...let's wait for her. For Treesi. So she knows it from us." He turned to face Treesi and Othi, who had just reached the tent.

Othi glanced at Arjin and stopped. "You're very serious. And new. Who are you?"

"Othi, I think this is one of the new healers I told you came into camp," Treesi said. She smiled at Arjin. "It's nice to meet you. I'm—"

"Treesi. I...we know. We know about you." Arjin looked at the others, then straightened and looked at Treesi. "Our teachers told us about you."

Treesi grabbed Othi's hand. "My brothers?"

Arjin nodded. "Elaias and Astur. Elaias was our main teacher. And Astur was our senior training partner. He's the one who told us about you. He's the one who got us away when the raiders came."

"But they took him," Pallas added. "He gave himself up so that we'd get away. He was afraid for us, for me and Selsi and Jesta."

Arjin nodded. "I'm not a good fighter," he admitted. "Astur tried to teach me to use a whip like he does, but...I'm not good at it. He knew I wouldn't be able to protect the girls."

"A...whip?" Treesi repeated. "Astur...uses a whip?"

"He was a drover when we met him, and that's how he learned," Selsi volunteered. "I...should we start over?"

"I think it will help," Treesi answered. She sat down at the long table. "Please. Sit. Tell me what you know, and what happened."

The four young healers moved around to the far side of the table to sit facing Treesi. Aria took a seat on Treesi's right, and Othi sat down on Treesi's left, taking her hand. Owyn sat down at the end of the table, feeling Alanar's hand on his shoulder.

Arjin folded his hands on the tabletop and took a deep breath. "Elaias told us that he was away from the healing center when whatever happened...well, happened. He was up in the hills, attending a birth. By the time he got back, everything was over. He never knew what happened. He thought the rest of his family was dead, so he moved on. I don't know how long he was alone. A few years, I think. Then he found us. I was first, and it was just him and me for a few months. Then we found Pallas." He smiled at the dark-haired girl on his right. "Then we found Astur—"

"Found Astur?" Treesi repeated. "He wasn't at the healing center when it was attacked?"

"No. From what Elaias told us, Astur was cast out after he helped you run away," Arjin answered. "We found him with some of the cattle tribes in the hills near the Solstice village, working as a drover and an animal healer." He took a deep breath. "We found Selsi and Jesta just after, and Elaias took us all back to the village where he'd been when the center was attacked, and started training us all." He took a deep breath. "We were out there...two years? Pal? Is that right?"

Pallas nodded. "Almost three. Elaias said we needed a better teacher. So we were going to go to Terraces. We'd heard about the Heir, heard that there was a healing center left there. So we were going there. Astur was hoping we'd find you." She paused and reached for Arjin's hand. "He made sure we got out. He made sure we got away." Her voice cracked, and Arjin put his arm around her.

"The raiders attacked our camp," Selsi said. "Elaias...he tried to bargain with them, but they wanted us." She gestured. "Not Jin, I mean. They said they wanted the girls. They called us breeders." She nearly spat the word, and Arjin shuddered.

"Elaias told Astur to get us out, and he'd meet us at the ruins of the healing center. And if he wasn't there in two days, to keep going and go to Terraces," Jesta spoke for the first time. "We waited for him there. But he didn't come. The raiders did." She clasped her hands on the table, but Owyn could see them shaking. "Astur made us run. He told us that he'd follow us, but he didn't. We heard him..." She stopped, her voice catching. "We heard him die."

"You didn't," Owyn said. He rested his hand on hers. "Listen to me. He's alive. And we're going to find him."

"I'm not a fool, Fireborn," Jesta snapped.

"No, you're not," Owyn said. He met her eyes and smiled. "You're part Air, aren't you?"

"A bit, yes. How did you know?"

"You've got an Air temper, like my husband. No, you're not a fool. And I'm not trying to make everything nice. I'm a Smoke Dancer. I saw Astur. Days ago. He's alive."

Jesta stared at him. "Really?"

"I can show you, if you want." He started to get up, but Alanar pushed him back down.

"Del, would you go and get Owyn's book?" Alanar asked.

"Allie, I'm fine!"

"You're slightly off balance. You need to eat more," Alanar said.

"You're checking me?" Owyn tipped his head back. "I couldn't even tell! You're getting sneaky."

"Good." Alanar kissed him. "I need to be, to keep ahead of you. Did Memfis go for food?"

"Memfis, Huris and Steward all went," Treesi answered. She turned in her chair. "Frayim?"

Frayim came forward, crouching next to Treesi's chair. "You want to know if they live?"

"We know Astur is alive," Treesi said. "And north of us. What about Elaias?"

Frayim patted her arm, then closed his eyes and tipped his head slightly to the side. His face went slack. Then he breathed in sharply through his nose.

"Yes," he said. He coughed and stood up. "Yes, he does."

"There's a but there, isn't there?" Othi said. "I think I heard it not being said."

Frayim nodded, resting his hand on the table. "There is a but," he said. "He lives, but he is in pain."

"They're hurting him?"

Owyn wasn't sure who was loudest — Treesi or Arjin. The two of them looked across the table at each other. Arjin closed his eyes and nodded.

"Hurts mend," he said in a harsh voice. "That's what he taught us. Hurts mend. We can find him. We can find him, and get him out, and heal him."

"We will find him," Othi said, his voice firm. "Now, I think I heard something said about food. You need to eat. Then we'll all go sing."

Arjin nodded. Then he looked up. "I...I'm sorry. Your name is Frayim?"

Frayim smiled. "It is."

Arjin licked his lips. "You're the one they call the Seer?" Without waiting for an answer, he looked at the other trainees. "Frayim is the name they said, isn't it?"

"They're looking for you," Pallas said. "When they first came to camp, they asked Elaias if he knew where you were. He told them he'd never heard your name before, and didn't know who they meant. But he was rubbing his hands together when he did it."

Treesi groaned. "He still does that?"

"What?" Aven asked. "He does what?"

"When he's trying to tell a lie, he rubs his hands together." Treesi rubbed her palms together, like she was rolling something between them. "He's always done it. Our parents always knew when he was trying to lie about something." She looked up at Frayim. "You didn't tell me you knew him!"

Frayim sighed and sank into another chair. "I stopped in the healing center once, before it fell. I met your parents. And when I spoke the truth to them about the coming of the Heir, they ordered me stoned for blasphemy and left me for dead. I didn't know his name then, but it was Elaias who saved me and brought me back to my own people."

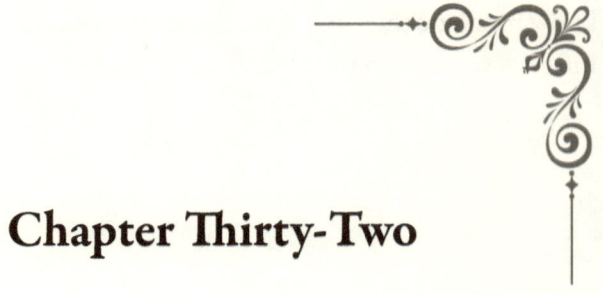

Chapter Thirty-Two

Treesi waited until after the morning meal before going to find the new healers. She meandered through the camp, watching as people packed their belongings away so that they could continue north. She finally found them in the first place she should have looked — with Jehan. All four of them looked nervous again, staying close enough to touch when walking, huddling together when they were standing still. Dark-haired Pallas noticed her as she came closer, and smiled as she touched Arjin's arm. He turned, and for a moment looked as if he wasn't sure if he should smile, faint, or run. For a moment, Treesi was thankful that Othi was off drilling with the guards.

"Good morning," Treesi said, stopping far enough back that she wouldn't be seen as a threat. She hoped. "Have you all eaten?"

"We're just finishing up, and deciding who was going to ride where today," Jehan answered. "We don't have enough horses, and I don't want to split them between carriages, but I was also hoping to work on finishing Othi's left arm today as we go, and he takes up most of a carriage all by himself." He turned to the trainees. "One of the things you're going to learn is how to remove tattoos."

"Off the big man? I was wondering why he looked unfinished," Jesta asked. "Why?"

Jehan smiled. "I'll explain as we go. To keep it short, he was forced into a current that isn't right for him, and now he's changing his course."

Arjin snorted. "You're not making sense."

"I spent twenty-five years living on the deep," Jehan answered. "I make perfect sense, if you know how to listen."

"Othi bears the marks of a Water warrior," Treesi said. "But that's not where his heart is. He's an artist, and they have different marks. So if he's going to be true to his heart—"

"He needs to have the old marks removed?" Arjin finished. "See, what she says makes sense!"

Jehan chuckled. "Good. Then you can listen to her when we work. Treesi, I'm assigning these four to you."

"To me?" Treesi repeated. "And all four at once?"

"To you because I think that the familiarity will help. You learned from Astur at the start, so you're familiar with how he and Elaias would have taught. And all four at once because I don't think I could separate them with a crowbar and a team of horses." He smiled as the trainees all laughed. "I think that they'll work together as well as you and Alanar did. Now, the other Healers will be there to assist, but you'll be their mentor until they go west. At that point, they'll work with Dyneh." He turned back to the trainees. "Unless you decide to stay with us, that is. You have time to make up your minds."

"We're not going back north," Arjin said.

"Jin, if they find Astur and Elaias, we won't be here," Pallas said. "They might need us."

Arjin looked at her. "They have three level five healers!"

"I meant Eli and Astur," Pallas murmured.

Arjin blinked, then licked his top lip. "Oh. I..."

"You have a few days to think about it, to talk with each other. And to get comfortable with us," Treesi said. "Now, come with me."

"Where are we going?" Selsi asked as they started walking.

"I want you to meet Karse, our Guard Captain. And properly meet Othi, before you help work on him." She led them down toward the practice grounds.

"Treesi, you're...expecting," Selsi said slowly. "Is he...?"

"In Water terms, we'd be building a canoe together," Treesi answered. "But I get seasick, so we're not going to the deep. Othi is staying on land, at the Palace. We haven't done any rites or anything yet. But yes, he's mine."

"You're paired, then?" Jesta asked. "And you're the Earthborn? And the Fireborn is married. His husband is Healer Alanar. He's like me — Earth and Air. And...is that allowed? Being a Companion and being married?"

Treesi nodded. "Aria wants us to be happy. So she's welcomed Alanar and Othi."

"That means her personal circle is...six?" Pallas looked thoughtful. Then she grinned. "Where did you find a bed big enough?"

Treesi giggled. "They had one specially made for us in Terraces. And they're building one for us in the Palace. But we don't always all share a bed at once. We all have our own spaces in the Palace, and our own offices. I think if we were all on top of each other all time, there would be arguments." She smiled. "What else would you like to know about us?"

"Pal, you're asking too many questions," Arjin murmured.

"Which is how you learn," Treesi replied. "I don't mind questions. And you shouldn't be afraid to ask."

"Then I have a question," Selsi said. "What am I hearing?"

"It sounds like it's coming from over there," Arjin pointed. "Is that where we're going?"

"It is," Treesi said, and headed for the source of the cheering and shouting. As they reached the barrier that separated the field from the guards who were watching, she could see what they were cheering.

Othi and Aven were sparring.

Treesi stopped by the cord barrier and watched them. It was the first time she'd seen Othi and Aven fight since the morning they'd left the Palace, when Othi had goaded Aven into attacking him, thereby proving to everyone that he could still fight. That fight had been beautifully, frighteningly, dangerously real. This one was far less dangerous, but no less beautiful. And it was clear from the laughter and smiles that for Othi and Aven, this fight was purely play. Aven had his hook swords, while Othi had somewhere found a pair of long-handled axes.

"And he's not a warrior?" Arjin asked. "If he walked into a fight, every other person would scream and run. Especially with those axes."

Treesi giggled. "You'd think that, with as big as he is. But he's really the most gentle man I've ever known. He'll fight to protect us, but killing makes him ill." The cheers grew louder, and she looked back to see Aven and Othi lower their weapons and embrace, laughing.

"They're both so pretty," Selsi murmured. "The Heir is lucky. You're lucky, Treesi."

Treesi smiled and brushed her hand against Selsi's. "I am. Thank you." She saw Karse bringing a waterskin out to Othi and Aven. "Now, what do you know about Waterborn?"

"Not a lot," Pallas answered. "We read the book about the other tribes, but that's it. And I don't think Sel got a chance with it before it got wet."

"You can ask Jehan about it," Treesi said. "He wrote it."

The four trainees all turned to stare. "Senior Healer Jehan is...Healer Jhansri?"

Treesi nodded. "And Aven is his son. Oh, and Healer Pirit, back in Terraces? That's his mother. Any of them can answer your questions. But the first thing you need to know is they drink salt water. Fresh water dries them out."

"Backwards from the way we are?" Arjin asked. "So that man just brought them salt water?"

"That man is Guard Captain Karse. I'll introduce you later. And yes. We keep salt on hand all the time. Waterborn also can't eat milk or cheese or anything that has milk in it."

Arjin grinned and nudged Jesta with his elbow. "You didn't tell us you were Water, Jes."

Treesi looked at the girl, who was blushing. "You can't have milk?"

She shook her head. "I've never been able to drink it. It makes me sick."

Treesi nodded. "That's good to know."

"Treesi!"

Treesi turned to see Othi coming toward them. She met him at the barrier, closing her eyes and breathing him in as he touched his forehead to hers. Then he kissed her and straightened.

"How much did you see?" he asked.

"Only the end," Treesi answered. "You looked like you were having fun. Where did you find those?"

Othi looked down at the axe in his left hand. "Cellan was watching me try to get used to the swords the Guard use. He said if I was going to swing them like axes, I should use real axes, and he gave me these. I'm not sure where he found them." He held one up so that Treesi could see it. "I like it. It feels more like a hook sword. The sword that Karse gave me didn't feel right in my hand."

"And that one is heavier than a sword, isn't it?" Arjin said.

Othi looked at him and arched a brow. "You know weapons?"

Arjin paled slightly. "Not weapons. I know axes like that, though. My family, my fa and my brothers, they were all woodsmen."

"We should introduce you to Cellan. He's a carpenter," Othi said. "I'm curious, though. You know axes, but you think you don't know weapons?" He looked down at the axes again. "If you had an axe like this, and someone was trying to get to Pallas over there, you could stop them."

Arjin looked startled. "But..."

"You were raised to be a woodsman," Othi continued. "This axe would probably feel right at home in your hands. Someone tried to tell you that a weapon was just a sword or a knife, it sounds like. That's not right." He held an axe out to Arjin. "You know how to chop wood with this? Then you know how to stop a man with this."

Treesi watched as Arjin frowned, then took the axe. He hefted it in his hands, studying it for a moment. Then he looked back over his shoulder at Pallas, straightened, and looked back at Othi.

"It can't be that easy, can it?"

Othi snorted. "I found out the hard way that killing is far too easy. It shouldn't be as easy as it is to kill a man. What you need to learn is how to be the one still alive at the end of the fight. You want to learn that? Karse can teach you. He's a good teacher. And you can use the axe." He smiled. "Looks like you're sure I'm not going to bite you now."

Arjin blinked. Then he laughed. "I'm sure of that now. And...can you introduce me to Karse? So we can see if I can learn?"

Othi looked around, then whistled, loud and shrill. It was answered by a bark, and Howl came running. Karse followed behind, laughing.

"You called the wolves?" Karse called. "Oh, he's got new friends now?" He nodded at Howl, who had rolled onto his back to allow Pallas and Selsi to rub his belly. "Othi, introduce me to your new friends."

"This is Arjin," Othi said. "And we have Selsi and Pallas with Howl, and Jesta over there."

"They're healers-in-training," Treesi added. "They came to us last night."

Karse nodded. "Steward told me. Nice to meet you, Arjin." He nodded toward the axe in Arjin's hand. "You know how to use that?"

"On wood," Arjin answered. "And it's been years since I did last." He looked down at his hands. "My calluses are gone."

"Karse, Arjin wants to learn to use the axe like I do," Othi said. "Think you can take on another?"

"Since Cellan is helping me with teaching you, on account of I don't know shit about axes? Of course." Karse turned to Arjin, shifting to clasp his hands behind his back. "Now, listen to me, lad. We're up at dawn, we work until the camp breaks to move, and we eat in the saddle once the camp rolls out. And that's on top of your healer training. Think you can manage?"

Arjin swallowed and glanced back at the girls. Then he straightened, holding the axe in a white-knuckled grip. "If I'd known how to fight, Astur would still be with us," he said. "I'll manage."

Karse smiled. "Good answer. Right, how about you?" He looked past Arjin at the other trainees. "Anyone else want to learn?"

"I do," Selsi answered. "But I don't think I can swing that thing."

Karse ducked under the barrier and walked over to her, gesturing for her to hold her arms out. Then he walked around her. "Not...yet," he said slowly. "I think we'll start you with knives. Treesi, do you think Del would be willing to work with her?"

"I can ask him," Treesi answered. "I haven't seen him this morning. Was he here?"

Aven came around the barrier and paused to kiss Treesi's cheek before answering, "He was here before we were."

"He told me he's been slacking on practice," Karse added. "Which is completely understandable since his primary teacher stayed in Terraces, but as blown as he was when we were done? He needs to get back into shape. Having someone to teach will help him." He folded his arms over his chest. "Archery. We'll get some butts set up when we make camp tonight, and tomorrow all of you can have a go at it. I want you all here at dawn." He looked out at the guards. "Right, we're done here! Get yourselves cleaned up and ready to move!"

EACH MORNING, TREESI woke at dawn, insisting on supervising her charges as they trained, working alongside them at the archery butts. She discovered that she couldn't even remember the last time she'd held a crossbow, and she was more than a little out of practice herself. To her amusement, after a week of training, Aria started joining them, teaching Pallas and Jesta to use Air javelins, and learning to use a blowgun.

"A blowgun is a healer's weapon?" Aria asked after practice on the first morning after they made camp at the Western Road. They were outside the camp, walking back toward the tents and wagons. "I've only ever seen you and Jehan use one."

"It can be. We can put potions on the darts. Jehan laces his with sleeping potions." Treesi held up a long length of tube-grass that she'd cut from a small stand near where they'd practiced. "If this dries without cracking, there's enough here to make a blowgun for each of you. I'm just not sure how we'll store it so it doesn't curl."

"We'll ask Steward. Who I have barely seen for the past several days." Aria looked around. "He works too hard. He needs help."

"Afansa is helping him. And Huris and Dyneh," Treesi pointed out. "It's a lot of work to keep this large of a group fed and moving. But we're going to lose more than half the group tomorrow, aren't we?"

Aria nodded. "I believe we will. Although I'm not entirely certain just how many will be going west. I can't be more specific than saying that a good number of the group will be leaving tomorrow." She stopped and sighed. "I'm tired, Treesi."

"You don't have to get up this early, Aria. You can sleep until it's time to leave." Treesi took Aria's hand with her free hand. "And we'll reach the Solstice village soon."

"That's not the comfort it should be," Aria admitted. "I'm telling the baby that she has to wait until we've reached the Solstice village before she comes. I hope she listens." She rested her other hand on her belly. "Aven is terrified. He tries to hide it, but—"

"But you can see through me as if I was clear water," Aven said from behind them. Aria and Treesi both turned, and Aria stepped into Aven's embrace. He kissed her, and lingered for a moment to share breath before laughing and taking her hand. "I honestly thought I was hiding it better than that!"

Aria smiled. "You have been. I don't think anyone would have seen it but me."

He made a face. "Fa saw it. I talked about it with him." He frowned. "Weeks ago now, I think. I'm losing track." He shook his head. "We'll make it to the Solstice village, though. I'm sure of that. And then..."

"We'll see what happens then. And how things happen," Aria finished. She rolled her shoulders and flared her wings. "Oh, I can't wait to fly again."

"Let's go back to camp," Treesi suggested. "We can eat something, and you can take a nap." She looked around, suddenly hearing raised voices. "Do you hear that?"

"Someone is arguing," Aven said. "Is that...Pallas?"

They followed the sound toward a far side of a stand of trees, where they found all four trainees. Arjin and Pallas were facing each other, and both of them were red in the face. Pallas had her hands balled into fists.

"We can't stay!" Arjin snapped. "It's not safe if we go back north. They want you, and they want Sel and Jes!"

"And if there's even a chance that Elaias and Astur are alive, that we can find them, how can we leave?" Pallas demanded. "They sacrificed so much for us! We can't just abandon them!"

"We didn't abandon them! They told us to run!" The anguish in Arjin's voice was clear and painful, and his breath hitched when he tried to continue, "They...I shouldn't have listened. I...this is all my fault."

Treesi shoved the tube grass stave into Aven's hand and went to Arjin's side. She held her arms open, and he stared at her before falling into her embrace and shattering into wracking sobs. Pallas bit her lip, then turned and ran.

"Pallas!" Aven shouted. He handed Aria the stave and hurried after the girl.

"Aria, leave that here and go find Dyneh?" Treesi said, keeping her voice low. "I need her."

Aria let the stave fall and hurried away, and Treesi turned her attention back to Arjin, stroking his hair gently as he cried.

"Selsi, Jesta, what happened?" Treesi asked. Selsi came and sat down on the ground facing her, with Jesta by her side.

"They've been arguing about this for days. Never where you could hear. That's why we're so far from camp. We came here after practice because Jin didn't want you involved. He said this was ours to decide," Jesta answered. "Pallas said she wanted us to stay. She wanted to be here when you found Astur and Elaias. Arjin wanted us to go. He said Astur wanted to make sure we were safe. He said that the only way he could do that was by taking us west. That Astur expected him to take us west. Pallas told him that she was staying. She wasn't beholden to him — he wasn't her father or her brother, and she didn't have to listen. Then they started yelling at each other."

"They've never fought like this before," Selsi added. "Argued, yes. But not screaming fights."

Treesi nodded, then looked over her shoulder when she heard footsteps coming toward them. Frayim and Dyneh were running toward them from the camp. Dyneh dropped to her knees beside Treesi and turned her attention to Selsi and Jesta. Frayim kept walking, going to meet Aven and Pallas and bringing them back.

Treesi took a deep breath, then looked back down at Arjin. "Everyone is here. All right. Let's go back to camp and discuss the options and..." For the first time, she realized that Arjin had started saying something, his words swallowed by his sobs. "Arjin?"

He raised his head, and in a broken voice whispered, "I'm sorry."

"WHAT ARE THEY DOING out here?" Huris asked, following Aria out of the camp.

"And what were you doing out here?" Karse added. "Wandering away from camp, when we know there are troublemakers around?"

"Treesi and I were here because she wanted to collect tube grass to make blowguns. Aven was with us." Aria headed for the stand of trees "And the trainees? I do not know why they were here." She frowned as the place where they'd found the trainees became visible. "And...here. We were here. Karse?"

"Oh, fuck," Karse breathed. He brushed past Aria and trotted forward, toward a patch of churned up ground. He stooped, picked up a splintered piece of tube grass.

"Fuck," he repeated. "Huris, take Aria back to camp. Find Steward and sound the alarm. The raiders came to us."

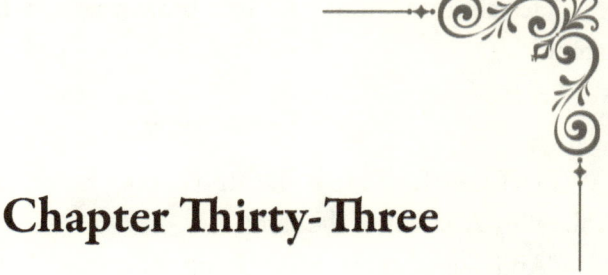

Chapter Thirty-Three

It was the pain shooting down Aven's arms that woke him, and the position that sent him into a near panic — his wrists were bound over his head, and his ankles anchored wide. For a terrifying moment, he could smell stale water and mold. Then he opened his eyes and saw bare rock, and felt the hot sunlight beating down onto his back. He looked up. His wrists were bound with rope, the end of which was fastened out of his reach to a wooden frame. He couldn't see the knots, and there wasn't enough play in the ropes that bound his ankles for him to pull himself up. He swallowed, licked his dry lips, and tried to think.

He remembered the attack, remembered the rush of men coming from the trees. Frayim had grabbed Treesi's long piece of tube grass, shattering it against one of the attackers as Aven drew his swords to try and defend the others. Then something hit him.

Hit him from *behind*.

How had someone gotten behind him? What had happened? Where was he? He coughed, his throat dry, and looked around. There were other, similar wooden frames, and one of them held another man. He'd been beaten, and his bruised skin was painfully scarlet where it wasn't purple. His long hair obscured his face. It was the shade of his hair — not quite brown, and not quite as bright a red as Treesi's — that gave Aven a hint as to who the man might be.

"Elaias?" he called, and the man groaned and raised his head to stare at Aven. Then he lowered his head again.

Aven took a deep breath and looked up again. There had to be a way to get out of this. He had to find the others. In the distance, he heard shouting from somewhere behind him, and someone crying out in pain.

"YOU TOLD ME YOU WEREN'T going to hurt them!"

Treesi flinched as Frayim screamed again, the whip cutting into skin already crossed with welts and blood. The raiders had herded her and the other female healers to one side. Arjin was with the raiders, and was currently shouting at the man who seemed to be in charge.

"He betrayed us," Pallas whispered. "How could he? He was our training partner. We were supposed to be able to trust him."

Treesi put her arm around Pallas' shoulder. "I don't know. I don't understand either." She looked around. She hadn't seen Aven since Arjin had hit him from behind and knocked him senseless. Frayim screamed again, and Treesi heard someone curse. She looked back to see Arjin grappling with the man with the whip.

"You told me you weren't going to hurt any of them!" he shouted again, then yelped as the man backhanded him across the face, knocking him to the ground. Arjin rolled onto his back. "Where is she?" he asked, his voice shaking. "I did what you said. Where is she?"

The raider cocked his head to the side. "Idiot," he drawled. "Gullible idiot."

"Where is she!"

"She's dead. She's been dead. She was dead before I came to you."

"No!" Arjin gasped. "You...you told me she was safe. You promised!"

"You served your purpose. Idiot," the raider repeated. He waved one arm. "Take the idiot out to the burning fields."

As the raiders dragged Arjin away, the whipman turned his attention toward Treesi and the other women. Treesi glanced at Dyneh, then stepped forward, putting herself between the raider and the other healers. He laughed and raised his hand....

"If you touch me..." Treesi barely recognized her own voice. "I will make you hurt in ways you never dreamed possible."

He paused. Then he laughed, sounding almost nervous as he lowered his hand. "What," he scoffed. "A little thing like you?"

"I'm a Healer." Treesi kept her voice low, even. Calm. "I can heal broken bones with a thought. It's so much easier to break them." She looked up at him. "Do you want to see?"

The raider took a step back, caught himself, then turned and snarled, "Move the blasphemer to the burning fields! And put the breeders in the wagon!"

"Do you think that's where they're keeping Astur?" Pallas whispered as the men started herding them away.

"We'll know in a moment," Dyneh murmured. "Now, you heard Treesi. If any of them touches you, break their bones."

Selsi gasped. "But—"

"Do it," Treesi whispered. "We need to protect ourselves until the others can find us." She nodded toward a wagon set off to one side of the camp. "We're going there, I think."

Someone went ahead, and unlocked the wagon door, gesturing for the women to enter. The trainees all looked at Treesi, who nodded; they climbed in one at a time. Then Dyneh entered, and Treesi went to follow, only to stop short when a man grabbed her arm.

"I'm going to enjoy breaking you."

Treesi looked at him, then turned her attention to his hand and focused her power. His face went pale, and he howled and clutched his arm to his chest.

"That's just a taste," she told him. "And when my husband finds you, you'll wish it was me hurting you." She climbed into the wagon, hearing the door slam behind her. Dyneh grabbed her and held her tightly, and Treesi gave in to her terror, burying her face in Dyneh's shoulder and shaking uncontrollably. Other arms encircled her as Pallas, Selsi and Jesta joined them.

"You did wonderfully," Dyneh murmured into Treesi's hair. "They'll find us."

Treesi nodded, sniffing and sitting up. She looked around, but there was no one else in the wagon. Jesta shifted, picking a battered sweater up off the floor.

"This is his," she whispered. "I made it for him." She hugged it to her chest. "Owyn was telling the truth."

Treesi smiled. "You still didn't believe him?"

Jesta blushed. "I was afraid to," she admitted. "I was afraid to hope." Her head shot up as they all heard a scuffling from outside.

"Come here," Dyneh said. "Against the back. Make them come to us."

They shifted, and Dyneh joined Treesi in front of the three trainees. The door opened, but it wasn't any of the raiders who entered. Instead, a man was thrown in bodily, tumbling over himself to come to a wincing stop halfway between the door and the wall. The door slammed again, and he shifted, chains clinking as he got to his knees. Then he noticed he wasn't alone and his familiar, expressive face shifted from surprise to recognition to shock.

"Treesi?" he gasped. "Is that...no. No...Jes?" His voice cracked, and Jesta pushed past Treesi and threw herself at Astur, wrapping her arms around his neck. He buried his face in her hair, wrapping one arm around her waist. Treesi sat back on her heels and smiled.

"You know, you all could have told me," she said. "Just Jesta?"

Selsi turned pink. "Ah...no?"

Dyneh laughed. "Then go on!"

Selsi and Pallas both joined Astur and Jesta, and Treesi looked away from the tearful reunion.

"You should join them," Dyneh said. "He's your brother."

"He needs to know they're safe first," Treesi answered. "I can wait. I waited this long."

Dyneh sniffed. "Safe?"

Treesi shrugged slightly. "Relatively safe." She looked out the dirty glass of one of the tiny windows. Outside, one of the raiders was brandishing a familiar hook sword. She bit her lip and turned back to see Astur wiping his face and looking at her.

"Treesi." His voice sounded harsh. Deeper than she remembered. "What are you doing here?" he asked. "I sent you to the main healing center."

"It's a long story, and I'll tell you once we're safe," Treesi answered. She hugged him, then rested her forehead against his in a gesture that had become nearly second nature over the past year. "I thought you were dead. When I heard the healing center was gone, and you didn't come west, I thought you were all dead."

Astur snorted and pulled away to sit down, pushing his long, matted hair back off his face. "I wasn't anywhere near the healing center. They put me out when they found out I helped you escape. Fa banned me as a healer. That's why I didn't go west — I couldn't be trained." He looked around. "Who's that?" he asked. "And...Jin. Where's Jin?"

"He betrayed us," Pallas said, her voice flat.

Astur sat up. "What?" he gasped, his voice cracking slightly. "No, not Jin! No!"

"It looks like they tricked him," Treesi said. "I think they told him that they had someone he cares about, and that if he did what they told him, they'd let her go. But she's dead."

Astur groaned. "It must have been his sister. He told me about her. She...well, she was older than he was, but not in her head. She was a child in a woman's body. He worried about her..." He paused, looking at the others. "He never told you about Searc?"

Pallas, Jesta and Selsi all looked at each other, and Pallas shook her head. "He never told me. But I know he wanted to learn about mind healing."

Astur nodded. "That was why. Where is he?"

"They took him to the burning fields," Selsi answered.

Astur closed his eyes. "He won't last long there. But he'll see Elaias."

"Elaias is alive?" Four voices chorused at once, and Astur chuckled.

"Good harmony," he said. "Yes. They use each of us to keep the other in line as their own captive healers." He looked at the door. "Elaias tried to distract them so I could escape. It didn't work. So..." he raised his hands, the chain between them ringing. "I get this, and he gets put out on the burning field."

"What is it?" Dyneh asked. She smiled. "I'm Dyneh. I'm another healer. I'd say it's a pleasure to meet you but—"

Astur grinned. "It isn't. I know. And the burning fields...it's a rock plain, up in the hills. They take you out there hooded, or unconscious. They put you into a frame, and they leave you here. No shade, no water..."

"No water?" Treesi swallowed. "Aven. He'll die out there!"

Astur looked at her, and blinked. "Trees, what are you wearing?" he asked, reaching out to touch the Earth gem at her throat. "This...is it true? There's an Heir?"

Treesi nodded. "Aven is her Water. He was with us when we were taken."

"And you're her Earth," Astur said, shaking his head. "And...what are you doing out here?"

"The Progress," Treesi answered. "Following Axia's Way. It's the lore."

Astur nodded. "Not that they'll believe it," he said, nodding his head toward the door. "They won't accept anyone except someone they call The Child. It's part of their lore. What I understand of it."

"Frayim told us about that," Treesi said. "Well, he told Aven. And Aven told the rest of the Companions. Because Aria is pregnant, and she's Air and Fire, and Aven is Water and Earth."

Astur went pale, his freckles standing out. "Don't say that!" he hissed. "Not where anyone can hear you! They've already wiped out entire villages in the name of this Child!" He glanced at the door. "There's no one there, I don't think. You keep that to yourself." He took a deep breath and let it out. "I don't know what to tell you about your Water. And...Frayim? The one they call the Seer? Is that the poor bastard they just beat the shit out of?" He shook his head. "They've wanted him, too. They call him the Blasphemer. They're going to burn him at the stake at sunset to cleanse the world of his tainted lies." He glanced at the door again. "Tell me help is coming?"

Treesi nodded, feeling slightly ill. "They'll find us," she said softly. "Help is coming."

DEL WENT TO ONE KNEE, studying the ruts in the dirt, the broken twigs and the scattered, mud-splattered leaves.

"*They came this way, and recently,*" he thought. "*The mud is still wet on the leaves.*" He looked up to see Owyn looking further up the trail. He had Del's crossbow in his hands, but if anything happened, Owyn was under strict orders from Karse to let Del do the shooting.

"Any idea how many?" Owyn asked, keeping his voice low.

Del shook his head, his braid falling over his shoulder. "*More than one, less than an army,*" he answered. Owyn scowled at him, and he shrugged. "*Best I can do.*" He deliberately left out that he could tell someone had been dragged through here. Or that some of the dark spots on the leaves might not be mud. He heard a rustling from down the hill, and held his hand out for his crossbow before he heard the identifying whistle and lowered his hand.

Karse appeared out of the trees. "Anything?"

"*They're close,*" Del signed.

"Close, hm?" Karse knelt next to Del, and looked at the spoor that Del pointed out. He sighed. "This isn't my regular terrain. Give me back alleys and streets any day. This? I couldn't find shit by smell out here."

Del snickered as he got back to his feet. He tucked his braid back down the back of his shirt. "*Let me scout ahead,*" he said to Owyn. "*I'll be careful.*"

"Yeah, you better be," Owyn whispered, and handed him the crossbow. "Allie will murder me if anything happens to you."

Del nodded and slipped through the trees. The raiders were either arrogant or careless — they clearly hadn't even made an attempt to hide that they'd come this way, leaving a trail that Del could read like print on a page. He stopped for a moment, stepping behind a tree and listening. No birds. No animals. Their camp must be very close. He leaned his back against the tree and gave a thought to Othi, waiting back with the guard and the horses, and worried out of his mind. He'd have been up here if there had been any hope of hiding his presence, and had been insistent on coming regardless; it had taken the combined efforts of Aleia and Jehan to calm him down long enough to listen to sense. Or at least, listen to Jehan promise that if he thought Othi was going to do something so infernally stupid that it would risk all of their lives, then Jehan was personally going to knock him out and leave him in camp.

The wind shifted, and Del heard voices, indistinct but definitely there. He followed the sound until he was sure, then retraced his steps.

"*That way,*" he signed, pointing up the slope. "*And close.*"

"How close?" Karse asked.

"*Close enough that I could hear them,*" Del answered. "*Close enough that they could hear us if we aren't careful.*"

Karse nodded. "Show me." He turned. "Owyn, you stay here, undercover. Del will relay orders through you."

"Are you going to be close enough?" Owyn asked. "If you go out of range, I can't tell you."

Karse scowled, looked at Del, then back at Owyn. Then he smiled. "You know how to whistle?" he asked Owyn. "Like a rock dove?"

Owyn looked puzzled. "Yeah. Why?"

"On account of they don't live this far north. When Del says something to you, whistle. We'll see how far we can go before you can't hear him anymore, and if that happens, I'll send him back to that spot."

"*What does a rock dove sound like?*" Del asked. Owyn whistled at him, and he nodded, then led Karse back up the slope toward where he'd heard the voices. He stopped by the tree and looked back down the hill.

"*Wyn?*"

An answering whistle. Del grinned, and they continued on. They were close enough to the camp that Del could almost pick out individual voices when he called to Owyn and got no response. He tapped Karse's arm, then touched his ear and shook his head. Karse nodded, then pointed to a rock overhang. They crept out onto it, and found themselves looking out over a camp full of men. Tents. A single wagon. A tall post that didn't seem to serve a purpose. Del counted men, then counted again, coming up with the same number both times. Then he glanced at Karse, who was studying the camp with ferocious intensity.

Del turned back to the camp, trying to see the best way to approach. How could they attack? Karse touched his arm, nodding back the way they had come. They left quickly, heading back down to the fallen log where Del had last heard Owyn whistle.

"Right," Karse whispered. "I need you to relay orders. Tell Owyn to bring them up to meet you. I need to take one more look. I'll be back."

Del nodded and looked down the trail. "*Owyn, bring them up. We've seen the camp, and we're very close. Be as quiet as you can.*"

He heard the answering whistle, then soft rustling that came closer until he was surrounded by their guards. Othi swallowed and rested his axes on the ground.

"Where's Karse?" Owyn asked.

"*He wanted to see something,*" Del answered. There was rustling behind him, and he turned and raised his bow, lowering it when Karse appeared. Karse nodded, then gestured to the others.

"Gather 'round," he called softly. He crouched and started sketching in the dirt with a stick. Del looked over his shoulder, and saw a representation of the camp growing, marked with boxes, lines, and x's.

"Right, this is what we've got here," he said, pointing with the stick. "This is the camp. No guards posted that I can see. Don't mean they're not there. Just I can't see them. Also, no signs of our people, but there's one wagon. Given what Owyn saw, I'm willing to put money on them being in there. It's also the most secure structure in the camp. Now, there's an approach here and here." He pointed. "Right, Del, you're taking the archers up to that rock where we scouted. When I signal, you start shooting. Two rounds, then we'll engage. After that, you just pick off the ones trying to escape." He looked up. "Owyn, you're with me. We're taking a team around this approach, coming at the camp from the rear. Your job is to get to that wagon and get whoever is in there out. Fara, you and Othi are taking a Water team up the main way. I don't expect this lot to fight. I expect them to run when we attack. You're going to stop them."

Fara smiled, baring all her teeth like a shark. "How permanently do you want them stopped?"

Karse grinned. "I'm leaving that up to you."

AVEN HAD ONLY EVER been sunburned twice in his life, both times when he was under the age of ten. It was something that Water children grew out of eventually. But he remembered the prickling pain of it, and he recognized that pain and the tightness of his skin under the unrelenting sun.

But the sunburn wasn't nearly as painful as how dry he was. He'd never felt this dry before, ever. Every breath burned, and it was getting harder to think, harder to stay conscious. It had been hours, he thought, since the raiders had come and gone. They'd brought Arjin and Frayim with them. Both were unconscious, and Frayim had been badly beaten. Arjin had been bound into another frame, but Frayim had been stretched out face-down on the bare rock, stripped, and bound in place. Then the raiders had left. None of them had seemed to hear Aven when he begged for just a drop of salt water.

He coughed, letting his head hang. He was alone, or near enough that it seemed to make no difference. Arjin and Frayim were both still unconscious, and Elaias hadn't moved save for that one time. Aven wasn't even certain if he was alive.

He wasn't certain if any of them were going to live, despite Owyn's vision.

He was fairly certain he was starting to hallucinate. He had to be.

He could hear shouting in the distance.

Chapter Thirty-Four

Del crouched on the rock and studied the camp, picking out targets. They went in and out of tents, milled around the post, dumping bundles of sticks into a pile around the base. He wasn't sure what they were doing, and wondered how much longer he and the archers would need to wait. No one seemed to be going to the wagon at all, and he wondered about that, too. Five women and five men would be cramped in Owyn's wagon, so Del assumed it would be just as cramped in the wagon in camp. Were all the prisoners in there?

How was Owyn going to get them out and keep them safe once the fighting started?

Someone crept up next to him, and Del looked to his right to see Leist.

"Any signs?" Leist asked. "Hear anything?"

Del shook his head, and Leist sighed. "Me neither. This is messy, Del. Hostage situations are always messy. And we've got no idea if they're all in the wagon, or if none of them are."

Del nodded, then blinked. A familiar whistle. He looked at Leist, who nodded.

"I hear it, too. Right." He raised his crossbow. "Archers, on my mark."

Del licked his lips and sighted, waiting. Another distant whistle, and Leist snapped, "Fire!"

OWYN SHIFTED, FEELING sick to his stomach.

"What the fuck am I doing here, Karse?" he whispered. "I'm not a guard."

Karse snickered. "I seem to remember someone insisting on coming out with us. Looked an awful lot like you."

"Yeah, well...you should have told me to get stuffed."

"One more time than I did?"

Owyn scowled at him. "I just..."

"You can fight," Karse said. "I've seen you do it. You're good with that thing." He nodded to the whip-chain in Owyn's hands. "But you're not the first line of attack. You stay back. Keep clear of the guard, let us do the fighting, and don't engage unless you have to. I told you — your job is to get to the wagon and get the hostages out. Bring them back through the way we came, and we'll meet you back at the fallen tree where we started. Now, give the signal."

Owyn nodded and whistled, then waited a moment and whistled again.

A heartbeat later, the camp erupted into screams as arrows hailed down on them from above. A second fall of arrows, and Karse shouted — he and the guard rushed forward into the camp. Owyn started to skirt around through the brush, working his way closer to the wagon. He could hear cursing, screaming, saw people dropping as they were felled by arrows from above.

Then he saw two men running toward the wagon, the both of them carrying burning torches. One of them fell screaming, an arrow piercing his back. The other kept running.

"No," Owyn breathed. "Oh, fuck, no!" He bolted out of the brush and ran, trying to intercept the raider. The man saw him, hesitated, then turned to flee. He stopped just long enough that Owyn could snap the whip-chain into motion, catching him from behind and pulling back sharply. He clearly heard the man's neck snap, and the body dropped to the dirt, the torch falling next to him. Owyn shook the chain loose and kept running, pulling up next to the wagon and shooting the heavy bolt on the door. He threw it open.

"Jax!"

Owyn sagged with relief. "Mama! Come on. We need to get you out of here. Everyone out, before they try to burn this down again or notice me." He turned, stepping away from the wagon as people started climbing out. Selsi. Jesta. Pallas. His mother. Treesi. The man from his vision.

And that was all. He stepped back, glanced inside, and decided to save the questions until they were safe. He pointed back to the tree line. "That way. Move!"

Treesi ran, followed by the others, and Owyn followed them, not looking to see what was happening behind him. He could hear more shouting, and he thought he heard Othi. But he had his orders, and he entered the trees behind Dyneh.

"There's a clearing a little bit up," he called. "Stop there!"

In the clearing, Owyn was hit from two sides by his mother and Treesi. He hugged them both tightly, kissed Treesi, then demanded, "Where's Aven? Arjin and Frayim?"

"The burning fields," the man answered. "They're all at the burning fields."

"Owyn, this is Astur," Treesi said. "But you knew that."

Astur blinked. "How did he know that?"

Owyn nodded. "I'll explain later, and I'll meet you proper when we're not all trying not to die. Where's the burning fields?"

Astur shook his head. "I don't know. When they brought me out there, they took me in a hood. The raiders are the only ones who know."

"Then I hope Karse leaves someone alive out there." Owyn pointed. "Come on. I'm supposed to get you all down to a safe spot, out of the way of the fighting. This way."

He took the lead, retracing his steps back through where the guard had waited, along the trail and around the camp, heading back to the fallen log that was their landmark. As they reached it, he heard a familiar voice.

"*Wyn?*"

He turned and whistled, and Del came trotting out of the brush.

"What are you doing down here?" Owyn asked.

"*I ran out of quarrels,*" Del explained as Treesi ran to him and hugged him. "*I saw you get everyone out and came to meet you. Where are the others?*"

"Someplace only the raiders know," Owyn answered. "Look, you got your lock picking things with you?" When Del nodded, Owyn gestured to Astur. "Get those off him. We might need his hands free."

Del reached into his pouch as he headed toward Astur. Owyn looked over his shoulder, up the trail, and turned to face that way. If anyone got past the Water warriors, he'd need to stop them. And maybe get some answers.

"Astur, what are the burning fields?" he asked, shaking the whip-chain out and draping it over his shoulders.

"It's a rock-plain, up in the hills. That's where they take you when they want you to die slowly." Astur winced, and Owyn glanced back to see that Del had gotten one manacle unlocked. The skin underneath looked raw.

"Oh, that doesn't look good," Dyneh murmured. "Let me see."

Owyn looked back up the hill, frowning as he heard the sounds of something coming toward them. "Get under cover," he called over his shoulder.

A man burst out of the trees, running wildly. He was battered and bruised, and his clothes were torn and streaked with blood. He almost fell when he saw them, catching himself on a tree to keep from landing on the ground at Owyn's feet. He stared, slack-jawed, then looked past Owyn and saw the others. His eyes widened, and he howled and launched himself at Owyn. There was no time for Owyn to use the whip-chain, and it went flying as he and the raider rolled down the hill. Owyn heard Del shouting in his mind, heard Treesi shouting aloud, but the voices were drowned out by a sharp pain in his side. He came to a stop against a tree, and couldn't move as the raider got up, his knife stained red. He spat on Owyn and turned...

Owyn saw a flash of metal as it caught the light, heard a crack, and the raider screamed and staggered backward, blood spraying everywhere. He swayed, then fell backward and didn't get up. Owyn could hear him groaning.

"Owyn!" Treesi dropped to her knees next to him, resting her hand on his chest. She closed her eyes and nodded. "It's not bad. Not deep enough to hit anything important."

"Hurts like fuck," Owyn growled. "He dead?"

"No," Astur answered, coming up to stand behind Treesi. He held up Owyn's whip-chain. "I like this."

Owyn closed his eyes and nodded. "I'll make you one. Once I have a forge again." He sighed as the pain faded to nothing. "Oh, that's good, Trees." He waved one hand toward the raider. "Use those chains on him. Chain him to a tree or something. And heal him. Don't let him die. We need to know where the others are."

Astur nodded. "With pleasure. Del, is it? Help me?"

By the time Treesi was finished healing the wound in Owyn's side, Astur and Del had the raider with his back against a tree, his wrists chained behind him. Owyn joined them, then turned to Del.

"Can I borrow a knife?"

Del drew one of his throwing knives, handing it to Owyn. Owyn took it and crouched down in front of the raider.

"Tell me about the burning field," he said. "Where is it?"

"I'm not telling you anything," the raider growled.

"Oh, you're going to tell me everything. In detail." Owyn looked up to see that the healers had come to form a semi-circle around him. The raider looked up at Treesi, and...flinched?

Owyn could work with that. Whatever that was. "Or," he drawled. "I'm going to give you to her." He smiled up at Treesi, flipped the knife, and offered it to her. She looked at him, and at the knife. Then she smiled, and Owyn stared at her in horror.

He'd never seen her smile like that, and he suddenly understood why the man had flinched.

"That's very sweet of you, Owyn, but I don't need a knife." She reached down and touched the raider's shoulder, and he howled in pain. "Now, you have something to tell us?"

"Keep her away from me!"

Owyn reached up and took Treesi's hand, tugging her back. "Then you tell us what we want to know."

"*Did I scare you?*" Treesi whispered in his mind. "*Your heart is racing. I'm sorry.*"

Owyn stood up and leaned in to kiss her cheek. "You're fucking terrifying, love. And I'm definitely not going to be teasing you about being horrible at making threats anymore," he whispered. She giggled. Then she looked back at the raider.

"Well?" she asked. "Do you need more convincing?" When he didn't answer, she reached out, and he screamed.

"Keep that bitch away from me!" He struggled against the chains, then slumped. "It's up in the hills," he murmured. "About a mile east of camp. The trail is marked with cairns. Just...don't let her touch me."

Owyn nodded, then turned when he heard voices. He saw Othi before anyone else —the big man was running. Behind him were Fara and the other Water warriors.

"We heard screaming," Othi panted as he came close. He pulled up, and his face lit up when he saw who was with Owyn. "Treesi!"

Treesi handed the knife back to Del and ran into Othi's arms. The raider moaned.

"That's her man?" he whispered, and Owyn watched as Astur turned to stare. "She broke all the bones in my mate's hand, on account that he touched her. Told him that when we saw her man, we'd wish it was her...fuck..."

"You could have played nice and just told us where to find our people," Owyn said. He turned to Astur. "You've got a lot of catching up to do. But later. Othi, where's Karse? I know where the others are."

Othi nodded. "He sent us on to check on you all, and take people back to camp." He frowned. "But not everyone is here."

"That's what we just got out of this one," Owyn said. "Look. You take Treesi and the girls and Mama back to camp. Take Freckles and Pewter and...and I'm not sure. You need one more horse, at least. Talk to whichever guard is still down with them. Astur, you up for staying with us?"

"I want to stay!" Treesi protested. "Elaias is out there. You might need me."

"To put the fear of all things painful into whoever we find?" Astur asked, grinning. "Never would have expected that of you, Trees."

"Fear of what?" Othi asked. "Treesi? What are you doing?"

"I'm staying," Treesi repeated.

"You're going," Owyn replied, then shook his head. "Wait. Let me rephrase that. You are taking that baby back to camp."

"Baby?" Astur gasped. He reached out and rested his hand on Treesi's shoulder, then laughed. "Oh, Treesi!"

Treesi scowled. "Owyn, that's cheating," she grumbled. "Fine. I'll tell the Senior Healer that he needs to be back here with all the salt water he can carry, too. Aven is going to need it. And carts. Othi—"

"I'll bring him back," Othi said. "And you can tell me why we need salt water. I missed something."

"What about him?" Selsi asked, pointing at the raider. "Are we leaving him here?"

"For now," Owyn said. "He's not going anywhere, and we're going to be busy. I'll tell Karse he's here."

"You can't leave me here!" the raider howled. "You can't!"

"Well, we can't take you with us," Owyn answered. "You already tried to kill me."

"Do you have something else we should know?" Dyneh asked. "Something to trade?"

"Mama!" Owyn turned to look at Dyneh. "I—" He paused, then turned back to the raider. "Well?"

The raider glanced at Treesi, then whispered, "You'll keep her away from me?"

"Yes," Owyn said, nodding. "She's going back to camp. So...Fara, would you go back and find the Captain?" He sat down in front of the raider. "You and me are going to have a nice, long talk while we wait."

RIDING IN FRONT OF Othi, Treesi could feel him watching her as they approached the camp, and the weight of the unspoken words grew heavier with every step Mountain took. She looked up at him, and he smiled.

"You can tell me when you're ready," he said.

Treesi looked away. She could see the camp. See the people watching. Waiting. She could see Jehan. "I had to protect myself. And our baby," she said. "And...and everyone. So...Owyn says he's not going to tease me about not being able to make threats anymore. Because I scared him."

Othi coughed. "You scared Owyn?"

Selsi and Pallas were riding double on Pewter, close enough that they could hear. "Treesi kept them off of us," Selsi said. "One of them tried to hurt her, and she broke him."

Othi's brows rose. "You did...what did you do?"

"Something I'm going to have to admit to the Senior Healer," Treesi said. "I broke my oath as a healer to do no harm." She looked up at Othi. "I'm not sure what he'll say."

"He'll say you did what you had to do," Othi assured her. "And I'm proud of you." He wrapped one arm around her. "My little warrior."

She leaned into his chest as he urged Mountain on, moving more quickly toward the camp. "Does that mean I get warrior marks?"

"If you want them, I'll be happy to give them to you. After the baby comes." Othi nodded. "Here comes Uncle Jehan."

"Where's Aven?" Jehan demanded as he reached them, with Steward and Memfis on his heels. "And Arjin and Frayim?"

"Still up there," Othi answered. "I'm supposed to bring you back."

"And you need to bring back all the salt water you can carry," Treesi added. "And wagons for the injured. And you need to hurry. Othi can tell you why on the way. I don't know about Aven and Arjin, but Frayim is hurt."

Jehan nodded and turned to Dyneh. "Take the girls and go on to camp. Huris is in a state. Aleia is with him."

Dyneh nodded. "Getting him calmed down will take all my attention." She turned to the trainees. "You're all going to be needed in the healing tent. Prepare for anything, just the way we taught you. Understood?"

"Yes, Healer," the girls chorused.

"Alanar will be there with you, and I'll join you in the tent as soon as I can," Treesi called after them. "Senior Healer—" She paused, looked up at Othi, then shook her head. "No, I can wait. You need to do what needs doing. We'll be ready when you get back, and we'll talk later."

Jehan frowned slightly. "Right. Let's go. And tell me what I'm walking into."

OWYN HEARD THE HORSES coming up the hill long before he saw them, and got to his feet. He saw Othi and Mountain first, and behind him were Jehan and Steward.

"You didn't bring a cart?" Owyn called.

"We couldn't get it up the trail," Othi answered. Owyn nodded and looked down.

"You told me everything else, Iantir. How do they get the cart into your camp?"

The raider nodded. "There's another trail, to the west. Sort of hidden, though. I know where it is and I still miss it sometimes."

"I figured that they have carts in the camp that they're not going to need," Othi said. "So we'll take that trail going out." He nodded. "What are we doing with him?"

Owyn snorted. "Yeah, here's the thing. Karse came up, then Del and Astur went back down to camp to help, because they thought they might need a healer fast. And I don't have a way to move Iantir here, on account of Del being the one who can open locks. So Iantir has been telling me all sorts of things about this group, and I've been telling him why they're wrong. We're getting on all right, and I'm not holding the fact that he stabbed me against him. And he's not holding the fact that Astur damn near split his face open against us." He looked at Iantir. "So, you convinced yet?"

"Still not believing you came back from the dead," Iantir answered. "I mean...dead is dead!"

"Not where Owyn is concerned. Now, who'd have the keys to those cuffs?" Jehan asked.

"Mitok," Iantir answered. "He's the chief."

Owyn nodded. "And if Iantir is telling me the truth, he's the one who's been taking orders directly from Risha."

Jehan growled softly. "Oh, I cannot wait to get my hands on that bitch."

"I think there's a line, Senior Healer."

"I'm patient. Show me how to get to the camp."

Chapter Thirty-Five

D el touched Karse's arm and pointed at the moss-covered cairn half-hidden near the edge of the trail. Karse nodded.

"I see it," he said. "Astur, how long did it take you to get up here?"

Del glanced back to see Astur behind them. He shook his head and pushed his hair back off his face. "It's hard to say," he answered. "When they drag you up here kicking and screaming and totally blind, it's hard to tell just how long the trip actually takes. But I think we're close."

"And no guards," Karse said slowly. "Why no guards?"

"*Because there's no way to get up here from anywhere else but the camp,*" Del signed. Karse chuckled.

"Too fast, Del," he said. "You scouted off the trail?"

Del nodded and pointed off to one side of the trail. "Cliff," he said slowly, trying to enunciate. He pointed the other way. "C...C...C..." The rest of the word refused to form, and he growled and picked another word. "Hole."

"Hole?" Karse looked at him. "Oh. Chasm?"

Del nodded, then pointed up the trail at another cairn. Just past it, the trail turned and opened out, and Del walked out onto the rocky ground, feeling the heat radiating up from below his feet. He could see six wooden frames like empty doorways standing stark against the sky.

"Elaias!"

Astur pushed past them and ran out onto the rocks toward one of the frames. Del started forward when he saw a familiar form hanging limp from another frame, only to stop when Karse grabbed his arm.

"Del," Karse said slowly. "Go back. Someone needs to bring Jehan up here when he gets here. That's you."

"But—"

Karse turned him, looking into his eyes. "I know. That's why I want you down there," he nodded toward the trail. "Let me take him down. Jehan will be here soon, and he'll have the salt water. You bring Jehan up. And guards. Litters. We're going to need to get them down from here. I don't think Astur is going to be good for much as a healer now that he's seen the state his brother is in. Remember Aven, back in Cliffside?"

Del looked back at the frames. How long had Aven been out here, in the sun? How long would it take Othi to get back with Jehan?

How long could a Waterborn live without water?

He nodded, turned, and ran back down the trail, trying not to fall over his own feet. If Jehan wasn't in camp, he'd go back down to the fallen log, to where Owyn was waiting.

He'd run back to camp if he needed to.

He hit the level ground and slowed, panting, looking around. Progress guards, standing watch over the surviving raiders so that they could be taken before Aria. Leist was among them, and he waved.

"You found them?" he called.

Del nodded and looked around, then pointed. Leist nodded.

"Othi might be back by now," Leist called. "If not, then soon."

Del nodded again, and trotted toward the trail that led out of camp. He'd only just cleared the tree line when he heard horses.

"Owyn?"

He was answered by a now-familiar whistle, and he stopped and tried to catch his breath. The horses grew closer, and Del saw Jehan first, with Owyn riding double with him. Behind them was Steward, but Del didn't spare a moment to wonder why his father was here instead of with Aria. He just started signing.

"We found them, but we don't have a lot of time. We need guards, and litters. Karse wouldn't let me get close, but he says we need salt water and a lot of it."

Jehan drew his horse in, his eyes wide. "What did they do to my boy?" he demanded.

"Is Frayim there, too?" Steward asked.

"I think so," Del answered. *"I didn't see Frayim."* Then he frowned. *"And I'd be better showing you. The trail is this way."*

"Del, ride with me," Steward called. "You can tell Owyn how to get wherever we're going."

Del swung up behind his father and pointed, and Steward urged Alabaster forward as Jehan shouted for guards to follow them and to bring whatever they could to carry people back down.

"Del, what's up there?" Owyn called. "Astur called it the burning fields."

Del hesitated, then answered. *"It's a rock plain, and it's like an oven. They're out under the sun, and the rocks reflect the sun back at them. There's no shade, and they can't get away from it."*

"Oh, fuck," Owyn breathed, just loud enough for Del to hear him.

"What?" Jehan demanded. "What did he say?"

"Jehan...I wasn't out in the deep very long," Owyn said slowly. "How well do Water deal with lots of sun? Like...lots and lots of sun? And no water?"

Del glanced back to see Jehan go pale. He pointed again. "Go," he whispered, and felt Alabaster surge forward.

When they reached the top of the trail, all of the frames were empty. Steward drew Alabaster in and shook his head.

"We're not going to have good footing up here," he said. "Dismount."

Del slid to the ground and went to join Owyn and Jehan, who had both dismounted. "*How can I help?*"

Jehan handed him a pair of waterskins, then handed another pair to Owyn. "Owyn, you have sweet water. Del, you have salt. Let's go." He started running toward the frames, and Del followed, feeling the waterskins sloshing and gurgling in his hands.

Karse met them halfway to the first frame.

"We moved them to the shade," he said, nodding toward the tree line. "Of the four of them, Frayim is the worst physically hurt. Arjin is a little battered, but fine. He's monitoring Frayim. Elaias is stable. Just exposure, dehydration and sunburned enough to nearly glow."

"And Aven?" Jehan asked. "Karse, where's my son?"

"He's over there, too, and I don't know. There's not a mark on him. Astur says he doesn't know enough to know what's wrong, so he's monitoring and waiting for you." Karse said, leading them toward the trees. Del could see Astur's bright hair standing out against the darkness under the trees. "Jehan, what happens when Water dries out?"

Jehan stopped. He closed his eyes, clearly trying to think of an answer to Karse's question. Then he swore.

"We need to get him underwater," he said. "We don't have a way to do that. But he needs to be underwater." He took a waterskin from Del, and ran toward the trees. Owyn looked at Del, who shook his head. They both ran after Jehan, who waved Del over as they approached. Del went to his knees next to Astur, his stomach churning.

Aven's skin was red, his lips cracked in places. His breathing was labored, and everything about him looked sunken and parched. Jehan laid the waterskin down and rested his hand on Aven's forehead. He took a deep breath.

"Del, I want you to work with Astur," he said. "You're going to get that entire waterskin into him. A steady stream. Astur, it's fine if it gets into his lungs. He needs to rehydrate. If we were anywhere near the sea, I'd have him underwater." He frowned and looked around. "Karse, when the guards get up here with the litters, I want them to search the camp for a...a basin, or a trough. Something big enough for a man."

Karse nodded. "We'll find something."

Jehan turned back to Astur. "Astur, are you ready for this?"

Astur swallowed and nodded. "I...I might yell questions at you. I've never worked on a Waterborn before."

"I'd be surprised if you had," Jehan replied. He started to get up, only to stop when Astur cleared his throat.

"Is he the Waterborn that they've been talking about? Or is it the other one? Othi, the big one that's apparently my new brother?"

Jehan sat back down. "I'm going to need some context."

Astur nodded, resting one hand on Aven's chest. "Del, start feeding him," he said. "And...we've only heard bits of it, when they came close to the wagon. Most of it didn't make sense. But this...we couldn't figure out why they were talking about Waterborn when we're so far from the sea. They were saying that there was one they wanted to catch...and...and dry like river snaps. Because the Lady wanted him." He closed his eyes and cocked his head to the side. "Interesting. That's something that never made sense in the book. I see what it means now."

Jehan smiled. "Let me guess," he said. "The extra fat layer?"

Astur nodded. "Exactly. Sometimes, I do better doing instead of reading. The book was interesting, but some of the differences didn't make sense. The extra fat layer in Water, and the shoulder musculature in Air. Elaias said I'd see it for myself one of these days." He opened his eyes. "Del, keep feeding him. He's absorbing it really well."

Del shifted, letting the slow trickle of salt water pour into Aven's mouth, watching as his throat worked as he swallowed. He'd drained almost the entire waterskin before Aven moaned and coughed, and took a painfully labored breath.

"Easy, Ven," Jehan said. He rested his hand on Aven's chest. "I thought so. Astur, define waterlung."

Astur blinked. "We don't get that much up here. It's too dry. But in damp places, it's inhaling liquids into the lungs and the lungs getting infected...oh! Do Waterborn get it in reverse? If they get too dry? It felt like waterlung, but I couldn't figure out why!" He looked down at Aven. "Show me?"

Jehan nodded. "Put your hand on mine. I'll guide."

Astur covered Jehan's hand with his own. Then he grinned. "Oh...you're a level five, aren't you?"

"He's the Senior Healer," Owyn said from behind them. "Litters are here."

Jehan nodded. "Aven is stable. Keep monitoring him, Astur. You've got a good touch. Del, keep getting the water into him. I want to check on Frayim and Elaias before we move them." Jehan stood up and sighed. "I'm getting too old for this."

"Are not," Del muttered, and Jehan laughed. He reached down and ruffled Del's hair, then walked away. Del reached out and picked up the other waterskin, looking away for a moment. When he turned back, Aven's eyes were open. Del smiled and brushed his hair back, signing with one hand.

"It's over. You're safe."

Aven grimaced and raised one hand. *"Can't breathe."*

"Owyn, tell him it's waterlung."

Owyn crouched down next to Del. "It's waterlung, Fishie. We're going to make it better. You have to keep drinking, and your fa is going to find some way for you to change. Will that help?"

Aven nodded. Then he reached out and tapped Astur's hand.

"I'm Astur. Treesi's brother." Astur smiled. "Thanks for being my first Waterborn patient."

Aven grinned weakly. Then he closed his eyes. Del poured more water into his mouth, and looked up as Jehan came back.

"Elaias is asking for you, Astur. Go see to him. We're going to move out."

Astur nodded. He patted Aven's chest and smiled. "I'll be back," he said softly. Once he was gone, Jehan sat down in his place.

"Did they tell you anything, Ven?"

Aven shook his head. Owyn came around to his other side and sat down. "Tell me, Fishie. I'll tell them." He frowned. "He says something hit him from behind, and he doesn't know how a raider got behind him. But when he woke up, he was here. The only time he saw any of the raiders after that was when they brought Frayim and Arjin up, and no one said anything where he could hear."

Jehan nodded. "Right. We'll get to the bottom of that once we're back to camp. And I'm going to figure out a way for you to change, Ven. You'll be more comfortable if you can sleep underwater, and your lungs will heal more cleanly."

Owyn looked up. "He wants to know about Frayim. And how Aria is, and who's with her?"

"Your mother and Memfis are with Aria, who is absolutely furious. And Frayim will be fine." Jehan grinned and looked back over his shoulder. "He's got a very attentive nursemaid."

"A very attentive...oh. Oh." Owyn chuckled. "Well, there's a shock."

Del twisted in his seat and looked across the clearing to where Frayim lay. On his left was Arjin.

On his right was Steward, and as Del watched, Steward reached out and ran gentle fingers over Frayim's forehead, brushing back his hair.

"Del, Aven needs to drink that, not wear it."

Del forced his attention back to his task, and away from the besotted look on his father's face. He hadn't seen that expression since before they'd left Terraces.

A shock indeed.

OWYN BENT AND GRABBED the litter poles, looking forward to see Karse doing the same.

"On three," Karse called. "One...two..."

They lifted together. Frayim, deep in a healing trance, didn't move as they started walking.

"So why did they beat the fuck out of Frayim?" Owyn called.

"Because he speaks the truth." Elaias answered. He and Astur fell in next to Owyn, walking slowly. Elaias leaned on his brother for support, but he looked better than he had. "And they don't want to hear the truth. They want the lies they've been taught, and they want others to believe those lies. So someone who tells the truth is a threat to them."

Owyn nodded. "Frayim told us about you getting him away from your parents. And Treesi told us what they were like."

Elaias sighed. "Possibly they still are like that. I don't know. I also don't care to find out." He sniffed. "Does that make me horrible?"

Owyn considered it while they walked, then shook his head. "I don't think so. So...they might still be out there?" He glanced at the brothers. "You going to tell Treesi that?"

Elaias nodded. "She should know. When I got back to the healing center, everything was ashes. I looked for survivors, but I didn't find any. Nor did I find any bodies. I don't know that they're dead. I assume that they are. I'm not going to check my theory by going to find them. That wouldn't end well." He looked at Astur and sighed. "I've had enough of things not ending well."

"It ended just fine. It was the middle that was the problem," Astur said. "We're alive. The girls are alive. Arjin...Eli, what are we doing with Jin?"

"I want to hear his side," Elaias said. "You know Arjin. He's made overthinking into an art form. He has a reason, and we need to know it. I need to hear it from him, not your theories about what the reason might be." He looked around. "Where is he?"

"With the Senior Healer and Steward, helping them bring Aven down." Owyn looked forward. "Now, before I have to pay attention to where I put my feet on that hill, what are you two talking about?"

"Arjin betrayed us," Astur said. "He was working with the raiders."

"The fuck you say!" Karse looked back over his shoulder.

"That had to be how someone got behind Aven," Owyn said. "Right. I'm interested in hearing what Arjin has to say for himself. But we have people to take care of first."

"Mind your step," Karse called. "It's a bit steep."

They made their slow, careful way down the slope, and Owyn was sweating and biting his lip by the time they reached level ground. "Hold up," he called as they came into the camp. "My hands are cramping."

"There's a cart," Arjin called as he came toward them. He pointed to where Owyn could see Jehan and Steward. "Can you make it, or should we bring it over?"

"I can make that," Owyn answered. Arjin started to turn away.

"Arjin," Elaias' voice was firm, and Arjin winced slightly. He took a deep breath and turned toward where Elaias and Astur stood.

"You know?"

"I want to hear the truth, Arjin," Elaias said. "Sit with me as we go, and tell me everything."

Arjin tucked his hands behind his back and nodded. "Yes, sir."

"And don't sir at me," Elaias chided. "I never wanted that from you before. I don't want it now. Come and tell me why."

Arjin joined Elaias and Astur, his head bowed. He somehow looked both terrified of what was going to happen and resigned to it.

"Come on, Owyn," Karse said. "Let's get him into the cart. And there's a way to get out of here?"

"Yeah, but we'll need Iantir. Did anyone find the keys?"

"I think Del went down the hill to fetch him and Othi," Karse answered. "I don't know if keys were involved."

They carefully maneuvered Frayim into the cart, and Steward came over to join them. He looked over the side and sighed.

"He looks so young when he's asleep," he said.

Karse looked at Steward and coughed slightly. "You...been watching him sleep?"

Steward looked up. He looked confused for a moment, then blushed. "I...no!" He looked down again. "He's half my age, Captain."

"So?" Karse replied. "My man is half mine. I'm just thinking of Rhexa. She's a good woman."

"She is a good woman. And she refused me," Steward said. "And I'm not looking to replace her, Karse. And we're not going to have this conversation."

"Not in front of me, you mean?" Owyn asked. Steward turned even more red. "Look. I'm the last person to tell you not to. If he makes you happy, then...you know, he might make Aunt Rhexa happy. But he isn't going to be happy if he wakes up before we get back to camp. So can you moon over him later, maybe?"

Steward scowled. "I'm not mooning over him." He looked down again, then back at Owyn. "Am I?"

"You're completely besotted," Karse answered. "And we all noticed."

Steward took a deep breath, let it out, then murmured, "Well, fuck."

Owyn snickered. "Right. Are we all loaded?" He looked around. "Where are the raiders?"

"The guards are marching them back to camp for Aria's judgment," Steward answered. "We'll probably meet them on the road." He looked past Owyn. "And there's Del and Othi and Iantir. Do we trust him?"

"Not really, no," Owyn answered. "But he's terrified of Othi, and even more scared of Treesi, so he'll behave."

"Terrified of...Treesi?" Karse repeated. "Did I miss something?"

"Apparently, Treesi put the fear of all things painful into them. At least, according to Astur. I don't know all of it."

Karse chuckled. "I need this story. Right. Let's go."

Chapter Thirty-Six

Aria stood at the edge of the camp and watched as carts and guards came closer. She fought the urge to look to her left — Aven wasn't there. None of her Companions were there — only Treesi was in camp, and she and Alanar were busy in the healing tent, getting ready for any injured.

A hand slipped into hers, and Aria smiled. Her Companions might not be with her, but her friends were. Trista stood on her right, and Afansa was on Trista's other side. Aria looked at her, and Trista smiled nervously.

"They're all going to be all right," she said. Then she bit her lip. "Aren't they?"

Afansa put her arm around Trista's shoulders. "They're all going to be fine. And if they're not fine now, we have the best healers in the world with us." She shaded her eyes with her other hand, and smiled. "Look, there's Owyn. Do you see him? In the cart? And there's Karse."

Aria studied the distant faces. "Can you see Aven?" she asked. "I don't see him."

"Not yet," Afansa said. She squeezed Aria's shoulder. "I'm sure he's fine."

By the time the wagons reached the camp, a small crowd had gathered around Aria. Aleia stood on Aria's left, with Memfis by her side. The wagons slowed, and Jehan jumped down from one. He looked around, saw Aleia, and waved at her, then started signing in broad gestures. Aleia tensed, then ran to the wagon.

"What happened?" she demanded, and Aria moaned. She started forward, only to be met halfway by Owyn.

"What happened?" she asked. "What's wrong with Aven?"

"Waterlung," Owyn answered. "It'll be all right—"

Aria stared at him. "My grandmother died from waterlung. How did Aven catch that?"

"From what I heard, Water can get it if they get too dry, and those fucks had Aven staked out in the sun. He's sunburnt, too. All of them are." Owyn looked back. "They beat Frayim near to death. We need to get him to the healers. Aven will be fine. Jehan says so. He's in healing trance, and Jehan wants to rig something so he can change and get some more salt water into him."

Aria nodded. "I want to see him. I don't care that he won't know I'm there. I want to see him."

Owyn nodded and offered his arm. "I expected that." They started toward the wagon. "The surviving raiders are being brought for your judgment. I think we have less than half of them. Including one who turned and helped us, after Treesi terrified the piss out of him."

Aria looked at Owyn. "How did she do that?"

"Ah...I'll let her tell you. She's not feeling all that good about it," Owyn said. He pointed. "Those are her brothers, by the way. Tall one is Elaias, and Astur is the one—"

"Who looks just like Treesi," Aria finished. "If Treesi was a man."

"Yeah," Owyn agreed. "You should see him when he smiles."

"Owyn—"

"I can look!" Owyn chuckled. "I'll have to describe him to Allie, later. Right. They're taking Frayim to the healing tent. Aria, did you know that Steward is sweet on Frayim?"

Aria watched as Steward trailed after guards who were carrying a litter. She shook her head. "Not before now, no. Are you sure?"

Owyn nodded. "Pretty sure."

"Do you want me to speak with him?" Aria asked.

"Nah." Owyn shook his head. "He's a grown man. And when I asked him, he pointed out that Aunt Rhexa did turn him down." He shook his head again. "They'll make it right between them. Or they won't. But as long as no one gets hurt, it's theirs to do." He stopped a few feet from the cart where Jehan and Aleia were both sitting in the bed. "Right. You want me to come with you, or you want to go on your own?"

She took his hand and held on tightly. "Come with me."

Owyn squeezed her fingers. "Of course."

They walked the rest of the way to the wagon together. Jehan smiled soothingly at her.

"He'll be fine," he said. "He needs to rehydrate, and we're working on how to do that. He'll feel like ten miles of bad road for a while, but he will be fine."

Aria nodded. "Owyn tells me that you want to set something up so he can change. How?"

Jehan put his arm around Aleia's shoulders and sighed, and Aria realized just how tired he looked. "We couldn't find a tub or a trough in the raider camp," he said. "So if there's nothing in our camp, Karse and Steward are talking about sending riders out to settlements within a day's ride of here, to see if they have something we can trade for. Once we have that, then I can match the proportions of salt to water to match sea water, and he'll be able to change and sleep."

"Do we have enough salt for that?" Owyn asked.

"We'll be bartering for that, too," Aleia answered. "Especially since we'll have to do this more than once. We'll need to change the water so the air doesn't run out."

Aria looked at Owyn, who frowned.

"Wait...like in a closed room with no vents?"

"Exactly," Jehan said. He dragged his fingers through his hair and took a deep breath. "Breathable air comes from plants. We don't have access to the right kinds of water plants to add them to a recovery pool. But we'll make it work." He looked down. "Now, I'm assuming you're not here to talk to me."

Aria stepped closer to the side of the wagon. To her surprise, Aven looked back up at her, his hazel eyes half-lidded with sleep. She cupped his cheek, and he sighed softly.

"I thought you were in trance," she said.

"I woke him up to see you," Jehan said. "You'll both rest better for it." Jehan rested his hand on Aven's shoulder. "Not too long, Ven."

Aven nodded and reached up with one hand, taking Aria's. He pressed a kiss into her palm — his lips were dry and scratchy. Aria shifted her hand back to his cheek and ran her thumb over his cheekbone.

"Oh, my Water," she murmured. "The trouble you get into."

Aven smiled, and she watched his eyes move, focusing past her.

"You do so!" Owyn laughed. "He said it's not his fault, and he doesn't get into any more trouble than the rest of us."

"Perhaps," Aria said with a smile. "Or perhaps not. But I hope that our children will not have this trait?" She looked up at Jehan and Aleia. "Is this something that he gets from you?"

Aleia burst out laughing. "Possibly," she admitted. "But I think it helps to be a troublemaker when you're a Companion."

"Speak for yourself," Jehan grumbled. "I wasn't ever a troublemaker until I met you." Aleia looked at him, and he laughed. "All right. Not much." He leaned forward and rested his forehead against hers.

"I'll ask," Owyn said. "Jehan, Aven wants to know if anyone found his swords. He had them when he was hit. I didn't see them, but I wasn't down in the camp for longer than it took to get people out."

Jehan frowned. "I'll find out," he said. "And if no one did, I'll go back out there and find them myself. And Owyn, you should go look in on your father. He was in a state, and your mother has been focused on him since she got back to camp."

Owyn straightened. "Where are they?"

"Either the healing tent or their wagon," Jehan said. He closed his eyes and took another deep breath. "We're going to take Aven to the healing tent, for now. And I'm going to have Alanar assess him and put him back into trance. I'm getting too old for this."

"Senior Healer?"

Aria turned to see Elaias and Astur had come up behind her. Elaias was horribly sunburned, but smiling. "Senior Healer, how can we help?"

"You can get your arse to the healing tent and let your sister see to that burn," Jehan answered. "Before it scars. Astur, sit on him if you need to."

Astur grinned. "Is that an order?" He looked up at Elaias. "It sounds like an order."

Elaias chuckled and gently punched Astur's arm. "You're such a troublemaker."

Jehan smiled. "Then you'll fit right in. Owyn, show them where. If your parents aren't there, then go find them."

Owyn turned to look at Aria. "My Heir—"

"You're the Heir?" Astur blurted. Then he winced as Elaias punched him again, harder.

Aria smiled. "I am. And I welcome you both. Now, go with Owyn, and I'll meet you properly later." She studied Elaias for a moment. "Go see the healers, Healer Elaias. That's an order from your Heir."

Elaias smiled and bowed. "My Heir," he murmured. He straightened, then elbowed Astur. "Manners!"

"Right," Astur stammered. He sketched a shaky bow. "Sorry," he added as he rose. "I'm not used to...well...people."

"You've been around cattle too long," Elaias grumbled. "Now, where are we going?"

Owyn grinned. "This way." He led them into camp, and Aria turned back to the wagon. Aven's eyes were closed when she looked down.

"Is he back in trance?" she asked.

"I thought it was a good idea, since we have to move him. You're welcome to come with us and sit and watch him sleep. Since, I think, that's what you were going to do anyway?" Jehan asked. Aria laughed, and Jehan smiled. "Thought so." He looked around and waved at the guards. "I need volunteers!"

OWYN LED ELAIAS AND Astur down the row of wagons and tents toward the healing tent, hearing Jehan's raised voice from behind them. "His bellow is almost as good as Karse's," he said.

"Karse. That was the man who cut us all down," Elaias said. "I need to thank him. And...where's Arjin?" He stopped and looked around. "I haven't seen him since we got out of the wagon. Where is he?"

Owyn turned and looked around, studying faces. "I haven't seen him at all since we left the raider camp. Who was riding with you?"

"The quiet one," Elaias answered. He frowned as he looked around. "And I don't see him, either."

"We'll send someone out to find them," Owyn said. "I'll grab a guard. You need to be seen by a healer, and I need to find my fa." He looked around again, then waved. "Fara!"

Fara waved and came toward them. "Just who I was looking for!" she said. "Othi and Del asked me to tell you that they were going to be busy." She pointed at Elaias. "Your boy slipped off and headed for the woods. Del and Othi are following him."

Elaias looked stunned. "He ran away?"

Fara nodded. "He's swimming in muddy waters, that one. Can't see his own way clear. Del and Othi, they'll find him and bring him back. Then Treesi and Dyneh can set him to rights." She frowned. "Lot of weight on someone that young. What happened?"

Owyn looked at Elaias, who shook his head slightly. "Healer business, Fara. We'll let them sort it out." He frowned. Did Del know? He couldn't remember. He shook his head and sighed. "Right. Del and Othi will find him. Come on, you two. Let's get you seen to."

DEL GESTURED TOWARD the cluster of thorn-bushes, and Othi nodded. Then he raised his voice. "You can keep going," he called. "Or you can come back, and we can fix it. Whatever it is." He folded his arms over his chest. "Or you can keep sitting inside a plant that stings. It's up to you."

The bushes rustled, and a scratched and battered Arjin crawled out. "Why did you follow me?" he asked, wiping his face.

"Because you're one of us now," Othi answered. "Because you're part of us, and it means you don't just get to run off without explaining why. Believe me, someone tried that, and it didn't work well for anyone."

Arjin frowned slightly. "Who tried that?"

"Aven," Othi answered. "He spent half a year out on the deep, because there was too much hurting and not enough healing. Which is kind of boneheaded—"

"*The word we use is fuckheaded,*" Del signed.

Othi's brows rose. "That's a word?" he asked. "All right. Kind of fuckheaded, according to Del. I mean, you'd think a healer would want to make things better, not make them worse." He paused, then cocked his head to the side. "So...why are you making things worse?"

Arjin sniffled. "I already made things worse." He frowned. "You don't know, do you?" He swallowed, then sighed. "I...I betrayed the others. I'm the reason that the raiders got them. I'm the reason the girls...and Treesi...and Owyn's mother...it's all my fault."

Del looked up at Othi, who looked stunned. "Arjin, why?" Othi asked. "You...you've been learning axe with me to protect them!"

Arjin nodded. "I have...I had...I had a sister. Searc—"

"Shark?" Othi grinned. "Good name."

Arjin smiled. "It does sound like that, doesn't it? Searc was older than me, but she never really grew up. She was a little girl, even though she was older than me. And I promised to take care of her. When we were close to my home village, I'd go see her and my brothers. Elaias and Astur, they knew. I never told the girls." He swallowed. "Mitok came to the village where we were staying when Elaias was off with the girls, attending a birth. He told Astur he needed healing, but when Astur left the room, he told me that they had Searc, and if I wanted her back, I had to help them. And that if I told Elaias, they'd kill her. I went back for my usual visit, and the entire village was gone. So I thought he was telling me the truth. It's all my fault." He waved his arms, then sighed. "All of it. Elaias and Astur being caught, and...and Frayim being hurt, and Aven..." He looked up. "Will Aven live?"

"He's going to be fine. And from where I'm sailing, I don't see it as your fault." Othi looked at Del. "Right?"

Del nodded. "*You were trying to save your sister,*" he signed. "*What happened to her?*"

"I...what was that?" Arjin asked. "I don't know a lot of the signs yet."

"Del says you were trying to save your sister," Othi translated. "And he asked what happened to her?"

Arjin looked ready to burst into tears. "She's dead. Mitok said she was dead before they ever came to me. I did all that...for nothing."

Othi nodded slowly. "I understand," he said. "I'm the little brother, too. And I was raised to believe that I had to be my sister's right arm, especially since she's Clan Mother of the Water tribe. If I'd been sailing your current, I'd probably have done the same thing."

Arjin stared at him. "You...you would? And...you're the *little* brother?"

Othi chuckled. "Yeah, I know. Hard to believe, right? But yeah. If someone had Neera, I'd have done exactly what you did to get her safe. And she'd have kicked my tail for it, but that's not the point. I'd have done it. So I understand why you did." He walked over to Arjin, who didn't move when Othi put his arm around his shoulders. "Now, tell me this. How are you going to fix it? Because running? That won't fix anything. It won't make anything better, or heal the hurt you caused trying to do what you thought was the right thing. Running will only make things worse."

"But you said Aven—"

Del started signing again, *"When Aven ran away, when we went to the deep, he was hurt. He needed to heal enough to come back and heal things here."*

Othi translated, then asked, "Did they hurt you? Do you need a healer? Did anyone ask you that?"

"Captain Karse did," Arjin answered. "I'm fine. Just sunburned, and a little bruised. It's not bad. If...if I go back, what will happen?"

"No idea," Othi answered. "We can go find out." He smiled. "Let's go find out."

Arjin nodded, then looked up. "I hit Aven. From behind, like a coward. That's why they got him. He's going to kill me, isn't he?"

"I'll stop him long enough that you can explain," Othi answered. "Or get a good running start, which should give Aria enough time to make him stop and think." Arjin went pale, and Othi chuckled. "I'm joking."

"You are?"

"Mostly. He'll probably be angry. But he'll understand, because I think he'd have done it, too." Othi tugged him forward, then let his arm fall. "Come on."

They walked back to camp, and the first person who noticed them was Karse. "There you are!" he called. "People were wondering where you'd gotten to. Othi, we're setting a watch schedule to oversee the prisoners until Aria has a chance to pronounce judgment."

Othi nodded. "Let me talk to Treesi, and then I'll come find you and see where you need me."

"Fair," Karse answered. "Oh, since you're going to the healing tent? If Aven is awake, tell him that we've got his swords. Leist found them, and brought them down. Jehan said he was worried about them."

Othi nodded. "I'll tell him."

Karse turned his attention to Arjin. "So. I'm told you did a stupid thing. I'm assuming you had a good reason?"

Arjin took a deep breath. "I thought so. They...they told me that they had my sister. That they'd hurt her if I didn't do what they wanted. But when I did what they told me to do, they told me they lied, and she was already dead."

"Oh, fuck," Karse breathed. "I'm sorry." He looked away. "I can take a team back out there. See if we can find her."

"Mitok will know," Arjin said. "And I'd really like to hear why they did this, and what they did to Searc."

"You're sure you do?" Karse asked. "It probably won't be pretty."

"We'll need to know," Arjin said. "Aria will need to know all of it."

Karse nodded. "Then we'll have him sit down with Healer Alanar, and we'll get the truth out of him. But you're not going to be there."

"But—"

"No," Karse said. "You don't need that. Not as young as you are. I'll be there. I'll tell you what you need to know, and I'll make sure that we find her and take care of her." They started walking again. "You said you wanted to know why. Why what?"

"Well, I know they wanted the girls as breeders. And I know they wanted Frayim because they wanted to stop him from talking to people and telling them the truth. I don't know why they wanted Elaias and Astur. And I don't know why they wanted Aven."

Karse turned to him. "They what? Wanted Aven? Specifically?"

"Mitok told me that if I could, I needed to help them get the Waterborn. I didn't know what they meant until we got here and I met him. I mean...we're days from the sea. What would a Waterborn be doing here?" He looked up at Othi. "No offense."

"None taken," Othi answered. "Honestly, if I wasn't here with Treesi? I wouldn't be here. It's too dry up here, and I haven't changed in..." He stopped and frowned. "I'm not even sure anymore."

"When we get back to the Palace, you and the rest of the Water guards can all go on leave and not surface for a month," Karse said. "Come on. I want to talk with Jehan, and I need to borrow Alanar." He smiled slightly. "I'm going to enjoy this."

Chapter Thirty-Seven

Frayim was still asleep when Treesi knelt next to the low cot. She rested one hand on his shoulder and considered how he was healing, then adjusted the healing trance to slowly taper. His back might be tender when he woke, but it was almost entirely healed. She got up and turned, and nearly bumped into Steward.

"How is he?"

Treesi laughed. "He'll be fine. But you're starting to worry me. You don't normally hover like a needlefly, Steward."

Steward scowled. He looked at the sleeping man on the cot, then sighed. "Treesi, am I acting besotted?"

Treesi looked at him, then at Frayim. "I...who told you that you were?"

"Owyn. And Karse," Steward answered. "I didn't think I was...but am I?"

Treesi tucked her hand into his arm and led him out of the curtained area. "Steward, I think you know the answer to that question."

He sighed and nodded. "I think I do. The minute I saw him, it was like I'd known him forever. And he said the same. More — he said he'd walk over hot coals to find me. I don't understand."

Treesi blinked, then looked back through the curtain at Frayim. She nodded. "I...don't know," she said.

"Sounds as if you have an idea?"

"One that I want to discuss with Jehan before I tell you," Treesi said. "So let me go and talk to him. I need to, anyway." She smiled. "If you want to sit with him, there are camp stools under the cot."

Steward smiled. "Thank you," he murmured, and disappeared back behind the curtain. Treesi shook her head and went looking for Jehan.

She found him outside the tent, talking with Alanar and Karse.

"I'm just worried about the risk," Jehan was saying. "There are how many raiders? And one Healer. If they try anything—"

"You really think I want Owyn to rip my head off?" Karse asked. "I'll take care of Alanar. We'll start with that Iantir, and maybe we won't even have to talk to Mitok."

"We can hope," Jehan grumbled. He turned and saw Treesi. "How's Frayim?"

"I set the trance to fade," Treesi answered. "He'll wake up and be tender, but the healing under the skin is done."

Jehan nodded. "Good. Your brothers are around here somewhere, with the rest of the trainees. I'll be speaking to Arjin when they're done with him. But you had something you wanted to talk to me about?"

"In private, please?" Treesi clasped her hands in front of her, suddenly nervous.

"Of course. Alanar, you're in charge." Jehan gestured for her to follow him, and they walked a short distance away from the healing tent. "Far enough?"

Treesi nodded. "Jehan...I misused my healing gift. I broke the healer's canon."

Jehan nodded. "Tell me."

"I...I needed to keep the raiders away the trainees," Treesi said slowly. "One of them grabbed me, and...well, you know the story about Alanar breaking Teva's arms? I did that. I broke the raider's hand. I shattered every bone."

Jehan whistled softly. "Impressive."

"And...when we had Iantir chained up, he didn't want to tell us anything, so I hurt him, just a little. Enough to scare him into talking." Treesi looked down at the ground. "Owyn says I put the fear of all things painful into him, and that he's not going to tease me again about how bad my threats are."

Jehan chuckled. "That would be a very poor idea, I think." He rested his hands on Treesi's shoulders. "Sweetheart, you're not in trouble. There have to be exceptions to every rule, and this is one of them. You didn't do anything that I haven't done myself."

Treesi looked up at him. "Really? You did it?"

"To try and get away from the Usurper, back when we were first going to Forge, when it was only Aven and Aria." Jehan snorted. "And it didn't entirely work. Aven and Aria got away, but I still got caught, and that's how I ended up on the green levels in Terraces. And Aleia ended up back at the canoes, not knowing that any of us survived." He shook his head. "No, my students are going to learn to defend themselves, because healer doesn't mean carpet. If there had been exceptions in place, we might not have had to put Alanar back together." He paused, then smiled. "Treesi, you did exactly what I would have expected of you, and I'm proud of you."

Treesi felt tears welling in her eyes. "You mean that?"

Jehan pulled her into an embrace. "I mean that, sweetheart," he said. "Now, you go ahead and have a good cry if you need it."

Treesi giggled. "I don't. I'm fine. I just...it's the baby, I know." She stepped back and wiped her face. "I had something else I wanted to bring to you."

"Which is?" Jehan looked around. "Should we head back?"

"Not yet," Treesi said. She looked over her shoulder at the tent, then back to Jehan. "Steward is very taken with Frayim. Have you noticed?"

"I think everyone in camp has noticed. And noticed that it's mutual," Jehan answered. "Why?"

"Because he's confused by it. But the way he described it...he *knew* Frayim, Jehan, and it sounds the same as the way I knew Aven and Owyn and Aria the first time I met them. I think it's the Companion bond."

Jehan stared at her for a moment. "You think Frayim would have been Yana's Earth?"

Treesi nodded. "It would explain how they knew each other immediately. Why they're so drawn to each other. It even explains Frayim's tattoo." She tapped the hollow of her throat, where her gem sat. Where Frayim had a tattoo of a stylized tree.

Jehan nodded slowly. "It's an interesting theory," he murmured. "And it would explain things. He's...how old?"

"I don't know. Owyn might."

Jehan looked around. "You know, I should check on Huris. So if anyone asks, that's where I'm going. Hold that close to your chest, sweetheart. Don't discuss it with anyone yet. Let me think on it. And I want to talk about this to Aleia and Memfis."

Treesi nodded. "Don't be surprised if Steward comes and asks. He was with me when I thought of it, and I told him I needed to talk to you first."

Jehan nodded. "I'll skirt around the camp. I don't want to answer his questions until I know more."

"Oh, you're not going to see him," Treesi assured him. "He's camped out next to Frayim's cot. I don't think we'll see him at all until Frayim wakes up and leaves the tent." She looked back at the tent. "Have the guards come back yet?"

"Not yet," Jehan answered. "So we'll just keep feeding salt water to Aven and keep him in trance. It'll be slower, but it'll work." He scrubbed one hand over his face. "Right. Let me go see to Huris and talk to Owyn." He walked away, and Treesi watched him for a moment before going back to the healing tent. There was still work to do.

OWYN LOOKED UP AS SOMEONE knocked on the wagon door, then rolled onto his knees and got up. He opened the door and jumped down, closing it behind him before turning to Jehan.

"Came to check on Huris," Jehan said. "How is he?"

"Asleep. He and Mama are both asleep," Owyn said. "He...Jehan, is panic something you can inherit from your parents? Like eye color?"

Jehan blinked. "That's an odd question. Why?"

"Because Huris was as bad as I used to get, and Mama says he just...does this sometimes. Even before he was hurt. He'd get upset or...or scared, and he'd panic." He looked back at the wagon. "She was surprised when I told her I did the same thing."

"You haven't, though. Not in a while."

Owyn shook his head. "Not since I came back, I don't think. I've been close. When Evarra died, I came close. But it's been a long time." He sniffed. "I didn't panic when Wren had me. I just realized that now. I was close again, but not like before."

"What does your mother say?"

Owyn shook his head. "She doesn't know. She says it's possible. It might be something with the way the brain works, she thinks. But she doesn't know." He looked back at the wagon. "She does say she thinks he'll be better when he wakes up. Which...yeah, I was like that, too."

Jehan nodded. "Can you spare a minute?" He looked around. "I was wondering if you knew how old Frayim is?"

"I..." Owyn thought about what Frayim had told him. "I'm not sure. He said he got sick when he was seventeen, and started having visions after that. But I'm not sure how long ago that was."

Jehan nodded, looking thoughtful. Then he looked down and counted on his fingers. "Thirty, at least. If I'm right."

"Frayim just turned thirty-one."

Owyn turned around to see Dyneh standing in the doorway of the wagon. "I didn't hear you come out."

"Your father is awake, and that woke me," she said. "He's a little disoriented, but he'll be fine once I get some food into him. Why were you asking about Frayim?"

"Trying to make sense of something," Jehan answered. "Once I do, I'll explain."

"Fair," Dyneh said. "How are the trainees?"

"That's my next stop," Jehan answered. "Elaias and Astur took them off, and I think they're having a long talk with Arjin about trusting your partners. Dyneh, when you're done, I'm calling all the healers for a meeting," Jehan said. "If you can't because you need to stay with Huris, send Owyn and let me know?" He looked around. "Dyneh, you know the Wanderers, so maybe you can save me some hunting around. Would any of them have a basin or a tub large enough for a man? Steward has been so distracted that I'm not sure if he ever asked."

Dyneh looked thoughtful. "I've seen one, I think," she answered. "Frayim insisted we needed it, but couldn't tell us why. When that happens, you learn not to ask questions. I'll find out where it is. Perhaps the blacksmith has it."

Owyn blinked and turned to stare at his mother. "There's a blacksmith?" he sputtered. "How did I not know there's a blacksmith? We've been traveling together for weeks, and how am I only just now learning there's a blacksmith?"

Dyneh laughed. "You never asked, and we've not been in any one place long enough for Kenta to set up his forge. But we have so many wagons, and so many oxen and donkeys needing to be shod. How did you think that happened?"

Owyn grinned. "I never once thought of it. Not once. And what do you mean oxen shoes?"

"I will introduce you to Kenta tomorrow," Dyneh said. "You can ask him about oxen shoes. It's quite interesting. And if you offer to help him, he might teach you to make them." She gently pushed his shoulder. "Go fetch some food for your father. And find your other father and tell him to come eat with us. Then you can stay with your father while I go to this meeting."

Owyn grinned. "Yes, Mama."

TREESI LOOKED UP AT Alanar, who was standing with his back against one of the tent posts. "What are we doing?" she asked.

"Not sure," Alanar answered. "Jehan said he wanted us all here. Healer business." He turned his head as the tent flap opened and Dyneh came inside.

"Is everyone here?" she asked. "And why here?"

"Because I wanted Aven to be part of this, and he's confined to his bed for the moment," Jehan said, coming out of the curtained enclosure where Aven was resting. "Come inside." He turned, going back through the curtain, and Treesi followed him. Inside, Aven was sitting up in bed, with a waterskin resting on his lap. Elaias and Astur sat on camp stools, while Pallas, Selsi and Jesta sat on the floor at their feet. When Dyneh came inside, Astur stood up.

"Healer Dyneh, please," he said, gesturing to the stool. "I can sit on the floor." He sat on the ground, putting one arm around Jesta.

"Thank you, Astur." Dyneh walked over and sat down, and Treesi looked around.

"Where's Arjin?" she asked. "He didn't run away again, did he?"

"No," Jehan answered. He went to the curtain and opened it again. "All right."

Arjin entered the enclosure, and Treesi saw Steward standing outside. Jehan nodded at him, and closed the curtain. Then he turned to face them.

"I'm willing to lay money on the fact that there are only two people in this room who know what a Healer Conclave is," Jehan said.

Elaias sat up straight. "If you're counting that as just you and Dyneh, you'd be wrong," he said. "Astur and I both know. It's how our father cast him out after he helped Treesi run away. So if you're seriously proposing casting out my trainee, then you're losing all of us. If you ban Arjin, we're all leaving!"

Treesi gasped and turned to Jehan. "What?"

"If you'd let me finish, you'd know that I'm not proposing that at all," Jehan said. "I've asked you all to join me to determine what consequences, if any, Arjin should face for betraying the trust of his mentor and his training partners." He spread his hands wide. "Discuss."

"I'm not sure if punishment on top of what he's already suffered is appropriate. He was used, and used badly," Aven said, and Treesi winced at how harsh his voice sounded. He coughed, then grimaced. "If any of us were in that position, would we have done any differently?" He shook his head and took a drink from the waterskin. "I think he's learned his lesson. Losing his sister was lesson enough."

"He hit you from behind," Alanar pointed out.

"Which was on me," Aven replied. "I'm supposed to be better than that."

"How would being better make up for letting someone you trusted stand behind you and have them hit you?" Astur asked. Elaias glared at him, and Astur paled enough that his freckles stood out. "What? I want to know! I need to be that level of better!"

"He's right," Pallas said. "Aven didn't make a mistake. Arjin did."

"And if he'd trusted us in the first place, we might have been able to do something about it," Selsi added. Arjin nodded and ducked his head.

"I thought...I'd hoped that we were far enough away from them, that they'd given up. I thought I'd be able to see you all far enough west...and then I was going to go after Searc myself. That way, you'd be safe, and no one would be hurt but me. But it all went wrong."

"You had a plan?" Alanar asked.

"It probably wouldn't have held up," Arjin admitted. "I mean...it didn't hold up. But...I didn't know Elaias and Astur were still alive, and once we were here, with you, I thought...I don't know what I thought. But Mitok told me that if they found out I'd told, that I'd asked for help..."

"They'd kill Searc?" Elaias asked.

Arjin nodded. "I tried to stop it. I really tried," he said, his voice cracking. "I threw the stone. I couldn't stop the avalanche."

Elaias winced. "You picked that comparison deliberately."

Arjin nodded. "Yes. It's just as bad. They're all dead. Fa, and Nil, and Tolly and Searc. I came to be a healer so I could go back and help them...and they're all dead because of me—"

"Stop," Aven said, holding his hand up. "Stop right there. You didn't do anything to them. You didn't kill them." He held his hand out. "Come here and sit with me."

Arjin stared at Aven's hand for a moment, then shuffled toward the cot. He perched on the edge of the cot, then squeaked in surprise when Aven pulled him into a tight embrace.

"It wasn't your fault," Aven said. "And I'm not angry at you." He smoothed Arjin's hair, then looked up. "And we're done here, Senior Healer."

Jehan arched a brow. "Are we really, Healer?"

Aven met his father's eyes, and Treesi wasn't sure if the growl in his voice was from anger or waterlung. "We are done."

Jehan slowly nodded. "Conclave is over. All of you, out. Aven needs to rest."

"Arjin can stay," Aven said, shifting and resettling Arjin in his arms.

Astur got to his feet and held his hand out to Dyneh. "Healer Dyneh?" he said. "May I?"

Dyneh took his hand, letting Astur help her up from the low camp stool. "Thank you. If none of you have duties, we'll need help in the kitchen tents."

"That sounds like a challenge." Elaias slowly got to his feet.

"Oh, no! You're not allowed to cook," Astur laughed. "You turn everything to glue or charcoal. I'll help cook. You stay and help in the tent."

"Elaias, how are you feeling?" Dyneh asked. "You're still a little pink—"

"It's better than it was," Elaias said. He looked down at his arms. "I'm not on fire anymore, and my skin isn't tight."

"Before you all run away, I have a question," Treesi said. "Eli, what happened in the healing center?"

Elaias took a deep breath. "I was wondering when you'd ask me that," he said. "I'm not sure. I was attending a birth out in Ruby Canyon. When I came back, the center was in ashes, and I didn't find any bodies. I don't know what happened, or if they survived. Mother and Father and Minnit might have gone off with that madwoman for all I know."

"Madwoman?" Jehan pounced on the word. "Risha?"

"Yes," Elaias answered. "Father...well, it doesn't matter what he thought. He was wrong." He shook his head. "Are they alive? I don't know. Do I want to know? No. Am I counting them as dead? Yes. And you should, too. Trees, if they find out you're paired with a Water man, and bearing his child? Girl, they'd worse than kill you and you know it."

"They'd have to go through all of us to do it," Alanar growled.

Elaias smiled. "I'm glad you made a life away from them, Treesi." He paused and frowned. "Did they ever tell you who they were going to marry you off to?"

"No," Treesi answered. "They ordered Astur to stop teaching me, and told me I was getting married and I wasn't allowed to waste my time on learning anymore. But they never told me who."

"It was Mitok," Elaias said. "At least, I think it was. He went on at length about the girl that he'd bought, but who ran off before he ever laid eyes on her. That's probably why he didn't recognize you. But he had plans..." He paused. "And that's something else you don't want to know." He rubbed his hands over his thighs. "But that's why he wanted the girls. To replace the wife he never got. Now, I'm still not sure what they wanted with a Water, but..."

"They what now?" Aven asked. "They wanted...me?"

Jehan nodded. "Astur told me. We knew that Risha had followers in these mountains. And we knew that she wanted to get her claws into you again. And everyone in the world knows we're on Progress. It's not hard to put two and two together—"

"Except that we didn't," Alanar interrupted. "If we had, Aven wouldn't have been out there alone." He cocked his head to the side. "Aven, is he asleep?"

Aven looked down at the young man in his arms. "Relief, I think. He was wrapped in knots. Now he isn't. And I don't want a guard."

"Tough," Jehan grumbled. "You're having one. Everyone out." He folded his arms over his chest, and as Treesi passed him, he snorted. "Ven, do I need to define insubordination for you?"

Behind her, she heard Aven laugh. "No, Fa. Do I get Del as a guard?"

"Well, considering that he's at loose ends right now since Owyn isn't trying to get himself killed anymore? We'll see."

Treesi shook her head and went to check on Frayim. When she came back, Jehan was gone, and Aven was asleep, Arjin still wrapped in his arms.

Chapter Thirty-Eight

Aria sat down and closed her eyes, listening to the sounds of the camp waking up around her. It had been impossible to sleep — the big bed was too empty, and the tent too quiet. Aven was in the healing tent, and Jehan had opted to keep all the healers on rotation overnight, seeing to guards and to prisoners alike. That had led to Dyneh asking Owyn to stay with Huris in order to prevent another panic spell. Del had joined Othi in the overnight patrols, which had left the Heir's tent with a single occupant in a cold bed.

"Why am I thinking that you didn't sleep at all?"

Aria smiled and opened her eyes to see Owyn coming toward her. He was carrying two mugs, and handed one to her. She wrapped her hands around the hot mug and sighed. "Because you know me, my Fire?" she answered. "I am no longer used to sleeping alone."

He tugged a chair closer so that he could sit with her. "Drink that," he said, gesturing with his own mug. "Carefully. It's hot. We're seeing to the raiders this morning?"

Aria nodded. "If I can stay awake."

"I'll tuck you back in when we're done," Owyn said. "You need to sleep."

Aria smiled and held her hand out. He took it, then raised it to his lips and kissed her fingers.

"How is your father?" she asked as he let her go.

427

"They're both fine," Owyn answered. "In the kitchen tent, bickering like they've been married for years. It's funny how well they get on. I was a little worried that they'd fight or...or rub each other wrong." He shrugged and sipped his tea. "Mem says that breakfast will be ready soon, and they'll bring it here. You should have asked Trista to stay with you. Or Afansa."

"It's not the same," Aria murmured, blowing on her tea and taking a sip. "Shall we talk about Trista?"

"I'm tempted to say it's none of your business, but everything I do is some of your business, so yes, we can talk about Trista." Owyn sipped his tea and leaned back in his chair. "We haven't had a chance to talk to her, but Allie and I need to." He paused, then put his mug down and folded his hands. "We want a child. Our own family. And since you and I are going to have children, if the Mother grants...we wanted to ask Trista if she'd be willing to carry Allie's baby." He looked down at his hands. "You...don't mind, do you?"

Aria laughed and rested her hand on his. "Mind? Why should I mind? That's wonderful. And I'm certain that she'll say yes. She loves you both."

"I know, I just...I don't want her getting her hopes up about more. And I don't want her to feel...like she has to. Or that we're taking advantage of her." Owyn frowned. "Maybe it would be better to not to? I mean, she wants a family. She wants her own family. And we're not going to be the ones to give her that."

Aria nodded, watching as people moved around the camp. She saw a newly familiar figure. She felt a tingle, a sensation...and she murmured, "Introduce her to Elaias."

"To...to Treesi's brother? Wh...Aria, what are you thinking?"

"It feels right," Aria said. "I'm not sure why, but it does." She nodded toward the healer. "He's coming this way."

Owyn stood up. "How are you feeling?" he asked as Elaias stopped at the edge of the tent and bowed.

"Elaias, stop that," Aria chided. "You do not need to bow to me."

"It's good practice, and a good example to my trainees," Elaias answered. "And I'm feeling much better, Owyn. Thank you." He looked around. "This is nice. I'm on my way to find food for the healers. I volunteered, just to get out of the tent. Alanar said that I couldn't miss the kitchen tent, but I saw you first."

"We'll walk over with you," Owyn said. "Aria needs to eat."

"Jehan says to give him an hour of warning before you do whatever it is you're going to do to the raiders," Elaias said as they left the tent. "He'll make sure that Aven is able to be there."

"I was wondering how we were going to manage having the entire Council," Aria admitted. "Aven should not be out of bed."

"He's insistent," Elaias said. "And has an impressive growl. Which...I don't know. Did he learn that from his father? Because Jehan has one, too."

"I think they both learned it from Aleia, to be honest," Owyn said. "You meet her yet? War Leader for the Water tribe. You wouldn't think it to look at her, though."

Elaias frowned slightly. "Aleia? Aven's mother? She's War Leader?" He shook his head. "I should know better than to underestimate a tiny woman."

"You should, with Treesi being your sister," Owyn agreed, laughing. Aria laughed with him, then saw Trista come out of the Heir's tent. She smiled.

"Trista!" she called. Trista looked startled, but came to join them.

"My Heir," she said, and blushed. "I know you told me to stop. It's habit!"

"I was not going to say a word," Aria said. "I wanted to introduce you to Treesi's brother. Elaias, this is Trista. Nominally, she is our servant, but we've gone past that. She is our friend, who helps take care of me and my Companions."

"And who has better taste in clothes than I do," Owyn added.

Elaias laughed. "I need a friend like that. Astur says I would wear a shirt with only one side if it was comfortable."

Trista looked puzzled. "A shirt with only one side? I...how would that work? The left or the right? Or just the front?"

"Oh, it was an entire shirt. It was just too worn out to have two sides," Elaias answered. "It was nearly see through, it was that threadbare. But it was comfortable." He made a face. "And it's what I was wearing when we were taken, so I don't have it anymore. Which should satisfy my brother. But we also don't have anything else, so—"

Trista looked up at him, an expression very close to horror on her face. "You have no clothes?"

"Nothing except these, and I'm not even sure who I should be thanking for them." Elaias held his arms out.

"Those were from Allie," Owyn said. "And Astur is wearing something of mine. We're about the same size. That reminds me. He wants a whip chain. I need to see about making one for him. Mama said she'd introduce me to the blacksmith, but it might still have to wait until we get back to the Palace."

"It would probably be best to wait, Owyn. I've seen the whip-chain, and that can't be a quick thing to make." Trista held her hand out to Elaias. "Come with me, and we'll find something for you."

Elaias smiled and took her hand. "Thank you. But...after breakfast? I need to arrange for the other healers to be fed."

Trista nodded. "I'll help with that. Then we'll get you dressed properly." They walked away, and Owyn looked at Aria.

"You're as bad as Granna," he murmured.

"Really? I thought that went rather well," Aria whispered back. "But we'll see if I have inherited Grandmother's gift for match-matching. Let's go find something to eat."

ARIA SETTLED INTO HER chair and closed her eyes again, and Owyn could feel how tired she was. "I'm not looking forward to this," she murmured.

"I don't think any of us are," Owyn said. "But it needs to be done."

She opened her eyes. "Where are the others?"

"I sent the boys for Del," Steward answered from behind her. "Treesi will be coming out with the healers. I'm not sure what's being done with Aven. He shouldn't be out of bed."

"He needs to be here for this," Aria said. "I'll try to keep it from running too long." She rubbed her forehead. "Iantir first, then the others. Steward, I agree that we can offer Iantir the same as we did Cellan, but the others...I'm not certain I agree. If we send them all as a group, they'll take over whatever place we send them. Nor do we have enough guards to send them anywhere under guard."

"They're murderers, the lot of them," Owyn pointed out. "We know how to deal with murderers."

"And yet I hate starting my reign with so much bloodshed." Aria sighed. "But I can't see an alternative. I don't know."

Owyn nodded, then smiled. "Here comes Del."

A moment later, Del joined them under the tent. He leaned down to kiss Aria's cheek, then straightened and yawned before coming to kiss Owyn.

"Did no one sleep last night?" Aria asked.

Del shook his head. *"Guard duty. But they were quiet."*

"What were they saying?" Owyn asked. "Any conversations?"

Del looked thoughtful. "*Lots of stories about the Child,*" he signed. "*They think they'll be delivered from punishment because they serve the Child.*"

"The Child?" Aria repeated. "Did I understand that correctly? What child?"

Owyn made a face. "We hadn't told you yet. There are folks out here that think that a child of all four tribes will be the one to set everything right." He turned. "Have I got that right, Fray? And don't you dare stand up! Steward will thump me if I make you stand up."

Frayim was sitting at the table, and he smiled slightly as Owyn chided him. "I wasn't going to," he said. "And yes. They believe that Axia will be reborn as a child of all the tribes, who will wipe the tainted tribes from the world and that they will once more live in peace."

Aria frowned slightly. "I...see," she murmured. "I...that may not be this baby, though. Aven may not be just Earth and Water. He may be Fire, too. But...perhaps I can use this to our advantage." She smiled. "Where is Trista? I need help."

"At the healing tent with Elaias, I think," Owyn answered. "Why?"

Aria stood up. "Even better," she said. "I'll be back. Have the raiders brought out. I'll be back shortly."

She walked away, and Owyn looked at Steward. "Any ideas?"

"Not a one," Steward replied.

"*Why do I have the feeling that this would make Aleia giggle?*" Del whispered in Owyn's mind.

"Oh, fuck," Owyn breathed. "I think you're right."

"Right about what?" Steward asked.

"Aria is up to something, and we all need to play along." Owyn took a deep breath. "Let me go warn Karse."

THE PRISONERS WERE ranged in front of the audience tent, and there was still no sign of Aria when Jehan brought the other healers out to witness.

"Aria came and took Trista off," Treesi said when she and Alanar joined Owyn. "When they came back, they had a bundle of things, and asked us to leave them. Elaias is with them." She looked back at the tent. "And when did that happen?"

"This morning, and it was Aria's idea," Owyn answered.

"So what is Aria planning?" Alanar asked.

"Del thinks that it's something that would make Aleia giggle," Owyn answered.

"What?" Jehan demanded. He came over and lowered his voice. "Del thinks that?"

Owyn nodded. "And whatever she's up to, we're all going to play along." He frowned, thinking. "She got Trista involved. Somehow, I think we're all underdressed."

"*Not for long,*" Del signed. Then he pointed, and Owyn turned to see Trista coming toward them, clearly on a mission.

"You all need to go change," she said as she reached them. "Your clothes are laid out in the Heir's tent. Once you're done, I'll go tell Aria it's time."

"Trista, what are they doing?" Treesi asked.

"She told me not to say. And if you insisted, she said you'd find out when you found out, but to take your cues from her when it's time to announce yourselves." Trista grinned. "Go change!"

Del grabbed Owyn's hand, tugging him out of the tent. Treesi grabbed his other hand, and they hurried off to the Heir's tent.

"Our ritual things?" Treesi said when they saw the clothes laying out on the bed. "Isn't that formal for this? We didn't wear them in Hearthstone."

Owyn tugged his shirt off over his head and picked up his black. "We're playing along," he repeated. "Get dressed."

They dressed quickly, and Owyn escorted them back to the audience tent with as much formality as he had during the procession in Terraces. As they approached, he saw Trista dart away, running back to the healer's tent.

"Looks like whatever is going to happen will be happening soon," he murmured.

"Should we follow, so we can be there to escort Aria?" Treesi asked.

"No," Del answered aloud. "Wait."

"Trista didn't say to go with her," Owyn added. "We wait here."

Owyn escorted Treesi and Del to their places, then went and stood in front of his own seat, clasping his hands behind him like a guard at rest. Del took the same posture at his own place.

They hadn't been standing for long before he heard the commotion coming from the prisoners. He could see movement, heads turning.

"*It's starting,*" Del said. Owyn nodded, watching the reactions. Then the crowd parted, and Owyn saw Aria and Aven. Aven looked tired, but he was standing tall, wearing the purple vest and dark kilt of his ritual wear. Aria was on his arm, and Owyn suddenly understood what she was planning — Aria's white ritual gown had been altered to show off her pregnancy, and her wings were spread wide as she and Aven walked slowly through the crowd of raiders, making their way to their places. Owyn bowed as they came under the canopy, and felt the wave of mirth from Aria.

"*When you introduce yourself,*" she said in his mind. "*Follow my lead.*"

Owyn nodded as he straightened, and faced forward as Aven left Aria at her place, kissed her hand, then stepped to stand in front of his own chair.

Aria folded her wings. She looked to her left, then to her right. Then she looked out at the raiders, all of whom were staring at her as if they'd never seen a woman before.

"I am Aria," she announced. "Daughter of Firstborn Milon, a child of Fire. Daughter of Liara, a child of Air. I am my father's Heir, given the Diadem by the hands of the Mother herself."

Aven's voice was gravelly but strong. "I am Aven, Waterborn Companion. Son of Aleia, child of Water. Son of Jhansri, child of Earth."

A moan rippled through the watching prisoners, and Owyn fought the urge to laugh. He wasn't sure, but he thought that it had started with Mitok.

"Owyn Jaxis," he announced. "Fireborn Companion. Son of Huris, child of Fire. Son of Dyneh, child of Earth. Adopted son of Memfis, child of Fire."

Treesi's clear voice rang out. "Treesi. Earthborn Companion. Daughter of Gisa, child of Earth. Daughter of Elan, child of Earth."

Del looked down, then up. "Del." He spoke slowly, and more clearly than Owyn had ever heard. "Of Air. Son of Yana of Air. Son of..." He paused. "Del...an...dri of Fire." He broke into a wide grin and looked at Aria.

"Well done," she murmured, just loud enough that Owyn could hear. Then she looked forward. "I am Aria," she repeated.

"I'm told you were waiting for us." She rested her hand on the curve of her belly, smiled, and took her seat. "Here we are."

Silence. Then, slowly, Mitok sank to his knees. It set off a wave of movement, as one by one, the rest of the raiders followed.

"The Blessed Mother comes," Frayim's voice rang out from the rear of the tent. "Prosperity follows where she walks, and peace shall come to those who swear to her."

Owyn looked to see Aria turn to Aven, reaching for his hand. He raised hers to his lips, kissed her fingers. She gently touched his cheek, then drew her hand back and turned to look forward once more. "Peace shall come to those who swear to me," she repeated. "As the Mother decreed when she granted the Diadem to me." She looked out at the raiders. "I know what you've been told. I know that you have been led to believe that I am less, that the Water tribe are less. But I want you to ask yourself this — if the Child you wait for is of all four tribes, and will bring balance and peace, how can any part of that child be less?" She paused, letting her words grow heavy between them. "The path you have chosen sets you against the Child. It sets you against the Mother's will, and against mine. Is that truly where you wish to be?"

Mitok rose slowly. He stepped forward, and stopped when Karse stepped in his way and leveled his sword at Mitok's chest.

"Let him come forward, Captain," Aria said.

Karse looked back at her. "If he so much as sneezes on you, I'm taking his head off," he snarled. Aria smiled, raised her left arm, and armed her wrist crossbow. She rested her hand on the arm of the chair. Karse grinned and stepped out of Mitok's way. The raider took two more steps, then sank to his knees once more.

"I was raised on stories of the Child," he said slowly. "Most of us were."

Aven looked at Aria, then leaned forward slightly. "How old is this story?"

Mitok shrugged slightly. "I learned it from my father. Can't say where he learned it. But it's all through these hills."

Aria nodded slowly. "And since you do not know Water, or Air, you believe these stories. Even knowing that we are all children of the Mother."

"Tisn't hard to think it," Mitok answered. "Not hard to look at someone who can fly and say they ain't like me. And I never saw a Waterborn before, ever. Still not sure what makes you different, other than the scars."

"Scars?" Aria looked at Aven. "Oh, you mean the gill slits." She nodded again. "And now?" she asked as she turned back to Mitok. "You have seen me. You have seen my Water. You know us, Mitok. What say you now?"

Mitok looked up at her. He frowned slightly, and his hands on his thighs flexed. He tensed, and Owyn knew what he was going to do a heartbeat before he lunged at Aria...

And fell with a crossbow dart in his left eye. In the silence that followed, Aria calmly set another quarrel on the string and looked out at the raiders.

"What say you now?" she repeated.

Chapter Thirty-Nine

The rest of the proceedings went quickly. Once Mitok's body was moved away, Aria turned to the rest of the raiders.

"You've terrorized these hills, murdering innocents for far too long," she said. "Was it you who destroyed the healing center? And how many villages have you razed?"

One of the raiders looked at the others, then stepped forward. "Healing center?" he asked. "We...that weren't us. They did that themselves." He looked around. "Bali, you had folk there, didn't you?"

One of the other raiders nodded. "My mother's sister worked the kitchens. She got out, but it weren't raiders. It was the Healer and his kin, fighting."

"Who was your mother's sister?" Treesi asked.

"Her name's Tarfa," Bali answered.

"Oh, I remember Tarfa!" Treesi nodded. "She made wonderful fruit pies. Did she get out? Is she well?"

Bali nodded, then blinked. "Wait. You said you were Healer Elan's girl?" he gasped. "I remember you!"

"We've met?" Treesi asked. "I don't remember."

Bali shook his head. "We never met proper. Aunt Tarfa said not to mess with the Healer's family the one time I visited her there. And I didn't realize it was you when you busted up Hila's hand. She's fine, last I saw her. Disappointed in me, but fine."

He frowned. "Aunt Tarfa said that it was a fight — Elan's second oldest wanted out. And Elan wasn't going to let them go." He shrugged. "Don't know how the fire started but it burned fast, Auntie said."

"And none of them got out?" Owyn asked.

Bali shrugged. "Don't know. We never saw them north, I know that. Maybe they went west? All I really know is that it weren't us. And Mitok, he was mad about it, because we'd go to Elan if we needed fixing. We didn't have a healer, and we didn't have a place to go."

"Is that why you wanted Elaias and the trainees?" Aven asked.

"Think so, yeah," Bali answered. "So...when you lay our crimes at our feet, Lady, that one weren't one of them."

Aria nodded. She ran one finger down the bridge of her nose, fighting the urge to yawn. "You have not answered the other question," she said. "How many villages razed? How many people killed?" She looked around. "There are children in this camp orphaned because of you. Women made widows. Men who have lost everything."

Bali nodded and stepped back among the others. "It...it seemed like it made sense at the time," he said. "That's about all I can say. It...made sense, when we were doing it. Now...yeah, my aunt isn't the only one disappointed in me."

The first raider who spoke stepped forward. "Fireborn Owyn, he told me I was wrong. Told me you'd been doing good, Lady. Been thinking on that, and...I think I want some good. If you'll have me."

Aria turned to Owyn, who nodded. "Aria, that's Iantir. He...well, after Treesi put the fear of all things painful into him, he was willing to listen. And he told us what we needed to know to find Aven and the others."

Aria nodded, turning back to Iantir. "Do you plead clemency?" she asked.

Iantir frowned. "What does that mean?"

"It means you will serve," Aria answered. "You will help us rebuild that which has been broken. Cellan?" She looked around, saw the carpenter standing near the edge of the tent. "Cellan pled clemency. Come and tell them what that means."

"I was just as much a jackass as you," Cellan called. He came closer. "Riding out, hurting people, on account of I didn't have the stones to stand up and say no and risk dying for it. Same as you, I conjure?" He waited for Iantir to nod. "Now...I'm helping the Heir to rebuild. And when I'm done serving my time, then I'm going back to Hearthstone. Maybe have something there, if she'll have me." He blushed. "You stay with the Progress and guard. Or you go west and help rebuild the towns and the roads. That's clemency."

Iantir blinked. "That's it?" he asked. "That's all?"

"Don't think it's an easy sentence," Steward said. "There are a lot of roads, and not a lot of workers."

Iantir took a step forward, and went to one knee. "Got one more, then. I'll serve."

A moment later, Bali joined him. "Me, too."

By the end of the proceedings, just under half of the raiders had pleaded clemency, and all of them opted to stay with the Progress. To Owyn's eyes, Karse looked completely disgusted.

"You're all mine now," he snapped. "And none of you better so much as fart in the wrong key. Understood?" The warning set off a wave of nervous laughter, and the men started to move to follow Karse.

"Captain," Steward called from behind Aria. "I have a question for them, before you go."

Karse nodded. "Right. Answer the man."

Steward walked around the Companions and bowed to Aria, who nodded. She wasn't sure what he was thinking, but from the wrinkle between his brows, it was important.

"When was the last time you saw Risha?" Steward asked. "And what happened when you saw her?"

The men turned to each other, talking softly, and it didn't surprise Aria that Iantir was the one they pushed forward to answer.

"Been...a month? Maybe two?" he answered. "Not entirely sure. But it was when she told us that we needed to catch a fish for her." He winced, and glanced at Aven. "Sorry."

Aven waved one hand. "She's called me worse. Go on."

"I...it was strange. There were times before when she used to send people to give Mitok orders. Usually a man named Teva. This was the first time I'd seen her. And she weren't alone." Iantir shook his head. "I...I think she brought him to scare Mitok. To make him mind her. She...she had him on a lead, like he was a pet or something. He didn't walk right, and I don't think he could talk." He shook his head. "It was...what she did to that poor fuck, it was *wrong*."

Owyn moaned softly, and Karse went pale. "This...he was blond?" Karse demanded. "Like...really light hair? And...and young?" He pointed at Owyn. "Young like Owyn?"

Iantir started to answer, then stopped. "I...your wrist. Is...is that what I think it is?" He stepped closer. "Is that a pledge bracelet?"

Karse held his hand out to Iantir, who stepped closer, looked at it, then met Karse's eyes and swallowed. "Fuck..." he breathed. "I...I'm sorry."

Karse lowered his hand. "He was wearing one like this?"

Iantir nodded. "I...I brought him something to eat, when she left him to talk to Mitok in private. I saw it. I.... I'm so fucking sorry. If I'd known...I would have...I didn't have to tell you like that." He scrubbed his hand over his face. "I shouldn't have told you like that. I...fuck. Is there anything I can do?"

Karse took a deep breath. Then he shook his head. "No. But thank you. Othi!" He looked around. "Take these boys off and get them berthed. Then take them to the practice yard. Have them drill. Ask Aleia to assess them, see who needs what. I need..." He looked around again. "Fuck if I know what I need."

Aria saw movement, and Dyneh walked out to take Karse's hand. She glanced back at the tent. "Jax, once you're done, tell Afansa that the Captain is with me, and we'll be in the wagon."

"Yes, Mama," Owyn answered. Dyneh led Karse away.

Iantir turned toward the tent. "I...anything else you want to know? Maybe there's someone else I can tear up one side and down the other?" he snarled.

"My Heir, do you need him anymore?"

Aria looked up to see that Astur had come up behind her. He wasn't looking at her, though. He was staring intently at Iantir. Treesi turned in her chair and looked up at him.

"Astur?" Treesi said. She glanced at Iantir, then back up at Astur. "Do you want help?"

Astur shook his head. "Thank you, but no." He smiled and leaned down. "Besides, you terrify him."

Aria fought to keep from laughing. She nodded. "I think we are done here. Steward, if you have any other questions, you may ask them later."

Astur walked over to Iantir. "Come with me," he said, holding his hand out. "Let's take a walk."

Iantir stared at him. "You...want to take a walk? With me?"

Astur nodded and offered his hand again. "Come on. I won't hurt you."

Iantir snorted. "It's not you I'm afraid of," he scoffed. He took Astur's hand, and let himself be led away.

"Othi, you're dismissed." Othi bowed and herded the rest of the new guards away. Aria waited until they were gone before turning to the remaining raiders. "How many are left, Steward?" she asked.

"Fifteen, my Heir."

She nodded, looking out at them. "You still have time to plead clemency," she said, raising her voice. "You still have a chance to change. You want peace. So do we. Why can we not build that together?" The raiders huddled together under guard. She watched them talk in low voices, and took advantage of the wait to rub her forehead and look around. "Is there something to drink?" she asked softly. "Aven, you should drink."

Frayim brought two cups over, handing one to Aria, and the other to Aven. Aria sipped hers and closed her eyes, trying not to yawn. The baby shifted and kicked, and she smiled, resting her free hand on her abdomen.

"Is the baby truly a child of all four tribes?"

Aria opened her eyes and looked up to see one of the raiders had stepped forward.

"Yes," Aria answered. "Risha ensured that."

The raider frowned. "I don't follow."

"We were not going to have a child," Aven said. "Not yet. It wasn't safe. But I didn't know how to set a contraceptive block. Risha said she would do it. But she did the opposite. She made it so that the first time we shared a bed, we created a child between us. We didn't know why until we learned of your beliefs." He looked at Aria, and reached to take her hand. "I am Earth and Water. Aria is Air and Fire. The child is of all four tribes, in balance." He looked back at the raiders. "We don't know if this child will be the next Heir. We won't know until it's time. But this child of all four tribes may one day be the Firstborn, when Aria and I return to the Mother. Isn't that what you wanted?"

"I…"

"Did you think you were somehow going to get a child of all four tribes without having two of them involved?" Owyn asked. "You all didn't really think this through, did you?"

The raider swallowed, then shook his head. "We've been waiting for our whole lives. My fa, he waited his whole life."

"And how did you know?" Owyn asked. "Where did your prophecy come from? I mean…was it a Smoke Dancer, or some visionary like Frayim? Where did it come from?" He shook his head. "The only prophecy on this scale that I can think of is the Prophecy of the Dove, and…well, that's us. Where did this one come from?"

"My people," Frayim answered. "To my shame. But I don't know who spoke the words first. It's not recorded. The stories of the Child started with the Wanderers, and spread through the hills to the people who never knew more than the hills and the people of Earth. They never saw the people of the high mountains, or those of the deep waters. So they thought that the ones who looked different were…less."

"No one is less," Aria snapped. "It doesn't matter what tribe, or what we can or cannot do. None of us are less. We are all the Mother's children, and we are all loved. Enough of this separation. Enough of making differences into something wrong. Our differences are what make us stronger!" She looked out at the raiders. "I am tired of the bloodshed. I am tired of fighting people who want the same things I do, but do not want them for me and the people who look like me." She swallowed, her throat suddenly tight. "I want to finish this Progress and go home, and have my child in peace." Her voice cracked, and she couldn't stop the tears. Immediately, Aven and Owyn were both on their feet. Aven pulled her into his arms, letting her cry into his chest.

"I think we're done here," Owyn announced. "Fara, Cellan, you two take this lot off and—"

"Wait."

Aria raised her head and looked at the raider, who was now standing with both hands raised, and the point of Fara's sword at his throat.

"My Heir?" Fara said. "If we were home, I'd ask if I could use his guts for bait."

"Let him be, Fara," Aria said. She wiped her face, but didn't move from the safety of Aven's embrace. "What is it?"

"I...is it too late to change my mind?" he asked. "To...to say I'm sorry, and prove it?" He frowned. "You...clemency, you called it? Can I do that?"

"You're changing your mind?" Aven asked. "Why?"

"Because...because she's right," the raider admitted. "Because seeing the truth right in front of me...and seeing that if I want what I was raised to want...then I have to say my fa was wrong. That I was wrong. And...and I can do that. The Child is right there." He pointed at Aria. "That's what I was told I wanted for my whole life. And if I want it...then I should be doing what I can to protect the mother of that child. Right?" He looked at Fara. "Isn't that right?"

Fara snorted and lowered her sword. "Sounds like you've gotten the idea." She glanced over at the tent. "My Heir?"

Aria nodded. "It does. Have any of the rest of you changed your minds?"

Two more raiders stepped forward, and Owyn came out from under the tent. "I'll take them, Fara," he said. "Come with me. We'll go catch up with Othi and he'll get you set up."

"Thank you, Fireborn." The penitents followed Owyn away, and Aria looked back at the remaining raiders.

"My Heir, what do you want us to do with them?" Fara asked.

Aria closed her eyes and leaned against Aven's warmth. "I..."

"Let them go," Aven murmured. Then he raised his voice, "Let them go back to their hills and tell their people what they've seen and heard, and what they've rejected. Let them go in disgrace and tell their people how they refused to follow. Tell the rest of the Wanderers that they were tested and found wanting. That they have no place in the world, because they turned from the promise made to them."

The raiders all started protesting at once, and Aven let go of Aria and walked toward them.

"Tell me I'm wrong," he said. "Tell me that this isn't the Child that you've been waiting for. Tell me how you know that." He folded his arms over his chest and waited as sudden silence fell. "Well? How do you know?"

"How do you know that the baby is the Child?" one of them asked.

Aven smiled and tapped himself on the chest. "Water and Earth." He pointed at Aria. "Air and Fire. All four tribes in balance, born to the mother chosen by the Mother." His smile grew wider. "Did we mention the baby is a girl?"

"Axia reborn," one of the raiders breathed, and dropped to his knees. "It is the Child!"

Aven shook his head. "But you already turned your back on her. On us. So go back to your hills and live with your shame. You had the chance to stand and watch your people's greatest dream come true...and you failed. Because you couldn't look past wings and gills to see the people we are." He turned back to the tent, returning to Aria's side. "Fara, escort them from the camp, and make sure they go."

"But..."

"You had your chance," Fara said. "Now move."

The protesting raiders were herded away, and Aria looked up at Aven.

"That was..." she paused. "I am not entirely certain what that was."

"It was almost as inspired as your maneuvering in the Hall at the trial of the Usurper," Steward murmured. "That's what that was."

"And what are they going to do now?" Treesi asked. "Will they go?"

"No, I don't think so," Steward answered. "I think they're going to follow us. And I think they're going to become the most devoted guards anyone has ever seen."

Aria blinked. "Guards?"

Steward nodded. Then he looked over his shoulder at the men walking away. When he looked back, he had a thoughtful expression on his face. "And perhaps priests. The temple does need to be rebuilt. Perhaps that might be the most appropriate place for them?"

"Priests?" Aven said. "But...do they even follow the Mother?"

"They might, just...under a different name." Steward turned to Frayim. "Frayim? How long have they been talking about the Child in the Wanderers?"

"As long as I can remember," Frayim answered.

"And...were you the first one to talk about the blessèd Mother?"

Frayim frowned slightly. "I...if anyone else spoke of the blesséd Mother, I don't know of it. There was only the Child. But the Child had to come from somewhere."

Steward nodded. "Del, you collect stories. Have you found any like this? Any about a child?"

Del frowned, then signed. "*The closest I can think of are the ones of Axia as a little girl. The High Meadows stories.*"

Aria laughed. "I haven't thought of those in ages."

"I don't know them," Aven said. "We don't tell those."

Del smiled. "*I'll tell you. But I want to see what stories they tell. See how they compare.*" He looked at Frayim. "*And I'm starting with you. Fa, will you sit with us and translate?*"

"I thought you wanted to nap," Aria said.

Del laughed. "*New stories? That beats napping. Let me go get something to write on. Fa, explain to Frayim what we're doing?*"

Chapter Forty

They camped at the crossroads for three days, giving Aven time to recover, giving the new guards time to learn their routine and to become acclimated. And by the evening of the first day, it was clear that Steward was right, and that the disgraced raiders were not going to leave. They lingered outside the camp, and Aria ordered them to be left alone. The morning after, Del and Steward visited them, and Del started recording their stories.

"*They're all variations on the High Meadows stories,*" he told them as he sat at breakfast with Aria and the other Companions. All around them, the camp was being packed, and wagons were already rolling north to set up the evening camp. Del sat on the ground with a bowl in his lap and a pile of notes on the ground next to him. "*Their legends of the Child are all retellings of the stories of Axia.*" He glanced down at his notes. "*It's really fascinating. And they didn't believe me that other people told those stories until I told them the entire story of Axia and King Frog without any of them telling it to me first.*"

"Did you say King Frog?" Owyn asked. "What is a King Frog?"

"The king of the frogs," Aria answered. "He wanted to take Axia to wife, and she had to beat him at riddles to escape him."

"Oh, I remember that one!" Treesi said with a laugh.

Owyn looked across at Aven, who was sitting at Aria's feet. "I'm lost. Do you feel lost? Because I'm lost."

Aven chuckled, then coughed. He grimaced and sipped his tea. "I can't wait for this cough to clear," he grumbled. "As good as it feels to change, I'm tired of sleeping in an oversized bucket. And yes, I'm lost. I don't know any of these stories. So...these people have created a...a what? A cult, based around children's stories?"

"I don't think so," Aria answered. "Because the High Meadow stories aren't children's stories. They're...well, they're lore. They're stories taught about the early days, before the Mother and Axia came down from the Mother's Womb to find the tribes. The stories the followers of the Child are telling are the same stories that we tell. They're looking at them from a different angle, but it's still the same. They're different facets on the same stone." She set her bowl down, then reached out and gently ran her fingers through Aven's hair. "When we reestablish the Temple, then we can reconcile all of the stories. But this is how they follow the Mother."

"Has anyone else noticed that there are more of them?" Treesi asked. "Astur and I went out to see if they needed anything last night, and I think there are more of them. And I thought I saw women."

"*You did,*" Del signed. "*There were more of them yesterday morning when we went to listen, and I asked. Some of them went out to the settlements close by, and told them that the Child is here, and they should come to see. So...they're coming. The younger ones, anyway. And some of the ones who were here are gone. The ones who stayed said the others went to spread the word to the rest of their people.*" He went through his notes. "*There were thirty newcomers, as of yesterday. Twenty-two men and eight women. Fa said that he'd talk to you about meeting with them tonight once we made camp.*" He grinned. "*They're calling themselves the Mother's Penitents.*"

"I'm not comfortable with them calling me the Mother," Aria murmured, not looking up as she started braiding Aven's hair. "Have you found if it was truly Frayim who began calling me blesséd Mother?"

"*I think it was,*" Del answered. "*I asked some of the older folks who came to see us the other day. No one remembers hearing it before he started talking about his visions.*"

"And honestly, he might be doing the same thing as the other Wanderers," Owyn said. "Retelling the stories. But he's got them all mixed up with his visions." He looked up. "Mem! Good morning!"

"Good morning," Memfis called as he came over to join them. "The coaches are ready, and your wagon, Owyn."

"Did you practice this morning, Mem?" Owyn asked.

"A bit," Memfis answered, sitting down next to Owyn. "The new boys need more teaching, so I'm getting to work with them. That Iantir, he's a good teacher. Patient." He nodded, smiling. "They're good boys, at the heart of it."

"Remind me. How many people did those good boys kill?" Aven asked.

"You're a good boy. How many people have you killed?" Memfis asked in response. "Aven, some of them weren't given a choice. They were born to that, and it's all they knew. Some of them are followers. They need someone to lead, and they'll do whatever they're told. And some of them...well, they were ignorant, and they're learning." Memfis shrugged. "I have experience with young men who start out ignorant, and I think I did all right." He grinned at Owyn.

"Yeah, Fa. You did just fine." Owyn got up and went to fill a cup with tea, bringing it back. "Are the healers packed up? I told Allie I'd come so we could say goodbye to Mama and Fa together."

"I think they're almost done," Memfis answered. "The tent is down, and I think everything is packed."

"Who else is going west, besides Dyneh and Huris?" Aven asked. "I've lost track. And what is going on with Elaias? It seems like he's changing his mind about which way he's going every five minutes."

"I was going to ask about Elaias," Memfis said. "When did he and Trista start spending time together?"

"Oh, is that why?" Aven laughed. "I'd missed that. But then, I've been in the healing tent the past few days. I think I've missed quite a bit of what's been happening outside."

Owyn grinned. "You can blame Aria for that one. She put them next to each other."

Aria finished braiding Aven's hair and smiled. "And what did Alanar say when you told him?"

"That Trista is probably pairing with Elaias? He likes it. It may put a stop on our plans, but...well, we'll figure it out." He stood up and brushed off his trousers. "I'm going to go find my husband. If Trista might be going west, then there's a conversation that needs to happen today." He lingered long enough to kiss everyone, then hurried away.

"Plans? What plans?" Memfis asked. "What conversation?"

"Owyn hasn't told you?" Aria asked. "If he hasn't, it's not my place to say. But he'll tell you when he's ready."

Aven tipped his head back. "You know?"

She smiled. "We discussed it. But it is still not mine to share. He will tell all of you when he's ready." She smoothed Aven's braid. "Let's go say our goodbyes."

OWYN FOUND ALANAR LEANING against the wagon that carried the healing tent and all of the supplies. He was talking to Jehan and Elaias, and he was frowning.

"Are you sure?" he said as Owyn approached. "The group going west will need a fully trained healer."

"And they'll have one in Dyneh," Elaias answered. "She's very good. And the trainees respond well to her. Arjin especially. They should be fine."

"But you're their trainer of record," Jehan pointed out. "You should be with them. And I know Pirit would appreciate having another healer of your skill in Terraces." He folded his arms over his chest. "Elaias, what is this about? Your head hasn't been here for days."

Elaias grimaced, then sighed. "Trista won't come west with me. She says her place is here with the Heir and the Companions."

Jehan's brows rose. "It's that serious? That quickly?"

Elaias shrugged. "I...I'm not sure. And I won't know if we're apart, which...we both know that's what we have to do. She has to go north. I have to go west. But...well, neither of us wants to leave the other." He sighed and shook his head. "So...that's where we are. I have to go west, but I want to go north. And I think she'd say the same in reverse."

"Trista hasn't spoken to us about going west," Owyn said. "I mean, I don't mind. We'll miss her, but I think we can dress ourselves."

Elaias looked at him. "I didn't hear you come up behind me," he said. "You...do you think Steward will let her go?"

"We can ask him. But Allie and I needed to talk to her, and...well, if you're that serious, then we need to talk to you, too."

Elaias nodded slowly. "Right...I...Jehan, I'll have an answer for you as soon as I can."

"Sooner," Jehan said. "We need to get moving." He walked away, and Owyn joined Alanar against the wagon.

"You still want to talk to her about this?" he asked.

Alanar nodded. "I can't not ask. I mean...I lit the candle. I can't unburn it. The thought is there." He straightened. "Let's go see what she says. Where is she?"

"I think she's overseeing the packing of the Heir's tent," Elaias answered. He fell in on Alanar's other side as they started walking. "May I ask what you're asking?"

Alanar smiled. "Let me ask her first." He turned his head slightly. "How are you settling in?"

"It's strange," Elaias admitted. "Not as...regimented as it was under my father. I was never allowed quite as much...flexibility, I suppose you'd say. Father had his methods, and that's how we were supposed to work. So what that raider...Bali? What he said about Minnit wanting out, and Father not being willing to let him go? I can believe that. I just didn't even know Minnit had someone." He shook his head. "Father...he was determined to control everything about us, about how we lived. He had a girl picked out for me, and he'd arranged Treesi's marriage. That's why Astur helped her to run."

"We knew that," Owyn said. "She told us."

"What happened to the girl?" Alanar asked.

"She's the reason I was out of the healing center. Father thought that she was pregnant with my child, so I was there to attend the birth." He grinned. "She was in love with someone else, and we played at being together so that she could be with the person she really wanted. Once she had the baby, they left for the west. I went home...and there wasn't a home left to go back to."

Owyn shook his head. "That's...I don't understand how that could happen."

"Neither do I," Elaias admitted. "I knew my father was...rigid. I didn't think he was insane. And I never thought he'd destroy everything to try to keep us in line." He clasped his hands behind his back and smiled. "There's Trista."

Trista was standing with her back to them, supervising the loading of a wagon with travel trunks and the bed boxes that Owyn recognized from the Heir's tent. She turned slightly and saw them, and her smile widened and warmed.

"Shouldn't you be getting ready to go?" she asked Elaias.

"Well, I apparently need to be here for a conversation," Elaias answered. "Of what, I'm not sure."

"A private conversation," Owyn added. "So...come over to the wagon." He led them all to his wagon, and opened the rear door. It was cramped inside with the four of them, but it wasn't uncomfortable. Elaias and Alanar sat on either side of Trista on the bed, and Owyn sat down on the floor facing them.

"This must be something serious," Trista said. "What is it?"

"Well," Owyn said. "First, I want you to know that anything we ask you, you can say no to. It's just...we both like you. And we trust you. And...well..."

"Owyn and I want a family," Alanar said. "A child of our own. And...well, he's going to have children with Aria. We know that. But those children won't be our children. And since neither of us are equipped to carry a baby, we were hoping that you might consider being a host for us?"

Trista stared at them for a moment. "I...you want me to have a baby? For you? But..."

"We didn't know you were getting serious with Elaias," Owyn said. "And...if that's really serious, if you're both going to start a family together, we understand."

Trista turned to stare at Elaias, who shook his head. "I had no idea."

"We weren't going to tell him until we talked to you," Owyn said. "The only person who knows is Aria, because...well, because she's Heir, and I'm her Fire, and she sort of needs to know about that."

"That's a heavy thing to ask," Trista murmured. "You know...you know how I feel about you both, right? About the three of you?"

"Three?" Elaias repeated. "Why do I get the impression I'm not included in that count?"

Alanar smiled. "You're not, and Trista can explain why later. And we know. That's why we wanted to ask you. Because we know you have feelings for us. And we love you, too." He sighed. "But we neither of us want to get in the way of what you're building with Elaias."

Trista smiled slightly. "Thank you. For thinking of that. I...Eli?"

Elaias smiled. "I don't think there's a deep enough foundation between us yet for me to have a say. But if you're asking me if I object? No. You had a life before I came into it. You had people who you loved, and who loved you, before I did. I appreciate you asking me, but you don't need my permission." He rested his hand on hers. "If you want this, then I support you completely."

Trista swallowed. "I..."

"And if you want to go west, we'll clear it with Steward," Owyn added. "No matter if you say yes or no." She turned to look at him, and he grinned. "We can dress ourselves, Trista."

"No, you can't." She sniffed. "I've seen how you dress when I'm not there, Owyn."

"Hey!"

Alanar laughed. "I promise to stop dressing him, Trista."

Trista giggled. Then she took a deep breath. "This...how long have you been thinking about this?"

Owyn frowned. "I...think...Cliffside? But Alanar only suggested you as a host...was it right after the whole mess with Wren?"

"Can we not ever say his name again?" Alanar asked. "Please? And yes. That was when I suggested we talk to Trista."

"And I talked to Aria a few days ago," Owyn added. "Because I wasn't sure how to talk to you without making a mess of things, since we talked about you wanting a family of your own."

Trista nodded. "And...both of you?"

"Me," Alanar answered. "We decided that since Aria wants children with Owyn, that if you agreed, it would be me."

Trista nodded again. Then she smiled. "And...when?"

Alanar blinked. "Is...is that a yes?"

"I...can it happen now? Can...." Trista's voice trailed off, and she looked at Elaias. "If we can...and then I can go west...and when the Progress is over and you're back at the Palace, I can meet you there."

Alanar held his hand out, and Trista slipped her hand into his. From where he was sitting, Owyn could see her hand shaking. Alanar closed his eyes and tipped his head to the side.

"I...not today."

"Can you make it today?" Trista asked. She looked at Elaias, then back at Alanar. "Can you...well, Aria said that Risha made it so that she'd get pregnant the first time—"

"And it hurt her," Owyn interjected. "When Risha did it, Aria was in pain afterward."

"Oh," Trista murmured. "I...I was thinking that if we did it now, then I could go west with Elaias, and we'd all get what we wanted."

Alanar licked his lips. "You...are you absolutely sure you want to do it this way?" he asked.

Trista hesitated, then kissed him. "Yes."

"Right. I'll go tell Steward you're going west, then," Owyn said, and got up. "Elaias, want to come keep me company?"

Elaias followed him out of the wagon, and Owyn made sure the door was closed firmly. Then he started walking, wondering just where Steward would be. He didn't think the man had left yet, so where...

"Any idea where Frayim is?"

"I saw him with the Wanderers who are going west," Elaias answered. "You think we'll find Steward with him?"

"Almost certain," Owyn answered. He looked up at Elaias. "You know, I think we all forgot to ask. Did you want to stay?"

Elaias shook his head. "No. This...this is for her, and for him. If there's a next time, then I'll stay." He looked back and smiled. "We haven't yet, you know. I wanted her to be sure of what she wanted. And now...well, I want her to be especially sure. Because if she wants to be with you, then I'm not going to get in the way."

Owyn chuckled. "We were worried about getting in your way," he admitted. "I mean...Trista wants a family. And...Well, we can't offer her that. Not the way she wants. But we all want her to be happy."

"And that's why Aria introduced us?" Elaias asked. "I appreciate that. I do like her. I—" He stopped, turning. "Did you hear that?"

Owyn nodded, turning to look. He could hear someone shouting Elaias' name. It was Astur, who came running toward them with a wild look on his face.

"Eli!" he gasped as he reached them. "It's Mam! And Min!"

"What?" Elaias grabbed Astur's arm. "Where?"

"By the wagon. The healing tent wagon. Trees is with them, and Othi and Aven and the Senior Healer." Astur took a shaky breath. "They need you."

Elaias went white, and took off running. Astur followed, and Owyn chased them back to the wagon where the healing tent had been. One of the cots had been set up in the shade of the wagon, and Jehan knelt on one side. Aven was on the other, and the both of them looked as if they were focused on the figure lying there. Treesi and Othi stood nearby; Othi had his hand on a young man's shoulder, while Treesi had her arms around an older woman.

"Min will be fine," Owyn heard her say. "Jehan is Senior Healer, and Aven is a natural five." She looked up. "And now we've got more help."

The woman looked up, saw Elaias, and burst into tears. "Eli!"

"Mam!" Elaias went straight to her and hugged her tightly. "I thought you were dead!" He drew back, looked at her, then hugged her again. "I went back and you were gone. Everything was gone." He looked over his shoulder. "Min. What happened to Min?" His pale face went ghostly. "His heart?"

"Her heart," the young man with Othi said.

"Her?" Elaias repeated.

"She told her truth?" Astur gasped. "She finally did it?"

Elaias looked at him. "You knew?" he asked. "I thought I was the only one who knew. I helped her hide from Fa." He looked at the young man. "Is that what happened? She finally told Fa? And... I didn't get your name?"

"My name is Versi. Mina and I have been married four years now."

Elaias blinked. "Four years? That's before the fire. You married her...and Fa allowed it?"

Versi sniffed. "Your father never knew about me. Mina was defiant? Well, I'm sneaky. We managed. Then...she got tired of only having stolen nights and half-truths. I didn't know she was going to do it. I'd have tried to talk her out of it. But she told your father who she really was. That she was Mina, that she was mine, and that she was leaving. And...well..." He sighed. "No one ever thought Elan would go as far as he did."

"Do we even want to know?" Othi asked.

Gisa shook her head. "I never knew he was capable of it. He said that we had to stay together, to prove that we were worthy. That the failures were gone, and that the righteous children of the Mother needed to stand firm against the evils of the world, and that we needed to cleanse ourselves of those evils." She paused, and Versi went and took her hand. "We couldn't stop him. It was all Mina could do to get me out."

"Mama, what did he do?" Treesi asked.

Gisa paused, then closed her eyes again. "Inferno oil. There was inferno oil hidden in all the buildings. When he realized that Mina wasn't going to bend, when he realized that the majority of the healing center were going to leave with us, he barred the doors and set the torch."

"Mam!" Astur gasped. "Wait...you were leaving?"

Gisa nodded. She looked at Treesi, then back as Astur and Elaias. "I lost three of my babies to his...superstitions and lies. Because I wasn't strong enough to stand up to him. I wasn't going to lose the last of them. I told him either he welcomed Versi, or he lost us all."

Versi continued, "She...after she and Mama Gisa got out, she got sicker. I mean, she was never well. But she was weaker after the fire. We stayed low, stayed quiet, in case anyone was looking for her. But she's been getting sicker and sicker, and we were going to go west, to the healing center. We been three days on the road…and she collapsed this morning and wouldn't wake up and…" He swallowed. "Healer, am I gonna lose my Mina?"

"She'll be fine, Versi," Treesi said, her voice low and soothing. "Owyn, where's Alanar?"

"Busy," Owyn answered. "But I can go get him. Do you need three in the merge? Four? I mean, you've got Elaias here now, and—"

"No," Jehan answered. He shifted to sit down and looked up. "No, she'll be fine. And I'm appalled. From the way it looks, her heart has been weak her entire life. Why was nothing done to repair it?"

"What?" Elaias gaped at Jehan. "Fa said nothing could be done!" He turned back to his mother. "Mam?"

"Elan said it was nothing," Gisa murmured in a broken voice. "That it was just…she was always so defiant. You all were, but Mina—"

"You're telling me that a Healer, and her own father, let her suffer?" Jehan said in a low voice. Gisa flinched.

"It was to make her mind—" she murmured. Then she stopped and closed her eyes, and when she spoke again, her voice was stronger. "Elan was a bad man. A bad father. And a bad healer. And…I'm not beholden to him anymore. He can't hurt us anymore. Senior Healer, will my child live?"

Jehan nodded. "She's in trance. When she wakes, she'll be weak, but we repaired the leak in her heart. She'll be fine. Elaias, are you going west or north?"

"West, and Trista is coming with me," Elaias answered. "I'll take on Mina's care, if that was the next question."

"It was. And good. This will be a good lesson for the trainees while you travel."

"How is the patient?" Steward called as he and Frayim came closer. "I talked with Huris and Dyneh. Healer Gisa and Versi and... was it Mina? They can stay in their wagon, if someone will ride with them. Dyneh can't drive and mind her at the same time."

"I'll stay with her," Elaias answered. "Steward, we wanted you to know. Trista is coming west with me."

Steward laughed and looked at Frayim. "Do you ever get tired of being right?"

Frayim grinned. "Not yet."

"You knew?" Elaias shook his head. "Why am I even surprised? She's busy with Alanar right now, but we'll be ready to leave soon. I can help with Mina."

"And I want to get to know this new son of mine," Gisa said, smiling up at Othi. "As much as I can before I leave."

Chapter Forty-One

Jehan searched the camp until he found Steward, who was overseeing the packing.

"Good morning. We'll be ready to roll out shortly. How's Aven this morning?" Steward asked.

"Better for having had a night in his own bed," Jehan answered. "Where's Frayim?"

"Helping Memfis and Owyn with the kitchen tent."

Jehan nodded. "Good. Walk with me."

Steward arched a brow, and fell in next to Jehan as they walked away from the bustle of packing. "What is it?"

"Treesi came to me with a question. I've been mulling on it for days," Jehan said.

Steward blinked. "I'd nearly forgotten. She told me that she had a thought and was going to bring it to you. What was it?" He looked over his shoulder, toward the camp. "And what does it have to do with Frayim?"

"Treesi says you told her that you knew him. You've never met him before, but you knew him. And he knew you."

Steward nodded. "It was the oddest thing. I've never experienced anything like that before. Attraction, certainly. But nothing like this. I..." He paused, and his face paled. "And Treesi knows exactly what happened, doesn't she?"

Jehan nodded. "She thinks so. And I agree with her."

"But..." Steward looked back at the camp. "He'd have been her Earth?"

"If Yana had survived to come find him. He was seventeen when she died—"

"Which is when his visions started," Steward murmured. "I... a Companion bond? But Yana died before she found him! How can there still be a bond?"

Jehan shook his head. "There's never been anything like this before. Nothing in all our history. I don't know. Neither does Aleia or Mem." He folded his arm over his chest. "But I have a theory. The gems? Those are just a visible token that shows other people the bond that already exists. Milon's circle? We didn't need the gems to know we were part of each other. And you've seen Aria and her circle. They don't need the gems either." He smiled when he saw Frayim appear at the edge of the camp. "And I don't think you need them either. But I'm intrigued that he gave himself the visible token that he should have had."

"The tattoo," Steward said. "Jehan, he'd have been a child. He's so young! What am I supposed to do?"

"I don't think that's up to me, Steward." Jehan clapped him on the shoulder. "And if you'd asked me that question twenty years ago? I don't know what I'd have said. There's never been a Companion come to their gem that young. But he's a grown man now. And so are you. This is for you both to decide. If you want to talk more about this, you can come find me later."

Steward nodded. He walked back toward the camp, and Frayim met him halfway.

"YOU'VE BEEN AWFULLY quiet since we left the crossroads."

Treesi took a deep breath and looked up at Othi, who was riding on her left. "I know. I'm sorry. I've been horrible to you for days now."

"No, not horrible," Othi assured her. "I understand. You barely had any time with your mother before she went west with the others. And I miss your brothers and your sister, too. And the trainees. I like them."

"They're your brothers and sister now, too," Treesi pointed out. "And they're going to be safe. They're heading west to Terraces, and they'll be safe there." She paused, uncertain if the person who needed to hear those words most was Othi, or herself. "And Terraces is so close to the Palace, if we go by canoe. We'll be able to go see them when we get home."

"Do you think your mother would want to come live in the Palace?" Othi asked. "Would you want her to?"

Treesi blinked. "I...would you want her to?"

"That's both not what I asked and not important," Othi said with a smile. "Do you want her closer than Terraces?"

"I..." Treesi sputtered. "I don't know what she'd want."

"Then we'll ask her," Othi said. "Once we're home. Which...I can't wait to go home. How much longer?" He tipped his head back, then pointed. "Look!"

Treesi looked up and saw the figures circling overhead.

"I was wondering when we'd be seen," she said. "Steward said it would happen any day now. We must be very close to the Solstice village." She nodded. "You ride up and see if Karse needs you. I'll go see if Aria has noticed." She rode back to one of the two remaining coaches. Aven was sitting at the window, and he smiled as Treesi drew her horse up alongside.

"We've been seen," Treesi called. "So we'll probably be stopping soon to meet them."

Aria appeared in the window. "Seen? Today? I wasn't expecting it until tomorrow." She looked up through the coach window. "I must have lost a day. If we're being challenged, we're very close. We'll probably be at the Solstice village by sunset."

"Have you told Alanar yet?" Aven asked.

"Not yet," Treesi answered. "I sent Othi up to Karse, and came to tell you. I'll ride back and tell the other coach, and tell Owyn and Allie." She looked up again. "Three of them. Can't tell if they're men or women."

"Men," Aria said. "The sentries are always men, and they fly set patterns based on their flock. This route would be flown by some of the men from mine. I wonder who is up there?" She tried to look up again. "I suppose I will know soon enough. Go and tell the others."

Treesi rode further down the line, stopping briefly at the second coach to tell Jehan, Memfis, Afansa, and Aleia about the sentries. Then she headed for the two Wanderer wagons that drove one right after the other. Frayim's wagon was in front, and he nodded when Treesi rode toward them and started keeping pace with Steward and Del.

"We see them," Frayim said. "Will they stop us, or meet us in the village? I haven't come this far north in some time."

"Aria says that they'll stop us, and that the ones who are watching us may be from her flock," Treesi said. "She wanted me to tell Alanar."

"Alanar has family in the mountains," Steward said. "We'll have to send word to his flock, too." He chuckled. "That's where they were going, when they came to the Palace the first time. When they met the Usurper. They were going to meet Alanar's grandfather to tell him about their marriage. They weren't sure if he was still alive." He looked back over his shoulder. "Looks like Owyn is coming up."

The second wagon drew up on the far side of Frayim's, and Owyn looked across at them. "What is it?" he called, then nodded toward the sky. "Who's up there?"

"Aria thinks it might be someone from her flock, and they'll be coming down to meet us," Treesi called back. "We can ask them to send a messenger to Alanar's flock too."

"Please!" Alanar's voice came out of the wagon. "My grandfather is Alanar, too."

"Did you tell me that?" Owyn asked, looking down at the tiny window. "How did they tell you two apart?"

"I was smaller, and a lot younger?" Alanar answered, and Owyn laughed. "He's Alanar the Elder. I'm not even sure if he's still alive. If he isn't, the head of our flock would be my uncle Einar."

"Looks like they're stopping," Steward said. He looked up. "And there's only one in the air. Shall we go and meet the sentries?"

THE TWO SENTRIES STOOD in the middle of the road, arms folded over their chests, wings flared out. Aven had lived with Aria long enough to know that it was a display for intimidation. With the two of them, it definitely worked, and he started to regret that he'd listened to Aria and left his swords in the coach. He glanced to his right, saw Aria's smile, and relaxed.

"Tiercel and Ionith," she said softly. "They're my uncle's sons. I've known them since I was a fledgling." She started forward, and he followed, hearing Owyn behind him and on his left. One of the two sentries looked at them, then blinked and looked again, his wings folding.

"Ari?" he called. "Is that...you did it?"

"Ari?" Aven whispered.

"You do not get to call me that," Aria whispered back. "I do not like it. I've never liked it. He refuses to stop." She smiled. "Tierce. Did you get taller in the past year?"

He burst out laughing. "Grandfather says I'm going to knock my skull on the ceiling if I don't stop. You did it. I..." He blinked again. "And that baby is coming when?"

Aria looked down at herself. "Soon. But hopefully not before we go to the Temple. Tierce—"

"We...we found her," Tiercel said, sobering. "When you didn't come back, we went looking, and...we found her." He swallowed. "We hoped...and you did it. Proud of you, Ari." He looked at the others. "Do I get to meet your Companions now, or do I have to wait for Grandfather?"

Aria looked up at Aven. "I think I should do this all at once. And we still have a distance to travel. Will you go up the mountain?"

"And when you do," Owyn added. "Would you send for Alanar the Elder? If he's still alive?"

Ionith snorted. "That one? He'll outlive us all. He's too mean for the shadowhawks. Why do you want him, if I might ask? He'll want to know."

"His grandson is part of my circle," Aria answered. "Healer Alanar the Younger, who is heir to the Senior Healer."

Ionith nodded. "I'll go. Tierce, I'll start out now. The Old Man is farther out than our roost."

Tiercel nodded, and Ionith stepped back and took off, flying toward the mountains. Tiercel turned back to Aria and smiled.

"I'm really happy to see you, Ari."

"Not enough to remember that I don't like it when you call me Ari," Aria pointed out, her voice tart. Tiercel laughed.

"That's habit," he said. "I'll try to stop. My Heir." He bowed, then winked and stepped back before taking off. Aven tipped his head back and watched as Tiercel joined the other sentry, before flying off toward the mountains.

"So...how soon is soon?" Owyn asked. "Because...well, I'm going to need to know this, eventually." He cocked his head to the side. "The baby settled—"

"Dropped," Aven corrected.

"Right. Dropped. The baby dropped...was it the day after we left the crossroads?" Owyn looked at Aria, who nodded. "So...how soon is soon?"

"Jehan says it could be as little as two weeks, or as long as a month," Aria answered. She rubbed one hand over her belly. "I'm hoping she waits that month. If she does, we might be home when she finally comes."

"Maybe," Jehan said as he came to join them, standing just behind Owyn. "We'll discuss plans after we go to the Temple. Perhaps you and the others can go back while we stay and search. You don't need to be here when we find Risha."

"I need to be here when you find my father," Aria said.

Jehan nodded. "I thought you might say that. We'll discuss it. And we'll see if there's a midwife in the Solstice village. Sending you back to the Palace is an option, but I should be here when they find Milon and Trey. I'm going to be needed. Which means you'll be without a healer who's actually attended a birth for the time it takes to get to the Palace. So we'll need to make some plans." He looked over his shoulder. "The scouts that went out with the advance riders just came back and reported in. We're almost there. We're almost finished."

Owyn snorted. "It won't be finished until we stop Risha and get Milon and Trey away from her. You know that."

"We all know that," Treesi said. "But we're that much closer to the end. To finding them and finishing it." She leaned into

Owyn's side as he put his arm around her. "It'll be good to go home."

"I'm jealous," Aria said. "You'll get to go through the heaviest part of your pregnancy in comfort. I couldn't take a full breath between Hearthstone and the crossroads."

"Is that why you stopped singing at moonrise?" Owyn asked. "I was wondering. Because that was fun, and we haven't done it in ages."

"Maybe tonight," Aria said. "I think I would like that. If I can stay awake." She chuckled and put her arm around Aven's waist. He slid his arm under her wings and pulled her close, and she sighed. "I don't want to get back into the coach, but I don't want to ride, either."

"Ride with me," Owyn said. "There's room on the driver's seat of the wagon."

Aria looked up at Aven. "Do you mind?"

"No, I'll ride alongside," he answered. He leaned down and kissed her cheek, then let her go. "I'll go get Pewter and meet you at the wagon."

DEL AND TREESI ALSO decided to ride, and Othi joined them, so there were two riders on either side of the wagon as the setting sun cast long shadows toward the mountains. Owyn couldn't see the camp, but he could see a lot of people in the air.

"We have an audience," he said, nodding upward. Aria tipped her head back and smiled wistfully. Owyn chuckled. "You'll be up there with them soon enough."

"A few months," Aria said with a nod. "Once my flight feathers grow back."

"So what's it like?" Treesi asked. "I've never asked you. What's flying like?"

Aria blinked. Then she frowned slightly. "I've never thought to compare it to anything," she said. "Flying just...is."

"Like being in the deep," Aven said. "Right, Othi?"

"Right. The things we do because they're how we do things...we don't compare them to other things because we don't have to." Othi shrugged. "So flying for Air is like being in the deep for us." He looked distant. "Treesi, what's healing like?"

"I...oh. Aven, is healing like being in the deep?" Treesi looked across the wagon to Aven. "You're the only one who can answer that question."

"Vir can answer it," Alanar called from inside the wagon. "And he says yes and no."

"That's not an answer, love," Owyn said, looking in through the window. Alanar was lying on his side on the bed, facing the window.

"No, he's right," Aven said. "It is, but it isn't. And...I'll have to think about it. Maybe tonight I'll talk to Virrik and see if we can decide why."

"If we have time tonight," Owyn said. "Is that the camp?" He looked over his shoulder. "Ummm...any chance that one here is going to think Steward looks familiar?"

Del shook his head, and Owyn heard his mental voice, "*Unlikely. I don't think he's been here in years, and the Air tribe doesn't come down to the lowlands or the Palace. Not often, anyway.*"

"We should still be careful," Owyn said. "Aven, maybe ride back and tell him and Frayim to keep their heads down? Or...I dunno...maybe get in the wagon, or a coach?"

"We're being watched," Aven pointed out. "If we stop and have him get in the coach, they'll wonder why. Better to brazen it out, I think."

"Aven has a point," Aria agreed. "And I do not think anyone will know him. At least, not enough to do more than think he resembles someone. Aven, go and warn him."

Aven turned his horse and rode back to Frayim's wagon; Owyn turned to look back, then faced forward. The road had turned just enough that he could see the camp, and people waving.

"Do we have a plan?" he asked. "For how long we stay here before we go on to the Temple? And how far is the Temple from here?"

"I'm not entirely certain," Aria answered. "I know it took us several hours flight from our aerie, but I was rarely allowed to come down to the Solstice village. Del, do you know?"

Del shook his head and raised his hands. *"I've never been here. Or to the Temple."*

"Mem might know," Owyn said. "When we see him, we can ask. Or we can ask Steward. Right, where's the picket? Allie, we staying in the tent tonight?"

"I doubt it. They'll offer us the guest houses," Alanar called. "At least, I expect that they will. And we need to agree to stay there, because it's an insult to refuse."

"Guest houses?" Aria turned slightly in her seat. "There are guest houses?"

"And we'll be expected to use them," Alanar said. "Generosity. Aria, you know the custom. Probably better than I do."

"Oh, of course," Aria said. "I just hadn't realized, but I've never stayed in the Solstice village longer than a few hours. I didn't know that's how it was done here."

"When I was here with my father, after my mother died, we stayed in one. They're comfortable, from what I remember. And there were four of them then."

"What do you mean, generosity?" Owyn asked. "That sounds important."

"It is, and I should have told you," Aria said. "If you are offered gifts—"

"And you will be!" Alanar called.

Aria looked back at the window and smiled. "And you will be," she repeated. "You must accept them. To refuse them would be an insult. It implies that you think that the gift, or the gift giver, is beneath you."

"Do we have to give gifts, too?" Treesi asked. "And...do we have gifts to give?"

"We probably do," Aria answered. "I can't imagine that Steward didn't plan for this." She leaned into Owyn's shoulder, and he could feel how tired she was.

"Whatever we do, you're going to nap," he said. "Or you'll fall asleep in your supper, and that'll be an insult, too."

"No, that will be funny." Tiercel swooped in overhead and landed lightly on the wagon roof. "Aria, I wanted to warn you. The entire flock came down. Grandfather is...well, not giddy. I'm not sure he knows how to spell giddy, let alone actually be it. But he's smiling, and I can't remember when that last happened."

"What about Alanar the Elder?" Owyn asked. "Or...what was his name, Allie?"

"Einar," Alanar called.

"They both came down as well," Tiercel answered, leaning forward. "There's someone in there? What is this?"

"It's a house on wheels," Aria answered.

"A Wanderer wagon," Owyn added. "My parents went west with the Wanderers, but this is mine."

"Wanderers?" Tiercel repeated. "I don't know who you mean, but the village might."

"Frayim did say that they'd stopped coming north," Aven pointed out as he joined them. "Because of the raiders. So it's probably been an age since there were wagons like this on these roads." Aven drew his horse closer to the wagon. "Did you have trouble with the raiders?"

"They're why we were flying sentry," Tiercel answered. "Because they were threatening the village, and the headwoman sent to us for help. But it's been quiet the past week or so."

"Because the raiders aren't there anymore," Owyn answered. "They fucked with us. They lost."

Tiercel snorted. "Ari, is he one of yours? I like him. But if he talks like that around Grandfather, he'll taste soap."

Owyn snorted. "Been threatened with that. Still hasn't happened." He turned and looked up. "I'm Owyn. Owyn Jaxis. Once we've stopped, I'll meet you proper."

"Once you meet our grandfather. I need to get back to him." Tiercel launched himself into the air, and Owyn shook his head.

"*He doesn't know a blasted thing about horses,*" Del said in Owyn's mind. "*Someone needs to tell him not to do that. He'll scare the horses.*"

Owyn nodded. "Aria, when you get a chance, take him aside and tell him that he shouldn't land on wagons or launch near horses? He'll spook them. I don't imagine he knows any more than you did about horses."

"I will tell him." Aria took a deep breath. "We're almost there. Almost done."

"Almost," Owyn agreed.

THEY REACHED CAMP, and took time to change and clean up before walking toward the walls of the village. There was a crowd waiting for them, and Aven could practically feel Aria's excitement. He squeezed her hand gently.

"I imagine this is what it's going to be like for me," he murmured. "Once we're back to the Palace, and we can see the sea again."

She smiled, looking up at him. "I can't wait for you to teach her to swim."

Aven raised her hand to his lips and kissed her fingers, then straightened and looked forward. An old winged man was standing in front of the crowd. Behind him was another old winged man, a winged man who might have been Steward's age, Aria's two cousins, and a wingless woman.

"Which one is your grandfather?" Owyn asked.

"In the middle," Aria answered.

"The other must be Alanar's grandfather, then," Owyn said. He looked back over his shoulder. "I hope they don't object to me."

"They're idiots if they do," Aven said, and heard Owyn laugh.

"I love you, too, Fishie."

Aven smiled, then looked at Aria. She nodded, and stopped walking.

"I am Aria, daughter of Milon and Liara—"

"Little girl," her grandfather interrupted. "I knew that before you knew that."

"Let the girl finish," the woman grumbled, loud enough for her voice to carry. "I've got bread in the oven."

Aria's laughter was clear in her voice when she continued. "I have been chosen by the Mother as Heir to the Firstborn."

Aven waited until she squeezed his hand to continue. "Aven Waterborn, son of Jehan and Aleia."

"Owyn Jaxis Fireborn, son of Huris, Dyneh and Memfis."

Owyn's announcement caused a ripple of whispers, so it took a moment before Treesi could continue. "Treesi Earthborn, daughter of Elan and Gisa."

Then Del spoke, slowly. "Del...Airborn ...of Yana...and...Del...an...dri."

Yana's name brought even more commotion than Owyn's three parents, and which faded to uncomfortable silence. Silence shattered by a single caustic voice.

"Is that the best she could do?" Einar demanded. "A wingless freak?"

Chapter Forty-Two

D el went hot, then cold. For a heartbeat, he wanted to turn and run.

No. He was past running. He walked forward, his eyes never leaving the face of the man who was now laughing at him. He stopped, stripped his shirt off, hearing it rip when it caught on his wrist sheath. He ignored it and turned, showing them his bare back.

Showing them the scars where his wings had been.

"Wind and Sky!"

There was movement behind him, then a man asked, "May I touch you?"

Del nodded, and felt warm hands on his back. He glanced back to see the other old man.

"Al...nar?" he stammered.

He smiled. "Yes. I am Alanar. Alanar the Elder. And this...I know what these are. My grandson bears the same marks. How old were you?"

Del considered trying to speak, then decided against it and held up six fingers.

"So young?" Alanar the Elder murmured. He moved away and Del turned to see him stalking toward the now red-faced other man. Alanar the Elder glared at him, then swung, and the slap echoed across the field.

"No!" Del gasped.

A hand closed on his shoulder, and he looked back to see his father. Steward held out Del's shirt, and when Del took it, started signing, "*Are you all right?*"

Del nodded and tugged the shirt on over his head. He smoothed it down, examining the torn sleeve where it had caught on his wrist sheath. He could mend it later. He nodded again, and answered, "*Angry.*"

Steward snorted. "*I can see that. I don't think I've ever seen you this angry.*"

"What is it that you're doing?"

Del looked over to see Aria's grandfather, Alanar the Elder, and the man who'd insulted Del. He wasn't sure who had asked, and looked at Steward.

"These are Water signs," Steward explained. "How the Water tribe communicate when they are underwater. Del lost his wings and his voice in an attempt on his life—"

"At six?" Alanar the Elder gasped. He glared at the other man, whose cheek was starting to show signs of swelling. "This is my son, Einar. Who owes you an apology."

Del glared at Einar, then looked at Steward. "*Will you translate? And say exactly what I sign? Don't soften it.*"

"Of course," Steward said. "I am going to translate for Del."

Del looked at Einar, starting to sign, "*I do not accept your apology. This is my first time meeting my mother's people, and on the way here, Aria told us about the custom of generosity, and how we should not refuse gifts because to do so would be an insult. And the first thing you do is offer me an insult. And you expect me to take it. No. I refuse your insult, and your apology.*" He dusted his hands off, as if he were brushing off dirt, and waited for Steward to finish.

Aria's grandfather smiled. "You definitely have Yana's spirit to you," he said.

"You knew her?" Steward asked.

"Not as well as these two did." Aria's grandfather folded his hands and nodded. "Since our introductions were rudely interrupted, I am Agragor." He paused, then looked at Steward. "And you have some Air in you, don't you?"

Steward blinked. "I...yes. My..." He paused. "I should introduce myself. I am known as Steward, but—"

"Steward!" There was a definite warning note in Aria's voice, but Steward continued.

"But before I abdicated and surrendered myself to Aria, I was also the Usurper, whose name has been forgotten. And...I was Yana's Air." He glanced at Del. "And I am Del's adoptive father."

Agragor blinked. "The Usurper...you're *Mannon?*"

"That name is no longer spoken, no longer recorded in our histories. The Usurper will never be recognized by the Mother," Aria said. "Steward is a good man, who serves me and mine well. We call him Uncle, and he is part of my family."

"You're more correct than you think, little girl," Agragor said. "Falla was the mother of the one you call the Usurper. Falla's mother was my mother's sister." He smiled. "Welcome home."

Steward looked stunned. "I..." He coughed, then blinked and stammered, "How...how did you know Yana?"

Alanar the Elder answered, "She was of my wife's flock. My niece, through my wife's sister. The last generation of that flock, they were all girls, so they have all married into other flocks, and that aerie lies empty and cold." He turned to Del. "I offer you not an apology, but an invitation. Yana's flock is gone. Allow me to welcome you to mine." He paused. "Think on it. Now, where's my grandson? It's been too many years."

"The pair of you are worse than old hens," the woman finally snapped. She turned to Aria and bowed. "My Heir, they'll have you out here until the sun goes down with this scratching and pecking. I am Sarita, and I am the headwoman of the Solstice Village. I bid you welcome, and offer you the hospitality of our guest houses."

Aria nodded, then came to Del. "My Air?" she murmured, resting her hands on his shoulders.

He smiled, took one of her hands and kissed her palm. She caressed his cheek, then turned to Sarita. "Thank you. We accept."

THE GUEST HOUSE ASSIGNED to the Heir and her Companions was large, with wide windows and low couches that reminded Owyn of their house in Terraces. Sarita had initially been confused when Alanar and Othi had joined the group, but she covered it well, saying only that they'd need to get more cushions from one of the other houses.

"It's late, so we'll let you rest," Sarita added. "I'll have supper sent in, so you won't have anyone fussing over you. Tomorrow is soon enough for the welcome feast, and we can meet tomorrow morning with your Council. There is so much to tell you. So many years of records and reports."

"And we have news to share with you as well," Aria said. "But it will wait." Sarita bowed and left, and Aria sat down on one of the couches. "It will be good to spend time here. I want to visit with my grandfather, and I think Alanar is wanting the same."

"I do. I have a nice, new husband to show off," Alanar said from his place on one of the couches. He grabbed Owyn's wrist, pulling him down onto the couch and putting his arm around him. "And I need to see when Grandfather would be able to arrange the ceremony to welcome him into the flock."

"There's a ceremony?" Owyn squeaked. "You didn't tell me that!"

Alanar laughed. "They call it a ceremony, but it's more of a party. The flock gets to meet you, you get to meet the flock, everyone gives gifts, and we eat far too much. It's fun."

"If you'd told me, I could have made something," Owyn grumbled. "I could have had things ready months ago. Something special." He looked up to see Alanar smiling. "What?"

"Wyn, what you give them doesn't matter," Alanar said. "They're going to see how happy you make me, and that's enough." He shifted. "Del, there's probably going to be something similar for you." He paused, then smiled. "And it will probably be the same ceremony — you're my flock!"

Del came over to sit down on Alanar's other side, leaning into him. Owyn reached across and took his head.

"That was impressive," he said. "The way you put Einar in his place. I'm proud of you, Del."

Del smiled. "*I was terrified,*" he said in Owyn's mind.

"You were terrified?" Owyn laughed. "Couldn't tell. Not a bit. Angry, sure. I think we were all ready to rip his head off. But you handled it."

"I wasn't expecting your grandfather to hit him," Aven said. "That seemed excessive."

Alanar blinked. "Grandfather hit Uncle Einar?"

"Right across the face," Owyn said. "Hard enough that it echoed."

"Was that what that was?" Alanar shifted so he could rub his hand over his face. "I...I didn't know. I never thought...but then, I haven't been around him since I was ten. I guess that means I never really knew him." He shook his head, and put his arm around Del. "Either of them. To say that..."

"It is troubling," Aria said softly. "Especially the fact that no one objected to it. Or even seemed surprised. Your grandfather's reaction was because Del did have wings once, not because Einar said it." She took a deep breath and let it out slowly. "I'm tired. Is this something we can think about in the morning?"

Someone knocked on the door, and Aven opened it to reveal a small crowd. Aleia, Jehan, Steward, Frayim, Memfis and Karse, with Howl at his heels. They came into the house, and Karse closed and locked the door behind him.

"Where's Afansa?" Treesi asked.

"Overseeing the camp," Karse answered. "Steward, you need to make it official that she's your assistant."

"Tomorrow," Steward said. He looked around. "The guest houses are very nice. They all seem to be the same floor plan and furnishings. Are you all comfortable here, or will you need more room?"

"I think we are," Aven said, going to sit with Aria. "But I haven't looked at the beds yet."

"We did confuse Sarita," Othi added. "She wasn't expecting Alanar and me."

Steward smiled, then turned to Del. "How are you feeling?"

"*Tired,*" Del signed. "*I don't know how people can be angry all the time. It's exhausting.*"

"You handled him well," Jehan said. "Now, we're in the next house. And Karse is staying in the camp."

"And tomorrow morning, would one of you healers come look in on Afansa?" Karse added. "I..." He grinned, and his face turned red. "She's been sick the past few mornings, and she can't stand the smell of her favorite tea. So I'm thinking that this whole baby thing might just be catching. And I'm not sure she believes it. She told me she was barren."

Jehan nodded. "I'll come see her first thing. Now...if she is pregnant, is this what you both want?"

"We'll talk in depth tomorrow, Jehan," Karse said. "But...to keep Owyn and Memfis from hunting me down, Trey and I talked about this, back when we first talked about Fancy. About maybe a family of our own. So...yeah, if she is...and if she wants the baby, then yes."

Owyn swallowed. "Trey is going to be giddy when you tell him. You know he is."

Karse nodded, clasping his hands behind his back. "And we're going to find him so I can tell him. He's close. I'm sure of it. I can feel him. He's close. And we'll find him." He smiled and looked down. "I'm going back down to the camp. I need to drill the guard, and the boys want chances to practice."

"Before you go, what were your thoughts about what happened today?" Aria asked. "With Einar?"

"That was the loudmouth who had his teeth handed to him by his father?" Karse asked.

"My uncle," Alanar said. "And my grandfather."

Karse nodded, then folded his arms over his chest and leaned against the wall. "Honestly? I don't think he expected to be heard. It was one of those freak silences. You know how the entire room goes quiet, all at once?"

"Someone told me once that when that happens, it's because everyone in the room is all thinking about sex, all at the same time."

Owyn's pronouncement was met with complete silence as everyone turned to stare at him. Then Othi snorted, and the entire room erupted in laughter. Laughter that was cut off when someone pounded on the door.

Howl growled, and Karse rested his hand on the hilt of his sword as he stepped closer to the door. "Who's there?"

"Agragor!"

Karse looked at Aria, who nodded her permission. He unbolted the door and swung it open. Agragor scowled at it.

"We don't lock doors here," he growled.

"When there have been as many attempts on the lives of the Heir and her Companions as there have been the past few months? We lock the blasted door." Karse stepped back. "And if you don't want people to lock the doors, why even have locks on them?"

Agragor paused, then looked puzzled. "You...have a point. You are who?"

"Captain Karse, of the Palace Guard."

"And you have a wolf." Agragor looked down at Howl, who was standing at Karse's side. "The stories you have to tell, little girl. Now, I am here to spend some time with my granddaughter." He stepped into the room, drawing his wings in close. He saw Aleia, and stopped. "I know you!"

Aleia smiled. "I wasn't sure you would. It's been a long time. Karse, close that door." She waited until the door was closed, then gestured to Memfis and Jehan. "Agragor, this is Memfis, who is Milon's Fire. And Jehan, his Earth."

"Is?" Agragor repeated. "Not was?"

"Milon is alive," Aria said, keeping her voice low. "My father is alive, and he is being held somewhere close. I was going to tell you tomorrow, and show you the maps." She took a deep breath. "There is so much to tell you."

Agragor smiled. "And you are falling asleep. I can see that. Tomorrow is soon enough, I suppose. I would like to meet your Companions properly, though."

Aven got up from the couch and bowed. "Aven, sir. Son of Jehan and Aleia."

Agragor arched a brow. "A Companion who is the child of Companions? Interesting. Has that happened before?"

"Ah...Elcam's Earth was the daughter of Destri, who was Riga's Earth. But I don't remember her mother., And Firstborn Tirine was Granna Meris' daughter," Owyn answered. He stood up. "Owyn Jaxis." He turned and held his hand out to Del, who took it and stood up. "And you've met Del."

"That leaves me," Treesi said. She stood up and stepped forward. "Treesi. It's nice to meet you."

"You're not the last, Treesi," Aria corrected. "We haven't introduced Alanar and Othi yet. They are not Companions, but they are part of my circle."

"Agragor knows me," Alanar said.

"He doesn't know me." Othi stood up, and Owyn watched Agragor's shocked expression when he realized just how large Othi was. But he didn't say anything. Instead, he nodded.

"It's good to meet all of you. I am overjoyed to see Aria home safe. Now...which of you sired the child?" Agragor looked around, as if waiting for the father of Aria's baby to step forward.

"Aven," Aria answered. "He was my first Companion, Grandfather. And he's saved my life...I don't even know how many times now."

"We've all saved each other's lives," Aven corrected. "The past year...well, it hasn't exactly been quiet."

"Frayim says we won't have boring for a while, but it'll come." Owyn looked around. "Steward, where is he?"

"He went back to camp," Steward said. "What happened before upset him, and he couldn't put it into words. He went to clear his head. I'll walk down with Karse and see how he is." He took a deep breath. "And I'll let Afansa know that tomorrow, I'm officially naming her my assistant. It's overdue."

"I will let you rest, then," Agragor said. "Tomorrow, we will welcome you properly, and then I want to spend some time with my granddaughter."

"Sir," Aven said. "Before you go...Einar insulted Del, because he thought Del was wingless. Are we going to hear more of that from your people?"

Agragor sighed. "Einar is...well, he is an ass. I can't say you won't hear more of that. There's always been a thread of...disdain, I suppose. The wingless are of us, but not entirely. They carry the Air bloodline, but they cannot touch the skies. They aren't truly Air—"

"That kind of thinking is getting people killed," Aven said. "Air and Water alike. And it's spreading."

"What?" Agragor looked around and gestured to an empty chair. "May I? I think this should not wait."

"Sit, and we will talk," Aria said. "Aven, will you continue?"

Aven nodded. "Outside these mountains, there's a growing belief among people of Earth and Fire that anyone not like them is something to be hated and feared. That winged Air and Water are not human. That we are less, that we are animals. That we're not the Mother's children after all. And that to be a part of the Mother's world, we must be saved. And they're including people who are disabled, like Alanar. Like Del. And if you can't be saved, if you die...well, it's no matter. You were never human to begin with."

"Saved? Saved how?" Agragor demanded.

"She got the idea from me," Alanar said. "To my shame."

"It wasn't your fault, Allie."

"She? She who?"

"Risha," Alanar answered. "The healer who took my wings. She's the one who tried to kill Del, and she took his wings, too. Then she tried to do the same to Aria, last year. Owyn got to her in time. But there were others. I don't remember how many of our people she mutilated in the name of saving us."

"We'll never know exactly how many of my people she killed," Aven added. "How many she tried to save by breaking the cycle of the change and crippling them. As far as we know, I'm the only one who survived the process, and after it, I couldn't walk or change without pain. It took four healers to rebuild my hip, and I still limp when I'm tired or there are too many stairs."

"Risha is also the one who has my father," Aria said. "And another hostage. Captain Karse's husband. We know she's in the mountains, and we can guess as to where."

"You had maps, you said," Agragor said. "You know where she is holding them?"

"Roughly," Owyn answered. "Based on what we know of where she took Trey, how fast a cart travels, and what I've learned from Milon in the past couple of months." He paused. "I haven't danced in a while..."

"No," Aria said. "We can't risk him knowing how close we may be, and having the information get into her hands. We know she wants the baby—"

Agragor held his hand up. "The baby...Aria, I know you are Fire and Air. Aven, you are Water and Earth. Mother of us all, is this about the Child that the hill people prattle on about?"

"You know that story?" Aria asked. "I'd never heard it before some of our guards told us."

"It's fluff," Agragor said, waving one hand. "But...it's powerful fluff, even among our own. Over the past ten years, there are wingless clans that have gone to war with the hill tribes over trying to control children that were supposed to be this Child. I don't think any of those children survived the fighting."

"Wait... if they had children who were supposed to be the Child, where did they get the Water blood?" Owyn asked. "I mean...Earth and Air and Fire, they're all easy to bring in new blood. Where'd they find Water?"

"Ah...I have a thought. You're not going to like it," Othi murmured. Aven bit his lip, but Owyn snickered.

"You already hate it, don't you?" he asked. "I remember."

"Whenever you tell me I'm not going to like something, I end up hating it," Aven agreed. "Go ahead, Othi."

Othi rubbed his hands up and down his legs. "What if you weren't the only one who survived?" he asked. "What if there were others? What if there were girls who were crippled but lived, and were brought up here to try and breed the Child?"

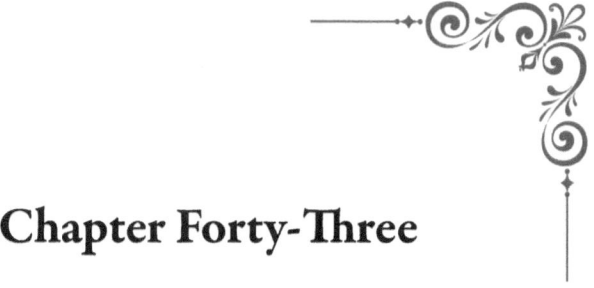

Chapter Forty-Three

A ven stared at his cousin, then croaked, "Thanks. I hate it."

Othi nodded. "Me, too. But it tracks. If they think we're animals, like those fuzzy things we saw south of here."

"Sheep?" Treesi asked.

"Those fuzzy things."

Agragor swallowed and nodded. "Oh, this is not good. And...tomorrow, you said we would speak on this? I...may not sleep. Not with this in my mind." He sighed and stood up. "Aria, I am so very pleased to see you, and see you well and happy. But this...I could have lived without this laid at my feet."

"You should see it from this side," Aria replied. Her grandfather snorted.

"Thank you, no. I will see you in the morning. For now, you've pointed out a deep flaw in all of our thinking. How... arrogant we've been. If the Mother made us as we are, then how can any of us be less? Wings or no wings, we are Hers. It's... I've been wrong. And if I've been wrong, then...I need to go and spend some time with Sarita, if she'll allow it."

"Grandfather?"

"She's my daughter, Aria. Your mother's half-sister. Never acknowledged because she was born as she is, and I was too stupid to see past that. I need to go and apologize. If she'll hear me.." He bowed slightly and turned to go. When Karse opened the door, Sarita was on the other side, carrying a tray.

"I heard that," she whispered. "I...let me put this down."

"May I help?" Agragor asked. "I can carry, if you tell me what and where to put it."

"I get to order you around, and hear you apologize? I might faint," Sarita said, and Agragor smiled. "Leave me with this. There's another tray in my house, on the table. And a basket. Bring one or the other, but not both. They're both heavy." She came inside and set the tray down on a table. "This is supper for the people in this house. Supper for the other guest house is waiting there. Unless you all want to eat together?"

"No, we'll let Aria and her circle rest," Steward said. "Karse, I'll walk back to camp with you."

THE NEXT MORNING, TIERCEL arrived as they were finishing breakfast, and escorted them to the meeting hall, where Agragor, Sarita, Alanar the Elder, Einar, and other tribal leaders were waiting. Aria told them everything they knew, everything they suspected, and everything that Risha had done. Then Owyn took from under his arm the rolled map that he'd started so many months before, and unfurled it on the table.

"Right," he said. "Near as we can figure, Risha is in this area here." He touched the circle. "Now, I'm a Smoke Dancer, and I have what are called heart visions. It lets me talk to other strong Smoke Dancers at a distance. So I've been getting information from Milon—"

"Milon? Tirine's Heir? Didn't he die?"

"That's what they wanted everyone to think. No." Owyn looked at Aria, who nodded. "No, the healers hid him first. They were trying to protect him from the Usurper. But then...well...something in the attack hurt Milon badly enough that he couldn't use his legs. And the steward at the time... ah..."

He looked at Agragor. "He was wingless Air. A lot of the Palace staff were wingless Air, we were told. And it looks like that lot decided that if them with wings were going to look down on the wingless, then the wingless had to find someone they could look down on, so they weren't the bottom of the pecking order.. So they had this fuckheaded idea that if your body was broken, you were useless. When they realized Milon wasn't going to walk again, it went from keeping him safe to keeping him prisoner." He paused. "And one of the healers who kept him that way was Risha. When the Usurper abdicated, and we were going to take the Palace, she attacked it, killed everyone who was in on the secret, and kidnapped Milon. But she don't know I can talk to him. What he's told me is that they're in the cellar of a house, or a building. It smells old, and it's damp. That sort of says ruin to me." He tapped the map. "So...what's in this area that fits?"

People clustered around the table, studying the map and talking. Owyn stepped back, and bumped into Memfis.

"You're doing fine, Mouse," Memfis murmured.

"Thanks," Owyn replied. "I just...I want them to tell us exactly where, so we can go find them already. I want Trey back."

Memfis nodded, resting his hand on Owyn's shoulder. "I know. So do I."

Owyn looked around the room, seeing Alanar and Del standing near Einar. Alanar was talking with his uncle, but Del was pointedly ignoring the older man. "I should go over there," Owyn murmured. "Before Del rips Einar's head off."

Memfis chuckled. "I'll come with you."

They walked over, and Owyn saw Alanar stop talking and turn, holding out his hand. "Uncle, you haven't met my husband yet."

Einar shook his head. "I haven't," he said, and held his hand out.

"Owyn Jaxis," he said, clasping Einar's hand. "But you can call me Owyn." He kept his smile on his face, even as Einar started to squeeze his hand. Owyn just smiled...and squeezed back, watching as Einar's eyes widened. As his lips pressed together. As he tried to pull his hand out of Owyn's grip. "May I offer you some advice?"

Einar coughed. "What?"

"Don't try to play silly power games with a blacksmith." Owyn let Einar's hand go. "Now go ask a healer to look at that. You've got hollow bones. I might have broken something." He folded his arms over his chest. "Now, if you don't mind my saying so, you need to get your head out of your arse. I mean, most of your tribe does, but you especially."

Einar's eyes widened, and he stalked away. Alanar turned toward Owyn.

"What the fuck just happened?" he whispered.

"Your uncle is a prick," Owyn whispered back. "You know that whole dominance thing some men do, where they test their grip on your hand? He tried it with me. I don't think he knew I'm a smith."

"And you broke him?" Alanar sounded stunned. "Is he still here?"

Owyn looked around. "Aven's got him. And since he's not yelling at me across the room, I don't think I broke him. But really, that's how he says hello to your husband?" He snorted. "Allie, he's a prick."

"And he's still my uncle." Alanar sighed. "I...and he went after two of the people I love best in the world. You're right. He's a prick. Is my grandfather free?"

"No," Del whispered. Then he signed, *"Don't tell him. He'll hit Einar again."*

"Del says we shouldn't tell your grandfather," Owyn said. "It's over, Allie. We'll let it be."

"Why...oh, because Grandfather hit him last night?"

"Yes," Del said. "Let be."

There was a sudden commotion around the table, and Sarita looked up. "My Heir? I think we have the place."

Owyn hurried over to the table, standing with Aria and Aven as Sarita pointed to the map.

"There was a healing center here," she said. "It's been burned out and abandoned for...five years? More?"

"Healing center?" Alanar said. "The one where my parents met? Grandfather?"

"Hrm...yes. That would be the same place," Alanar the Elder said. "It was abandoned when the Usurper razed the healing centers."

"Which he actually didn't do," Jehan said. He looked around. "Best to have this out before Steward gets here. Those orders came from Risha. She destroyed anyone who could have challenged her place as Senior. Murdered her own trainees if they were too strong." He looked down at the map. "It makes sense. Where would she go to ground? Someplace she knows no one would ever go."

"Especially since the hill people in this area think it's haunted," Sarita said. "They say that people who trespass there vanish, and are never heard from again." She frowned down at the table. "Given what Agra...what my father told me of the conversation he had with you last night? That makes sense. She's been killing people under our noses for years."

"Right, we need to get a..." Owyn paused, then shook his head. "Not going to say it."

"A bird's eye view?" Tiercel offered, looking like he was trying not to laugh. Owyn grinned.

"I wasn't going to say it, but yes. We need eyes on that place, and we need that today. We need a full survey. Who's out there, and how many? What weapons? And we need to do it without them knowing. So how do we do that?" He frowned. "Wish Marik was here. We really could have a bird's eye view on it, from real birds." He looked up to see people staring at him. "We have a friend with the Earth sense. He talks to birds. They talk back. You don't have anyone like that up here, do you?"

"You just said you were a Smoke Dancer," Einar snapped. "Why don't you go look in your visions?"

"I could," Owyn said. "If I'm careful. I'm willing to try. And maybe we can ask Frayim what he sees."

"Nothing."

Owyn looked over his shoulder to see Frayim and Steward in the doorway. Frayim shook his head. "There's no clear path. There are too many threads that come together in this place and time. All I can see is mist."

"Oh, that's not good," Aven said. "Probably means that Owyn won't see clearly either."

"Grandfather, how soon can we get patrols in the air?" Aria asked. "And how would you suggest they proceed?"

Agragor stepped back from the table, then turned. "Tiercel, answer the question."

Tiercel looked startled, but stepped forward and studied the map. "I...fast fliers, staying above the clouds as much as we can. It'll give us some preliminary information, let us plan things a little better." He frowned slightly. "We're not going to be able to get low, not without warning them. That's not an area that we usually patrol. Flying over it now, and in large numbers? That's going to alert them." He turned to Agragor. "Grandfather, permission to proceed?"

"Granted. Safe skies."

Tiercel bowed, then hurried out.

"Einar, go with them," Alanar the Elder snapped. "Make yourself useful, and stop antagonizing people."

"Father, I—"

"Did you think I didn't notice your little stunt with your new nephew?" Alanar the Elder asked, his wings flaring slightly. "I saw you try him. And I saw him best you. Did he break your hand?"

"No, sir," Aven answered. "Minor bruising."

Alanar's grandfather looked at Owyn. "You let him off too easily," he said, then turned back to Einar. "And it would have served you right. He's the Fireborn. Fireborn means Smoke Dancer. If you'd paid any attention to the lore, you'd have known that Smoke Dancer means blacksmith." Alanar the Elder gestured to the door. "Now go make yourself useful, you overgrown cockerel."

Einar bowed, his wings pulled in close to his back. He hurried out of the room, and Alanar the Elder sighed.

"What else is there to tell us, my Heir?" he asked.

"Milon isn't the only hostage in there," Aria said. "One of our guard squadrons was out on a patrol, and came on her and her men by accident. She wiped out the entire squadron, and took the commander hostage. What we know is that he's hurt. We do not know how badly."

"Milon said that the bitch broke him," Owyn growled softly.

"The commander is Captain Karse's husband," Aria continued. "He is a dear friend to all of us. I want them both returned to us."

"Did Milon tell you anything else?" Agragor asked. "About men, or their arms?"

"He can't see," Owyn answered. "It had to have been done to him. He kept journals, and he was still writing when they took him from the Palace. The last page in that book weren't finished. She blinded him to control him."

"I hate to say it, but it's been months," Alanar murmured. "We may not be able to undo what she did."

"That hardly matters right now," Alanar the Elder said. "First we need to get to him. It will be a few hours before the patrols return. What now?"

"Village reports," Sarita said. "News of the high ranges, and the Temple. The feast tonight. My Heir, when will you go on to the Temple?"

"How long will it take us to get there?" Aven asked. "And how? Can we take a coach, or is it better to ride?"

"The road to the Temple is still good," Sarita answered. "You can take a coach or a wagon. And it's about three hours."

"Tomorrow, then," Aria said. "We'll go to the Temple tomorrow."

PEOPLE LEFT THE MEETING house slowly, and Owyn stayed at the table to roll up the map.

"It's so strange," Alanar said. He was sitting at the end of the table, his chin resting on his stacked fists. "I never thought that it might be the healing center where my father served. Where he met my mother." He snorted. "Where I was made. Mama was pregnant when they moved back to Terraces."

"Why would you think about it, Allie?" Owyn asked. "I mean, were you ever there?"

"Once, when we came back after Mama died," Alanar answered. "And Fa took me to see it. I should have thought of it. I just...I suppose that since we knew all the other healing centers were gone, that it didn't even occur to me that there was any part of it still standing." He sighed. "What are we doing now? Where is everyone?"

"Well, Aria and Aven went off to talk to the village midwife. Jehan and Treesi went down to camp, so that they could talk to Afansa. Del is behind you—"

"I knew that."

Owyn chuckled. "So I think we're at loose ends for a bit. We could go back to the house and take a nap, if you want?"

The door opened, and Alanar the Elder came inside. "There you are," he said. "Del, where is your father?"

Del frowned. "*He may have gone back down to camp, I think?*" he signed. "*Or he may be meeting with Sarita about the feast. The Waterborn can't eat some of the things we can.*"

Owyn translated, and Alanar the Elder nodded. "The ceremony to welcome you and Owyn into the flock will be held right before the welcome feast for the Heir. I don't know what Agragor is planning for your father. But for us, is tonight acceptable to you?"

Owyn walked around the table to rest his hand on Alanar's shoulder. "That sounds fine," he said. "But...ah...are we supposed to bring gifts? For how many? And...well, what kind of gifts?"

Alanar the Elder smiled. "Aria coached you well. On the night you're welcomed, you needn't worry about giving gifts. You're being welcomed as a new member of the flock, and it's on us to welcome you and provision you appropriately." He smiled. "Don't be surprised if Sarita comes to take your measure."

Owyn chuckled. "This is going to be a little strange. I mean, it was a year ago that the only person I had in the world was Mem. Now...well, I have Aria and the other Companions, and you, and Aunt Rhexa, and now my real parents. This..." he snorted. "I went from having no family to having too many to keep track of!"

Alanar laughed and put his arm around Owyn's waist. "And more to come."

Owyn looked at him. "You're sure?"

Alanar shook his head. "No, but I'm hoping. And if not, Trista says she's willing to try again." He smiled. "And I shouldn't say more, although Grandfather has probably already put together what we're talking about."

Alanar the Elder smiled slightly. "It sounds as if you're talking about a baby?"

Alanar nodded. "Owyn and I want a family of our own, and since he'll probably be having children with Aria, this one is mine. A friend of ours agreed to carry the baby for us."

"Is she in your camp?" Alanar the Elder asked. "I would like to meet her."

"She went west, back to Terraces," Owyn answered. "With my parents. We weren't sure what kind of trouble we might find before we finished what we have to do, so we sent a bunch of people west."

Alanar the Elder nodded. "Wise. Bring her and the child. I want to meet them. I have no great-grandchildren yet, and I would like one. Several."

"We'll work on that," Alanar said. "But you have to promise to wait to meet them."

Alanar the Elder laughed. "I have no intentions of meeting the shadowhawks yet." He reached out to ruffle Alanar's short hair, then left.

Owyn leaned against the table, folding his arms over his chest and thinking about what he'd said about his family and how it had grown.

"I'm going to need to make a list," he said. "I need a list, or I'm never going to be able to keep all of my family straight. I'll never remember."

"*Owyn, do you think we're going to have any more problems with Einar?*" Del asked, coming to sit on the table next to Owyn

Owyn looked at him, then turned to Alanar. "Allie, Del wants to know we're going to have any more trouble with Einar."

Alanar went quiet, then started drumming his fingers on the table. "I...I don't know," he admitted. "Probably. If he's willing to do things like he's been doing around Grandfather..." He folded his arms over his chest and sighed. "Did you have to break him, Wyn?"

"I didn't. Aven said so," Owyn protested. "I only bruised him a little. I know he's got bird bones, same as you and Del. I know I have to be careful."

Alanar shook his head. "Still, it might make things harder for Aria."

"You think so?" Owyn asked. He gnawed his lip. "Do you think I need to apologize?"

"*No,*" Del signed. "*If you apologize, he wins.*"

Owyn sighed. "This is complicated."

"What did Del say?" Alanar asked. He stood and came around the table, standing on Owyn's other side. "Did he say anything?"

"That if I apologize, Einar wins."

Alanar nodded. "That's about right. And I'm not sure what's going to happen when he's the head of the flock."

"We'll worry about that later," Owyn said. "We need to pick out what we're wearing tonight."

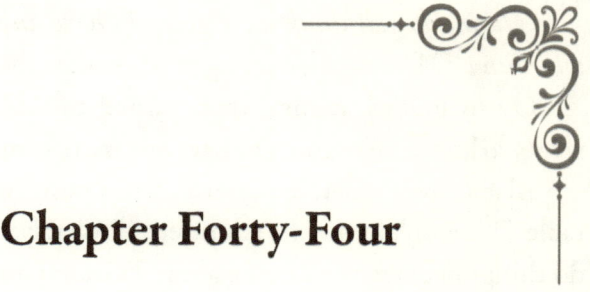

Chapter Forty-Four

"You're going to be fine," Memfis said.

Owyn smoothed the front of his black shirt and looked up at Memfis. "I'm just...this is important to Allie. I don't want to fuck this up."

"You're not going to," Alanar said, coming out of the bedroom. He was wearing his wedding finery, and looked wonderful. As if he knew what Owyn was thinking, Alanar held his arms out. "How do I look?"

"You look wonderful. Did you trim your beard?" Owyn asked.

"Del did it. Hair and beard both." Alanar turned his head slightly. "He'll be out in a moment. He's finishing up."

"And everyone else is getting ready for the feast," Owyn said. "So the ceremony will sort of spill right over into the feast." He glanced at the door. "Where's Steward?"

"He said he'd be here," Memfis said. "I think he needed to go back to camp for something."

Owyn nodded, smoothing his shirt again, and smiling as Aven came out of one of the other rooms. He was wearing his dark kilt and purple vest, and his hair had been braided in a multitude of tiny braids.

"That looks good on you," Memfis said. "The braids."

"Aria did it," Aven said. "Took her most of the afternoon." He looked back at the door. "I think going to the Temple tomorrow is a good thing. She feels...different. And she won't let me examine her to see why." He turned back, smiling. "The midwife said that Fa's prediction of a month could be accurate, but that for a first baby, it might not be. And right now, I don't think she's going to wait that month."

It took Owyn a moment to realize that Aven didn't mean Aria, and he laughed. "You think...how soon?"

"Ask me later," Aven answered, shaking his head. "Aria explicitly said I was to wait until after the feast to examine her. But given these?" He shook his head again, making the braids dance. "Fa says that there's something women do right before birthing. He called it nesting behavior."

"I remember reading about that." It wasn't Alanar who spoke — the Water accent said clearly it was Virrik. Owyn turned to him and smiled.

"You've been quiet, Vir. You haven't come up for ages."

Virrik shrugged. "I've been feeling...I don't know. Tired? Which is strange, because Alanar isn't tired, but I am. So I've been asleep. Missed a bit, but Allie told me what happened while I was sleeping. Told me he might be a father." He smiled. "I like that. That's a good thing."

Owyn glanced at Aven, who shrugged. "Vir, are you all right?"

Virrik laughed. "I have no idea. It's kind of hard to answer the question. What's all right for a dead man?" He smiled. "It's...I don't know. Maybe it's almost time for me to move on? Which I'm ready for. But I'm not. So I don't know if I'm all right." He shrugged. "I just...wanted to be a part of things for a moment. And now I'm tired again. I'll go back now." A moment later, he shook his head, and Alanar said, "Virrik says he wanted to say hello."

"Has he been quiet for you, Allie?" Owyn asked.

Alanar nodded. "He has. Occasionally, I'll hear him and he'll ask me about what he's missed. He isn't sure why he's sleeping so much."

"What's going on?" Treesi asked as she came out to join them. Othi followed her into the room.

"Virrik came out to say hello, and he's acting strange," Aven said. "He says he's tired."

Othi coughed. "Dead men can get tired?" he asked.

"Ones who live inside a person's head do, apparently," Alanar answered. "And...I heard him say it. Maybe it is his time to move on? Maybe the Mother noticed he's missing, and is fixing it?" He shook his head. "I don't know. And...well, we have enough things to think about. So I'm not thinking about it now. Is Del ready?"

Owyn opened his mouth to say something and saw Aven looking at him. He arched a brow, and heard Aven's voice in his mind. "*Let him be. You have things to do.*"

Owyn nodded. "I'll go check on Del," he said, and went past Alanar and down the corridor. Del met him just outside the bedroom.

"*Is something wrong?*" he asked.

"Maybe," Owyn whispered. "We'll talk later. It's about Virrik."

Del nodded slowly, then took Owyn's hand. They walked back down the corridor, and were in time to see Steward, who was dressed in his formal livery.

"Best thing I have with me," he said when he saw Owyn looking at him. "That I have left, anyway. I think some of my clothes went west."

"Well, here's hoping it won't matter. We'll be on the road to the Palace soon," Treesi said. "Tomorrow the Temple, then home."

"But first, we have things to do," Memfis said. "We'll see you at the feast."

"Where are we going?" Steward asked as they left the guest house. "Alanar?"

"I...let me get my bearings," Alanar answered. He closed his eyes and tipped his head. "Unless they've moved things around, there should be a large common area right in front of us. The meeting house where we met this morning is over there..." He gestured, then continued, "So there should be a large...pavilion, I guess you'd call it. That's where the feast will be. We'll be going past that. Someone should meet us on the far side."

"Right." Owyn took Alanar's hand, and they started walking again, skirting around the bustle of activity under the pavilion as people ran back and forth to get things ready. He could smell roasting meat, and something that tickled the back of his throat.

"I hope you like lots of seasoning," Alanar said. "It's harder to taste things up higher, so they make the food spicy."

"You know how I cook," Owyn said. "And how I season."

"More than that," Alanar chuckled. "My father used to have to eat with a glass of milk next to his plate. It was the only thing that would stop the burn."

"That won't be good for Aven," Memfis said. "Alanar, I see your grandfather."

Owyn looked where Steward was pointing, and saw Alanar the Elder and Einar. "Oh, fuck," he murmured. "Your uncle is with him."

"That means the patrols are back," Steward said. "I haven't heard anything."

"We'll find out during the feast," Memfis said. "We're busy now." They walked up to the two men, and Alanar the Elder moved to bar their path, spreading his wings.

"You shouldn't be here," he said, pointing at Memfis.

"What?" Owyn looked at Memfis. "Why not?"

"He was not invited."

"He's my father," Owyn protested. "He should be here to see this."

Alanar the Elder frowned. "Your father went west. No...you said you have two fathers. I remember now." He sighed. "This is a...dilemma."

"Why?" Steward asked. "You didn't say anything about not including family, or those who weren't being welcomed to the flock. What's the issue?"

Alanar the Elder hesitated. Einar did not.

"He'll taint the ceremony."

Owyn coughed. "He'll...he'll *what*?"

"He's deformed—"

"Einar!"

Alanar went pale. "I...Memfis lost his arm to a snakebite. It was lose his arm or lose his life. I know. I was one of the attending healers." He licked his lips. "He's no more deformed than I am. And...and that's the truth of it, isn't it? I'm deformed in your eyes. But I was already part of the flock, so you couldn't put me out." He paused. "Or could you? Grandfather?" He stepped forward, and his voice went hard and cold. "Were you going to put me out? When I came back to you, broken and blind? Were you going to abandon me?"

"No. I always wanted you," Alanar the Elder protested. "My namesake, my grandson. I see Alane in you. I always wanted you, even though you could no longer touch the sky with me."

Alanar turned toward his uncle. "I don't think I even have to ask you the question. I have another one for you. When Grandfather goes to the shadowhawks, are you going to put me out?"

"He would not dare!" Alanar the Elder gasped.

"You wouldn't be able to stop him. No one would," Alanar told his grandfather. "This is the future of our flock."

"*And we're not going to be part of it.*"

Owyn turned at the sound of Steward's voice, and saw Del signing, fast enough that his fingers were snapping. Surprisingly, he could hear nothing of Del's voice, only Steward as he translated, "*You were there. You heard Aria this morning talking about the way things are outside the mountain. You heard how we're fighting to bring the tribes together, to stop people from looking at others and seeing them as less because they're different. But they learned it from you, didn't they? Air does it to their own. And you're doing it to us. You thought I was wingless, and didn't deserve to be the Airborn. You thought Memfis was deformed, and didn't deserve to be a part of this ceremony. You're as bad as Risha. And I want nothing to do with you.*" He stopped, shook out his hands, then turned and walked away.

"Mem, go with them," Owyn said in a low voice. "I don't think you want to be here for this."

Memfis nodded. He reached up and squeezed Alanar's shoulder. "Don't do anything you'll regret, son."

Alanar smiled. "Where you're concerned? That's impossible. Go on, Fa."

Memfis' jaw dropped. Then he smiled. He let Alanar go and turned to follow Steward and Del. Alanar turned back to his grandfather, and his smile was gone.

"So, this is what I have to look forward to," he said. "Grandfather, I hope you realize that the minute your mourning is done, the minute the rest of the flock recognizes Uncle Einar is head of the flock, he's going to throw me out."

Alanar the Elder turned to look at Einar. "Is this true? Is this your plan?"

"If he doesn't, it's only because he wants the status of being able to say that a member of his flock is the Senior Healer's heir," Alanar snapped, and Owyn watched as Einar's eyes widened.

"The look on your face..." Owyn said. "Jehan told you this morning!"

"I'm pretty certain he heard it," Alanar said. "He just didn't believe it. He thinks I'm less. He thinks I'm broken. Del is right. You're no better than Risha." He paused and Owyn knew what he was going to do before he started to speak.

"Allie—"

"I have no flock," Alanar said, as if he hadn't heard Owyn. He paused, closed his eyes, took a deep breath, then continued, "I fly alone. My family are those who love me as I am. Who want me as I am. Who have never thought of me as broken, or less." He stopped again, and Owyn heard the shake in his voice as he added, "I'm sorry, Grandfather. Owyn, let's go back."

Owyn took Alanar's hand, and they walked away. He heard footsteps behind them, and looked back.

"Your grandfather is following us."

"I know," Alanar said. "And I'm not going to let him try to change my mind."

"Are you sure that's what I was going to do?"

Alanar stopped and turned to face his grandfather. "You're not?"

"No, my namesake. I followed you to apologize." He sighed. "I think...that perhaps before I die, I should dissolve the flock."

"Grandfather!"

"It would be the right thing to do," Alanar the Elder said. "And...I think it would be the only way to stop him. Because there is no one to challenge him. I will speak to Agragor. We'll end this. I just wish..." He stopped. "May I come visit you?"

Alanar swallowed, and Owyn saw tears in his eyes. "I'd like that, Grandfather." He held his hand out, and let his grandfather pull him into a tight embrace.

"I'm sorry."

"Thank you, Grandfather." Alanar held his hand out to Owyn. Owyn held his other hand out to Alanar the Elder.

"I'm sorry," he said. "I'm not sure what else we could have done, but...I'm still sorry."

"It's none of your fault, my new grandson." Alanar the Elder smiled. "You chose a fine man, my namesake. I approve of him."

"Thank you."

"Now, you should go back. Tell Agragor I will need to speak to him in the morning, will you?"

"I'll tell him," Owyn said.

Alanar the Elder nodded, then turned, walking a few steps before taking to the air.

"Allie..." Owyn started. Then he stopped and shook his head. "Fuck. I have no idea what to do. I...should I get Treesi? Or...or someone?"

"No," Alanar said. "No, I just need...let me be? I can't go to the feast. Not now. Take me back to the house and go to the feast. And...and don't say anything. Not yet. Let Grandfather do what he needs to do. Tell Aria I have a headache, and went to lie down."

"Do you?"

"Have a headache?" Alanar snorted. "Enough that my teeth ache."

"Let me get you back to the house, then. You can lay down, and I'll take care of you."

"You have to go to the feast. I can take care of myself."

AVEN STAYED CLOSE TO Aria's side, and could feel her getting more and more restless.

"Are you all right?" he whispered.

"I'm not used to this many people in close proximity," she whispered back. "It feels close. It should not feel close. We're outside." He took her hand, and led her toward the edge of the pavilion, away from the people. She sighed and nodded. "This is good, thank you."

"I can always make an excuse, if you want to go back to the house," Aven said. He saw his parents entering the crowd, and Karse and Afansa and the boys. "I wonder how the ceremony is going?"

"You can ask Owyn," Aria said. "There he is. He's alone. That's odd."

Aven looked, and saw Owyn coming toward them. He looked troubled, enough that Aria started walking toward him, tugging Aven along with her.

"Hey," Owyn said as he met them. "Allie asked me to tell you that he's having a lie-down. He has a headache."

"How was the ceremony?" Aria asked. "I haven't seen anyone else yet. Where are Steward and Del?"

"They and Mem left first," Owyn answered. "They might have gone down to camp. Or they're in the other house. I'm not sure." He looked away for a moment. "I'm not really good company right now. I'm sorry."

"Mouse, what is it?" Aven asked. Owyn shook his head.

"Nothing," he answered. "Just...worrying about Allie. It's been a while since he's had a bad headache." He looked around. "There's Mem. I need to go talk to him. Back in a bit." He walked away, and Aven looked at Aria.

"It's bothering him quite a bit," Aven said.

Aria nodded. "It is. Have you dealt with Alanar's headaches before?"

"Back in Terraces. It's a problem with the nerves behind his eyes. Residual damage from the fire. I should go check on him." He looked around. "Come with me? It will give you a break from the crowds."

"Let me tell Aunt Sarita."

Aria spoke briefly to the headwoman, then took Aven's hand as they walked back toward the guest house.

"Look," Aven said. "Owyn was right. Steward and Del are coming up from camp. They must have gone to get Frayim. Is...is that Wanderer formal dress?" The green robe that the tall Seer was wearing over his clothes was covered with bright embroidery in complicated patterns that Aven knew he needed to see more closely.

"It's very pretty," Aria said. "And that color suits him. Let's go see to Alanar, then we can meet them."

Aven opened the door of the guest house and held it for Aria, then they went down the corridor to the closed bedroom door. Aven tapped it. "Alanar?"

Shuffling on the other side, and the door opened. Alanar looked rumpled, and his eyes were red. "What are you doing here?"

"Aria needed a break from all the people, and Owyn told us you had a headache. So we came to see if you needed help."

Alanar smiled. "I should have told him to tell you to leave me be. I just want to be alone right now."

"Alanar? What's wrong?" Aria asked. Alanar gave a soft, watery laugh.

"I have no flock," he whispered. "I fly alone."

The words meant nothing to Aven, but the effect they had on Aria was astonishing — she reared back as if she'd been struck, and her wings flared wide. "What? What happened?"

"I'm not telling you now, because you have to go back out there," Alanar answered. "Grandfather is handling it. And he needs to speak to your grandfather, so I want to give him the time he needs. He's as upset as I am. And...I'm just going to go to bed."

Aven touched Alanar's arm, then pulled him into a tight embrace. "Whatever it is, we support you," he murmured.

"Thank you," Alanar said. "I..." He stopped, raising his head, turning. "Aven...?"

As Alanar said his name, Aven felt it — there were people in the house. "Who's there?" he called.

A loud slam from the front room made Aria jump, moving closer to Aven. Two men stepped into view, blocking the head of the corridor. And from the other end of the corridor, Aven heard a soft laugh that made his blood run cold.

"Well now," Risha murmured. "Isn't this a lovely reunion?"

Chapter Forty-Five

Owyn was talking with Sarita and another woman when the screams started echoing in his head, hard enough that he nearly doubled over. One moment, he was talking about bread recipes, then next, he was on the ground, trying to block out the sounds that only he could hear. Aven's voice. Aria's. Alanar and Virrik.

"Owyn!" There were hands on his arms, shaking him. He coughed and looked up, seeing Karse in front of him. "What happened?"

"Aria," Owyn stammered. "Aven. Where are they?"

"They went back to the guest house," Sarita answered. "Aven wanted to look in on your man, and Aria needed a moment away from the crowd. What's wrong?"

Owyn shook his head, trying to make sense of what he'd heard. The voices had all jumbled together, making things hard to understand. He closed his eyes, trying to focus as the voices slowly grew more indistinct.

"*Owyn!*" Aven's mental voice sounded slurred, almost drunk. "*Risha...find...*"

"Risha," he spat. "Fuck! She's here!" He scrambled to his feet and ran, dodging around people, heading for the guest house.

He could smell the fire before he saw it, and by the time he reached the door, there were flames breaking through the roof tiles. He heard someone shouting behind him, ordering a bucket brigade, getting people in the air to fight the fire, to stop it from spreading.

"Owyn!" Karse grabbed his arm, pulling him to a stop. "Are they in there?"

Owyn stared at him for a moment. Then he swallowed. "No. No, they're not in there. Risha has them. She...she took them." Oddly, there was no panic. No desperate fear. Only...calm. This was Terraces all over again. He found them before. He'd find them again. And this time, he'd end Risha for good. He looked around, seeing Agragor landing a few feet away, followed by Tiercel. "We need fighters in the air now!" Owyn snapped. "Risha's been here. She has Aven, Aria and Allie, and I think she's drugged them. That means a wagon just left here. Tiercel, what did your group find?"

Tiercel looked shocked. "Einar volunteered to report. He didn't?" He shook his head. "The ruins are definitely inhabited. It was hard to say how many from how high up we were, and how fast we were going, but there was smoke from the chimney, and we saw horses. Einar came back ahead of us to report."

Agragor turned and roared at the top of his voice, "Alanar!" Then he turned to Owyn. "When did you last see Alanar the Elder?"

"Before the feast," Owyn answered. "The ceremony...didn't go well. And he needs to talk to you about it. But Einar was there." He looked up to see Alanar the Elder overhead, and raised his voice. "Grandfa! Where's Einar?"

"He should be with the water brigade!" Alanar called back. "Where's my namesake?"

"Come down!" Agragor called.

Alanar the Elder landed, and Owyn turned to him. "Risha was here. She took them — Aven and Aria and Allie. We need fliers in the air now to follow, and guards to follow on the ground. Karse, get down to camp and get the guards ready to ride."

"It'll be full dark soon, and there's no moon tonight," Agragor said. "She could not have timed this better. We cannot fly in the dark. And riders...there are no trails. We can't send anyone until dawn."

"Oh, that's lovely," Owyn snapped. "So we're just going to let her take them off and kill them all and destroy the fucking world? Because she's got what she wants now. She's got the baby." He turned to Alanar the Elder. "Einar didn't report to you, did he?"

"Report? Report what?" The old man turned, almost hitting Owyn with his wings. "Einar!"

"Tiercel, find him," Agragor said. "And bring him here. Do what you have to."

"I need to get the others. Treesi and Othi and Del. And Mem and Jehan and Mamaleia." He turned, and nearly ran into Steward. Frayim, Del and Treesi stood with him, and all of the others were behind them.

"We're here," Steward said. "What's happening? In ten words or less, Owyn."

Owyn blinked, then counted on his fingers as he answered, "Risha was here. She's got them. We're all fucked."

"Not yet we're not," Karse snapped. "What do we know?"

"Fuck all," Owyn snapped. "We know fuck all."

"No, we have a lot of loose ends that are suddenly making more sense," Aleia said. "She had people in the Palace. We know that. She knew when we left. She knew we'd be coming here. She's been waiting for us the whole time. And..." Aleia caught her breath, and Owyn realized what she was thinking a heartbeat later.

"She has someone here," he whispered. "She had an informant here."

Alanar the Elder moaned. "I think we know who," he said. "I have a very good idea who."

"Einar," Agragor said softly. "Alanar—"

"Grandfather!" Tiercel called from above. "I...think we found Einar."

"You *think*?"

"There's a body on fire down in the gorge behind the guest houses," Tiercel answered as he landed. "We're not sure, but...we can't find Einar in the water brigade, and no one has seen him since the ceremony. And he's the only one not accounted for. Sarita has been assigning people to the water brigade, and counting off the rest as she sends them back to their aeries or out of the way. You know how she remembers. She says he's the only one she hasn't seen."

"Then he's either the informant, or he was in the wrong place at the wrong time." Owyn scrubbed his hand over his face. "We need answers. We need information. Frayim, tell me you can see something? Anything?"

Frayim closed his eyes for a moment, then wheezed and stumbled, catching onto Steward for support. "I..."

"Fray?" Steward steadied him. "What happened?"

"Fog," Frayim answered. "I see only fog. I...I can't see anything." He looked at Steward, then at Owyn. "Twiceborn, this is the moment. This is what we have been preparing for."

"And we need more information." Owyn closed his eyes, trying to think. "I need my blades."

"Mouse, are you sure?" Memfis asked.

"This is the moment," Owyn repeated. "I need my blades."

"*I'll go*," Del said, and took off running. Owyn tried not to wince — Del's mental voice had felt raw.

"Agragor, where can I dance?" Owyn asked. "It needs to be level, and people need to stay out of my way. Where can I go?"

"Back where the ceremony was supposed to be," Alanar the Elder answered. "Come with me."

Owyn followed him through the pavilion and back down the path, hearing the others behind him. They passed the point where Einar had challenged them.

"Alanar," Owyn said. "Grandfa, I'm sorry about Einar."

"Are you?" Alanar the Elder answered.

"I...yes?" Owyn stammered. "I mean...I may not have liked him, but he was still your son. He was family. And...well...I might not know a lot about families, but when someone dies, someone is going to miss them."

Alanar the Elder stopped and turned to face Owyn. He reached out, took him by the shoulders, and kissed him on the forehead.

"My namesake picked wisely in you, Owyn Jaxis," he said. "I'm proud to call you my grandson. The place to dance is there." He gestured, and Owyn walked off to find a small, grassy meadow.

"Oh, this is good," he murmured. He walked back and sat down to take his boots off. By the time he was done, the others were standing with Alanar's grandfather. Except for Memfis.

"Memfis is waiting for Del," Treesi said. "Owyn—"

"We're going to find them," Owyn said. "We just need more information. Which we'll hopefully get once Del gets here with my blades."

"He's coming!" Tiercel called from overhead. "But I have your...what are these?" He landed, and handed the smoke blades to Owyn. "I'm faster, so I offered to carry them."

"Thank you," Owyn replied. "These are smoke blades. I use them to dance for visions. Which...excuse me, I need to go get started."

He trotted out to the middle of the meadow and set his feet, ignoring the people behind him. He closed his eyes and took his first, deep breath.

Second.

Third, and he started moving, feeling the all-over tingle of a strong vision rising to meet him.

But it wasn't what he thought he'd see.

A woman sitting on a rock, in a meadow very similar to the one where his body was dancing. Familiar. Older than Rhexa, younger than Meris. She reminded him a little of Aleia. She smiled, and her smile was full of warmth and love and laughter, and her eyes were the bluest he had ever seen.

"It's time to remember, Owyn."

All at once, he did — the vision when he was retested, and the Mother pulled him out of the smoke to talk to him. Warning him.

"We no longer have the luxury of time. Because Adavar has lost patience. He began to wake when our daughter Tirine died. He is awake now, and He is not pleased. If nothing is done, if the Firstborn falls, or his Heir, then Adavar will rise."

Owyn heard his own voice. "Father Adavar rolling in His sleep. That's what the Water tribe calls a quake. Aven said we don't want Him to wake. And...and Mem said He was close to it. Close to waking. He's awake already? What...what happens if He does rise?"

"He is awake. And watching. And if He rises, then everything ends."

The words 'everything ends' echoed in his ears, in his mind.

"Right, so that wasn't me being dramatic when I said that about the world ending," he muttered. "That was me remembering.

Mother!" he shouted into the smoke. "Are they alive? Let me see them! Please!"

"They live, my son." An image rose — Aven, Aria and Alanar, all sprawled together in the back of a cart like the one he'd once driven in Forge. All of them were unconscious.

All of them were breathing.

"Thank you," he called. "Right...any advice?"

That warm, rich laugh. "You'll know what to do when you get there. Now go back."

He felt the slight push against his chest, and opened his eyes to find himself kneeling in the middle of the dark meadow. He slowly got back to his feet, staggering toward the waiting crowd.

"That was it?" Tiercel asked. "Did you see anything?"

"Yeah," Owyn answered. "They're alive. I saw them. I need to eat something. And...you all need to sit down. Because if we get this wrong, we're more fucked than we thought."

AVEN WOKE UP PROPPED against a wall, feeling someone else's pain, sharp and stabbing as if someone were poking him with a knife. He groaned, tried to move, and realized that he couldn't. There were manacles on his wrists, and short chains that ended in rings just over his head. He took a deep breath, trying to clear his head as he looked around.

There was a lamp hanging from the ceiling that gave just enough weak, wavering light that he could see Aria and Alanar against the wall across from him. He couldn't see how they were bound, and he couldn't tell if they were awake.

"Aria!" Aven called, trying to keep his voice low. "Allie!"

"Be still, son," a man said, his voice coming from the darkness to Aven's right. "She'll hear you."

"Who..." Aven stopped and realized that he knew exactly who. "Firstborn Milon."

A warm chuckle. "I'm not standing on formality, son," Milon answered. "I'm not standing much at all. Who are you?"

"Aven. Son of Jehan and Aleia. I'm your daughter's Water."

"And you're here. My Aria is here. And...who is Alanar?" Milon asked. "No, wait. I remember. Trey told me. Owyn's husband. The blind healer."

"Yes, sir."

"That's almost as bad as calling me Firstborn. Aven, you should have grown up with me as one of your fathers. I'm not having titles from you. I'm Milon."

Aven shifted, the chains holding him clashing loudly in his ears. Across from him, he heard Alanar moan, and called, "Allie?"

"Aven?" Alanar sat up slowly, shaking his head. "What...where are we?" He shifted around. "I...who put boots on me? Aven, these are locked on me. There are chains...where are we?"

"Risha has us, and I don't know," Aven answered. "Allie, how is Aria? She's next to you, on your right."

Alanar moved, and Aven heard chains clattering. "She's waking up," Alanar answered. "And...I hope Owyn does something quickly. I don't think this baby going to wait for a lengthy rescue. Aria's waters have broken. She's in labor." He coughed. "Risha has us. Is Milon here?"

"I'm here," Milon answered.

"Can you reach Owyn? Tell him where we are?"

Milon sighed. "I've tried. I can't. I can't reach the visions the way I am now."

Alanar growled softly. "And...who's in pain? I can't tell. Aven?"

"I think it's Trey," Aven answered. "Milon, where is he?"

"She chained him as far from me as possible, so I'm assuming on the opposite wall from me. Where he can see me, but not help me."

Aria moaned softly, and Aven jerked against the chains. "Alanar?"

"She's waking up. Aria, I've got you." Alanar helped Aria to sit up. Aven could see her shaking her head. Her wings looked strange, but he couldn't tell what was wrong.

"Aria?"

She jumped, looked at him. "Aven. I...I thought I was having a nightmare. I'm not. We're here." She looked around. "What...she's bound my wings. I...wait. If we're here, then...Father?"

"I never thought I would hear that word," Milon said. "I never thought I'd meet you." A moment, and he sighed. "I still haven't. Tell me what is likely to happen...no. She's coming."

The door creaked and squealed as it opened, and light filled the room. For the first time, Aven saw Milon. Emaciated and filthy, his graying hair was hanging in greasy clumps around his narrow face, he was bound to a chair near the wall. Risha ignored him as she came into the room, followed by two guards. Alanar lurched to his feet and put himself in front of Aria, but Risha ignored him, too. She came to stand in front of Aven, shook her head, and sighed.

"I examined you," she said. "You've gone and undone all my work. That was inconvenient." She folded her arms over her chest. "I can't replicate the experiment anymore, so I can't even see if you surviving was an aberration or not. It is interesting what they did to your hip. That's a level of healing I've never seen before."

"Of course you haven't," Aven snapped. "It's something you can't do."

She chuckled. "Oh, I couldn't put you back together again. That's true. But I can certainly take you apart again. And I'm looking forward to that." She turned and walked toward Aria and Alanar.

"Stop," Alanar growled. "I will kill you if you try to get past me."

Risha laughed. "Oh, I don't need to get any closer to you, Alanar. I already examined Aria. My dear, you progressed so well. I'm very pleased you chose to carry the baby to term. I will admit, that was a major risk in my plans. But you did exactly as I hoped you would. And now...well, now I'm very excited for the next stage. For the Child."

"Risha, if you so much as breathe on our baby, I will feed you to the sharks myself," Aven growled. Risha just laughed.

"Aven, how do you think you're going to stop me?" she asked. "You're not going anywhere. None of you are. Alanar, do try to do a better job with this birth? The last one...well, that didn't end well, now did it? I hope you've been studying." She turned back to the door. "Leave them the lamp."

OWYN FOLDED HIS ARMS over his chest and tucked his chin down, closing his eyes and trying to ignore the tumult going on throughout the camp. He mentally poked himself, looking for the panic that should have been there. He kept expecting it to appear, to surprise him with waves of incapacitating fear. But there was still nothing.

Where was it?

Then again, maybe he should be thankful — he didn't have time to fall apart. Not now. The horses were ready. The weapons were ready. The two rescue parties were almost ready, and there were Air warriors ready to take to the skies at dawn. There were wagons set to go with each group, to bring back the wounded. They had guides from the Solstice village who knew the trails well enough to lead people through them in the dark. They were leaving.

It was almost over.

"You're doing an exceptional job."

Owyn opened his eyes, straightening as he said, "Thank you, Mamaleia." She wasn't alone. Memfis was with her, his face unusually solemn. Owyn could guess why.

"We're going to find him, Mem. We're going to bring him back."

"Find them all, Mouse. Bring them all back."

"That's the plan," Owyn said. He took a deep breath and looked around. Del, Frayim, and Steward were with Jehan, Treesi and Othi. He could hear Karse shouting orders in the distance. Owyn took another deep breath, then raised his voice. "Can everyone hear me?"

The buzz of conversation died down, and Owyn nodded. "Right. We've got two places she could have taken them. The ruins of the healing center, and the Temple—"

"How do we know they could be at the Temple?" Othi interrupted.

"Had the same vision twice," Owyn answered. "Part of this happens at the Temple. So...we're going to get people in place there. If they're not there, find cover and wait. They're coming. If they are there, we'll meet you there once we clear the healing center." He looked around. "Right. Treesi, you're staying here. I want you to get the healing tent ready, because once we come back, we're going to need you."

Treesi nodded, her eyes wide. "Be careful, Wyn," she murmured. Owyn blew her a kiss, then turned back to the others.

"Mamaleia, take Othi, Frayim and Steward to the Temple. Take the Penitents. If they're there, surround the Temple, hide and wait for us. If they're not there, they're coming, and let them come. Don't engage. Don't let them know you're there." He paused, thinking about the vision. "The baby is coming. By the time we get to the Temple, Aria will have had the baby. Which means that Risha will have a hostage. Do not go into the Temple."

"He's reminding me of you," Jehan said as he came to stand by Aleia. "Another Little General."

"Thank you," Owyn said. "You're with me and Del. We're going with Karse and the guard." He licked his lips. "Mem—"

"I know I'm staying here. Afansa already told me that she has orders to sit on me if I try to follow you," Memfis said. "I'll be fine. I might kill the turf in one area from pacing, but I'll be fine."

Owyn nodded and turned. "Now, we'll have Tiercel and his fighters in the air as soon as it's light enough to fly. But since I don't know how long it will take us to get to the ruin, or how long it will take you to get to the Temple, don't count on them. We might be done before they get in the air." He looked around. "Are we ready?"

"*No, but when has that ever stopped us?*" Del said, and Owyn laughed.

"Stop that." He looked around. "Right. This is it. I told you all what the Mother told me. If we fail, if we lose Milon, Aria, or the baby, we're done. Everything is done. So don't fuck it up." He licked his lips. "Let's go bring them home."

Chapter Forty-Six

Every midwife they'd spoken to since before they left the Palace had all said the same thing. First babies take their time. First time labor takes a long time. For a first baby, the initial stages of labor can go on for most of a day.

Apparently, the baby hadn't been listening. Either that, or she was as stubborn and willful as her mother. Because Aria's labor started in earnest shortly after Risha left. And as her contractions grew stronger, so did Alanar's panic.

"Allie, you can do this," Aven crooned, his voice hoarse. He had lost count of how many times he'd already said it. "You know what to do. I know you worked with Zarai and with Marzi." He took a deep breath and pulled against the chains, feeling blood running down his arms. "Is she asleep?"

"Yes," Alanar whispered. "Aven...the last time—"

"This isn't the last time," Aven interrupted. "This is now. I need you here, now. Alanar, I can't take this from you. I can't help you. You have to help her. You know what to do!"

"And I killed her!" Alanar wailed. "I killed Calline! I killed Virrik's son, and I promised myself I'd never put myself in that position again. I can't. I can't...I'll kill her. I'll make a mistake and I'll kill her." He curled up and whimpered. "Aven, I can't. I..." His voice trailed off abruptly. He sat up, and there was something different in the way he was sitting.

Aven stared for a moment, then whispered, "Virrik."

"I should have stepped forward sooner," Virrik answered. "I apologize. Let me...Aven, tell me which way?"

"To your right," Aven answered. "She's asleep."

Virrik nodded and crawled over to Aria, resting his hand on her arm. "On her left, too. Good. That can slow labor. Oh, this baby is galloping into the world, isn't she?"

"Aven?" Milon called. "What just happened? How did we get someone new?"

"It's a long story," Aven said. He glanced at the door. "And...I'm not telling you right now. Not where I can be overheard."

"Understood. I'm looking forward to story time." Milon took a deep breath. "Virrik, is it? How is she?"

"Progressing very well," Virrik answered. "Her body is ready, and the baby is in the right position. I think once she wakes up, it won't be too long." He hummed softly. "Aven, tell me about the room."

"There's nothing in the room," Aven answered. "You're chained to the wall on one side. I'm across from you—"

"And chained."

"Yes. Milon is to your left, bound to a chair, and Trey is to your right, chained to the wall."

"Ah, that's who I was missing. I couldn't tell who was in pain. No furnishings, no table, nothing overhead?"

Aven looked up. "There are beams, but they're too high up to touch. There's nothing else."

"And it's just me over here," Virrik said. He growled softly. "Right. Swaying, squatting, kneeling. All right. She hasn't been complaining of back pain, has she?"

"No," Aven answered, and heard Aria catch her breath and moan.

"That was a strong one," Virrik murmured. "All right. Aria, are you awake?"

"I am now," Aria mumbled. "I do not want to be. I'm tired. I...oh..."

"Breathe, Aria," Virrik said in a low voice. "Breathe through it. Zarai taught you that, didn't she?"

Aria nodded and started panting. Aven found himself copying her, and tugged hard against the chains again. He was supposed to be with her for this, holding her, helping her. All he could do was watch as Virrik did everything that he was supposed to do. Holding Aria as she stood and swayed, walking with her as best they could. Helping her breathe. Helping her focus. Helping her balance as she squatted. There wasn't anything Aven could do for her.

No, there was one thing he could do.

He cleared his throat and started to sing the chants his father had taught him. He hadn't even known Jehan knew them — his father had resisted any part of the Water rituals, arguing that he had no right to them. But he'd known the chants that a father sang to welcome a child, and Aleia told Aven that Jehan had indeed sung them the night Aven was born.

What he wasn't expecting was for Milon to join in, adding the counter chants sung to welcome a grandchild. The harmonies spiraled and dove, rising and falling as Aria's voice rose and fell.

As the cry of a newborn rose.

"Easy, Aria," Virrik crooned. "Easy." He helped her to lay down, placing the baby on her chest. "Easy. Oh, she's perfect. She's beautiful."

Aria giggled, and it sounded tired. "You can't see her!"

"Doesn't matter. I can tell she's beautiful." He turned to Aven. "She has gills, Aven. And wings. Congratulations."

Aven shivered. His daughter. She'd swim with him. She'd soar to touch the sky with her mother.

"Aria, tell her her name," he called.

"Just a moment," Virrik said. He stripped off his shirt and draped it over the baby, then rested his hand on Aria's lower belly. "Aria, when I tell you, push."

"Again?"

"One last time," Virrik assured her. "Then you can rest."

A few minutes later, Aria was reclining against Virrik, holding the baby as she nursed.

"My daughter," she murmured. "Your name is Aeris. Aeris, daughter of Aria. Daughter of Aven." She looked up at Aven. "Your father wants to hold you."

"Once we get out of here, I will," Aven said. "Virrik, thank you."

Virrik smiled. "I think we have an answer now. I was needed for this." He kissed Aria on top of her head. "I'm going back now. Alanar was with me through all of that. He knows. He's so happy. And he's sorry."

"He has nothing to apologize for," Aven said. "Virrik, is he right? Treesi told me you didn't sleep with girls. But she wasn't sure if Calline's baby was yours. Neither was Alanar."

"Treesi told you true." Virrik sighed. "Calline was my friend. She wasn't carrying my child. I never slept with her. She asked me, but I only wanted Alanar. No, the baby wasn't mine. It was Teva's and he didn't want to be a father. I think that's why...." He took a deep breath. "Aeris is a beautiful name," he murmured. Then he took another breath, a sharper one. He shook his head, and his arms tightened around Aria.

"Allie?" Aven called. "Are you back?"

"Yes," Alanar answered. "Exhausted. Aria, you're wonderful. And...I'm sorry I panicked."

"You're forgiven," Aria murmured. "Can we sleep now?" She yawned, then chuckled. "I'm sorry about your shirt."

"I'm not. It's been sacrificed for a wonderful cause."

They sat in silence, until Milon cleared his throat.

"Is she asleep?"

"Both of them are, yes," Alanar answered.

"Her name is Aeris," Milon said. "Aven, my grandmother is dead, isn't she? The name is a tribute?"

Aven swallowed hard. He wasn't going to tell Milon that Mother Meris had been murdered. Not now. "Mother Meris died just over halfway through the Progress. But we were already going to name the baby Aeris. We chose the name months ago." His chest felt tight. "She wanted to meet her great-great granddaughter. She was so excited. She was so happy when we told her the baby was a girl."

Milon nodded, then turned toward the door. "They're coming."

The door screamed as it opened, and the baby woke wailing. Risha stood by the door and smiled.

"You did better than I expected, Alanar. Well done," she said. Then she gestured, and armed men entered the room. Half went to Milon, and the others to Aria, dragging her and the baby out of Alanar's arms.

"What are you doing?" Alanar demanded. "Stop it! Leave her alone!" He struggled to his feet, reaching out and grabbing the sleeve of one of the guards. Before he could do anything, another man struck him, hard enough that he fell. Aven heard the dull thump as Alanar's head hit the wall; he slid down, and didn't move. Aria screamed as she was dragged from the room, calling Aven's name. And for the first time, Aven heard Trey's voice, raised in a wordless wail.

"Aria!" Aven shouted as the other guards left with Milon. Risha laughed and closed the door behind her, leaving Aven behind.

"THEY'RE COMING," AVEN said aloud. He wasn't sure who he was saying it to — Alanar hadn't woken, and Trey was curled in on himself against the far wall. He was silent, and he hadn't moved – even as the room grew brighter, Aven still had a hard time picking him out of the piles of trash and debris against that wall. "They're coming," he repeated. "Once they can see, they'll come." He looked up at the tiny, high window, at the sliver of sky that he could see. It was brighter. They were coming.

He blinked hard, unwilling to fall asleep. He was tired, angry, and scared to his bones. But they were coming. Owyn was coming. He remembered Owyn telling him about his vision in the Temple. They'd go from here to the Temple. They'd find Aria and Milon and Aeris.

He was going to finish the welcome chants.

He was going to hold his daughter.

He was going to teach his daughter to swim.

He heard voices, and the door screeched open. Four unfamiliar men entered the room, all of them carrying swords. One of them looked at Aven and laughed.

"Been a while since I last gutted a fish," he said. "Kill the rest, then we'll go meet the others." He started toward Aven.

He never made it. Aven heard a snap, and the man jerked and fell forward, a quarrel in the back of his neck. The other three turned to the door, and one of them fell with a bolt in his chest. Before the last two reached the door, there were two more snaps, and both of them fell. Del stepped into the room, his crossbow raised. Behind him, Aven saw several armed guards and Owyn.

"There were only four," Aven called. "Tell me my Fa is out there! Alanar needs him!"

Owyn followed Del inside, carrying his smoke blades. "Only four in here. There were seven more outside. He's coming. Risha probably took the keys with her. Del, get him unlocked." He looked around. "Where are they?"

"Risha took Milon, Aria and Aeris away hours ago," Aven answered. Owyn and Del both stared at him. Then Owyn smiled.

"You named her for Granna?" he said. "Oh, that's good. That's wonderful. I...if I go to Allie right now, I won't want to leave. I'll be back in a minute."

"Mouse," Aven called as Owyn turned. When he looked back, Aven nodded his head toward the far wall. "Trey is there. Do not let Karse in here. Tell Fa."

"Oh...oh, fuck. Del, hurry up. He needs to see to Allie, so Jehan can see to Trey." He hurried out, and Del pulled his lockpicks out of his pouch. He grimaced as he started working, no doubt at the state of Aven's wrists.

"I'll be fine," Aven said. "It's just another scar."

The manacle cracked open, and Aven winced as he lowered his arm. The muscles in his shoulders were painfully stiff. Del moved to the other side, and started working on that manacle as Jehan came in.

"Aven!" Jehan blinked. "Triage?"

"Alanar hasn't woken up since they took Aria and Milon and the baby away. I can't tell how badly he's hurt. Trey is on the far wall, there, and all I know is he's in pain. Start with Alanar, get him stable, and I'll take over once I'm free." He turned as he heard Karse's raised voice.

"What do you mean I can't go in there?"

OWYN STOOD IN FRONT of the door, trying not to flinch. "You have to let the healers work," he said. "Karse, right now, if you go in, you'll be in their way. Let them do what they need to do. They'll come and get you when you can go in. Now, are you sure you got everyone?"

"There were eleven horses. Four inside, seven outside. All dead. We'll throw the bodies into the gorge." He closed his eyes. "Owyn—"

"I know," Owyn said. "I know. It's been months, and he's in there. I know. But we have to let them work. I...Karse, we've got company." He pointed, and they both watched as a familiar Air warrior landed a few feet away.

"Report," Karse snapped.

"Wagon," Ionith answered. "It was most of the way to the Temple when I saw it. They left a clear trail back here."

"That's Risha, and she's got hostages," Owyn said. "Aria, her father, and the baby. Follow them. Watch them. Don't engage. And try not to let them see you."

Ionith nodded and looked up at the sky. "The clouds are starting to burn off. It'll be harder. We won't have cover soon."

"Do what you can, then go and join Aleia," Owyn told him. Ionith saluted, then took back to the sky. Karse closed his eyes and took a deep breath.

"We need to get moving. But we can't yet. Who's inside still? Jehan, Del, Trey and who else?"

"Aven and Allie. And Allie is hurt."

He stared at Owyn. "And you're standing here that calm?"

"Two of the best healers in the world are in there with him. In there with them." Owyn started spinning one of his blades. "And honestly, if I fall apart now? I'm not getting myself back together. So I can't fall apart yet. I'll cry on Allie later."

"Wyn." Owyn turned to see Del standing in the doorway. *"Jehan says you and Karse can come in."*

"Karse, Del says that we can go inside," Owyn said.

Karse looked at him, then at Del. For a moment, Owyn wasn't sure if Karse was going to move. Then he lurched toward the door. He stopped just outside, said something, then disappeared into the ruin. Aven came out into the light, blinking in the sun.

"Alanar is fine. At least, he's fine now," he said. "When they hit him, he hit his head on the wall. He's awake, but he's still a little dazed. He wants to talk to you before he goes back with Fa. And...he's making my father make interesting noises."

"Why?" Owyn asked. "I'll go see him in a minute. I need to talk to you first."

Aven smiled slightly. "Because apparently, if you have a dead healer inside a live healer, the dead one can work on the live one. If Virrik hadn't been able to do that, Alanar wouldn't have woken up at all. His skull was broken, and his brain was bleeding. Owyn, he wasn't unconscious. He was in a healing trance."

"Wait...what happened to six arms and no noses? Or whatever it was? Rule one."

"That's why Fa is making interesting noises." Aven looked back at the door, then sighed. "I know that I need to give Karse a chance, but I want to grab him and throw him on a horse. Aria's out there. She needs us. Aeris is out there." He looked back at Owyn. "I sang her into the world, Owyn. And I still haven't held her. My daughter, and she doesn't even know me yet."

"And it's tearing you up one side and down the other. I know. We'll go as soon as we can. We know they're going to the Temple," Owyn said. "And Ionith just came and reported that they're keeping an eye on the wagon. We'll get them, Aven." He took Aven's hand and pulled him into an embrace.

"I knew you were coming," Aven said, his arms tight around Owyn. "I knew you'd find us."

"Always," Owyn murmured. "And we'll find Aria. Now, let me go see my man."

They went back into the ruin. Owyn could hear Karse's voice, coming from the far wall. He couldn't make out the words, but nothing would mask the pain in them. He tried to ignore it. If he fell apart now.... He shook his head and focused on Alanar, who was sitting with his back against the wall. He was naked from the waist up, his wedding shirt missing.

"Allie?"

Alanar smiled. "I was wondering when you'd come," he murmured. He sounded dazed and sleepy. Owyn knelt next to him and leaned in close to kiss him.

"Virrik confusing people again?" he asked. "Tell him I said thank you, will you?"

"He hears you," Alanar said. "And yes. And...we think we know, Wyn. We think we know why he's been in my head. We needed him. Risha thought I'd kill Aria. And I thought so, too. I panicked, and Vir took over. He knows how to deliver a baby. Remember, I told you? After Calline, he studied everything he could. He knew exactly what to do. He helped Aria have the baby. That's why he was with me. The Mother put him where he needed to be. With me. Because She knew this was coming." He closed his eyes. "She's a perfect baby, Wyn. And she's Air and Water. She has gills and wings."

Owyn caught his breath. "Oh. Oh, that's amazing." He looked over at Aven, who was standing by his father. Del was there, too, kneeling next to Karse. He couldn't see Trey. "I...I should go see Trey."

Alanar nodded. "Go see him. Then...go save them."

"Go save everyone," Owyn murmured. "Have I got shit to tell you, Allie."

Alanar smiled. "Later. When we're all safe."

Owyn kissed Alanar again, then stood up and started toward the others. Aven met him halfway.

"Fa says you need to go outside," he said in a low voice.

"What? Why?" Owyn looked past him. Jehan met his eyes and shook his head.

"Trey doesn't want you to see him," Aven said. "He didn't want Karse to see him either." Aven licked his lips. "Come outside."

Owyn stared at Aven, then raised his voice. "Trey? I know you can hear me. I'm listening. I'm going out. We've got you now. You're safe. It's over." His voice cracked. "Almost over."

"*I hear you, Wyn,*" Trey murmured in his mind. "*Go out.*"

Aven put his arm around Owyn's shoulders and led him back out into the sun. "Don't break, Owyn," he whispered. "You can't break. I need you."

Owyn nodded. He swallowed, and turned around, looking at the guards. "Right!" he shouted. "Move the wagon up here! We've got wounded men to go back to the village. Two guards to go with them. And get the horses ready. We're leaving—"

"Now." Karse came out into the light, his face stony and chalk-pale. Del was behind him, and the expression on his face would have frozen a glass of water. Karse glanced at Del, then looked back at Owyn. "We're going now. I want that bitch to burn."

Chapter Forty-Seven

The cart was very similar to Owyn's wagon. But where Owyn's wagon was clean and neatly furnished, with a bed that Alanar assured Aria was very comfortable, this wagon smelled dirty and moldy, and the bed where the guards had unceremoniously dropped Milon had no mattress or cushioning, only bare boards. Aria curled on the floor, cradling Aeris in her arms, trying to calm the crying baby, trying not to cry herself.

"Aria, come up here," Milon said gently. "Sit with me. Let me take her."

"I don't know what to do with her," Aria said, moving onto the bed. Everything hurt, and her hips and back were stiff. She winced as she sat down, and laid Aeris in her father's arms. He bounced the baby gently.

"She won't nurse?"

"She's too upset," Aria answered. "And I don't know how to calm her."

Milon nodded. Then he sighed. "My hands are dirty. But I remember the midwife telling me a trick of putting your smallest finger in the baby's mouth, touching the top of their mouth. It makes them suck, and helps them calm down."

"Let me try it." Aria took Aeris back, and did as Milon explained. Aeris cried around her finger, then started to suck. As she calmed, Aria shifted Aeris to her breast, and sighed softly as the baby started to nurse. "How did you know that?"

Milon chuckled. "I was preparing for you," he answered. "Aria, I wanted you so much. And I never got this. I never got to hold you when you were born. Or see you take your first flight. I missed your entire life." He shifted, turning toward her slightly. "I am sorry."

Aria looked down at the baby, smoothing back her wispy dark hair. "I understand Owyn now. When he found his parents again, he had trouble remembering that they were his parents." She leaned into Milon's arm. "I will have to remember to call you Fa." She paused. "I've never said that before. Never had anyone to say it to."

"Liara never married?"

"She had offers, but she refused all of them. She never stopped missing you." She chuckled and shifted the baby to her other breast. "Such a hungry little girl."

Milon nodded. He rubbed his hands together. "Will you tell me about...you? About everything I missed? I regret it so much. Have been regretting it, since Owyn first told me you were alive. Since I knew that they'd lied to me. They told me all of my Companions died. That Jehan and Aleia and Memfis all died that night. That they never got out of the Palace. That Liara miscarried. And that she came back down from the mountains, and that Mannon killed her." He frowned. "What did you do with Mannon? Is he alive, or has he been executed?"

"We call him the Usurper now," Aria said. "I ordered his name struck from the records and the histories. He is known only as the Usurper, and the Mother will never know him."

Milon's brows rose. "That's...and what happened to the man?"

"The man we now call Steward saved Memfis from a Widowmaker snake, and dragged him for four days on a sledge to find help."

"He...he did *what*?" Milon covered his face with his hands. "I...that's hard to reconcile. If not for him..."

"I know. If not for him, none of this would have happened. And at the same time, when we put this to trial, everyone in the Palace and in the surrounding towns spoke for him. They swore that he did his best to take care of them, that he tried to undo the damage he'd done. Because he understood that he was wrong. That was why I did what I did," Aria answered. "Because the man who was the Usurper, the man who caused all this? That is not the man who stood at Yana's side as her Air. He is not the man who stands by my side as my steward, and who we call Uncle."

"Yana?" Milon closed his eyes, then shook his head. "I think I should know that name. But it's not coming to mind."

"You had an Heir before me, Father," Aria answered. "Yana was injured fighting the Usurper's forces, and when she woke, she had the mind of a child. But she recognized him as her Air, and he cared for her for the rest of her life. Until Risha murdered her. Her son now stands as my Air."

"And that would be...did Owyn tell me his name? I can't remember." He closed his eyes and hummed softly. "Aven is your Water. Owyn, your Fire. I should know this."

"Treesi is my Earth and Del is my Air."

Milon nodded. "I don't remember if Owyn ever told me. It's no matter. I'll meet them." He smiled. "I will meet them. They'll come for us." He took a deep breath. "Man...the Usurper saved my Mem?"

"He did." Aria looked down at the baby. "She's asleep."

"Then let me take her so you can rest," Milon said.

"Do you know where we're going?" Aria asked as she laid Aeris in Milon's arms. Milon just laughed.

"Aria, my darling girl, for most of your life, I've had no idea where I've been! I most certainly have no idea where we're going! Nor how long it will take to get there. Rest. You can lean on me."

Aria rested her cheek on Milon's shoulder and closed her eyes. "I...we're going to the Temple."

"Why do you say that?" Milon asked.

"Owyn has had the same vision twice. Him and Del and Aven in the Temple, and hearing a baby crying. We're moving to that vision."

She felt Milon shift. "How does it end?"

"We're going to find out." Aria yawned. "We found your journals. I was reading them. And I have your writing desk. Jehan and Aleia and Mem told me stories about you. So did Mother."

She felt him kiss the top of her head. "I can't wait to get to know you, Aria."

The wagon shook as it rolled to a stop, and Aria sat up. She heard the bolt on the door shoot back, and a guard stepped into the small space. He looked at them, but said nothing; instead, he reached out, took the sleeping baby out of Milon's arms, and turned to leave.

"Where are you taking her?" Aria demanded.

"Risha wants her," the man answered. He looked back, then smiled slightly. "I'll watch her, blesséd Mother. Don't you worry. Your Penitents are here. And we'll watch her."

He stepped out, and the door closed. As the bolt shot home, Milon turned to Aria.

"Blesséd Mother? Penitents? What does that mean?"

Aria bit her lip and tried to collect her thoughts as the wagon started moving again. "There are people in the hills who believe that a child is coming who will be Axia born again, a child of all four tribes in balance. They think Aeris is that child, because I am Air and Fire, and Aven is Water and Earth. The ones who have realized that they can't hate Air and Water and still follow the Child have sworn themselves to me, and have been calling themselves the Mother's Penitents. And some went back to the hills to spread the word. They... they must have spread the word into Risha's guards." She paused. "Aeris can't be the Child, because Aven isn't just Water and Earth. He's Fire through Jehan."

Milon frowned. "They're still saying he's Elcam's son? Even though Pirit said he wasn't?"

"*The Book of Silver* says so," Aria stammered. "Pirit says she's never been certain—"

"She's still alive?" Milon asked.

"Yes, and I like her very much," Aria answered. "She told us that Jehan's father was either Elcam, or the Palace Healer. But Jehan and the Usurper resemble each other. I saw them together, and they had the same facial expressions sometimes."

Milon shook his head. "*The Book of Silver* says it because Elcam wouldn't take no for an answer. He wanted to claim Jehan, especially after Jehan showed how good a healer he really was with the mountain fever outbreak. Did you know about that?"

"According to the healers, Jehan wrote the definitive text on mountain fever."

Milon laughed. "Did he really? That shouldn't surprise me. Aria, I remember Elcam's Palace Healer. Jehan is Hargat all over again." He frowned slightly, then nodded. "Elcam and Hargat shared...a grandmother? An Earthborn grandmother, I think. So that may be the resemblance. But I'm almost certain that Jehan being listed in the book as Elcam's son was the result of Elcam wishing it was so."

Aria took a deep breath and rubbed the bridge of her nose with one finger. "Does it matter?"

"I don't think so. Not in the long run." Milon shifted, put his arm around Aria's shoulders. "Rest, Aria. I have a feeling that when we get where we're going, things will start happening very quickly."

THE TRAIL FROM THE ruin to the healing center was nothing more than a wish and ruts carved in the turf by the recent passing of a wagon. Karse led them on at a maddeningly slow place. Aven understood why, but he still wanted to kick Pewter into a gallop. He shifted, feeling the weight of his swords on his back.

"How much longer?" he called.

"No idea," Karse called back. He drew his horse in, waiting until Aven was alongside before starting forward again. "I also don't know how well the sound carries out here, so keep your voice down. Owyn, you saw the map. How far?"

Owyn drew up on Aven's other side, with Del on his other side. "Not sure," Owyn admitted. "It was...maybe about the same distance between the village and the ruin? But we rode that as fast as we could. So...hey, is that Tiercel?"

Aven looked, and saw Aria's cousin waiting for them. He stepped back as they rode up, and walked with them until they could stop.

"We lost our cloud cover, so we had to break off," he said. "Ionith was up high, and saw them taking Aria into the Temple. And a man they had to carry in. My flight is with the other guards, and we have the Temple surrounded. They're not coming out. But we're not sure how we're getting in either."

"How much further is it?" Karse asked.

Tiercel frowned slightly. "Not a long flight. I'd barely be in the air before I had to land where Aleia is waiting." He looked up the trail. "Ah...it looks different from down here. Two rises? Maybe three?"

"Let's get moving, then." Karse urged his horse forward. Aven heard Tiercel take to the air behind him, and watched as the man soared overhead and up the trail.

Aleia and Steward were waiting for them as they crested the last rise. Karse dismounted and led his horse over to her. "And?"

"And we're at a standstill," Aleia answered. "There's enough of the Temple still standing that it's secure. We know some of what's happening, but not enough. And Risha just did a strange thing."

"What?" Aven asked, dismounting his horse.

"Just ordered half of her followers executed," Aleia answered. "The Penitents told us that they had people in Risha's guards. I don't know what happened inside, but I think if there were Penitents inside, there aren't anymore. And I'm not sure what disturbs me more — the fact that Risha ordered it, or that the rest of her followers followed those orders."

"We're dealing with fanatics," Steward said. "Who will follow orders blindly. The only good that came of this is that she's down to seven or eight guards."

"Easier to handle, once we get inside," Karse said. "Show me what we're facing."

They walked up the trail, into a copse of trees. Several of the Penitents ran up to take their horses, and Aleia led them on to a place where they could look out at the Temple. Karse whistled softly.

"That's a fortress, that is," he said. "Even as it is. Right. How are we getting inside? And once we're inside, what's the layout?"

Del took out one of his throwing spikes, kneeling and using it to sketch in the dirt. Owyn came and crouched next to him.

"Del says that the Temple plans haven't changed at all since the Temple was first built. They're in the Palace archives. There are two ways in — the main door here, and the entrance to the Priest's living quarters around the back. There's the one big space in the front, the crypt down below, and a long corridor that leads to the priest's quarters and the archives. Which he's dying to get into, I'll have you know." Del looked up and grinned.

Karse crouched next to Owyn and studied the drawing. "Not a lot of cover, and if she's gone to ground in the crypt, we won't get her out easily."

"She wouldn't," Steward said. "It would be dark down there, and she's never been fond of the dark, not even with candles. She'll want to be in comfort. I'll lay you a wager she's in the priest's quarters."

"Which has another entrance. Right. We need to get people in place up against the walls, ready to go in. She's got...how many? Seven or eight?" He sighed. "Even one would be a disaster, if they were in the wrong place."

"We need a diversion," Steward said slowly. "And I have an idea." He glanced at Owyn. "What was it that you called Aven's ideas?"

Owyn stood up. "Fuckheaded?"

"That's it." Steward looked down, took a deep breath. Then he looked up. "I'm going to betray you."

"You're *what*?"

The words seem to come from four different directions, and as many different pitches. Aven and Karse in the lower register, and Owyn and Aleia in the higher. Aven hadn't realized that Owyn could get quite that shrill.

"Steward, I think you need to explain," Karse said. "And then you're going to explain why you think Frayim is going to let you do whatever this fucked up plan actually is." He looked around. "Where is he?"

"Watching the Temple, and trying to see through the fog that's all he's seen all day." Steward gestured. "And I discussed this with him. He agrees with me that this may be the only way to distract Risha enough to break her hold."

"Explain," Aleia said.

Steward rubbed his hands together and nodded. "She...was obsessed with him. With the Usurper. Enough that she murdered Yana and attempted to murder Del." He hesitated, then said, "I can be that again. Be him again. And I can go to her and try to convince her that I've decided she was right. That I'm in love with her."

"She's not going to believe it," Aven said. "Uncle, she'll kill you."

Steward shrugged. "The thought did occur. And we think it's worth the risk."

Del started signing, *"You didn't discuss it with me!"*

"I discussed it with Frayim, because I didn't want him following me down there. She might give me a chance. She'll kill him. I don't want that." Steward looked back over his shoulder. Frayim had come out of the trees; Steward held his hand out, and Frayim came to join them.

"Fray, if Steward does this, what happens?" Owyn asked

Frayim shook his head. "I don't know. It galls me to say it, but I cannot see anything past right now." He took Steward's hand. "I don't like this plan, but I have no others."

"And honestly, if it's a choice between my life and theirs? How can I not?" Steward added. "I'm going in there, and I'm going to distract Risha, and get her out of the way long enough that you can do what needs to be done. And if we all walk out of the Temple at the end? I'll be content. And if I lay down my life to finally pay for my crimes? Then I will still be content."

"I won't be," Frayim muttered. Steward smiled at him.

"I know, Fray. But this is something that I have to do."

"She's not going to believe you," Owyn said softly. "Not if you go in there alone. Maybe..." His voice trailed off. Then he nodded. "I have an idea. A fuckheaded one."

IT WAS DEFINITELY A fuckheaded idea.

Owyn tossed his head, trying to get sweat out of his eyes. He couldn't use his hands — his wrists were bound together in front of him, and tethered to the back of Alabaster's saddle. The ropes were just for show. Aven had worked at them with a knife until they were almost frayed through, and Owyn could break them with very little effort. But they looked the part, with the cut portions hidden underneath the tether. If only Steward would remember to look the part — he kept looking back over his shoulder. Owyn would have yelled at him, if he hadn't been gagged. He did growl, loudly enough that Steward looked forward. Then he kicked Alabaster into a faster walk, leaving Owyn to trot along behind him up to the Temple door.

Risha was already waiting for them, her arms folded over her chest. She looked older, rougher, and her narrow face seemed even narrower. She scowled at them as Steward reined in Alabaster. Owyn dropped to his knees, panting.

"So you've decided to commit suicide?" Risha asked. "There are faster ways. Certainly less painful ones than how I'll kill you."

Steward snorted, and for a terrifying heartbeat, Owyn almost believed that he was Mannon. That the entire Progress had been an elaborate plan. Then Steward looked back at him and winked.

"Hardly," Steward said. "I've come to prove to you who I truly follow." He tugged on the rope, nearly pulling Owyn over. "And I've brought you a gift. Teva's murderer."

Risha smiled. "That is an attractive gift. One that I didn't think was possible. I thought he drowned, too." She cocked her head to the side. "Bring him in." She disappeared into the Temple, and Steward followed, with Owyn stumbling after him.

The inside of the Temple was just as Owyn remembered it from his vision, right down to the baby crying somewhere out of sight. Steward led him into the center of the space, then put his hand on the back of Owyn's neck. "Kneel, boy," he growled, making Owyn shudder. "You were a slave. You know how it's done."

Risha chuckled. "I thought you'd gone over to her," she said. "I thought you'd decided to follow, like a good dog. So why are you here, Mannon?"

"I told you," Steward said. "I'm here to show who truly commands my loyalty."

"How many times have you rebuffed me?" Risha snorted. "How many times did you tell me you'd never have me?"

"I was wrong. And I'm man enough to admit it." Steward walked over to her. "I've finally seen how wrong I was, Risha. I'm here. And I'm telling you that there is no other woman in this world that makes me feel the way that you do." He held his hands out to his sides. "I'm here. I'm yours. If you'll have an old fool who didn't see what he had until it was gone?"

Risha chuckled. "You're serious, aren't you?" she murmured. "You mean it. All of it." She stepped closer, looking up at Steward. He ran his hands up her arms, and leaned down to kiss her...

Owyn heard the sharp breath, saw Steward continue to bend, to fold in on himself as he fell. Risha stepped back, and he saw the bloody dagger in her hand.

"You really are an old fool," she snapped. Then she shouted, "Guards! Come clean up this mess!"

Chapter Forty-Eight

Owyn felt as though his heart stopped. All he could do was stare at the man lying on the ground, a pool of blood growing underneath him. Then he heard the clamor of guards coming down the corridor, and twisted his wrists. He felt the ropes resist, then pop as the last threads parted. With one hand, he tugged the gag out of his mouth. With the other, he pulled his whip chain from the pouch at his belt. By the time the guards burst into the room, swords bared, he was already moving, the whip chain singing for blood.

"*Stay to the left!*" Del ordered. Owyn moved left, taking down a guard who ventured too close. He heard the snap of a crossbow. Another snap. Then...

It was over. Owyn slowed, letting the whip chain clatter to a stop as he turned back to Steward.

Aven was already there, on his knees in the blood, one hand on Steward's chest. Owyn heard a low moan as Del dropped to his knees on Steward's other side. He went to crouch next to Del.

"He's fighting the trance," Aven growled. "Del, tell him to let me work!"

"Fa?" Del whispered. "Fa—"

"I...I heard," Steward mumbled. "No. Go. Go save them." He gestured with one bloody hand, and Del caught it and clung to him. Owyn put his arm around Del's shoulders.

"Uncle, I'm putting you in trance," Aven said. "It will hold until we can get back to camp. Stop fighting me."

"Not important," Steward answered. "They are. Go." He smiled slightly. "My son. Proud of you." He closed his eyes and moaned softly. "Avenge your mother. And me."

Del shivered, then kissed his father's hand. "Yes, Fa." He laid Steward's hand down and shook off Owyn's arm. Then he picked up his crossbow, putting his foot in the brace so that he could draw back the string.

Owyn rested his hand on Steward's shoulder. "We're finishing this. We'll be back. No sneaking off while our backs are turned, you hear me?" Steward reached up, patting Owyn's hand. He said nothing, and Owyn walked over to join Del, Karse, Aleia and Othi.

"We killed six," Aleia said. "She has one or two guards left."

Owyn nodded, trying not to look back. It had gotten very quiet behind him. "So what's the plan? There's another door, you said?"

Del nodded and signed, "*The plans for the Temple show a door into the priest's quarters.*"

"Windows?" Karse asked.

Del frowned, then nodded. "*I think so.*"

Karse looked toward the door where the guards had come from. "She has to know they're not coming back. She can't not have noticed. And if she tries to leave out that door, the Penitents will get her."

"She can't leave with Aria and Milon and the baby. She's trapped. So we need to move now," Aven said as he joined them. He nodded back toward Steward. "He's finally in trance. But he's failing fast. I don't know what she did, but the wound isn't behaving properly. He's bleeding heavily, and it won't stop.

He...he's not going to survive if I don't stay with him, and I can't stay with him." He licked his lips. "Del, I'm sorry."

"Do we have a plan?" Owyn asked. "She's trapped, but she's got hostages. What do we do?"

"I think I have a plan," Aven said. "Owyn, you go with Ama and Karse around to the back. Othi, you stay here with Del. But I want you outside until I do what I need to do. I don't want anyone out here. I want her to think I'm alone." He frowned. "Del, give me one of your spikes? And Owyn, that cloth that you were using as a gag?"

Owyn blinked and untied the knot, holding the cloth out. "What's this for?"

"Camouflage," Aven answered. "Wrap my wrist, like a bandage." He held his arm out, and Owyn wound the cloth around and tied it. Aven nodded, then slid the throwing spike Del offered him underneath the bandage.

"You go get into place," he said.

"And you'll be where?" Aleia asked. Aven shook his head. Then he flinched as the baby started to wail once again. He didn't answer, closing his eyes, and Owyn went cold.

"Aven, just how fuckheaded is this plan of yours?" Owyn asked.

Aven smiled. "Might be at the very top of the list. But that's my daughter in there. If it works, it'll be the last fuckheaded idea I'll ever need to have. Now, kiss for luck?"

AVEN WAITED UNTIL THE others were gone, then counted to one hundred to give his mother time to get into position. Only then did he start toward the corridor. "Risha!" he shouted. "Do you hear me?"

"You'll stay out there if you value their lives!"

"It's hard to bargain when we're shouting at the top of our lungs," he called back. "So either I come in, or you come out. I'm alone."

He heard rustling, then Risha's voice. "Leave your swords and come in."

Aven stripped off his sword harness and laid it down, then started down the corridor. There was an open door at the end, and he entered what looked like it once might have been a space like the sitting room in the Heir's suite in the Palace. It had been ransacked a long time ago, though. There were no furnishings except for pallets on the floor. Milon was sprawled on one of those pallets, his hands bound behind him. Aria was on another, on the far side of the room from Milon. She was also bound, and Aven could see that she was crying. Aeris was laying on her back on the pallet next to Milon, and her wails made Aven want to kill. And.. fuck. Three guards — one standing guard over Aria, one near Milon, and a third with Risha. He took a deep breath and tried to stay calm, holding his arms out and turning to show he was unarmed.

"*Owyn,*" he thought. "*There are three guards. Tell Karse to take the one by Milon. I'll get the one by Aria.*" He lowered his hands and turned to face Risha, who was aiming a loaded crossbow at Milon. "I'm here to bargain," he repeated.

"So you say," Risha replied. "And yet I've no idea what you think you're going to be bargaining with."

"Let them go," he said. "Aria and Milon and the baby. Let them go, and I'll stay." He heard the strangled protest from Aria. "That's my coin. The only adult who survived your experiments, Risha. If you want a chance to figure out what you did right where every other experiment failed, you'll let them go." He shifted, flexing his hand, feeling the spike slipping out of the bandaging and into his palm. "You said you wanted to see if I was...what did you call it? An aberration? And you said you'd never seen anything like what they did to put my hip back together. If you want to study me, in depth, and with my full cooperation, then you'll let them go."

Risha studied him for an uncomfortable time, then laughed. "So your bargain is them, or you?" she asked. "Honestly, Aven, I'm not seeing why I have to make a choice." She started to turn the crossbow on Aven...

"*Now!*" Aven threw the spike at the guard standing over Aria, then dove at Risha, hearing a snap as Karse fired through the broken window. A second snap, and Aven felt something slam into his thigh. He stumbled, and saw Risha heading for the pallet. For the baby. He grabbed her discarded crossbow, but the string was slack. Of course it was — the quarrel was in his own leg!

"Enough!" Risha shouted as she picked up the baby. "I am leaving. You are going to let me leave." She rested one hand on Aeris' chest. "Am I understood?"

The door burst open, and Karse and Aleia stepped inside. "Give me the baby," Aleia said. "And you can walk out of here."

"Do you think I don't know that if I do that, I'm not leaving?" Risha skirted around Aven, around the bodies of her guards, backing toward the door out into the Temple. "The baby is mine. She was always supposed to be mine. I planned for her. I made her. And when I'm through with her, she'll be perfect. The Child was always supposed to be perfect." Aven staggered to his feet, and Risha laughed. "I don't need you anymore. I don't need any of you anymore. I have what I wanted." She looked down at the crying baby. "You and I, we're going to fix everything, aren't we?" she asked, still backing toward the door. "We're going to rid the world of the animal tribes, and we'll be happy. Yes, we will."

Aven felt hands on his arms and looked back to see Owyn. Owyn wasn't looking at him, though. He was staring at Risha.

Past Risha.

Aven saw Risha stop, saw her jerk. Then Owyn was moving, grabbing the baby out of Risha's arms as she stumbled. As Del shoved her forward, and Aven could see the bloody tip of a long knife as it broke through the skin and pierced her chest. Once Owyn and the baby were clear, Del shoved Risha forward; she collapsed onto the floor with a scream of pain. Del took a deep breath, then walked around to where she could see him.

"You?" she moaned.

He spat on her. "For...my...mother," he said the words slowly, clearly, and with more anger than Aven had ever heard from him. Risha's eyes widened, and she whimpered. Del ignored her. "For...my...fa." He stopped, licked his lips, then spat again. "An...for...me. Fuck...you."

Aven closed his eyes, trying not to shake. Over. It was over. "Someone give me a knife," he said. Del handed him one of his throwing knives. Aven took it, and limped over to Aria. Kneeling hurt, but he didn't care. He cut the ropes binding her wrists and her wings, then pulled her into his arms. She clung to him, sobbing into his shoulder.

"It's over, love," he whispered. "I've got you. It's over."

"I hate to bother you two," Owyn called. "But I have no idea what I'm doing here. Help?"

Aven snorted, shifting to sit on the ground, his left leg stretched out. Now he could see the rest of the room — Aleia and Karse were with Milon, and his mother and Milon were both crying. Del was with Owyn, his forehead resting against Owyn's back as Owyn awkwardly bounced the baby.

"Owyn, bring her here," Aria called. "Wait...I have something I need to do." She slowly got to her feet, her movements stiff as she walked across the room. "Father?" she said. "Firstborn, I ask permission as your Heir to pronounce sentence on the traitoress Risha."

Milon put his arm around Aleia. "I...granted, my daughter." He smiled. "My Heir. Granted."

Aria bowed. Then she turned and walked over to Owyn and Del. She murmured something to Del before taking Aeris out of Owyn's arms. She did something that Aven couldn't see, and the baby quieted.

"Risha, once Senior Healer," Aria pronounced. "You have betrayed your oaths as a healer. You have betrayed your Firstborn, you have betrayed the tribes, and you have betrayed the Mother. For the crimes of treason and murder, you are sentenced to death." She turned to Del. "If you would?"

Del frowned slightly. Then he turned to Othi and started signing. Othi's brows rose.

"For this, yes," he answered. He set down one of his axes, and handed the other to Del. "Carry this for me?" Once Del had the ax, Othi reached down, picked up Risha by the back of her shirt, and dragged her out of the Temple. Del followed him.

When they came, Othi looked a little green, and there was blood on the ax.

"Done," Del pronounced.

"And we leave her for the shadowhawks," Milon added. "The Mother will never know her name."

"The Mother already can't see her," Owyn said. "She's so far gone in her hate that the Mother couldn't see her anymore."

A smile blossomed on Milon's face. "Owyn! Your voice is just the same!"

Owyn grinned. "Yours, too. We'll meet proper once we get everyone seen to. And...fuck, Steward's dying out there."

"Not if I can help it," Aven growled. He slowly got to his feet, trying not to put any weight on his left leg. "Othi, help me?"

Out in the large Temple room, the only sound was Steward's harsh breathing. Othi helped Aven sit down next to Steward; as soon as he was settled, he rested his hands on Steward's chest and dove into healing with all the power he could.

It wasn't going to be enough. He could tell immediately. Risha had somehow corrupted the wound — there was infection setting in, far too quickly to be natural. Steward was already burning with fever. Aven set the strongest healing trance he could, and opened his eyes to see fewer people than he was expecting.

"Where's Owyn?"

"He and Karse and Othi rode back to the village. Tiercel and Ionith went ahead of them, so they know what to prepare," Aleia answered, coming over to him. "We need the rest of the healers, and..." She looked over at where Milon was sitting with his back against the wall. "And we've got a long overdue reunion waiting."

"Where's Aria?"

"Trying to put Del back together," Aleia answered. "And Frayim is outside. The last I saw him, he was throwing rocks at Risha's head. He has... remarkably good aim. Aven, can you save him?"

Aven sighed and shook his head. "Not by myself. She did something. I'm not sure what, but the wound is already poisoned."

"Did she poison him?"

Aven shook his head. "There's nothing unusual in his blood. As far as I can tell, she did something to prevent clotting, and increased the rate of infection. It's not responding to anything I'm doing. All I can do is slow it. Maybe when the others get here, we can stop it. But for now? I'm holding him stable, and he's comfortable."

Aleia nodded. Then she smiled. "Milon told me that you sang her into the world."

"I'm surprised I remembered how. I still have to welcome her and give her a name. I haven't held her yet," Aven admitted. "Ama, Milon sang to her, too."

"He still remembers the chants? I taught him, because you weren't supposed to be my only child," Aleia answered.

"Ama, he knew the counter chant. The grandparent chant."

Aleia frowned. Then she called, "Milon, how did you know the counter chant? I didn't teach that one to you."

Milon turned at the sound of his name. He looked puzzled. "I honestly don't know. I know they're not the ones you taught me, but I am not sure where I learned them. I may have read them somewhere."

"Not likely." Aleia went to sit with Milon, leaning against him as he put his arm around her. "We never wrote those down."

Milon shook his head. "I don't know, then. It just...seemed to be the proper words."

Aven laughed. "I'm honestly not surprised that the Mother is giving you the right words at the right time. Aria? Where are you?"

"Behind you." Aria settled down onto the ground next to him, kissed him, then looked at his bandaged leg. "Del is in the crypt. He said he would come out when he was able. How are you?"

"Oh, this leg hurts like fuck," Aven said. "But it was worth it." He smiled. "Let me have her. There's something I need to do and it's hours past when it should have been done."

Aria laid the baby in his arms, and he ran one finger over Aeris' soft cheek. She was still wrapped in Alanar's shirt, but he could see her tiny wings over her shoulders, the soft down pale against the black cloth.. He leaned down and touched his forehead to hers, feeling her breathing. Breathing with her. Then he sat up and took a deep breath.

"Your name is Aeris," he sang in a low voice, translating the ritual words so that Aria would understand. "Aeris, daughter of Aven, of Neera's canoe, of the line of Abin. Daughter of Aria, of Agragor's flock, of the line of Liara. You are a child of the Mother, born from her dreams and her wishes. You will do wonders."

Chapter Forty-Nine

Getting back to the Temple seemed to take much less time than it had to get down to the village. Owyn slid off Freckles' back and watched as the healers all rushed for the Temple, with Treesi leading Alanar by the hand. He needed to stay out of their way, so instead he went the other way, to where Memfis was still sitting in Dasher's saddle.

"Need some help?" Owyn asked.

"Hold his head," Memfis answered. Owyn took Dasher's bridle and held the horse still as Memfis dismounted.

"You could have come in the cart with Karse," Owyn said.

"And it's not here yet, and won't be here for a while," Memfis said. "I need to be here now. I need..." He stopped and stared at the Temple, then turned back to Owyn. "He's really in there."

Owyn nodded. "He is. And he's waiting for you." He smiled and held his hand out. "Come on, Fa."

Memfis took Owyn's hand, and they headed into the Temple. Once his eyes had adjusted to the dimmer light, Owyn could see the healers all gathered around Steward, with Del and Frayim both pacing back and forth behind them. Aleia and Aria were standing near the wall, and when Aleia saw them, she smiled and stepped back. Owyn could see Milon, sitting against the wall. Saw him sit up straight, wonder plain on his face.

"I'd know that footstep anywhere. I can't come to you," he croaked. "And I've waited this long. Get yourself over here."

Of all the reactions Owyn would have expected from Memfis, having his father burst into tears was the most disturbing. Memfis stumbled to the wall and dropped to his knees hard enough that Owyn winced. Then he stopped, looking almost terrified.

"Mil—"

"Guppy warned me. I don't care. Mem, I don't care how broken you are," Milon said softly. "I mean...look at me." He paused. "You...can look at me, can't you? No one said anything about you going blind."

Memfis moaned softly and reached out to touch Milon's cheek, and Owyn remembered his own reunion with Alanar. He glanced over to see his husband bent over his work, looked back, then decided he needed to be looking anywhere else. He turned to study the dust-covered carvings on the far wall. Then he heard footsteps, and Aria came up next to him.

"They need some privacy," she said. "Aleia has gone outside. Who came with you?"

"Your grandfather should be outside by now. Karse and Othi are coming with the wagons." Owyn scrubbed his hand over his face. "I think Alanar the Elder is coming, too. How's Del been?"

"He isolated himself for a long time. Then he came out and helped me make Aven rest." She took a deep breath. "Which may have been a mistake. Steward got worse when Aven slept."

Owyn sighed. "I was afraid of that. And...how are you?" He turned to look at her. "What do you need? What can I do?"

She smiled. "I would like to go outside and see my grandfather. And I hope someone thought to send supplies for the baby with the wagon. None of the healers thought of it. Alanar's shirt is well and truly ruined."

"He'd say it was for an excellent cause," Owyn said.

Aria giggled. "He did say that. Almost exactly."

Owyn smiled and tipped his head to look at Aeris. "She's so little and wrinkly. Can I...can I hold her again?"

Aria laid the baby in his arms, and he laughed as her face scrunched up. "Oh, so fierce!" he crooned. "You're going to tie your father all in knots. You cry, and he'll fall all to pieces." He laughed. "If she cries, I might fall all to pieces."

Aria laughed. "I'm hoping that she's seen enough crying over the past few hours."

Owyn nodded. "From your mouth to the Mother's ears. Let's go...oh," He stopped in mid-sentence as the healers all stood up. Frayim sat down to take their place, and Aven leaned on his father as they came to join Aria and Owyn. Del followed, standing next to Alanar, who put his arm around him and hugged him tightly.

"Treesi, would you go get Aleia?" Jehan asked. Treesi nodded and left the Temple, coming back shortly with Aleia and Karse.

"You made it," Jehan said.

"Just got here," Karse answered. "How is he?"

Jehan shook his head. "He's failing fast. She...twisted her powers, and it's killing him. His entire body is shutting down, and all we can do is block the pain." He looked down. "I hate that it's ending like this. I hate that he's come so far, and he's dying like this."

"He chose it, though," Karse said. "You heard him. He said that if he died today, and Aria and Milon and the baby survived, he'd die happy."

Del nodded. *"He atoned,"* he signed. *"Everything he did before he was Steward, he's atoned for all that. I think he's at peace."*

"We're going to wake him up," Jehan added. "So we can say goodbye, so he can see the baby, and know that he did what he set out to do. Then...I'll send him on to the Mother myself.

He was the Air Companion, so we'll arrange sky burial with Agragor."

Aria nodded, then looked past Jehan and blinked. "Jehan, who is that with Frayim?"

Owyn looked, and nearly dropped the baby. A familiar woman sat next to Frayim, holding his hand. Her other hand rested on Steward's chest.

"Fuck me!"

The Mother looked up and smiled at him. "Owyn Jaxis, such language around the baby!"

Jehan looked at Her, then at Owyn. His eyes widened. "I..."

"Yeah," Owyn said, nodding slowly. "Yeah, that is exactly who you think it is."

Jehan turned slowly, and went to one knee. "Mother," he murmured. "You...you came for him yourself?"

"On rare occasions, I will come to claim my own. And I am claiming him as my own. But not to come to me. Not for many years." She smiled down at Steward. "Are you awake, my son?"

"Mama?" Steward mumbled. "I..." He pushed himself up on his elbows. "What...wait...I was dying. I...I..." He sat all the way up, looking down at himself. "I'm not dead?" He turned, and gasped as Frayim threw his arms around him. "It's all right, Fray," he said softly. "It's all right. I'm fine. I..." He fell silent and turned, realizing there was someone on his other side. "I...Mother?"

She smiled and stood up. "I see you, my son. I know you. And I claim you. Steward, attend."

"Fray, help me up," Steward croaked. He got to his feet, leaning on Frayim's arm for support. "Mother, I hear you. How may this completely unworthy son serve?"

She smiled. "You may serve me here," she answered, and gestured to the Temple. "My home is in disarray, my son. I charge you to put it to rights."

Steward paled slightly. "I...of course. This...this will take me the rest of my life." He smiled. "But it will be worth it. I was willing to lay down my life to serve. I should be willing to live it and do the same." He licked his lips and nodded. "I accept this charge, Mother."

"And I'm staying with you," Frayim added. He rested his hand on Steward's shoulder. "This is where my road led. This is why I could see no further. This is where I am supposed to be. No more roads to travel. I've arrived."

The Mother nodded. She turned and walked over to Memfis and Milon, kneeling down and taking their hands. Owyn took advantage of her inattention to give Aeris back to Aria, and went to Alanar and Del.

"Del?" he whispered. Del looked at him and smiled, his face streaked with tears.

"*He's alive. And she knows him. She forgives him.*"

Owyn nodded. "Go on, then."

Del slipped out of Alanar's arms and went to Steward, who hugged him tightly. Owyn took Del's place, leaning into his husband's side.

"That's really the Mother?" Alanar whispered. "Really?"

"Really," Owyn said. "I've seen Her before. When I tested, I talked to Her. And She made me forget until last night. I danced to find you, and She let me remember."

Alanar took a deep breath. "She has a wonderful voice," he said. "Aven, let me work on that leg. It's making my teeth ache."

"How is my leg making your teeth ache?" Aven asked.

"Sit down, Aven," Alanar ordered. Aven laughed and sat down on the ground, but as Alanar went to crouch next to him, the Mother came back.

"Virrik," she said. "It's time to go."

"Go?" Owyn sputtered. "Go where? You're taking him?" He looked at Alanar. "Allie was right? Virrik was in his head because we needed him to be there for Aeris?"

"It was a contingency I'd hoped we would not have to use," the Mother said. "If you had taken another path, taken another route back to the Palace, it would never have come to pass."

"Because we both would have been dead," Owyn finished. "The other path was taking the cutter, and Risha would have killed both of us, and no one would ever have known."

The Mother nodded. "Exactly. You took the road that led to this place, and this time. And now it is time that Virrik moves on." She held her hand out. Alanar took it, bowed his head, then staggered back and fell into Owyn's arms. Owyn lowered Alanar to the ground.

"Allie?"

"I..." Alanar shook his head, then sat up. "It's...it's so quiet!" He turned toward Owyn, shock and confusion clear on his face. "It's...Owyn, I'm alone in here!"

"Owyn?"

The round tones were familiar, even if the voice wasn't. Owyn looked up, and saw a Water warrior standing with the Mother. He was shorter than Aven, almost the same height as Owyn himself, but with Othi's solid bulk.

"Vir?" Owyn croaked. "Is...is that what you looked like?" He snorted. "You like them short, don't you, Allie?"

Virrik smiled. "Well, you like them tall, so it balanced. I wondered what you looked like. What any of you looked like." He stopped when his gaze reached Aven. "Cousin, thank you. For bringing me home."

"I wish I could have done more, Virrik." Aven shifted, and Virrik pointed at him.

"Don't you dare stand up!" He laughed. "Get that leg taken care of." He looked around again. "Thank you all. I'll miss all of you."

Alanar got to his feet. "I'll miss you, too, Vir. I love you."

"Love you, too. Silly bird." Virrik turned toward the Mother, who held Her hand out.

"Mother," Aria called. "Thank you. For saving him."

"Thank you, my daughter. You did well. You all did so well." The Mother started to fade into the shadows. "You will have peace now."

"We still need to rebuild," Aleia said. "There's so much work to do."

"But we have the time to do it now," Memfis said. He looked at the man next to him. "And we have each other again."

The Mother vanished, but her voice whispered from every corner of the Temple, "And now it's time for you to go home."

OWYN STOOD AT THE RAILING, watching as the dock grew larger. The first thing that Aria did once they were back in the Palace was send him to Terraces. They hadn't sent advance word, and Owyn wasn't sure how they'd known, but he could see people waiting for him on the dock. And, from the looks of things, it wasn't just Rhexa. Owyn saw several flashes of red hair among the people on the dock, and as the cutter stopped moving, he heard his mother's voice, "Jax!"

Owyn waved, waiting until Destria signaled, then trotting down the gangplank. Dyneh was waiting at the bottom, and hugged him tightly.

"I've been so worried!" she said. "Are you all right? How did the Progress end?"

"It was...interesting," Owyn said. "And I have a lot to tell you. And you all have a standing invitation to come to the Palace. You have a sort-of granddaughter to meet." He turned and hugged Huris, then let his father go and hugged Rhexa.

"You!" she gasped. "Do you have any idea what you did?"

Owyn blinked. "No. Not a single one. What did I do?"

"You...you found them! And you sent them home! And I had no idea if you were even still alive out there!" Rhexa hugged him again. "You..." She sighed and shook her head. "I'm so glad to see you."

He smiled. "I'm glad to see you, too." He paused long enough to welcome Elaias, Astur and Gisa. "Where's Trista?"

Elaias grinned. "Horribly morning sick. She stayed with Mina and Versi, and I'm to bring you around to see her when you're done with whatever you're doing."

"Allie and I will come to see her once we finish getting things sorted in the Palace," Owyn said. "We've got a lot of work to catch up on, and he's...well, that's part of it."

They walked up through the tunnels, and through familiar streets to the healing center. Inside, Elaias excused himself for rounds, and Astur for lessons. Gisa also excused herself, going back outside.

"How are the trainees?" Owyn asked as they went down the corridor to the Senior Healer's office.

"They're all doing quite well," Rhexa answered. She knocked on the door, and Owyn heard Pirit's voice.

"Come in!"

Inside, Owyn took a seat in one of the chairs, and opened his carry-bag. "First things first. Risha is dead. Executed on the orders of the Firstborn, with sentence carried out by the Heir's Air Companion."

"I'm sorry?" Pirit asked. Then her jaw dropped. "You found him?"

Owyn smiled. "That's the second thing." He reached into his bag and took out a sealed packet. "For the Senior Healer and the Governor, greetings from the Firstborn, Milon. He invites you to the Palace at your earliest convenience."

"And?" Pirit asked. "Could the healers undo the damage?"

Owyn paused. "No. All the healers in merge couldn't give him his legs back. But he says he's fine with that. He's had twenty-five years to get used to it. And I don't remember if I told you, but when I was talking to him in visions, it was always dark. It was always dark because Risha blinded him when she took him."

"Mother of us all," Rhexa murmured. "Could they undo that?"

"Not entirely," Owyn answered. "It's been months, and they couldn't reverse it entirely. They managed to give him a little bit of sight back. Enough that he can tell who he's talking to, and see the baby if she's really close." He grinned. "Your great-granddaughter's name is Aeris and she's beautiful. And...fuck, there's no easy way to tell this. Granna Meris died in Hearthstone."

Rhexa nodded, reaching out to rest her hand on his knee. "We know. We got word of that from the headwoman. I'm so sorry, Owyn. How is Memfis?"

"Getting used to being Head of the Fire tribe until they reconvene the Council," Owyn answered. "And it's the weirdest thing. He giggles now. I think because he's got his Milon back. He...he giggles, and it's weird."

Rhexa laughed. "And the baby's name is Aeris. That's good. What else?"

"Virrik isn't in Allie's head anymore," Owyn said. "The Mother took him back with her. And..." Owyn took another sealed packet out of his bag. "This is for you., Auntie. It's from Steward. And...he's sorry, but he's not going to be coming back."

"Not..." Rhexa took the letter. "Owyn, he isn't...?"

"No, he's not dead," Owyn answered quickly. "He's High Priest. Claimed by the Mother's own hand. He asked me to bring you this, and apologize, and ask if you'd write to him."

"He's up there alone?" Rhexa asked.

"No, Frayim is with him. The Seer. And a bunch of former raiders who swore themselves to Aria, too." Owyn rubbed his hand against his trouser legs. "He's not alone. But he's happy. And we'll see him again." He leaned back in his chair. "We'll see him again."

Epilogue

The Firstborn was dead.

Fifteen years had passed since Milon was rescued and restored to his place as Firstborn. Fifteen years in which he'd ruled wisely and well. His remaining Companions had resumed their places at his side, each of them representing and ruling their respective tribes. There had been only one exception — Milon refused to seek another Air Companion. In the Hall, the chair that should have been Liara's remained empty, while Aria took her mother's place as the voice of the Air tribe. And the halls of the Palace that overlooked the sea were once more filled with light, the scent of flowers, and the sounds of children's laughter.

Now, Aria dismounted her horse and looked up at the Temple once more. She and her oldest daughter had ridden ahead of the funeral procession, to have a private moment at the Temple.

"They've rebuilt so much," she murmured. "I've read the reports. But it's different, seeing it for myself."

"We were here before, Mama?" Aeris asked. She led her horse over to Aria. "I don't remember it."

"I'd be surprised if you did, my dove," Aria said. "You were born near here. The last time we were here, you were only a few hours old."

Aeris blinked. "Oh. I imagine you don't like thinking about those days."

"You're the best part of those days, my dove," Aria answered. "Now, how far behind us is the carriage?"

Aeris handed her reins to her mother, walked away, and launched herself into the air. She soared overhead, circling for a moment, then swooped back down and landed. "The cart and the carriage just came through the pass."

"Then we have a moment or two." She turned toward the Temple, and saw the old man standing in the door.

IT WASN'T OFTEN THAT he heard horses anymore. Or voices that he didn't know. Steward stepped out into the sunlight and saw the winged women standing outside the temple. For a moment, he thought the older woman was Yana. Then she smiled, and walked to meet him. "Steward."

He blinked, then laughed, realizing who it was. "Aria. You haven't changed at all. Not a hair. Not a feather." He opened his arms. "It's so good to see you."

Aria dropped all decorum and ran into his embrace. "I've missed you!"

He laughed and hugged her tightly. "I've missed you as well." He let her go and turned to the young Air girl standing nearby. "Now, who is this young lady?"

"Uncle Steward," Aeris laughed. "It's me!"

He blinked. "Oh, no. You can't possibly be my little Aeris! Who told you that you could grow up beautiful? It was your father, wasn't it? He spoils you outrageously—" He left Aria's side and went to embrace the giggling girl. "Come inside. Frayim and I were just planning our next report on the rebuilding, but you can see it for yourself. How long will you be visiting?"

"Uncle," Aria said. "This isn't a visit."

Steward frowned. Then his eyes widened. "It's not?" He looked past them, and saw the funeral cart, and the carriage behind it. "Oh, Aria."

"He died in his sleep, Uncle. We were all with him," Aria said. "He knew. He knew it was time." Aria reached into her coat and took out a packet of papers. "He asked me to give this to you."

Steward took it and looked down at it. "A letter?" He broke the seal, and held the pages close to his face. Tiny handwriting that couldn't quite make out, and he sighed and lowered the pages. "Frayim has started reading to me," he grumbled. "My eyes are old. I can still see distances, but reading..." He frowned and squinted again, then blinked and shook his head. "Did you read this?"

Aria shook her head. "It was sealed when he gave it to me."

"Then you can read it to me later. Now...Fray!" He turned and shouted. "Fray!"

Frayim appeared in the Temple door. "High Priest?" He blinked in the sunlight, then laughed. "The blesséd Mother! And the Child!" He came out and knelt in front of Aria, taking her hands in his and kissing her fingers. "You honor us!"

"Frayim, after all these years, you've forgotten that you can call me by name," Aria said.

He blushed slightly. "Aria." He got to his feet and turned to Steward. "High Priest?"

"The Firstborn has passed to the Mother, Frayim," Steward said. "They'll be here soon."

Frayim sobered. He nodded. "Blesséd Mother, I share your grief. He was a good man, your father. A very good man. The Mother will hold him close, I'm very certain."

"Thank you, Frayim," Aria said. "If you think that, then it must be so."

"We have work to do, Fray," Steward said. He closed his eyes, ordered his thoughts, then nodded. "The...blue book. Fourth shelf in the records. On the left."

"Yes, High Priest," Frayim said, and hurried into the Temple. Steward held his hand out to Aria, who took it and squeezed his fingers.

"You brought the children, I imagine. For the ritual. I can't wait to meet the rest of them. You write and tell me about them, but meeting them..." he said. "I'm looking forward to that."

"They'll be here soon," Aria said.

Steward tried to remember, then shook his head. "I can't think. How many now? The last time I was at the Palace, there were only four."

"In total, or mine?" Aria laughed. "I have Aeris and Mila with Aven, and Fisher is Owyn's son. Treesi has Neri and the twins with Othi, Jaxsyn with Owyn, and Leihan is Aven's. And Owyn and Alanar have Dyna and Vir." She smiled slightly and counted on her fingers, "In order, Aeris, Neri, Dyna, Fisher, Jaxsyn, Vir, Leihan, Mila, and Agati and Gira. Treesi says she's done with babies, but I don't think she is."

"And you? Are you done?" Steward looked at her, then laughed. "No, you're not. Aria, are you pregnant?"

She smiled. "You can tell? I didn't think it was obvious yet."

"I remember when you were carrying this one," Steward said, nodding towards Aeris. "And you've the same glow. Who's the father? Aven or Owyn?"

"They're here, Mama!" Aeris called, taking off and flying down to the carriage. The first person out was Aven, and Steward winced as he watched Aven limping across the uneven ground toward them.

"That limp is worse than I remember," he murmured.

"Because my Aven is stubborn, and keeps trying to do things he should not," Aria answered in a low voice. "He knows he should not ride anymore, but three years ago, Leihan wanted to learn, and as you said, Aven spoils his daughters outrageously." She took a deep breath. "He fell off the horse and rebroke his hip."

Steward winced again in sympathy. "He's lucky to be able to walk at all."

"Alanar is very good at what he does. And Aven is very lucky. Now, once he stretches, he'll move more easily," Aria said. "He slept poorly last night. He never sleeps well when we're away from the Palace."

Steward nodded. "I'll see if we can make him comfortable tonight," he said. Then he stepped forward to accept Aven's embrace.

"Uncle," Aven said. "It's good to see you. I wish it could have been for another reason."

"We all do, my boy. We all do." Steward looked past him, and realized someone was missing. "I see Memfis, Jehan and Aleia. Where's Alanar?"

"In Terraces," Aria answered. "There was another tremor the day my father died, and Terraces took damage. One more message from Father Adavar."

Steward sniffed. "We all learned our lessons. He didn't need to punctuate it."

"He felt otherwise, apparently," Aven said. "But Alanar, Dyna, and Vir are all in Terraces, and they send their love. Aunt Rhexa does, too. We have a letter for you from her."

Steward nodded. He looked past Aven and blinked, seeing the horde of children walking up the slope, followed by Owyn, Treesi, Othi and Del. "Mother of us all. You told me all the names, but somehow...how do you keep track of them all? You're outnumbered!" Behind the children were Memfis, Jehan and Aleia, all of them walking slowly. At the very rear, walking with Aeris, were two young men who seemed familiar. One was tall and graceful, while the other had the solid build of a fighter. Steward frowned. "Those two young men with Aeris. Do I know them?"

"It's been a good number of years, but yes. The taller one is Danir, and—"

"Is that Copper?" Steward gasped at the sight of the young warrior. "Look at him! He looks like he could chew nails for breakfast and spit tacks the rest of the day." He watched them with Aeris. "They're both a bit older than she is..."

"There's nothing sordid, Steward," Aven assured him. "Danir and Copper are paired."

"Are they?" Steward smiled. "I missed that news."

"They married a year ago at Turning. Aeris calls them both Uncle," Aria answered. "They're very protective of her. I'm thinking that I see our future Steward and Captain of the Guard when Afansa and Karse both stand down."

Steward arched a brow. "I thought Marik would follow Afansa?"

"Marik and Esai went back to Serenity. He's headman there now. Danzi decided she'd rather be grandmother than headwoman. Marik and Esai have four, all boys."

Steward nodded. "And how is Karse? And Trey?"

Aria sighed. "Trey...he has his good days and his bad. More good days than bad now, although the day Fa died...that was not a good day for him. They were so close." She took a deep breath and looked up at Aven. "The healers did all they could for his body, and Karse and Afansa and Treesi do what they can for his mind. It helps—"

"Until it doesn't?" Steward finished. He sighed when she nodded. "A blasted shame."

"He's alive," Aven said. "And he is loved. He knows that."

"High Priest."

Steward turned to see Frayim had come back out of the Temple, carrying the blue book. "I have it. I'll go and speak to the attendants, have them bring him to the Temple so we can prepare for the ceremony." He looked up at the sky. "It's traditionally held at sunset. We should have enough time."

Steward nodded. "Thank you, Fray."

Frayim smiled and bowed before walking down the hill.

"Steward, have you ever formalized what you have with Frayim?" Aria asked softly.

"We've never felt the need. He's here for me. I'm here for him. That's enough. And don't you go worrying about an old man, Aria. He's good to me. Good for me." He paused. "He keeps me from maundering in the past, which is what would have happened if I were here alone those first few years." He smiled broadly. "Now, introduce me to this tribe of yours, Aria!"

The children swarmed up and around them, competing for Aria and Aven's attention. For a moment, it was a cacophony of voices and movement, then Othi's voice rang out.

"Enough!"

Immediate silence, followed by a peal of giggles from the smallest ones, two identical girls who ran to Othi, laughing as he scooped them into the air. Aeris joined a darker-skinned boy who had a solid build, barred gray wings, and bright, ember eyes under dark curls.

"Fisher is Owyn's very image," he said. "Having them all in the Hall must make for interesting echoes."

"You have no idea," Owyn answered. He came up to hug Steward. "You look good. You look really good. This whole high priest thing, it suits you."

"I'm rather enjoying it," Steward agreed. "The long hair suits you, Owyn. And the twists look good." He turned to the bearded man who was standing next to Owyn and smiled. "Oh, my son. Look at you. When did you decide to grow a beard again? You look wonderful."

Del broke into a wide smile, and wound his way through the children to hug Steward. He swallowed, then slowly answered, "You...lll...look...g...good." He swallowed again, then went back to signing. *You look wonderful, Fa. And the beard was Allie's fault. He dared me to try it again, and I decided I liked it this time.*

"It looks good on you." Steward beamed at him, then gestured to them all. "Come inside! Come inside. The guest house is ready. It...well, it won't hold all of you, but it's ready."

"We'll have tents put up in the meadow," Memfis said. "We came prepared to take care of ourselves. How are you, old man?"

"Who are you calling old?" Steward shot back, then laughed. He turned to Aleia and shook his head. "Jehan is a lucky man. You get prettier every time I see you."

"Flatterer," Aleia chided, a fond smile on her face. There was sadness in her eyes, and Steward sighed.

"He died in his sleep, Aria said?" he asked.

"In his own bed," Jehan answered. "In his own time, and with the people he loved around him. He knew his daughter, and his grandchildren. And the grandchildren of his heart. He had fifteen years with us, and his only regret at the end was that Liara wasn't alive to share it with us." He took a deep breath. "Did Aria give you the letter?"

"I'll have to have her read it to me," Steward answered. "Then we'll probably have a good cry together." He saw movement coming up the slope. "Let's move out of the way, let Fray and the attendants work. Come inside and see the repairs, then I'll take you to the guest house while the tents are set up."

THE SUN HAD JUST TOUCHED the western peaks when Steward came out to meet the mourners. He smoothed the front of his robes, cleared his throat, and raised his voice.

"It is time," he called. "Come inside." He turned, hearing them following him into the Temple. Inside, Milon's body had been laid on a bier and draped in gold silk. The Crown rested on his chest. Aria and her Companions stood in a line facing the bier, two steps behind Memfis, Jehan, and Aleia. The children were all quiet, standing behind Aria and the Companions with Othi, Danir and Copper. Steward nodded, and a soft bell sounded, echoing through the Temple.

"Mother of us all," Steward began. "We surrender to Your arms a son of Fire. Your son, a Firstborn of the line of Axia and Nerris. Milon, son of Varia and Tallin, grandson of Meris and Versin, of Grigette and Martis. We return him to Your arms, and inter him alongside the Firstborn who came before." He turned to face the bier, and tried not to shout, hearing Memfis moan behind him.

The Mother stood on the other side of the bier.

"I have looked into his heart," she said. "And there is nothing wanting. He will return to me, and he will be at rest." She rested one hand on Milon's chest, picked up the Crown...

Then she vanished.

Steward blinked. He blinked again. Then he coughed.

"I...I don't think we need anyone to speak for the dead, then?" he offered, turning to face the others, and tried not to react. Aria had been wearing the Diadem when she came into the Temple. But it, too, had vanished.

"I hadn't expected to see Her again," Memfis said. "Not before I went to Her myself." He swallowed. "I'd like to speak for him, anyway. If no one minds?"

"I think we should," Owyn added. "I think it'll help."

Steward nodded. "Memfis, will you speak?"

The remembrances went on long into the night. Stories were told, and laughter and tears both were shared. After a time, Aeris and Fisher took the younger children out. Finally, only Aria and her Companions, Memfis, Jehan, and Aleia were left.

"They'll take him to the crypt once we go?" Aleia asked. "And?"

"And at dawn, Aria will go into the crypt. Then the children will," Steward answered. "In what order?"

Aria glanced over her shoulder. "I'm not sure. I think...I suspect I know who'll find the Diadem. I think we all know. But I don't know if we should send her first, or last."

"You can't be sure it'll be Aeris," Aven said. "We can't be sure of any of them. I mean, someone being sure and being disappointed is what got us into the mess in the first place."

Steward winced. "She's been raised far better than that one was, I'm certain. Fray, how is it usually done? What does the book say?"

"Let me look," Frayim answered. He got up from his seat on the floor and left the room, coming back a moment later with the blue book. He opened it and started turning pages. Then he shook his head. "It doesn't give a specific order. Just that the chosen candidates shall enter the crypt one at a time."

Steward sighed. "I suggest we start with the youngest. They won't have to stand for the entire ceremony, then."

Aria nodded. "We'll do it that way. I need to sleep now." She got up. "Oh, Steward. You asked me earlier, and I never had the chance to answer." She rested her hand on her abdomen and smiled. "You wanted to know if this one was Aven's or Owyn's. Neither...Grandfather."

Steward frowned. "Neither?" Then the last word registered. "Grandfather?" he repeated. "I...*grandfather*? Really? *Really*?"

Del rose to stand with Aria. He smiled at her, then nodded. *"We talked about it for a long time,"* he signed. *"Years, I think. And...yes."* He smiled again. *"We know this is a girl. And her name will be Yana."*

"Oh..." Steward breathed. "Oh..." He looked up to see Frayim looking fondly down at him and started giggling. Which quickly changed to crying on Fray's shoulder.

"Fa?"

Steward barely heard Del's voice, but he did hear Fray.

"He's fine," Frayim assured them. "Too much joy bubbles over. He's fine." His hand smoothed over Steward's shoulder, down his back. "He's fine."

AT DAWN THE NEXT MORNING, Steward waited in the now-empty Temple, with Frayim by his side.

"I'm surprised I slept at all," he said. "A baby. A grandchild. I...I never thought I'd have a grandchild."

"We'll go to the Palace in the spring to meet her," Frayim said, taking Steward's hand. "And to Terraces. I want to finally meet Rhexa. I feel like I know her from her letters."

Steward nodded. "We'll go in the spring. Iantir will be ready by then to manage things while we're gone. You'll like Rhexa. And maybe we'll be able to convince her to come back with us." He looked toward the door, seeing movement outside. Aria came in. Behind her were her Companions, and behind them, Othi, Danir, Copper and all of the children. Jehan, Memfis, and Aleia brought up the rear.

Steward stepped forward and took Aria's hands. "The time has come," he said. "The door is open to you, Aria, daughter of Milon. You enter as the Heir. You will emerge as the Firstborn."

She smiled at him, kissed his cheek, then walked to the crypt door and went inside. The door closed. When it opened again, she was wearing the Crown. She had an odd look on her face, and Aven came forward to meet her.

"Firstborn?" Steward said.

"She's in there," Aria answered. "I was not expecting Her. And...she's not alone." She looked up at Aven as he reached her side. "You look like him. Just like him."

"I..." Aven looked toward the door. *"Abin* is in there?"

"All of them are in there," Aria said. "The Mother and Axia and all the first Companions. They're all in there." She looked back over her shoulder. "It was *crowded.*"

Frayim left Steward's side and went to the door, looking inside. "They're gone now," he said. "Or at least, they're not showing themselves to me."

"If they show themselves to the children, that will be...interesting." Aria murmured. "Now, youngest first?"

"Youngest first," Steward said, and gestured for the children to come closer. He looked at the twins. Both of them had Treesi's fiery hair, and both had gill slits. "Which of you is the younger one?"

"I am," one of the girls said. "I'm Gira."

"Gira, you go first, then," Steward said. "If you find anything waiting for you, bring it out. If you do not, come outside and it will be your sister's turn."

Gira nodded and skipped toward the door. Then she came back out. "Nothing here!"

Agati went next, then Mila. Leihan barely walked through the door before she walked back out. Jaxsyn took nearly five minutes before he came back out.

"What took so long?" Frayim asked.

"The carvings in there are really intricate," Jaxsyn answered. "They're interesting. Can I go back in and study them when we're done? And can I draw them?"

Steward glanced at Owyn, who grinned. "Jax is my artist."

Steward chuckled. "Of course you may. But you have to let the others go first."

Neri went inside, and came out again shaking her head. Fisher just looked at the door, then shook his head, folding his wings against his back.

"It's not for me," he said. "That's not my road. Aeri, you go."

"Fish?"

"Trust me, Aeri."

Steward looked at Owyn and signed, "*Smoke Dancer?*"

Owyn nodded, draping his arm over his oldest son's shoulders.

Aeris folded her hands together, her shifting wings the only sign of her nerves. She looked at her mother, then squared her shoulders and walked into the crypt. Steward watched as Aria took Aven's hand. Treesi took her other hand, and the other Companions moved in close.

They heard Aeris' laughter clearly through the door.

Then the door opened, and the Heir to the Firstborn walked out of the crypt.

⌘

WORLDS BEGIN. WORLDS end. Worlds begin again. So it is with worlds.

The world begins again.

BONUS CHAPTER

Worlds Begin:

The Heir to the Firstborn Creation Myth

Worlds begin. Worlds end. Worlds begin again. So it is with worlds.

The world Adavar began, lush and green and alive, and the Maiden Goddess was pleased. She walked the face of the new world, studying creation. She sang with the birds, swam with the great water cats and the dolphins. She ran with the deer and the great, gray wolves. She explored the caves beneath the mountains, and watched the heart of the world burn, delighting in the antics of the tiny fire mice. Then she returned to the surface, and realized that that throughout all of this new creation, there was no one like her. There was no one to sing with the birds, or swim with the water cats. No one to run with the deer, or watch the fires at the heart of the world. She was alone. There was no one to share her world with her.

The Maiden pondered this as she lay in the soft meadows, and passed into sleep. In her sleep, she dreamed of her love for this new world, and her desire for someone to share it. And such was the power of that dream, and of her desire, that the world responded.

"Wake," the world called. "Wake and come to the high places, hidden between the sea and the stars, and there you shall find what you seek."

The Maiden woke, and heeding the call of the world that she loved, she searched for the high places hidden between the sea and the stars. For ten months she searched, and her belly swelled like the silver moon. Finally, she found the hidden fields, and as she reached her destination, the waters of her womb burst, flowing down the mountain to the sea. And in the hidden fields, the Maiden bore the Firstborn, the Eldest daughter. Maiden no longer, the Mother rejoiced in the life that her love for the world had created. She named the child Axia, in honor of the world that sired her.

The Mother and her daughter lived in peace for many years, until one morning Axia went to her mother and said, "I have dreamed of people who are like us, but who are not like us. People of air and of water, of the earth and of the fire. They live in the cliffs over the sea, and in the sea, and in the caves overlooking the sea, and all along the ocean's shore. We must go and find them."

The Mother was confused, and told her daughter that there were no such people. But Axia insisted, and the two left their home, and went down the mountains toward the sea. And there, they found people. Not many, but people, where there had been none before. There were people of the air, who sang with the birds and who flew through the air on great feathered wings. There were people of the water, with long tails and gills, who swam with the dolphins and the water cats and who changed to walk like men on the land. There were people of fire, who harnessed those fires in forges and turned the gifts of the earth into wondrous creations. And there were people of the earth, who brought forth food from the land, and who had healing in their hands. They greeted the Mother and Axia with great joy, calling Axia "Firstborn" and "Oldest Sister." The Mother looked at these people, these living embodiments of her dreams, and asked, "Where have you all come from?"

It was Adavar who answered her. The world rumbled and spoke, "These are our second-born children. I have created them from your dreams, and from the waters of your womb, to populate the world. From them shall be born all the races of men."

The Mother and Axia tarried among the people, spending time with each of the tribes. And in each tribe, there was one who became close to Axia, and who chose to leave their people and follow where Axia went. From the Fire tribe came Nerris, who courted Axia by crafting roses made from silver and gold. From the Air tribe came Liara, who taught Axia to call birds to her hand, and who sang to rival nightingales. From the Earth tribe came Mika, merry and laughing. Last, from the Water tribe came Abin, quiet and thoughtful, and ever at Axia's side.

And so they lived. The tribes looked to Axia and the Mother for guidance, and to those of their own number who counseled Axia so that they might have a voice. And the Mother was pleased to see how her children had grown, and returned to the hidden places between the sea and the stars.

Years passed, and a small group came seeking the Mother. At their front was a young woman, quiet and thoughtful, and with Axia's sparkling eyes. The Mother welcomed them, and asked their purpose.

"I am the Firstborn of the Firstborn," she said to the Mother. "My name is Alaine, and my mother has sent me to you, so that you may never know loneliness."

A temple grew, in the fields where a Mother had once raised a daughter, and the place came to be known as the Mother's Womb. Over time, it became traditional for the heirs of the Firstborn to come to the Temple, to find which of them would be chosen to lead their people when their time came. And it also became tradition for the heir to choose their companions, one each from each of the tribes, as Axia did at the beginning.

Worlds begin. Worlds end. Worlds begin again. So it is with worlds.

The world begins.

Don't miss out!

Visit the website below and you can sign up to receive emails whenever Elizabeth Schechter publishes a new book. There's no charge and no obligation.

https://books2read.com/r/B-A-KGBH-MAUBC

BOOKS 2 READ

Connecting independent readers to independent writers.

Also by Elizabeth Schechter

Heir to the Firstborn
Worlds Begin
Written in Water
Forged in Fire
Bones of Earth
Wings of Air
Visions in Smoke
Children of Dreams

Rebel Mage
Counsel of the Wicked
Haven's Fall
Where Home Lies

Swords of Charlemagne
Hidden Things
The Lady and the Sword
Ashes and Light
Table of Stone
Swords of Charlemagne: The Complete Series

Standalone
The Rape of Persephone
Fools Rush In
Her Captive
To Market
Infernal Machine
Chains of Light

Watch for more at elizabethschechterwrites.com.

About the Author

Elizabeth Schechter has been called one of the top erotica and alternative sexuality writers in the world. Her writing credits include the award-winning steampunk erotic romance *House of Sable Locks*, the Celtic fantasy *Princes of Air,* and the dystopian fantasy *Rebel Mage* trilogy. Her shorter work has appeared in anthologies edited by D.L King (*Carnal Machines*), Laura Antoniou (*No Safewords*), and Cecilia Tan (*Jingle Balls*; *Like a Prince*).

With *Written in Water*, the first in the *Heir to the Firstborn* series, Elizabeth is exploring new ground, with her first new adult romance that was written entirely in real time on Patreon.

She was born in New York at some point in the past. She is officially old enough to know better, but refuses to grow up. She lives in Central Florida with her husband and son.

Elizabeth can be found online at http://elizabethschechterwrites.com, or on Facebook at https://www.facebook.com/Elizabeth.A.Schechter. You can also find her on Patreon, at https://www.patreon.com/EASchechter.

Subscribe to Elizabeth's newsletter at https://www.subscribepage.com/k4u7k2

Read more at elizabethschechterwrites.com.